Along
Temptation's Eage

AKKADIA

Nik August

Art and Design by
Jason Buhagiar

NIK AUGUST

Along Temptation's Edge: AKKADIA

By
Nik August

Nik August and Phoenix Illustrations and Publications

Printed in the U.S.A.

ISBN-13: 978-0-9840110-0-1

Thanks

I would like to thank my faithful volunteers, who read through my rough drafts every week, then begged for more. You know who you are. I must mention my #1 fan, Marlene Tannenbaum.

Marc Caravella, for his relentless copy reading and editing. The ability to know just how much to correct and when I should get my way.

Tristeen Caravella, for helping me with a beautiful cover and choosing the best music for the movie that played in my head, and giving me the supportive feedback I needed.

I'd like to thank Lauri Jon, for the fabulous layout of the original cover. You made my artwork look wonderful.

To Jason Buhagiar, for the digitally remastered illustrations for the interior cover layout and design. I couldn't be happier with the finished product.

Bruce Sconzo, who encouraged me to self-publish.

To Arial Burnz, for showing me how to bring my world to life and kept me plugging away!

I could not have written this story if not for "Danny." So, thank you, to the man that made me angry enough to write it all down and let the healing begin.

Lastly, I wish to apologize to the beauty of the Hamptons, which I so thoroughly destroy.

NIK AUGUST

Dedication

This is a book of fiction. Danny and Ilmar are not real, but the love they shared was, and based on real people. So thank you "Danny and Ilmar" for being who you are.

As for love, I must remember the most wonderful person that I've known. The sunrise must always make way for the sunset. I learned the joy of happiness and the sadness of loss. A soul that taught me deep love was about giving and not just taking. That any heart, no matter what age, is capable of it.

A restless soul that wanted to live life as an adventure...

But never found the time.

Table of contents

NIK AUGUST

A sleepy Hamlet on the east end of Long Island... A peaceful playground, but what lies beneath may change human civilization, even human evolution... forever. Danny, a self-centered playboy, has finally fallen in love. Or, is he an unwitting pawn in the young woman's quest to save her ancient, secret world? Unsure of her motives, he follows her even when his own memories are suspect. Danny, his best friend, Aaron, and Aaron's girlfriend, Sarah, get caught in a tangled web of sexual pleasure and deceit, as they try to save another society from imminent extinction.

Their search takes them into the deep into an uninhabited section of the Earth's inner crust. Danny gets caught in Ilmartutar's subterranean world and takes chances that could cause his end. With the entire city of Akkadia chasing after him, the different worlds collide in a massive war that must bring peace.

Sympathetic Akkadians might side with Danny and Ilmartutar – although they might pay the ultimate price for their treason. The East End of Long Island must survive the confrontation between the two sides. But with their memories compromised, the possibilities of a favorable outcome are hopeless.

NIK AUGUST

Southampton

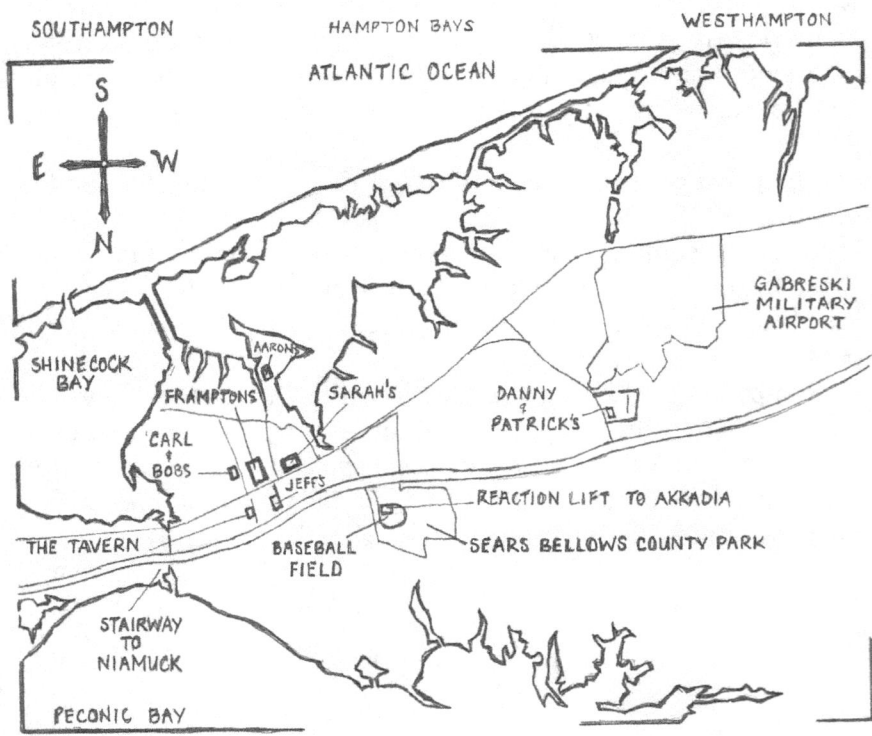

Akkadia

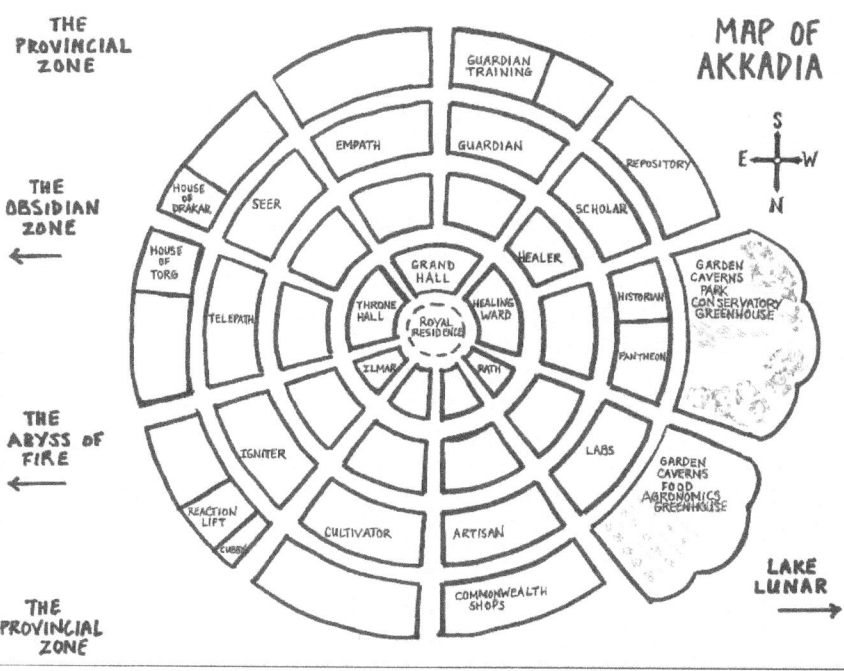

THE PROVINCIAL ZONE

THE OBSIDIAN ZONE ←

THE ABYSS of FIRE ←

THE PROVINCIAL ZONE

MAP OF AKKADIA

LAKE LUNAR →

Akkadian Guilds

Artisans: They can create anything desired from nothing. Clothing, décor, or whatever is needed. There are at least 80 of these talented people.

Cultivators: They only need touch a seed, and it will grow.

Empaths: These people can feel whether or not another is well, or centered. They can experience and share another person's pain. This Guild's members number in the 100's.

Guardians: Have the power to grow twice as large as a normal human, or morph 12 feet tall and are fully armored. The Guild has at least 60 members at any time.

Healers: A small group in the Akkadian ranks, numbering only in the low teens. They are the doctors called Mage's, keeping everyone healthy with their warm glowing light.

Historians: Only four may be alive at a time. There are usually only two. They keep the memories of all the Akkadians of the past. When someone dies, they perform the Absorption Rite.

Igniters: This Guild runs the Kingdom. They power the lights and household workings, also the Chariots. All they need to do is come into "contact" with an object. There is an Igniter in every House. The members number 200.

Scholars: They are the teachers of Akkadia. They help mold the younglings into their Guild. They possess the highest intelligence. Members number only 20.

Seers: They have the gift of prophecy. They can go into a trance and see the future, or possible futures.

Telepaths: There are 5 Levels of skill. #1 being the least powerful and #5 close to omniscience. They communicate via a bond or mental link.

Glossary

Abyss of Fire: Deep within the crust of the earth, where the molten core has broken through into a deep cavern.

Akkadia: The Ancient Kingdom run by a Monarchy. The city lies 15 miles beneath the surface deep into the bedrock; founded by people who went underground during the volcanic age.

Agronomic Greenhouse Cavern Gardens: Where the Cultivators grow the food that feeds the Kingdom.

Conservatory Greenhouse Cavern Gardens: Flora and fauna growth to keep the air in Akkadia fresh. A place to relax.

Grand Hall: Dining area.

Lake Lunar: the subterranean lake.

Obsidian Zone: A Geographical area where the rocks created from smooth, black, sharp stone are deadly. Just one touch from their edge could cut right to the bone.

Pantheon: Where the Absorption Rite takes place.

Plantings: A time frame of gauging Akkadian age, akin to 10 human years.

Provincial Zone: The uncultivated area outside of the city of Akkadia. A place of hard bedrock and tunnel caverns.

Reaction Lift: An elevator that can take the Akkadians 15 miles to the surface. It opens in Sears Bellows Park.

Repository: Ancient machinery storage.

Throne Hall: Where Council meetings take place.

NIK AUGUST

Conspiracies

prologue

The two combatants worked each other over, throwing punches, slamming into walls, shaking the very bedrock of the foundations of the practice room. Their metal bodies crashed together with a resounding clang. The giant twelve-foot Guardians attacked each other with vigor as each massive armor clad individual wrestled the other in a battle of wills and superiority. The noise level alone deafened anyone watching the exercise. The Guardians were the defenders of Akkadia. No need arose for their use in the passing of eons, as the Akkadians lived fifteen miles below the earth's surface, unbeknownst to the humans that lived their lives above.

As the Guardians practiced, a notification siren blared throughout Akkadia. Prince Pikkar nodded to General Nutrion, the Guardian Guilds First Council, pulling him away from the commotion to the other side of the training facility. Even with the general's immense height, he needed to gaze up at the prince to meet his eyes.

"You wish words?" the General asked.

"The Reaction Lift with the envoy of women goes to the surface again this eve. We could not have asked for a better distraction," Pikkar stated.

"Indeed," General Nutrion agreed and thought about the ramifications of that ascension. "I have spoken to Drakar. He alluded to a coming of a crossroad. Our time is almost upon us."

Wickedly Pikkar smiled as he eyed the old Guardian. Nutrion edged the periphery of his golden years, but his body held incredible muscle tone. Pikkar guessed his physique rivaled other Guardians much younger than himself. Familiarity wasn't the prince's strong suit.

On the other hand, Nutrion made it his personal job to know his prince. Besides being the Queens husband, Pikkar was First Council of the Igniter Guild. Controlling the entire illumination system of the subterranean city engaged most of his time. Strikingly impressive, with the blackest of eyes, but with white skin and hair, some would consider him an albino. He was not. His colorings were the markings of all true Igniters, except for his eyes. Other Igniters shared the ice blue eyes of their Guild.

Pikkar made sure his words found his General's ears but unheard by others. He leaned in lowering his voice. "I have longed for this day, Nutrion. To play at complacency is... more difficult each day."

"Victory shall be ours, my Prince," Nutrion assured him. "We have waited patiently for our time to expand our borders and subjugate the people on the surface."

"Indeed, and our catalyst seeds itself even deeper. At this time, she defies me, again and again. If there is one person I know better than myself, it is her. The unyielding tenacity of my own daughter, Ilmartutar." General Nutrion would have said more, but the Prince walked away from him and continued to watch the Guardian gladiators.

The practice arena held approximately fifty Guardians, all intent on proving their prowess to their General. For any out-Guild observers, the hand-to-hand combat, which the Guardians participated, often proved dangerous.

Prince Pikkar focused on Lieutenant Thorium and his opponent. Thorium was a beast of a man. In his non-Morphed state, he stood head and shoulders above all others. With his Guardian Ability activated, he was a mountain. At the moment, he was more concerned about the Prince's scrutiny, then his opponent's ferocity.

With renewed intent, Thorium charged his adversary. "Grrrargh!" He growled in a low inhuman voice as he threw himself at the other Guardian. Both sailed across the practice floor, ripping a few floor tiles in the process. They crashed into the adjacent stone wall, again, shaking the infrastructure.

Thorium's practice foe had no intentions of being beaten in front of the Prince, either. Forcefully, he reached out with both hands and pushed Thorium backward. The two-ton Guardian flew into the air and landed with a loud rumble. Their action caused the floor tiles to crack and split, but before Thorium could recover, his opponent was upon him again.

The other Guardian slammed into Thorium's body armor. Thorium staggered briefly, managed to hoist the other over his head, and then tossed his competitor backward. The thrown Guardian slammed into another duo of combatants. All crashed to the floor. The room shook violently from their massive weight.

Pikkar stepped backward as the ceiling cracked and crumbling stone fell to the practice floor. Glancing around the room, he searched for someone. "I thought I saw Yanni? You DO have her here, Nutrion, do you not?"

The General nodded and smiled. "There is always need of a Level 4 Telepath after a training session. And there is only one sympathetic to our cause. Yanni."

As the practice session continued, the wear and tear of the facility took its toll. Yanni made herself useful and used her Telepathic Ability to reconstruct and reinforce the walls, ceiling, and floor. Effortlessly, she raised her hands and manipulated the rubble as it replaced itself, nudging into the open cracks the broken pieces of stonework, and floor tiles. She knitted each piece with her Telepathic Ability, returning the Guardian training facility to a fair state of repair. Yanni lifted herself into the air with just the power of her mind. She sailed over to Prince Pikkar and General Nutrion.

Yanni bowed her head slightly in reverence to the prince, causing her raven black hair to fall into her eyes. "My Lord, Prince. The altercations between the Guardians seem intense this day. May I raise a force shield to protect you from any unwanted potential accidents to your person?"

Pikkar scowled. "You presume I can not remove myself from the path of a fighting Guardian?"

"No, my Prince," Yanni answered quickly. "I only wished to offer my services for your peace of mind."

"Hum..." Pikkar dismissed her with a wave of his hand.

It was a mistake. The ground under the prince's feet trembled, and his attention drew to its cause. Three Guardians stood at the end of the practice room. Each stomped their feet in unison, creating a physical vibration that Pikkar experienced at the opposite end of the cavern.

General Nutrion witnessed the Prince's confusion and smiled. "I have been working in secrecy with those three." He pointed to the Guardians who marched in place. "I hoped their skill would one-day rival the Telepaths in earthquake creation."

"Ha!" Yanni scoffed. "It shall be a cold day in the Abyss of Fire for that to happen!"

"Now, now, Yanni," Pikkar began. "A bit of friendly competition is healthy."

As they watched the Guardians move, the practice floor visibly shook, causing the rest of the fighting Guardian's to stop and check their footing. The earthquake makers picked up their pace and mashed their armored feet into the floor. Slight vibrations shook and intensified. It wasn't long before stress cracks reappeared on the ceiling and walls of the training facility.

Pikkar nudged Nutrion. "Perhaps we should halt their disciplines for the time being before I must summon the complete Telepath Guild for repairs."

General Nutrion held his hand up to curtail the Guardians, but it was too late. The entire wall behind the threesome collapsed, and they watched in horror, as the corridor beyond it crumbled as well. Springing into action, Yanni levitated to the destruction and attempted to hold the falling hall and adjoining caverns back, but the amount was too vast for her to bear alone. The people of Akkadia fled in all directions, as the upper crust of the caverns caved in on the Commonwealth emporiums and shopkeepers.

"Goddess, Nutrion!" Pikkar growled. "*Look* at what your Guardians have done!"

"One thousand pardons, my Prince." The General bowed, swiftly. "I had no idea things would get so carried away."

Unable to hold the canopy back any longer, Yanni retreated from the falling boulders before their weight crushed her. When she approached Nutrion, wrath covered her face. "Why do you presume we Telepaths carry out this task, instead of Guardians? I shall let you know! Simply because we can control our beam to a specific area!" She brought her lips close and whispered to the prince. "Now, Torg has been alerted to the incident."

Pikkar barred his teeth. "Torg!" *Oh, now I must endure that insufferable bore!* He thought to himself.

Yanni caught his meaning, and he heard her laugh inside his head. He shot her a glance of disapproval that might have cut her in two, making her avert her eyes. Pikkar had heard Torg's arrival inside his mind before he saw the Level 5 Telepath float toward the rubble in the corridor.

Rarely smiling, Torg's mental acuity was sharp as a tack, perhaps among the greatest of the current Akkadians, excluding those which belonged to the Scholar Guild. Not a piece of his dark hair moved from place as his light green eyes gathered information from the scene.

When Prince Pikkar spied Torg, he attempted to massage the Chancellor's ego. "Thank the Goddess for your swift arrival, my Lord Chancellor."

"Indeed?" Torg raised an eyebrow at the prince's praise. "The entire kingdom of Akkadia felt the seismic activity. Speaking as First Council for the Telepath Guild, I advise you to curtail the Guardians from this line of instruction. Leave the earthquake making to the professionals."

"As you wish, my Lord Chancellor," Bowing low, General Nutrion promised his cooperation.

The Prince and the General managed to keep their thoughts closed to him which caused Torg to doubt their sincerity. Not many could master the ability. Infinitely suspicious, Torg would have pressed the issue, but the whole Igniter Guild approached to help fortify the caverns over the Commonwealth.

The Chancellor shook his head at the Prince. "The Queen is beside herself with concern at this. She commands the Guardian Guild to cease training at once!"

Torg turned away from the prince, unable wait for a response. Extending his hands outward, he immediately lifted the rubble with the power of his mind, orchestrating their replacement.

As soon as Torg restored the granite stones to their proper place in the cavern canopy, the Igniter Guild went to work with their mending-mesh machine guns. The hardware showed its ancient craftsmanship – each cannon-shaped object, pitted, scarred, and tarnished with age. As the Igniters aimed and shot a web-like substance of adhesive organic material into the ruptured terrain, they used their Ability to activate an accelerated growth of living rock.

The Guild member's hands glowed white, activating their Abilities to transition their energy to the gun. Viscous elements erupted from the barrels, sealing the breaches and repairing the collapsed area. They repeated the process again and again until they healed their world.

Torg lowered himself. When his feet touched the ground, he approached the prince. "I am unsure of both your intentions in this... Be aware; I shall be watching." The Chancellor turned, rose into the air and sailed down the corridor. Pikkar and Nutrion locked eyes, but no words passed between them.

***

The room was dark, and the moonlight created shadowy landscapes, as it broke through the slatted window shades. The rhythmic breathing of the other person in bed told her he slept. The woman threw back the covers, rose carefully, and redressed. She did so in relative quiet, hoping not to wake the man who lay next to her.

Continuing to the bathroom, she checked her face and hair. Brushing her fingers through the blonde locks to tame her unkempt ends, she checked her reflection in the mirror. As she ran the faucet and brought the water to her cheeks, it revitalized her. With a new confidence, she dried her hands on the towel hanging on the rack. She headed back to the bedroom, but when she entered, he was awake.

"Lacara," he said weakly, calling her to him. "Are you leaving already?"

Lacara smiled and sat on the bed next to him. "You know I shall return." She got up to go, but he grabbed her hand. Consumed with guilt, she glanced down at it, feeling his pain. *I have done this to him.* Her thought referred to his bruises, open blisters, and sores, covering his face and body.

Jeff Donaldson didn't look his twenty-five years. The sallow skin and dark circles under his eyes bemoaned his suffering. Hunger grabbed at his intestines, and he found it hard to gather the energy to get up and go to work. His condition deteriorated right before Lacara's eyes.

"Hush, my love," she said. Using her Empathic Ability, she soothed away his pain with her voice. "Lie back and return to sleep."

He did as she told him. He ran his fingers through his hair, and the corrosive blisters on his forehead throbbed with pain. When he pulled his hand away, some of his hair came with it, wrapped in his fingers. "Okay, I'm not feeling great right now, anyway."

"I shall see you again tomorrow night. I promise." Lacara smiled again, but tears ran down her cheeks.

She turned, walked to his door, but paused for a moment. She faced him one last time to blow him a kiss, and then walked out of his room, closing the door behind her. When her mind refocused, she found herself out on the street in the warm summer night air. She walked for two miles while she marveled at the stars in the sky.

So beautiful, yet so alien, she thought, as she reached a sandy path.

She bent down, took off her shoes, and trekked through the parkland barefoot. Lacara hurried because she was late. As she approached the open field, she ran toward the bright light – her eyes gauged everyone inside waiting for her. She joined the other women in the Reaction Lift as the doors closed behind her.

"You are late again, Lacara," Ilmartutar stated, full of disappointment.

"I know. Forgive my delay," Lacara apologized.

"Mother shall not be pleased," Ilmar warned, shaking her head as the giant elevator descended on its way miles below the surface.

Above, in the abandoned human baseball field, nothing remained of the strange visitors, except the blowing sand erasing any trace of their footprints. As the only witnesses of their passing presence, the scrub oak, the sand, and the breeze tried to warn – whispering, whispering, whispering to no one.

NIK AUGUST

I
Danny The Bouncer

(A day, or so, in the Life)

Danny woke in a cold sweat. The recurring dream haunted his waking world. Flashes of light assaulted his subconscious. Fleeting glimpses of things he should know about, or remember, but couldn't. A woman's face, maybe? Intense heat, burning his skin. A bizarre scenario, bordering on reality, ending with him walking around the town nude. To make things more unbearable, each time he ran into his boss from the bar.

Whatever, he thought, yawning.

Danny shrugged it off and glanced over at his alarm clock. 3:15 PM, Saturday afternoon. A substantial amount of sleep, considering he didn't get home from Frampton's until 5:00 AM.

Bouncing is a tough job, Danny thought, *but someone's got to do it!*

Darkness shrouded his room with the help of thick curtains, and the lack of any sun struck windows, but he liked it that way. Danny threw back his sheet, revealing his naked body. He sat up in bed – every muscle rippled from each movement. He created that body with hard work and dedication. A seven-year project to perfection.

His physical appearance pleased him to the point of narcissism. At six foot two, two hundred and twenty-five pounds, Danny portrayed a picture of physical beauty. Crystal blue eyes, light sandy blonde hair, and a killer smile. That Dudley-Do-right smile which made many women fall for him.

Danny's gaze lowered and shook his head. *A morning rod.* He laughed to himself. *Well, I can take care of that easily enough.* He grabbed his robe and made his way to the bathroom. As he stared into the mirror on the wall behind the john, he drifted off into a daydream.

***

She was a recent conquest, already naked on his bed – his body glistening from the heat of their previous encounter. Beads of sweat graced his brow and caught in his hair. He didn't notice or care, as they dripped onto the sheets. He took her in with his eyes. Her expression barely visible, with her hair, drenched, wet and hanging.

A wicked smile spread across her face as she straddled him, accepting his throbbing manliness. He glided into her again and again, with deep thrusts. She threw her head back and roared a moan loudly as she sunk her fingernails into his chest, moving against him faster. He grabbed her hips to help pull her forward and push her back, matching his motion. A raging inferno rose within him which ignited a fever, and...

***

That's absurd! He thought as he broke from his revery. Danny eyed his hand. *What the hell am I doing?*

Laughing, he flushed the toilet. After a quick shower, he dressed. Nothing fancy. Just jeans and a white wife-beater, his usual uniform. Stopping at the fridge, he grabbed a Miller Lite.

Drinking was his first love, his greatest pleasure, and a major pastime. As an original Canadian National of Irish blood, relocated to Long Island, his love was understandable.

He headed to the front of the house where he and his brother, Patrick, ran their small business. Sutters' School of Aviation. Danny entered the shop and tilted the bottle to his lips, sucking half of it down. Engine parts and machinery scattered throughout the large, hangar-like garage in a clutter. A testament to Danny's ability to compartmentalize. Placing three fingers to his lips, he blew a kiss to the autographed pictures of two Penthouse Playmates hanging on the wall before he went outside through the bay doors to find Patrick.

Pat landed the Cessna on the main thoroughfare of the landing strip. As a certified flight instructor and plane enthusiast, Patrick spent most of his time in the air. Their business consisted of the aviation school and attached hangar repair shop. Neither of them had wads of cash in their pockets nor did they expect riches, but at least they didn't have to answer to anyone. They wrote their schedules, which left Danny considerable time for fun.

Pat recognized Danny's confident swagger walking toward him. "Oh, Sleeping Beauty awakens," he said sarcastically, as he exited the small plane.

"Thanks for letting me sleep in. I really needed it." Danny took another swig of beer.

"No problem, little brother. It's a Saturday routine, right?" Pat laughed, causing Danny to glare at him. Pat clarified. "It's no problem, Danny. Although, my four o'clock appointment will be here soon, so do you feel like checking over the plane?"

Danny held out his freshly washed nails and gazed at their level of cleanliness. *Oh well.* "Sure," he lied. Working his way deep inside the engine, the rest of the afternoon passed quickly.

Around 4:15 PM, Danny slammed the engine compartment to the Cessna and wiped the grease off his hands. Tossing the dirty rag in the corner of the shop, he unzipped his coveralls, hanging them on the wall. With his work finished for the day, Danny's thoughts turned to food.

It's about time to fire up the barbecue!

He arrived at the kitchen, opened the fridge, and took out the thawed chicken legs, grabbing another beer. With his bounty intact, he exited into the backyard and lit the coals. After setting the food on the grill, he took a few swigs of his beer. As Danny shoved the chicken around on the grill grates, the fire mesmerized him, mindlessly. As the flames grew in intensity, a slight sweat broke out all over his body. His gaze drew him deeper into the blazing fire, entranced...

***

She removed her clothing. Her full, firm, and high breasts, called to him. His mouth salivated at the thought of their bodies meeting. As she moved closer, he reached out to pull her to him, his tongue caressing her erect nipple. He placed his entire mouth over one, surrounded it, nipping and sucking. His tongue sent shivers along her skin. He brought his hands up, and she moved hers down. It wasn't long before her skilled fingers removed all and any trace of his clothing.

Her warm breath caressed the tanned skin of Danny's inner thighs. Intense pressure built inside him as she ran her smooth hands against his shaft. Her mouth touched his throbbing lance and engulfed him; her tongue played his instrument like a flute...

***

"Jesus!" Patrick yelled, breaking Danny's torrid reverie. "I know chicken's supposed to be well done, Danny, but this is ridiculous!"

Danny came back from the world of illusion and found his dinner on fire. "Shit!" he cursed. Reaching for the garden hose, he let the water run over the grill. A huge plume of steam and smoke rose from his crispy feast, sending the odor of charred flesh to his nostrils. "Oh well, I wasn't that hungry."

"Since *when*?" Pat laughed.

The alarm on Danny's watch beeped. "Since I gotta go, or I'll be late for work. You mind cleaning up?" Without waiting for an answer, Danny threw the garden hose, ran down the driveway and jumped into his Camaro.

Pat shook his head. "Why should I? I'm used to it by now. HEY! Don't work too hard!" Pat yelled, waving as his brother drove away.

"That'll never happen!" Danny yelled back. His huge grin spread across his face as he drove away. Spraying dirt and gravel into the air, the tires of the car dug into the driveway.

At Frampton's, the night took forever to fall. Danny kept his concentration on the crowd at the door. Waiting for someone to show made his blood boil. He didn't wait for anyone. To make matters worse, he and his boss, Brad, had words that evening, which usually never happened. He took an attitude, a little short with the patrons as well, and that never happened. He was a people person, happy, charming, but the suspense of not knowing killed him.

He bottled up his apprehension and shifted his weight from one foot to the other as he scanned the parking lot from the front door of the bar. There she was – walking through the parking spaces with her friends following close behind. They giggled as they paraded along, tossing their hair. Their hips swayed as they got closer and closer. Hypnotizing him, she walked right up to him. Danny's pulse quickened. The beating of his heart pounded inside his head. Just the memory of their two nights together brought an ache deep within him. She must feel the same way.

"Hi!" Danny said to her, his throat dry and tight.

"Hi," she replied back before passing him to continue inside.

Danny was dumbstruck. *Well, that didn't go as planned.* He hardly believed it. He wanted to follow her in, but he had to tend to the rest of the girls. *I'll just try again, harder.* He was determined.

After the door was clear, he yelled to his boss. "Brad, I'm taking my break." Brad waived him an "okay," so Danny wandered up behind her, grabbed a stool, and sat next to her.

"Hey, Lisa." He got the bartender's attention. "Her drinks on me."

"You got it, Danny," Lisa responded.

Danny took a moment to scrutinize her. She was hot, but not unusually gorgeous. Her hair gleamed a halo of blonde as bright as the sun on a bright day, but her skin remained untouched by that same sun. Its milky white softness radiated as an unblemished canvas. Her brown eyes smoldered, with hints of red flecks in the center of the iris near her pupils, "this close" to setting her countenance on fire.

A certain air swirled around her, a self-confidence that overwhelmed him when he neared her space. Each time they made love, she captivated him under a magic spell. No other woman made him burn with as much desire, but the mystery of her drew him in.

Of course, it doesn't hurt that she's well put together, either, he thought, smiling.

She sat through his conversation politely, but they chatted about nothing in particular. She paid attention more out of moral politeness than anything else. As much as he wanted to concentrate on her words, his eyes fixated on her lips. Fresh memories of tasting those lips, of having them explore his body, probing, warm and wet – obsessed him. Heat burned between them as she spoke. No one made him feel so vulnerable. He found himself checking the clock more often than he should have, wishing he didn't have to go back to the door.

But Danny's break was over too quickly, and Brad summoned him back to the door. Danny excused himself and said he'd see her later on. During the night, the bar got busy, and Danny finally lost track of her. At his first convenience, he searched for her, but she and her friends had disappeared. He left that night a little disappointed. Danny bid good-night to the staff and headed out the back door to his car. He fumbled with his keys, when the sound of grating sand against asphalt from behind, startled him.

He spun and came face to face with her. She waited for him. The thrill pleased him beyond belief at the sight of her. She wanted him again just as much as he wanted her; he knew it in his heart.

"Hey," Danny whispered, afraid if he spoke too loudly she would disappear.

She held her hand up to make sure he didn't approach her. "Stay where you are."

Danny chuckled. "You're not afraid of me, are you?"

It was her turn to laugh. "Not likely. It is you who need the fear."

He shook his head. "Me, afraid of you? What are you? A hundred pounds soaking wet?"

"What does my weight have to do with your safety?" she asked confusedly.

"Don't change the subject," Danny told her. "Why did you wait for me if it wasn't too... Well, you know."

"I have come to warn you. Stay away from my friends and me."

"What? Why?"

"I already told you it is for your safety."

"Look, I appreciate your concern, but you're really not in any position to tell me what to do with my – uh, with my life. Who are you anyway?"

"Someone dangerous." She reflected, sadly.

Danny took advantage of her while her guard was down and reached for her. Grabbing her by the arm, he spun her around and pushed her against the car. He pressed himself against her to keep her from squirming away. As his body leaned against her with their closeness, his crotch tingled. The scent of her – fresh and earthy, enticing his nostrils. He brought his lips close to hers, attempting to excite her.

"You want *dangerous*, honey?" He smiled smugly but noticed her reaction. Fear, concern, and determination crossed her face. Genuine panic gripped her. In the silence of their heat, his car engine started and revved at an extremely high RPM. His hands burned hot where he held her, which momentarily stunned him. He let go of her, turned toward the car, perplexed at the engine sound. His action gave her the opportunity to break away.

She sighed. "You have been warned."

Danny reached for her again, and this time she didn't struggle. "Okay, so I'm warned, now shut up."

No more words passed between them, they didn't need to. She wanted him again just as much as he wanted her. He didn't need her to speak it out loud. She brought her open mouth up to his and kissed him, pressing against him roughly. She pulled his shirt off with ease and pushed him down onto the hood of his car.

"No, not here!" Danny said.

"Yes," she breathed. "Here! Now!"

Alright, he thought to himself, *but we do this my way*.

He quickly picked her up and placed her gently on the Camaro's hood. Ripping at her attire, he removed her clothing. He practically tore his off. She watched him move as he undressed. His body, silhouetted against the darkness and the overhanging light in the parking lot, showed his hard muscles and reflected the glow of those same lights.

Danny found her desirable, and willing. Her body was comfortable against the cool steel of his car, and she radiated heat wherever he touched her. His blood rushed its way to the very place he needed it, making him able to carry out her demands. Her outstretched arms reached for him and pulled him into her. Where ever she touched him, his body burned as if it caught fire.

He waited long enough. As he lowered himself onto her, she wrapped her legs around him. He entered her, and they became one, over and over again – each moving together with only one purpose. They worked each other, faster, deeper, and harder, to a fevered pitch, a heated frenzy, to which there could be one end.

She clutched his back, dug her nails deeply into his skin, and arched hers. Bringing him deeper inside, she took his fullness. The Camaro's engine turned over for the second time. The motor shuddered under him. It didn't matter, his mind remained elsewhere, and he soon forgot about it. As they both reached their peak, they slowly released each other, exhausted.

She didn't bother to catch her breath before she gathered her clothes, and slid off the hood. Danny reached out to her, grabbing her arm to stop her. His eyes searched hers as if he wanted to say something.

I think I love you! I love you, dammit! His brain screamed inside his head. Instead, his mouth managed to utter the words, which fell short of his actual opinions. "I – good night."

Ilmartutar gazed back at him, smiled that knowing smile, and walked away, leaving him naked on his car.

"SHIT!" Danny swore, kicking his car. He leaned over and stroked the Camaro, apologetic for his outburst. "I'm sorry, baby... Ah, WOMEN!" Danny dressed, slid into the driver's seat, and drove home, utterly disappointed.

***

Danny bounced at Frampton's Friday nights, Saturday nights, and Sunday nights while the planes monopolized his weekdays. The family business was butt up against the Gabreski Airport, on the east side, located nearer to East Quogue than Westhampton, easily accessible from County Road 104. Danny possessed the ability to fly the planes; he was a great pilot, but he wasn't that interested in being the teacher. As likable as Danny presented himself, Pat dealt with the customers. His older brother's patience with people drew the customers into the school. They respected Patrick's greater age as well. For Danny, dirty hands, painful muscles, uncomfortable positions, and hard work filled his life.

He spent his days alone with the planes. A quiet and lonely place – the hanger allowed his mind to wander. The week moved slowly for Danny. He went to Frampton's three times to see if he'd run into "that" woman, but he was unable to find her. He didn't even know her name. He chuckled in his head at that thought.

Well, that's nothing new, he thought. *How many women had I slept with without knowing their names?* He held up his greasy fingers and counted. After he had used both hands, he gave up. *Nah, it's easier to count the ones with names.* He laughed out loud.

"Do you always amuse yourself when you're alone?"

The voice startled Danny, and he hit his head. He jumped, creating a loud bang that echoed throughout the garage. He thought he was alone. Peeking out of the plane, he spied his best friend, Aaron. Standing with his hands jammed into his jeans pockets, Aaron smiled.

"Dude!" Danny hollered.

The sight of Aaron brought back memories. Aaron and Danny shared their age. Both twenty-eight, they were old enough to be somewhat responsible, yet young enough to still have a good time. They established their friendship in middle school when they found they shared a sense of humor. Ever since then, they were inseparable, hanging out together at every opportunity. They shared everything, and those lines blurred from time to time, which created quite interesting scenarios. In their younger years, some things shared were better off forgotten. When Danny left high school, he went straight to work for his brother, Pat, opting to forgo college.

Aaron, on the other hand, went to college – a SUNY College, Southampton campus. If Danny was honest with himself, he was jealous of Aaron's family conditions. His friend graduated with a Marine Biology degree, all paid for by his parents. When Aaron found work close by, it enabled the duo to keep their friendship going while they both did their own thing.

Jumping down from inside the plane, Danny joined Aaron on solid ground. Aaron stood taller than Danny by a few inches, but that brought him well over six feet tall. His shaggy light brown hair got into his dark brown eyes every so often. His eyes, so dark you couldn't discern the pupils from the irises.

Danny gazed up into those dark eyes, as he wiped his greasy hands on a rag. "You scared the shit outta me, Aaron! Thought I was *alone!*"

"Then I'm glad I didn't catch you doing something we'd both regret!" Aaron joked.

"Right?!" Danny laughed. "Chances are 50/50 that I might have been self-stimulating." He smiled; a big grin spread across his face, and he patted Aaron on the shoulder as he walked by to the toolbox.

"Hey dude," Aaron protested. "Watch the hands! Really nice white shirt, here!" Aaron referred to the shirt he wore.

"Sorry! We can't all be as unsoiled as some people," Danny yelled, with his back turned. He finished up, before unzipping his work suit, stepping out. "Hey, where'd you get those bruises?"

Aaron examined his bicep. "Huh, funny. I don't have a clue."

Danny took a closer look. "It's like someone grabbed you real rough."

Aaron laughed. "It does, doesn't it? I think I would have remembered that!"

"I would have too!" Danny attention fell to his hand, and he fingered the blister there. "So, what's up, Buttercup? Why are you here?"

Aaron smiled. "I was wondering if you wanted to head out to Frampton's tonight?"

Danny cocked his head and stared directly at Aaron. "I know I look dumb, but I saw you with that chick last weekend, you know." He scolded with his finger. "I hate having this much info. Gives me a headache."

Aaron appeared ashen. "Don't tell Sarah; it'll kill her."

"You mean, it'll kill *me!* Do I look like I want to die? No way would I make my life that miserable. She'd blame me for your indiscretion," Danny warned. He didn't want to lie to himself. He wanted to go; he needed to go. "Okay, we'll go! I owe it to myself for all this hard work I've been doing." As they made their way to the house, Danny turned to Aaron. "Come on, bro... Want a beer to go?"

II

The Mystery of Akkadia

Ilmartutar awoke to the artificial light or lightning, all courtesy of her father's power. It signified the arrival of the morning and heralded the new day. She spied the pile of clothes on the floor. Her "human" clothes. She smiled.

I love those clothes, she thought. As she turned her head, she witnessed her attire for the day. Her robes hung where her House Telepath left them. Ilmartutar rolled onto her back. The trappings of who she was, those robes. She ran her hand down to her abdomen in full knowledge it was empty, barren.

Not yet, she thought. *I'm just not in the mood for this today.*

She dreaded the confrontation with her mother and father. Ilmartutar slid out of bed to prepare for her day. With herself washed, her hair done, and robes in place, she left her bedchambers. She headed out on her way to the first meal, and a meeting with her parents.

As she walked through the white halls in her home of Akkadia, she contemplated her predicament. For hundreds of centuries, she and her people lived in peace, fifteen miles below the earth's surface. They survived by way of her species special Abilities. Communing in harmony with each different Guild, so each person, in his or her own way, created a bond with their underworld paradise.

The humans above used technology to make everyday living a comfort to them. Her people needed no such help. Ilmartutar entered the Grand Hall, where most of her people took their meals. Immediately met by her father, Prince Pikkar, Ilmar sighed at his impatience.

"Your Mother is waiting." He motioned her to the chair next to her mother. She nodded reluctantly to her father.

So much power in this man, she thought.

So blonde was his hair, as to be thought white, and his eyes of the darkest brown scrutinized openly. He stood over two meters high, brought himself quick to anger, had a temper, but exerted self-control often. He supplied almost the entire kingdom with their artificial light. Other subjects in the monarchy had the Illumination Ability, a power of the Igniters Guild, but none as powerful as Prince Pikkar.

The Grand Hall supported the entire number of inhabitants of Akkadia. Although, not all took their meals at the same time. Sending her gaze around the massive columned hall, Ilmar noticed many tables empty. Her eyes fell to her mother.

Alkara, the most beautiful woman Ilmartutar had ever seen, lived her life in complete serenity. Her jet black hair hung past her waistline. Tall and athletic, with emerald green eyes, she stood out from the crowd of her people. When Alkara turned her eyes on another, she could tell in a minute if they were not telling the truth, and her eyes could see deep into a person's soul. She was the Queen and ran the matriarchal society. Queen Alkara was a formidable force. Intense, confident and enchanting.

Ilmartutar walked toward her mother and sat beside her. "Good morning, Mother." Ilmartutar bowed her head.

"Ilmar." Her mother smiled at her as she used her daughter's shortened name.

Her father joined them and sat on Alkara's other side. "Have you accomplished your task?" he questioned Ilmar.

Ilmar looked shocked. "Father," she breathed, "this is not the time nor place to address this issue!"

Alkara placed her hand on her daughter's arm and looked deep into Ilmartutar. Alkara was an Empath. She could sense another person's emotions as well as see inside, gaining insight into their inner turmoil. She was not a Healer but could alert a Healer to a problem. Her Ability made her a great Queen, but an annoying mother.

"She has not," Alkara replied before removing her hand.

Ilmar dropped her shoulders and sighed. "I *am* trying."

"This is very important, Illy." Her father used her nickname.

"I know this, Father." Under this scrutiny, the meal on her plate became unattractive, and she realized she wasn't hungry anymore.

What else could happen to make this the worst day ever? She mused. As if in answer to her question, Azewrath strode into the Grand Hall. *Oh, my Goddess!* She screamed inside her head. Ilmar watched her father rise to meet Azewrath, accompanying him to the seat next to her.

"My love," he cooed with a deep voice, smiling as he took her hand and brought it to his lips. The short bristles of his goatee poked her skin as he did.

Ilmar forced a smile in return. She never understood why he preferred to wear the facial hair. No one else in Akkadia did so. It was as if he enjoyed some silent rebellion with its presence.

"My intended," Ilmar responded. *I'm not in the mood for him right now!*

Azewrath moved closer to Ilmar. "How have your trips to the surface fared?"

Pikkar broke in. "Unsuccessful, I am afraid. She must continue for at least another month."

Ilmartutar stood up. "Please excuse me, my family, I am not feeling well."

Pikkar checked Alkara's face for confirmation on that, and his wife nodded. "Our daughter is not centered at this time, she is correct," Alkara stated.

Ilmar stole away. Leaving the Grand Hall behind, she hurried down the corridor, but her father followed. "Illy," her father called after her. When she turned to face him, hands on hips, he continued his oratory. "Our situation in Akkadia is dire! You know this!"

"I do." *I know this... Why must we repeat ourselves?* She thought, frustrated.

"Well," Pikkar scolded, "I am not sure you do realize how serious this problem is."

Ilmartutar sighed. "I have been schooled in this most of my life, Father." She went through it in her mind.

Our beautiful home is dying, she thought. *The poisons that the surface people have created and let spoil their lands has leached into the crust, slowly seeping into the surrounding ground, and water supply, thus festering in the people of Akkadia. The Healers say it is what caused most males to become sterile. After only three live births in seven plantings, it was decided all young women MUST make trips to the surface. All aged eighteen to thirty-five plantings would mate with the males in the human world to strengthen the species. And I have done so!*

Pikkar firmly grabbed her by her shoulders. "Yes, you have

been schooled, but it is harder to carry out your charge. You shall be Queen, and Azewrath, your Prince. You must have an heir!"

Ilmar looked at her father. *He will never understand!* She fumed, turned, and stormed wildly down the corridors.

***

Ilmartutar spent the rest of the day in quiet reverie. She walked the Garden Caverns for hours. *So beautiful*, she thought. *But how long before the damage from above will also destroy this paradise?*

Stalactites and stalagmites along with all forms of flora and fauna linked the giant hollow caverns used to help produce oxygen and grow all their agriculture. No animals survived deep inside the world's crust. The Akkadians didn't need any. Everything they needed to cultivate their crops of food came to them naturally. Most meals consisted of small teleostei – fish-like creatures that swam in the underground lakes.

Ilmartutar stayed out as long as she could. She needed to head home eventually, as she couldn't stay out in the Commonwealth forever. Azewrath would be waiting for her. Not that they had plans, but he would make sure their paths crossed. As she wandered the corridors, her anxiety level grew.

Azewrath wasn't unpleasant to look at, dark hair, dark eyes, all wrapped into a dark demeanor. He wasn't tall, but not short either. Unremarkable would be the way she would describe him.

It pained Ilmar to contemplate her future. Her destiny to spend the rest of her life with him upset her thoughts. Much older than she, Azewrath lived thirty-eight cycles of the planting season while she saw twenty-three. He was her father's friend and now her future husband.

Taking a deep breath, Ilmar walked toward the housing. Her heartbeat quickened, and butterflies entered her stomach which caused a sickness deep inside.

One more turn and I will be at Azewrath's quarters. She sighed, as she spied him in front of his chambers. He stood in wait for her.

He motioned her to come to him. "Please," he said, "come inside."

Ilmar went into his lodgings, without making a scene. It was frowned upon to show ill behavior, and she didn't need another reason to disappoint her parents. His rooms were sparse. Azewrath chose to keep a minimalistic approach to his life's surroundings. With a lounge, two tables, and a floor to ceiling shelving unit to house his tablets, the room gave a larger than average impression.

As Azewrath moved closer, his mouth came down to graze her lips. Ilmar quickly turned her head. Shrugging off her snub, he grabbed her face and kissed her roughly, forcing her lips apart. She broke away from his embrace.

Azewrath smiled. "You know it upsets me when you are not a willing participant. I would very much like you to spend the night," he firmly suggested.

"What is the point?" she replied and turned to walk away.

He grabbed her arm and pulled her to him. "The point is… it is what I *want!*"

His eyes burned right into hers as they faced each other. Her breath came deep and angry. She hated him, hated who he was, especially when she was with him. She affected him adversely, yet he would never let her go. Azewrath released her for the moment and sat on the bed.

"You know what I wish," he stated, as he leaned back. "Come, let us not waste the term."

Her nails bit into the palms of her balled fists as she tried to control her anger. Even her father's earlier words rang hollow in her ears. She disrobed unceremoniously and walked toward him. He grabbed her hands and made her untie his tunic trousers. After, she opened his tunic shirt to expose his chest and went to slide it off his shoulders.

"No," he interrupted. "Leave it on. I shall not undress. I shall have you just like this." He attempted to humiliate her. To show her she was his plaything, and she must obey him.

I will not let him make me less than I am, she repeated to herself.

Ilmartutar did what he asked. Taking her place above him, she lowered herself onto his engorged manhood. Azewrath reached up and grasped her ample breasts. He worked her nipples until they were erect. She cursed her body for responding to him and moved over him as if in a trance. Her mind focused on one thing. So blanched white was his chest, his skin, soft and thin. If she dug her fingers deep into him, she was sure she could reach into his chest cavity and pull out his still-beating heart... watching as he bled to death.

Ilmartutar woke early to escape Azewrath's presence. She dressed quietly, but from previous experience, she was aware he observed her. His Ability, a sixth sense about things that were about to happen, made it nearly impossible to accomplish anything without his foreknowledge. Azewrath held the position of First Council Leader of the Seer Guild. Nothing she did surprised him. If she tried to leave, he knew before she did.

Ilmar revealed her knowledge of his Ability. "I know you are awake and watching me."

"And I know you planned on sneaking out."

"Azewrath..." She turned to face him. "I do not love you."

He roused himself up against his pillows and smiled a wicked sort of grin. "And, I do not care."

"Then know this, if I must spend the rest of my life with you, I will surely die!"

"So dramatic, Ilmar! We all must do things that are distasteful, at times."

"That is easy for you to say."

"Yes, it is." Azewrath laughed. "And in fifteen cycles, or so, it shall be easy for you as well. You are still very much a child. When you age, things that seem as if it would be the end of the world shall appear different to you. And you shall wonder what all the fuss was about."

"I hate you!" She seethed.

"That shall change as well." He laughed out loud. She fumed, fastened her robes, and stormed out.

***

Ilmartutar took the days meals in her bedchambers. *I hate my life*, she thought. *And now I hate myself for hating my life!*

She moved around her room and readied her clothes for the trip she must take to the surface. After she had laid them out on the bed, Ilmar sat down in front of her mirror, to fix her hair and make-up. She stopped to admire herself. Dark circles appeared under her eyes, belying her wellness.

Too much responsibility, she thought. Water welled up in her tear ducts, and she grabbed a hanky to blot the moisture from the corner of her eye. *Do not cry; you shall ruin your make-up*. Noise from behind alerted her to an others presence, but she didn't turn around. Instead, the reflection of her mother as she entered the room, projected itself in the mirror.

Alkara sat beside her daughter. "I missed you today in the Grand Hall."

"Hmmm," Ilmar hummed, "I was not in the mood for company."

"I see," said Alkara. "Shall you be in the mood tonight, in the world above?"

"Mother!" Ilmar yelled, and then composed herself. "May I ask a question of you?" Her mother nodded. "Is there truly a chance that our Healers are right about the after effects of our co-mingling with the surface males?"

Alkara paused to think before she answered. "It could be true, my dear, which is why you should do what you must and find another. As quickly as you can."

"But Mother," Ilmar stressed, "I have found someone that is perfect in *every* way. I am just afraid our prolonged union might kill him."

Concern crossed Alkara's face. "It *shall* kill him, Ilmar," she promised. "You must find another, tonight!"

"No!" Ilmar adamantly protested. "There must be something our Healers can do."

"My little one." Alkara wrapped her arms around Ilmartutar. "The Council Leaders of the Healers Guild are doing their best. Our unique physiology is much stronger than the humans. We can not come into physical contact without draining some of their life-force." Alkara took Ilmar's hands into her own. "We can not be responsible for leaving dead bodies behind in the wake of destruction." Alkara kissed her daughter's cheek before rising to leave. "Think of this as a survival mission. It must be discrete, and covert. Do you understand?"

"Yes, Mother, but..."

"Ah-ah!" Her mother interrupted – her finger wagging in the

air. "No more discussion. The other girls are waiting for you. It is time to ascend to the surface."

Ilmartutar dressed in a hurry and met the group of women making the trip topside. Tonight, their idle chatter held no excitement for her. Something nagged at her memory, more important than the prattle of young women. Something she read about a possible aid in the mating process.

Perhaps it shall come to me; she thought as the Reaction Lift took her the fifteen miles upward.

III

Dangerous Encounter

Danny and Aaron crashed Frampton's on a Thursday night, both hoping to run into their respective trysts. With the place packed and the music loud, people stood shoulder to shoulder – not a regular occurrence for a weekday night. Women galore danced everywhere, but the duo turned down all who approached them. Instead, they decided to drink their beers and check out the patrons in the room.

"Dude, this blows!" Aaron shouted over the music.

"What'd ya mean? This place is hopping, tonight!" Danny yelled back, but he understood the real meaning behind Aaron's statement. "Okay, bro, I know what you mean. Let's go." He downed the last of his beer and waved goodbye to Brad, his boss. "See ya tomorrow night!" Danny called back. They exited the bar into the warm Summer evening. "Wanna hit another place?"

"Yeah," Aaron said. "I told Sarah I'd be with you all night anyway."

"You dog!" Danny teased.

"Aw, shut up!" Aaron slid into the Camaro's passenger seat. "Let's try the Tavern."

"Okay, but that place is a dump," Danny remarked, starting the engine. They pulled up to the Tavern, parked, and exited the car. "What a dive!" Danny stated. "Glad I don't work here. You sure you wanna go in?"

"It's not *that* bad. Come on." Aaron opened the door. "We'll just have one. I'm looking for something."

"Yeah... trouble!" Danny shook his head.

It took a few seconds for Aaron's eyes to adjust to the dim light, but as soon as he could see, he spotted her. The woman from the other night. He punched Danny in the arm.

"Oh-ho!" Aaron winked at Danny and walked away. "I'll check you later, bro."

Danny observed Aaron sit at the bar next to the same girl he saw him with last week. Her long, dark hair pulled back into a braid accentuated her slim neck and regal posture.

"No thanks," Danny said out loud to no one, in particular. "I'm good; you go ahead."

Danny settled at the bar and ordered another beer. He took a swig, scanning the room. A few huge guys playing pool, a couple making out oblivious to their surroundings. Two more women were hanging all over two more guys, a guy with his arm around a woman, a blonde woman, an old guy...

Hey! Danny stopped short. *The blonde! It's her! What the hell?!*

She sat closer to the other man than Danny liked. From where he sat, she seemed to laugh, but her laughter didn't spread to her eyes.

Do I go over there?

Danny wrestled with the idea before a brainstorm hit him. The digital jukebox stood on the other side of the bar. For him to play music, he needed to walk right by her, and she would have to see him. He jumped off the stool and walked by, watching her do a double-take.

So, she recognized me. Danny put money into the machine, pushed a couple of buttons, and the song played.

Danny went back to his bar stool and drank his beer. Their eyes met over and again. He gazed over the rim of his mug and caught her watching him more than once. She couldn't take her eyes off him.

Annoyed with her behavior, the guy she sat with finally raised his voice in a derogatory statement. He got to his feet and tossed his coaster across the table. When he left the booth, he gave Danny a dirty look as he passed. She stared at Danny with slitted eyes, and he took that as an invitation to join her.

Her expression was anything but happy when he scooted in beside her. Danny leaned in to kiss her, but she turned away. "No, don't," she said, using the human contraction.

Her reaction confused him. "Hey." He touched her face to regain her attention. He encountered that specific heat they shared with each other. "I thought we were working on something special here."

"What made you believe that?" she asked.

"Oh, I don't know," Danny answered. "Maybe because we hooked up at least three times so far? I'm kinda looking forward to our fourth time."

"I can't." She averted her eyes. "WE can't anymore." She stressed her word and stared him directly in the eyes. "If you value your life, you'll leave me alone." She attempted to get up and get passed him.

He put his hand on her shoulder and pushed her down. "Wait just a minute. What's all this talk about life-threatening? You're not as scary as you think."

She put her hands to her head. "You just don't get it. Why can't you take no for an answer?"

"Call it a character flaw." Danny chuckled.

His wit did not amuse her and she stood again to get around him. "Let me go."

"I don't think so."

She pushed against him. "Let me pass, or I'll have to call my friends for help!"

"The HELL you say!" Danny grabbed her as she tried to pass, threw her over his shoulder, and waved at Aaron as he walked out. She kicked and screamed the whole time which made it difficult for Danny to keep a grip on her.

"Put me down! Let go of me! Let go of me!" she repeated, as she banged her fists against his back.

"Yeah, yeah," Danny taunted. "Blah, blah, blah." He opened the Camaro door and threw her into his car.

"How dare you!" she fumed.

Danny wasted no time. He launched himself at her and held both sides of her head in his hands. When he planted his lips on hers, fire met his skin. She struggled, fought, and thrashed against him, but he never let her go. Slowly her hostility lessened, and she surrendered to his embrace.

More receptive, her desire strengthened, deepening, and she finally demanded his tongue to probe every inch of her mouth. She seized his back, and his body exploded with fever. The heat between them intensified until he broke away from her. Turning the key in the ignition, he jammed his car into gear.

"Where are we going?"

Danny didn't even glance sideways. "Home."

As he drove, the yellow lines in the center of the road blurred. He blinked his eyes, squeezing them shut in an effort to see straight. A little lightheaded, he focused his attention on driving. He didn't need to get pulled over by the police. Unmarked cars hid behind bushes and blind drives for unsuspecting tourists.

Now? Now I can't hold my liquor? He thought. *Shit, I only had three beers!*

He pulled into the driveway of their airport, passed the hanger and sped the car to his back door. He jumped out but had to steady himself on the fender of the Camaro until his strength returned. He opened the passenger door, picked her up in his arms, and stumbled his way through the house, almost dropping her once.

He kicked his bedroom door closed a little too loudly. *Oops, I hope I didn't wake up Patrick.*

Danny plopped her on his bed unceremoniously before he fell over as well, causing them both to giggle. She caught her breath just in time for his lips to cover hers and suck her air away, again. She returned his embrace with an urgency.

As if a man driven, Danny took her shirt in both hands and ripped it down the front. Exposing her ample, heaving breasts, he dove in, exploring the soft skin that burst from her lacy bra. She grabbed handfuls of his hair, leading him to investigate every erogenous zone of her body.

He unzipped her pants and slid them down as his tongue dampened her skin. She moaned and helped him push them off her feet. He threw off his shirt, dropped his pants, and heaved himself on top of her. They met as water and fire.

Their heat so intense, he was sure steam rose from their skin. His mouth had a mind of its own. It searched, probed, and brought her pleasure. An aching hit him hard – his blood engorged his manhood. She reached for it, wrapping her fingers around his shaft. He rolled onto his back as her other hand cupped his generous globes.

Oh, God! Danny thought. "Oh, baby!" Was what he said.

She smiled and brought her ruby lips down to taste his salty, throbbing strength. Dominant in her skill of manipulation, she brought Danny to the brink of insanity. She stopped long enough to maneuver her way above him, straddling his largeness.

He seized her hips and pulled her with all his muscle onto him, as he thrust upward. She rocked herself back and forth, over again. Her breath came heavy, working up a sweat. Danny's entire body was aflame! From where she was above him, she captivated his attention.

So beautiful, he thought.

With her head tilted back, and sweat beaded on her shoulders and breasts, she personified lust. Overcome with desire, Danny couldn't wait any longer. He used all his energy, and in one swift motion, swung her around. Lying her on the bed, while Danny replaced her on top, he mounted her. He thrust deeply, and she wrapped her legs around his waist. They never missed a beat.

Danny leaned on his palms and worked feverishly to reach his pinnacle. With his strength waning, he lowered himself to his elbows, allowing for a more relaxed position. Her body shook with the first signs of rolling pleasure that closed in on her release. He moved his hips faster, entered her deeper, bringing about his climax. She arched herself and dug her fingers into his back. He was on fire where her hands met his skin. With his discharge, he threw himself onto his back, spent, and weaker than ever before.

As they lay there, both tried to replace the oxygen in their lungs. Their heaving chests and heart rates finally returned to normal. After Danny's exertion, he had trouble finding his voice. Gazing into her eyes, he lifted his arm to gently stroke her face.

"I don't even know your name. I think it's about time I do." Danny propped himself up on an elbow. "I can't call you lover forever."

Ilmartutar grinned. "Illy," she said, using her nickname.

Danny brushed her bangs away from her forehead. "Lilly," he said, speaking it softly.

No, Illy, she thought, but he continued to speak.

"Lilly," he said, and kissed her cheek. "Such a beautiful name."

Lilly is a beautiful name, she reflected.

"Lilly," he repeated and kissed her neck. "Lilly," he whispered it again while he kissed her shoulder.

Ilmar giggled as he progressed ever downward with his kisses. She reached up and snatched handfuls of his hair, guiding him to pleasure her again – which he did without hesitation. After, they lay wrapped in each other's arms and slowly drifted off to sleep.

Ilmar woke with a start to the dark. *Oh no!* She worried. *Did I spend the night?* She could see some light through the covered windows. *Let me think; the sun comes over the horizon in the Summer at 5:30 AM.* She remembered from her teachings. *Good Goddess! The others must have gone back down without me. Mother will be beside herself with worry at my absence, and Father will be so angry, he might consider punishment. I am a dead woman.* She sat up as panic gripped her heart.

Danny lay with his back to her. She shook him gently. When he didn't respond, she tried with more force. He grumbled, but eventually acknowledge her.

"Man, I'm burning up." He turned, wiping the sleep from his eyes. His large smile disappeared when he witnessed the dismay on her face. "What's wrong?"

"I didn't go home last night." She breathed, frenzied.

"Is that all?" His smile returned.

Ilmar responded sternly. "There shall be *terrible* repercussions!"

"Lilly," Danny started, "I think you're old enough to stay out overnight."

Lilly?! Oh, that is right, I remember. I am Lilly. I like the name, anyway. Ilmartutar would be too hard to explain, right now. Something caught her eye on Danny's chest. "What's this?" She examined the mark. More appeared on his shoulders. She pushed him over and checked out his back. *Yes, there also. Oh, no!* She thought.

"Hey, what's all over me?"

Ilmar stumbled over her words. "It looks like... I think... I don't know; maybe you're allergic to something?" *I am killing him!* She fretted upset.

"No, can't be. I haven't eaten anything or touched anything." He inspected the marks. They were like small bruises. At the center of each bruise, there appeared to be a blister or burn mark. Almost as if actual flames touched his skin.

Where have I seen this before? Danny thought. He flashed back to the day he and Aaron were in the hanger together. *Aaron had bruises just like this!*

"I've seen these before," he admitted to Ilmar.

"Where?" she asked stunned, worry furrowing her brow.

"My best friend, Aaron, you know him. The guy who hung around one of your girlfriends." Her eyes opened wide as he went on. "He had a few of these on his arm the other day."

Ilmar didn't know what to say. *Multiple incidents are bad! Mother was right. Oh, what trouble I have caused.* "Do they hurt?"

"Yeah," Danny said. "A little, but I'm a big, strong guy." He leaned forward to kiss her. When dizziness overtook him again, he fell face forward. Missing her, he face-planted into the bed. Next thing he knew, Ilmar's fingers tapped him on the cheek. "What happened?"

"Oh my, Danny, you passed out!"

"WOW, I must be worse off than I thought." He leaned back against a pillow. "Maybe I'll just take the day off. I mean, my brother is my boss!" He laughed. "You want to spend the day here with me? I don't know how much fun I'll be... I'm dizzy."

Thoughts of her misfortune rushed back into her mind. "I better not. I think I'm going to be in trouble when I get home." She picked up the remnants of her ruined shirt and put it on.

Even in his weakened condition, she aroused him as she dressed. "Do you really have to go?"

She sat beside him on the bed, full of guilt. He was in pain because of her. *I wish I could make you well.* She thought about his safety and placed her hand on his arm to comfort him. *I wish I could make you well.*

"Wow, your hand feels warm."

Ilmar pulled her hand away from him as if something stung her. "Oh, I'm sorry, Danny." She stood up. "I must go."

"Do you need a ride?"

"You're in no shape to take me anywhere. I can find my way."

He called after her. "Lilly, when will I see you again?"

Ilmar turned to him. "You worry about getting better. I'll come see you soon." She walked out and closed the door behind her.

Ilmar walked the whole way back to the rendezvous point. She took off her heels and swung them in her fingers, walking barefoot. It took her hours to get from Danny's house in one town to the park in another town where she should have met the other girls.

She entered the County Parkland through the power lines.

From there, it wasn't too far down the trails to a defoliated area. A truly beautiful place, the County Park was protected by the humans. Protected not for the wildlife, although there were native animals there, but for the area's trees. The park encompassed the region of the "pine barrens." Humans set aside 693 acres of land for the preservation of the pine trees growing there. The humans lived under the impression the pine trees had special abilities to keep their ground drinking water clean.

Ha! She scoffed. *If they only knew how futile their attempts have been. Everything they touch becomes poisoned. Do they not realize that they are eventually bringing about their destruction?*

The clearing must have been a baseball field years ago when the humans frequented the park. Now overgrown, it homed partially grown scrub pines, red and white oaks, and wild blueberry bushes.

Ilmar inspected the area and sighed in relief. *Thank the Goddess no one is here waiting for me!*

She walked to the center where the sparse vegetation sprouted and reached for a large rock, picking it up. On the bottom was a small switch. She flicked it, and the turf beneath her feet rumbled. The sand moved upward, and an audible whoosh of air escaped as the Reaction Lift rose from the ground.

After the doors had opened, she put the rock back on the ground and stepped inside the Lift. When Ilmar pressed a button, the doors closed, sending the elevator into the depths.

What do I say...What do I say? Her mind raced.

Ilmar repeated those words to herself the entire ride down to Akkadia. Fear welled up inside her, causing her adrenaline to circulate throughout her body. *I do not think I have ever been this scared in my life.*

Her heart beat wildly. The closer the Lift fell to Akkadia, the worse her anxiety grew. When the alarm sounded to alert everyone to its arrival, her mother and father were sure to meet her as soon as the doors opened. She wrung her hands together in anticipation. The Lift stopped, and the door locks released.

Ilmartutar let out an explosive breath as Mage' Rom was the only one who met her at the rise entry. "Mage' Rom." She sighed in relief, "What –?"

He cut her off. "Your mother turned off the Reaction Lift

alarm."

"Oh." She let her voice trail off.

"You, your mother, myself, and the other girls you went topside with are the only ones that know you did not *return* last night. Your best friend, Reeglar, informed your mother, quietly, of the situation when she arrived." Rom took her by the elbow. "Come with me to the Healing Ward."

Relieved she was with Mage' Rom, Ilmar relaxed – growing up he was her favorite Scholar. She used to follow him around, was always right behind him, sometimes underfoot, but he didn't mind. He gave her a cute nickname, just for her. Prime. He did it because she was his favorite, always correct in her studies, always first with the right answer to all his questions, always eager to learn more. She was his Prime.

Prideful of her accomplishments, Rom protected and nurtured her growth. In Ilmar's youth, they both found an aptitude for Healing in her bloodlines. Ilmar's schooling revolved around the teachings of a Queen, the trade of a Healer would conflict with her stately affairs, and take too much of her valuable time. The lengthy education of the Healing Arts wasted Ilmar's time and resources.

Born with a secondary Ability, Ilmar's gifts of an Igniter likely came from her father's side. An Igniter took care of the successful running of the Kingdom. So again, not a possibility for a Queen. And surely not a necessary skill. Unschooled in her Abilities, Ilmar functioned without any useful Queenly Abilities at all.

When Mage' Rom and Ilmar entered the sterile walls of the Healing Ward, he ushered her into a private room. Ilmar sat on a cushioned slab. When Mage' Rom put both hands on Ilmartutar, she glowed with a slightly yellow light. It surrounded her entire body while it enveloped her in warm comfort.

"I think I have done something wrong," she confessed.

The Mage' raised an eyebrow. "Well, you have not yet conceived." He removed his hands, and the glow disappeared.

"Ugh." She sighed in frustration. "That is the least of our worries right now."

"Is there something you need to tell me, Prime?" he asked encouragingly.

She warmed to the affection in his tone and gazed down at her hands resting in her lap. "Yes, Rom, I have disobeyed you."

"Me?" he questioned. "I have given you no charge."

Ilmar shook her head, still unable to make eye contact. "The Healers... All the Healers. It is about the human I lay with."

Rom corrected her. "You mean humans, correct? More than just one. You have been to the surface four times, Prime."

"Yes," she admitted slowly. "Yet, I have been with only one human four different times, Mage'. I know it is wrong, but I could not help myself. My heart burns as the Abyss of Fire for him."

The old Healer seized her by her shoulders and forced her to look at him. "Ilmar, what have you done?" Her eyes welled with water, as she shook her head again. Rom continued his questioning. "What have you done? Is he still alive?"

Ilmar managed to nod through her tears. "Yes. Uh, he was, but he is not well, Mage'. He is weak." She finally met her mentor's gaze. "And he has bruises and blisters all over his body where I touched him."

"Oh, my dear, Prime." Rom cradled his young student in his arms and let her cry.

IV

A Captive Duty

Ilmartutar left Mage' Rom with a special gift. She held it up and turned the jar around, hoping it was all he said it was. She slid it into a pocket in her jeans before running to her quarters to clean up and change. She had joined her family by the time the Hall served mid-day meals.

She smelled the cooked food as she entered the Grand Hall. *I am starving*, she thought. Ilmar hadn't eaten at all yesterday and missed the first meal as well.

Ilmar nodded at her father and Azewrath. She locked eyes with her mother as she took her seat. A knowing glance passed between them, and Alkara gave her daughter a sad smile.

Ilmartutar dove into her food as if she had never eaten before. The freshness of it pleased her taste buds. As she ate, she made noises to show how much she enjoyed her food. "Mmmmm." She moaned. Azewrath and her father gazed over at her, questioningly. "Sorry," she apologized, food still in her mouth. "This is good!" Ilmar pointed to her plate and giggled. *I have had a lot of exercise lately*, she concluded.

Pikkar addressed his daughter. "How did you fare yesterday? We have not seen much of you of late."

"I have had to catch up on some sleep, Father," she answered. "I have been out late."

"Pikkar," Alkara interjected, "this is neither the time nor the place, for an interrogation, remember? Our gathering is shared family time." She placed her hand on his, and patted it, which calmed him. "Our daughter shall make time for us later, in our chambers." She brought her stare to Ilmar. "We shall take an audience with you on your progress after the evening meal." The statement was not a request.

Ilmar understood her mother was her ally, but her leniency went only so far. She resigned herself to the fact her evening grew complicated. "Yes, Mother," she promised.

Azewrath addressed Ilmar. "I would also appreciate your company after this meal."

Oh, Ilmar shrieked in her head, *how much more can I take?* She answered him. "Of course, Azewrath."

"Since you have slept most of the waking hours away, we shall not have much time together."

"It is best you get used to that," she stated flatly. "When I am Queen, we will have even less time together." *I hope!* But Ilmar hadn't slept. She was going to have to face the day exhausted.

With the meal over, Azewrath and Ilartutar excused themselves, left the Grand Hall, entering the corridor that opened into the Commonwealth. The pure beauty always took her breath away. Between her Queenly teachings and her frequent excursions to the surface, she hadn't had any time to explore and enjoy the wondrous, secluded expanse of the caverns.

They strolled past the shops of her subjects. Each person crafted objects needed by the people in their daily life. Markets lined the vast caverns and invited all to experience a harmonious enterprise.

There is the shoemaker. Ilmar waved to the stout little man with great talent.

Everyone had something to trade: textiles, services, building crafts, and entertainment. Some people of the Commonwealth had the Ability get inside your head and make you believe anything. After a visit to their shop, your memories were not your own.

Or so I have heard.

Ilmar let herself doubt the rumors. She was not allowed to go into those places. While life for her people bordered on the routinely mundane, their existence remained easier than in the world above. Although Akkadians missed the excitement of the fast-paced human society, the serenity of Akkadia pleased most.

As they continued, they passed the prosperous Food Agronomic Greenhouse Gardens. Again, her subjects went about their business of supporting the Kingdom's grocery stock. Each greenhouse encompassed sizeable cathedral-like area full of exotic vegetables and fruit.

When they strode by, Azewrath reached for her hand and wrapped his strong fingers into hers. She acquiesced. *I just do not have the strength to fight him today.*

She returned her attention to the wonders of the caverns, all aglow and full of life so far away from the power of the sun. The energy in Akkadia came from geothermal vents. Heat waves distorted the scenery, causing her eyes to search beyond the easily observed.

While she thought the caverns a magical place, sustainable life followed a natural path and made it easier for her people to tap into the well of wonders of the lower world. It all brought a smile to her face.

Azewrath sensed her elation. "What is the reasoning behind that big smile?"

"Just soaking in the beauty of this place." She beamed at him genuinely with a skip in her step as she trekked down the passageways through the catacombs. Ilmar wrapped her arm in Azewrath's, leaning her head on his shoulder while they walked on.

As they left the crowded empire behind, they witnessed a soft glow of light at the end of the tunnel they entered. Their footfalls echoed throughout the stunted cave and gave an endless loop of sound to the darkness. Azewrath and Ilmar emerged to arrive at a breathtaking subterranean lake.

The most extensive lake in the underground caverns, Lake Lunar, encompassed the entirety of the open space. So enormous, Ilmar struggled to see the other side. She fell into her fond memories of the lake. The magnificence of the bio-luminescent creatures housed within the domed canopy above the lake lit the area. Their glimmering lights reflected on the veil of the water's surface.

With the lake as the life-blood of Akkadia's food supply, workers covered its subtle waves. The laborers that caught many aquatic teleostei or fish, to sustain the people of the kingdom, held a prominent position. Different varieties of fish swam the lake's depths.

It wasn't a busy day at the reservoir, but they were by no means alone. Many fishing vessels sailed the lake with their nets. Azewrath guided Ilmar to a quiet cove away from the commotion of daily commerce. As they walked, the grinding of gravel under her sandals assaulted her ears.

You could never sneak up on anyone out here, she deduced. She approached a blanket, laid out with a fruit basket and a bottle of an intoxicant elixir. "What is this?" Ilmar motioned with her arm.

Azewrath grinned proudly. "Our alone time." She gave him a dower look, which made him explained further. "Most women would call this a very romantic gesture."

I would call it, presumptuous, she judged, yet didn't repeat her thought out loud. "Sorry, Azewrath. It is an indulgence fit for a Queen."

He lowered himself to the quilt, took her by the hand, and pulled her into his arms. He squeezed her so tightly he crushed her breasts into his chest. His lips met and captured hers as he lowered her to the mat.

Ilmar quickly broke their embrace. "Can I have a drink first?"

Azewrath sighed before reaching for the flask and glasses. He poured both and handed one to Ilmar. He took a sip. She placed the rim to her lips, tilted her head back, and downed the liquid in one gulp.

"Hit me again," she ordered and waved her finger. Azewrath glared at her, confused. "Fill it up again," Ilmar clarified. He did, and she shot her drink the second time. She glanced up at Azewrath. *Well, maybe I will be able to tolerate him, and our marriage, if I stay intoxicated the entire time. He truly is not harsh on the eyes.* She giggled out loud and hiccuped. Snatching the bottle out of his hand, she poured another cup full and drained it for the third time.

Azewrath stared at her, shocked – his first drink still in his hand. Ilmar stole it from him and tossed it on the ground. She propelled herself forward and tackled him to the blanket. Her emotional state shifted from all kinds of happy to lustful. He gazed up at her and watched her face descend to connect with his. He accepted her advance and returned her desire in kind. He firmed beneath her.

Ilmartutar embraced her intoxication and let her inhibitions fall away. She liberated his virility with both hands, rising to spread herself over him to accept his fullness inside her. She rode him, used him, and enjoyed him as her body ruled her mind. She let go of all her doubts and fears, of all the right ways to behave and concentrated on the pure joy that her physical form experienced. She rocked her hips, met his thrusts, and took him at his full swelling until the moment of sweet release. Then, spent, she fell to the ground beside him.

He turned to her and brushed her bangs from her forehead. Such a simple gesture, but one she had experienced before. *Oh my Goddess*, she panicked. *I forgot about Danny!* She rolled over, away from Azewrath. *Is he even still alive?* Ilmar wondered. The rippling water of the lake called her attention as one tiny tear rolled down her cheek.

***

As soon as Ilmartutar closed Danny's bedroom door, his head hit the pillow, and he passed out cold. His sleep, fraught with unsettling images brought forth his dreams again. The vision, the one that haunted his rest. Only it was different. He wandered around town at night in the dark. Still nude, but unsure of his surroundings. He limped, hunched over in pain. Pain all over. His flesh fell from parts of his body, exposing bone and muscle. Confusion and disorientation gripped him to his inner core. A distant banging grew louder as he struggled to discern the information – banging again and again. He sat up and screamed.

***

Danny's eyes flew open as his brother, Patrick, opened the door to his room. "Hey, you all right?" Patrick asked. "Still in bed, and it's 9:30."

Danny's heart rate dropped back down to a reasonable level. "I'm feeling like crap today, Pat. Dizzy, aching. What about giving me the day off?"

"Well, you don't look good... If that makes you feel any better." Pat laughed.

"Ha, ha!" Danny threw his sheets back over his head as Pat closed his door. He shut his eyes, hoping to fall back to sleep and not dream. *I should call Aaron,* determining, through his ever-growing grogginess. *See if he's okay.* But unconsciousness crept under the sheets with him.

***

Ilmartutar body sweat out the liquid intoxicant during her coupling with Azewrath, yet she moved sluggishly. The walk back to the city brought her the rest of the way to sober. She couldn't shake the dread about her ability to get to the surface to help Danny.

Tired and shaky, all she wanted was to get some rest, but her presence was requested, quite emphatically, by her mother and father. A confrontation Ilmar would have avoided at all cost. Besides everything on her plate, she must spend another night topside. She wasn't going to join the others at a bar; she was going directly to Danny's.

Please, Goddess, let me get there in time! She just had to make it through a few more hours.

Azewrath's gaze followed Ilmar from behind. She walked like a dancer, fluid in flux, her robes swaying in rhythm with her hips. She was beautiful, she was his, but he understood he would never be able to control her.

"I know you are planning something," he stated.

She tensed. "I am just thinking about my strategy with mother and father."

He didn't believe her. "You seem a million miles away."

"No," she replied absentmindedly. "Just fifteen."

"What does that mean?"

"Nothing, never mind. I am just tired," Ilmar covered. They both remained silent for the rest of the journey.

***

Ilmartutar took her last meal in her quarters. Her scheduled audience with her parents later troubled her; she needed to relax and unwind. Only with great difficulty was she able to keep her thoughts out of her head during her outing with Azewrath. When she brought herself back to center, Ilmar took the long walk to her parent's chambers with great trepidation.

The stark white of the corridors presented a less than welcoming embrace for her. It was as if she walked the last mile – the end of the line. Facing her parents held only emotional torture. She stood in front of the giant doors, knuckles raised, and knocked.

"Come," her father's deep voice called through the door.

She pushed open the large door and entered. Both her parents sat on an ornate chaise lounge, their expressions impossible to read. Ilmar approached, and her father motioned her to rest.

"Please, Illy. Relax with us."

"Of course, Father." She did as he told her, choosing a chair across from them.

"We know this has not been easy," Alkara started. "We are sorry we even have to ask you and the other girls to do this."

"But, this is important," Pikkar interrupted. "So far, there have not been many positive results."

"Father, it has only been two months for me!" Ilmar attempted to defend herself. "Did you or the Healers think that maybe there might be something wrong with our women, too?"

"All females have been checked, Ilmar. The Healers tested you, did they not?" Pikkar's question was more a statement.

"Are you insinuating I am not trying hard enough?" Ilmar cried. "You must be kidding me, Father!"

"Please, my loved ones," Alkara broke in, "I need this to be a civilized conversation."

"I am sorry, Mother," Ilmar apologized as she rose from the chair. "But I am doing the best I can, and I must go up again tonight. If I have suffered enough, I am leaving."

"Ilmar!" her father screamed at her. The lights in their chambers flickered twice as bright with his anger. "You shall not defy us!"

"What are you going to do to me? Punish me?" She opened the door. "I think what I am doing on behalf of our survival is adequate punishment!" She slammed the door.

Alkara faced Pikkar. "Why must you always be so hard on her?"

"Why must you always be so easy?" he returned.

***

Ilmartutar rushed through her usual motions of getting ready and was first to arrive at the Reaction Lift. *All this waiting is making me crazy!*

With her impatience unbearable, she paced the corridor. Eventually, all the women gathered, and she spotted her friend, Reeglar, make her way through the crowd. Ilmar smiled at her and received one in return. They entered the Lift as it journeyed to the surface.

Ilmar regarded her best friend. Growing up together, they held no secrets. They spent cycles upon cycles helping each other with their studies. As Chancellor Torg's daughter, Reeglar rivaled many as a strong Telepath among them. Her father, the Chancellor, was highly valued as the Queens most celebrated Council member. One of the most powerful Telepaths in Akkadia, he earned that title as an essential part of the Ruling Class.

Reeglar sensed Ilmar's eyes on her. The picture of refinement – tall, graceful, and pleasant, the young Telepath was far too smart for her own good. Her straight, dark brown hair would lie against the small of her back except for the fact she always kept it in a braid. Even while dressed in her human clothes for the evening, she sported her braided hair. Her eyes sparkled the most fantastic shade of golden brown.

"What have you done?" Reeglar's question was just a formality.

"I have created quite a problem for myself," Ilmar confessed.

"So I have seen." Reeglar referred to when Danny carried Ilmar out of the Tavern.

"Well," Ilmar asked, "what about you and Aaron?"

"I have lain with Aaron only once, as commanded," she stated. "And left marks, so I had to move on. To his dismay." Reeglar gave Ilmar a sly smile. They both giggled.

When they reached the surface, all the girls piled out and sent the Lift back to ground level. They removed all pairs of shoes, trekking through the thick sand of the parkland toward the town. When they hit the asphalt, everyone stopped to brush the sand from their feet and slipped their heels back on.

It is so strange, the way the sand gets stuck between my toes, Ilmar thought to herself. Then she heard Reeglar's laughter in her head. *Hey!* Ilmar thought back. *No fair peeking.*

I could not help it, Reeglar continued. *Your thoughts are so loud!*

Ilmar immediately panicked. *Reeglar will know. She will find out. Stop, stop, stop thinking,* Ilmar chided herself.

You are a terrible liar, Ilmar.

Ilmartutar experienced the sensual rush of Reeglar's search into her mind. It was impossible to hide anything from Reeglar, even if she wanted to. All the things Ilmar had done and what she planned to do was laid bare to Reeglar's mind. The Telepath scrutinized Ilmar's mind before bringing her gaze deep into her eyes.

"Oh, Ilmar, it is even worse than I thought. I can see your heart burns, as the Abyss of Fire." She took Ilmar's hand. *"I can not help you, my dear, but I shall not stop you either. Good Luck!"* Reeglar gathered all the women and led them into town and away from Ilmar and her task.

***

Ilmar exited the car and slammed the door. The stranger who gave her a ride to Danny's house drove away and left her standing at the head of the long driveway. She examined her surroundings and surveyed the hangers, the planes, and the house. Ensuring she was alone, she took her first tentative steps.

I am almost there. Ilmar sighed, hoping Danny still drew breath. *Did I make it in time?*

Ilmar hurried toward the house, unsure of what she would do next. Danny's car wasn't in the driveway, but he was in no shape to drive the last time she was there. Ilmar stood in front of the door she entered the night before. She knocked, waited, and then knocked again louder. Soon the door opened.

A strikingly beautiful man greeted her. The resemblance to Danny was uncanny, but Danny's features were more masculine than the man in front of her. This man was perfection, with flawless skin, and pleasing features, the kind that caught you by surprise. She immediately liked him.

He must be Patrick, she assumed. *Oh, my!*

"Can I help you?" Patrick asked.

"Yes, hi," started Ilmar. "I'm Lilly. I came by to see Danny. I know he's not feeling well." She used human contractions, attempting to mimic human speech. It was easier to go unnoticed as an outsider in their society.

Patrick smiled. "Sure, I'm his big brother, Patrick. Come on in." She followed him into the house. "He's been sleeping all day. I guess he really *is* sick."

Ilmar studied Patrick. His very dark hair and ice blue eyes which seemed almost white complimented each other. A spectacular specimen of a human man, she found herself captivated by him.

"I brought him something to make him feel better. Can I look in on him?"

"Yeah, go ahead. Can you find his room?"

"I remember where it is, thank you. Very nice to meet you, Patrick."

"Nice to meet you too, Lilly."

Ilmar practically ran to Danny's room and burst through the door. Bundled up in his sheets, a tiny tuft of hair stuck out, the only thing on his body exposed.

Is he breathing? She wondered.

"Danny! Danny!" Ilmar gently urged as she shook him. She made sure to touch his bed sheets and not his skin.

"Huh?" he replied.

"Hey, it's me, Lilly." Danny rolled over to face her. "Hi, there!" She smiled at him. "How are you feeling?"

"Like I've been hit by a truck." He tried to make a joke.

"I brought you something." Ilmar pulled out a small jar from her jeans pocket. "It will help you Heal."

Danny propped himself up on his pillows and took the small container from her. The bags under his eyes were dark and deep – his appearance, gaunt and drawn. "What is it?"

"Old family secret," she instructed. "You'll just need a little. Rub it all over your injuries, and you should be feeling better in no time."

"Maybe you should rub it on me," he teased.

"Oh, no!" She smiled and shook her head. *I should never touch you again*, she thought, putting on a brave face. "It works best if you do it yourself."

Danny scooped a tiny bit with his index finger and went to apply it to his arm. He stopped short. *Where'd the bruises go?* All the injuries on his arm healed. "What the hell!? What happened to the marks on my arm? They're gone."

Ilmar examined his arm. "You're right. That is weird." She checked his back. "They're still back here, and on your other arm and chest." *How did he Heal?* "Just rub it on somewhere else."

Danny applied the lotion to his chest. It cooled his skin where he spread it. "Wow!" he said. "It feels soothing." His chest took on a slight yellowish glow. "Hey, I'm feeling better already. What's in this stuff?" He studied the jar.

Ilmar shrugged. "I don't know… I just know it works. So, put on some more."

He did, and when the rest of his body took on the glowing hue, his strength returned. "Oh wow, Lilly, I feel great! I feel so much better."

She took the jar and screwed the cap back on. "Let's keep it here on your nightstand." Ilmar placed it down. "You never know when you'll need it again. *Thank you, Rom, for making this cure. It worked.* With so many variables as to whether the Healing Power infused into the lotion would help Danny, she rejoiced it worked like a charm.

Ilmar watched Danny stretch his muscles to get the kinks out. "I've spent all day in bed, and I'm so stiff."

"Uh-huh," Ilmar responded. "I'm not going there!" She giggled.

"But I'm getting my energy back," he tried to coerce her. "And I didn't get any exercise today."

"I think you'll survive one day without exercise," she told him. "Plus, I have been disciplined for not coming home last night." She stood, bent over to graze her lips across his forehead. "I just came by quick to make you feel better."

"You're leaving?" Danny sounded disappointed.

"Yes, I must." She turned to go. "I'll see you again soon! Promise." Ilmar blew him another kiss and stepped out the door.

***

Ilmartutar returned to the rendezvous point before any of the other women. Everyone seemed light and cheery, smiling and laughing, except Lacara. Ilmar noticed the woman appeared downright miserable. She moved closer to her as they entered the Lift.

Ilmar put her hand on Lacara's arm. "Is everything going well with you, Lacara? You seem disturbed."

The older woman practically popped right out of her skin. "Yes, Ilmartutar!" Lacara spoke too loudly.

"I am glad you are all right then," Ilmar said.

Almost immediately, Lacara's whole attitude brightened, and she smiled. "I am all right," Lacara stated and gazed off into space.

All right? Ilmar thought. *I do not believe you are all right. I must speak with Mother.*

As she mused about Lacara's odd behavior, her thoughts came back to her problems with Danny. She remembered something that would help her. Something she heard one of the women speak of a few months ago. She would take time to visit that friend.

V

Life and Death

It shall be a fabulous day. Ilmartutar imagined. She got herself together and sailed out of her quarters to meet everyone at the early meal. Even the sight of Azewrath, as he waited for her, didn't sour her mood. She would solve her problems with Danny today, she just knew it.

Ilmar nodded to everyone. "My family," she declared and received greetings in return. As she sat next to Azewrath, she brushed her lips across his cheek. So startled by her behavior, he almost jumped out of his chair.

"Well!" he announced, regaining his composure. "You are exceptionally affectionate. What do you want?"

"Nothing! I wished to say hello. Am I not allowed?"

"You most definitely are allowed, and I welcome the gesture." He bent over and kissed her gently.

"Mother," Ilmar began. "I think you should spend some time with Lacara today. She was not quite right when I saw her last."

"What do you mean?" Alkara questioned her.

"I am not sure. She was – *uncentered.* One moment she was almost vibrating, and then, when I said she would be all right, it was almost like she became calm and was... *all right.*"

"Was she intoxicated?" Alkara asked.

"I do not believe so," Ilmar answered.

"Did you touch her when you spoke to her?"

"Humm..." Ilmar tried to think back. "Yes, I believe I did." Alkara nodded her head. "Do you know what is wrong with her?"

"I shall command an audience with her. I do not know why she is stressed, but I think you must have Healed her into that calm state."

"I did?" Puzzlement gripped Ilmar.

"Part of a Healer's Ability is to 'channel' a cure for whatever is not right inside the body. When you touched her and said everything would be all right, you *Healed* her to peace."

"Oh, I see." Ilmar truly didn't understand. *I know so little about my Abilities.* "I would like to know more about my gifts."

Pikkar interrupted the conversation. "Ilmartutar shall be Queen, not a Healer. That Ability is something you need not know."

"But if I could help people –?"

He cut her off again. "You are also an Igniter. Would you like to learn how to run the Reaction Lift as well?"

Azewrath changed the subject. He sensed Ilmar wasn't forthcoming with something... something she didn't want anyone else to find out. "You have plans today." He made the statement, and it was not a question.

Ilmar's heart leaped into her throat. *Oh Goddess, help me to be steadfast in my mind.* "I do," she agreed. "It was not my intention to make it public knowledge, but since you have brought it up." Both her parents contemplated her suspiciously. "I have seen some very appealing styles in the human world. I planned to have a tailor and shoemaker design new clothes for me."

Her father laughed. "Big plans, indeed!"

"It is not that important." She sighed. "I can postpone it."

"No, my dear," her mother encouraged. "You go ahead and shop today. Create something beautiful."

"Thank you; I will." Ilmar smiled. Azewrath gave her an evil gaze, but the rest of the meal continued without issue.

***

Danny woke full of life. *I feel like a million bucks!* He jumped from the bed and went to enjoy a hot shower. On his way out of the bathroom after his wash, he ran into Patrick. "Hey bro!" Danny slapped his hand on his brother's shoulder.

"Looks like you're feeling better." Pat noticed.

"Like a new man! And ready for a full day of work."

"Hope you stop to get dressed first." He laughed at Danny.

"Hey, this towel is the latest in summer wear." Danny laughed as well. "It would do you well to get yourself one. You'd catch more ladies if you sported one of these now and then, and ran around half naked."

"I don't need any help in the lady catching department, thanks. And if I did, I wouldn't take any advice from you! From what I've seen, looks like you've gone off the market yourself."

"You never know…" Danny trailed off.

"She was very concerned about you last night," Patrick informed him. "I think she's lovely, too."

"Hands off my girl, bro," Danny warned, but still smiled.

"Wouldn't think about it."

"Okay, well I'll see you in the shop." Danny took off to get dressed.

Once in the shop, Danny fiddled with the Teledyne TCM Continental A-65 piston, from a Cessna 172RG Cutlass. He halfheartedly watched News 12 Long Island on the flat screen in the shop, his mind, distracted by thoughts of Lilly. A big smile crossed his lips.

Patrick walked in, joining him at the mechanic's table, and shook his head. "You know, you been walking around with that stupid grin on your face for the past three days."

"Well, you can't count yesterday."

"I don't think I can stand hanging around with you if you're going to continue to be this happy every day."

"You're just jealous."

"Have you been drinking already?" Patrick jokingly asked.

"Yeah," Danny answered, and raised a cup in his dirty hands. "I'd love to have a beer, but as it's only nine o'clock, I'm substituting with coffee. Anyway, I have to catch up on all the mess you left me." While he bantered with his brother, something on the TV snagged Danny's attention.

"Whatever…" Pat said.

Danny held up a greasy finger. "Shush!" he ordered. "Shhhh, hold on, Pat. Stop talking." His eyes transfixed to the broadcast.

The TV showed a close-up shot of someone's skin, the arm, covered with dark bruise marks and large blister-like pustules. *Oh my God!* Danny thought in a panic. The news anchorman, Doug Geed's, face replaced the arm on the TV. He spoke.

"The man was found in his complex, the Town and Country Apartments, off Montauk Highway in Hampton Bays, behind the Villa Paul Restaurant. Authorities were directed to his address by a 911 call."

"What's going on?" Pat asked.

The news team played the 911 tape:

> **911** – "911, what's your emergency?"
> **Caller** – "He is dying… Or dead…"
> A small voice reported.
> **911** – "What's the situation? Are you hurt, ma'am?"
> **Caller** – "He needs a Healer…Um, medical attention, I mean."
> **911** – "Stay on the line, and we'll get someone out to your location."
> **Caller** – dial tone

The anchorman, Doug, came back on the screen. "The call ends there, and the police found no one else at the scene. We've been told the CDC has taken over the case. They're asking anyone with information to please call the hotline number:"

1-(770) – 7100 The number flashed on the screen.

Confused, Patrick turned to Danny. "Danny, what's going on?" But Danny ignored him, transfixed by the screen.

"… To recap," the anchorman went on. A picture of the dead man replaced the anchorman. "Jeff Donaldson, age twenty-five, found dead in his apartment, late last night, under suspicious circumstances. The police aren't ruling out foul play, or a possible contagious disease development. Call the CDC's hotline number at the bottom of the screen if you have any information."

I know that guy! Danny thought. *We went to school together. He's a regular at Frampton's. SHIT! We're all screwed!*
Danny finally addressed Patrick. "Look, I gotta go." That was the only information he gave his brother.
He put down the plane parts and grabbed a rag to wipe his hands. Patrick observed his brother drop everything and take off. He ran straight to his car. Danny jumped in the Camaro, jammed it into reverse before spinning a quick U-turn in the driveway. He

whipped out his cell phone to call Aaron.

What the hell? Was all Patrick could think as he watched Danny screech down the driveway.

***

Aaron woke at Sarah's house. He stretched, reached for her, but came up empty. She wasn't in bed next to him. She worked the graveyard shift, and he wanted to be there when she came home, so he spent the night. He thought she'd be in bed to snuggle with him in the morning. Disappointed, he slid out of bed, threw on a pair of boxers, and headed out to the kitchen to make coffee.

As he exited the hallway, he noticed Sarah sat on the couch with her coffee already in hand, staring at something intently. "Hey, baby." He greeted her, bending over to give her a big kiss.

"Ugh," Sarah groaned and made a face. "Thanks for the morning breath!"

"You didn't come to bed!" Aaron yelled as he shuffled his way into the kitchen to make his cup of java.

"We had a big case pop up last night," she answered back.

Aaron's gaze shifted to the kitchen shelf and all of Sarah Halsey's awards. As a Southampton town detective on the force for ten years, she was one tough cookie. Being short in stature, she made up for it with gritty determination.

She twirled her wavy red hair and squinted her light green eyes. Her outward appearance belied a femininity which hid the competent police officer – a contradiction in itself.

He turned to stare at her while he took his first sip of coffee. The few freckles that speckled the bridge of her nose gave her a Pippy Longstocking air, adding charm to her harshness. The Halsey's were one of the first families to colonize the towns out on the East End. With her years of service in the police force, her family still gave back to the community.

Aaron met Sarah one early morning, driving back to the college housing after a hard night of drinking with Danny. She pulled him over, but let him off with just a warning – and her phone number. Sarah's attraction to him was immediate, and she wasn't able to reprimand him. At twenty-five, she was three years his elder, but that didn't get in the way of their dating. They spent the last seven years together, more or less.

As he made his way back to the living room, his cell phone rang. He left it on the TV stand the night before, so he changed direction to see who called. The phone displayed a picture of Danny on the LED screen.

Just woke up, partner. He used a Western accent in his head. Aaron hit the "ignore" button.

Sarah stared at the photos intensely. Aaron took a giant gulp of his coffee, placed it down on the table and tried to kiss her again. "Aaron, no! I just got off work, and I haven't had a shower yet."

"I love you dirty!" he teased her, but she still ignored him. "Okay, no more Mr. nice guy." He grabbed her and threw her down on the couch. "We're just gettin' started, so I'm not through with you!"

"Hey!" she yelled, as he kissed her neck. "Oh, what the hell!" She reached up and grabbed him by his ears. He loved that.

"Oh, baby," he mumbled, crushing his lips between her bosom. She moaned with pleasure. He removed her blouse, slowly, pulling it over her head. Wrapping his big hands around each of her breasts, he gently massaged them. Aaron slid the straps from her bra off each shoulder and peeled her bare. "My beautiful little girl!" he complimented her, taking his mouth and enveloped her full mounds.

"Not so little, you beast!" she swore back.

He ran his mouth all the way down to her jeans. Aaron opened her button deftly with his teeth and tongue before he grabbed and pulled down the zipper. He gazed up at her triumphantly. Sarah helped him pull her pants down her thighs and off her legs altogether. Her thong joined the cascade of clothes on the living room floor. Aaron, intent on stripping off his boxers, caught his toe in them as he went to fling them with his other foot. He tripped and crashed on top of Sarah.

She laughed, as he regained his composure and propelled his fullness inside her. "Well hello, big boy!" she managed to say, as Aaron thrust himself into her.

Grinding, they attacked each other with a fervor – mouths searched, and hands groped. Their sex was like a circus act, acrobatic and aerobic. Aaron on top first, and then Sarah on top. They lay on the couch and performed; they sat upright as Sarah rode him. They threw each other around until they ended up on the floor, covered in sweat and completely spent.

Sarah reached for her shirt and pulled it on. Her nipples, still erect, protruded through the material. She stood and danced her way into her undies. Pulling up one side, and then the other. Partially redressed, she returned to the couch. She grabbed the rest of her now, cold, morning cup of "joe" and went right back to studying the photos.

Aaron peeked over at the pictures Sarah had spread out on the coffee table. The photos showed the body of the man lying on a bed. *Excuse me;* he thought as he corrected himself. *Young man.*

The guy in all the pictures was Jeff Donaldson. Aaron knew him. Apparently, Jeff was dead; his body covered in marks. Marks with which Aaron was all-too-familiar. Hyperventilating, his heartbeat drummed inside his head. His breathing quickened and suffered extremely lightheadedness. Aaron hit the couch next to Sarah with a thud.

Immediately, she worried about him, under the impression the graphic photos affected him adversely. "Well, honey! I didn't think you were that sensitive. I'll put these away for now." She gathered the pictures and brought them into her office.

Normally, he would watch her hips as they swayed back and forth when she walked away, fantasizing about her incredible ass. Not that morning. Instead, he jumped up, ran to the bathroom, and got dressed in record time. He zipped back into the living room and snatched his cell phone, just as Sarah returned. She puzzled at his appearance.

"You're leaving?" she asked.

"Yeah, sorry, Danny called." He held up his phone and shook it.

"I didn't hear it ring," she challenged him.

"Before," Aaron said. "He left a message," he lied. "Something about serious shit going down, and he needs me to meet him, now."

"Oh, okay," Sarah said. "Are you alright?"

"Yeah, hon." He kissed her cheek. "I'll call ya later."

"Bye..." Sarah closed the door behind him, bewildered.

***

Aaron ran to his Dodge Ram truck with his phone to his ear. Danny didn't leave a message; he lied to Sarah. But that's who he called.

Hurry up! Answer the damn phone! Aaron thought impatiently.

Danny finally answered. "Aaron!" Stress colored his words. "Thank God! I'll be in, in a second."

"In? In where?" Aaron asked.

"Inside... Your job, remember? I'm in the Atlantis parking lot." Aaron worked on staff at Atlantis Marine world, in Riverhead. "When I didn't hear from you, I drove here as fast as I could."

"I'm not at work today, *ass!*" Aaron's exasperated reply met Danny's ears. "Shit's going down, bro!"

"Yeah," Danny answered. "I know. Okay, meet me at Frampton's, ASAP."

"Okay, bye."

"Bye."

Danny hung up, threw his cell phone on the passenger seat and headed back to Hampton Bays. Twenty minutes later, both men sat in the empty bar with Lisa, the bartender, as she prepared the bar for the day.

She set them up with two beers, but Danny grabbed her hand. "We'll need two shot glasses and leave us a bottle of Jack on the bar, will ya?" Danny told her. She shook her head but gave it to them so that she could open the bar in peace.

Danny poured the shots of Jack Daniels. "We're in some deep shit here, Aaron. Jeff Donaldson's dead. I saw it on the news this morning."

"I know," Aaron confirmed it. They both did their shots and slammed the empty glasses down on the bar. "Sarah is working the case." He practically sounded hysterical. "I saw the damn pictures, Danny." He rubbed his hand across his forehead. "The shit... The bruises on Jeff were surely the same kind I have on me!"

"You still have 'em?" Danny asked.

"No, they're finally gone, but what does that mean, exactly?"

"What do you think we should do, call the CDC number?" Danny filled the shot glasses again.

"I don't know. Would you sit here with me if you thought this thing was contagious?"

Danny cleared his throat and downed another Jack. "Until last night, I was covered in those things too."

"What?" Aaron's eyes opened wide in disbelief. "What the hell? How? And when were you gonna tell me?"

"Uh, I've got no idea how I got it. It's got a be contagious, right? I probably caught it from you."

"Me?" Aaron asked.

"Well, you had it first," Danny argued. "Why didn't it kill you?"

"Why didn't it kill *you*?" Aaron yelled back, emptying his glass.

Danny reached for the Jack and poured again. *It didn't kill me, 'cuz of Lilly's medicine. What was in that stuff? Should I show it to the CDC?* "More importantly, why did it kill *Jeff*?" He threw back his head and drained his drink. "You're the God damn biologists, what do *you* think?"

Aaron drank another Jack shot. "I'm a marine biologist, you idiot! How the hell would I know?"

Danny stared Aaron right in the eyes. "A body is a body, what difference does it make if one stands and the other swims?"

"Are you going to tell me all your engines work the same way?"

"Basically! It's all the same. It don't work, so you make it work. It's that simple."

Aaron poured another shot. "Well, the human body is just a little bit more complicated."

Danny took the bottle of Jack Daniels from Aaron and poured the very last drop into a shot glass, watching the drip, drip of the alcohol as it splashed into the small shooter. *What a mess,* he thought, mesmerized by the dark amber liquid as it swirled around and around. He drank it before capturing Lisa's attention. "We'll have another bottle over here."

"Whatever you say, Danny," Lisa replied.

By 2:00 PM, eight beers, and 17 shots each later, both men

still hadn't come up with a solution to their problem.

"I think I've had enough," Danny slurred. "Iss time for sum fresh air."

"Yeah," Aaron agreed. "Lesss go." They stood and wobbled to the door.

"You guys all right?" Lisa shouted to them.

Danny waved a shaky arm without turning around. "Isss all goood, honey!"

When Danny opened the door, the bright sunlight accosted him. As he shaded his eyes, he stumbled to the curb and unceremoniously plopped down on his butt. "Think I'm gonna just sit here, a while," he mumbled to Aaron while his body swayed back and forth.

"Great idea!" Aaron agreed, hitting the pavement as well. "I think I'll join ya!" He leaned back, but his arms buckled and he passed out, flat on the cement.

VI

Love Ruins Everything

Ilmartutar set out on her errand of necessity. She hurried down the corridors of Akkadia until she reached the marketplace. She wandered from shop to shop. Keeping a sharp lookout, she made sure no one followed her. She wouldn't put it past Azewrath to have someone stalk her every move.

He knows something is up with me. I can tell.

Ilmar spent an hour roaming the Galleria of the Commonwealth. She hoped it was long enough to be sure she could hide her true mission to any unwelcome, spying eyes. She secretly made her way back through the hallways to the newest places in the kingdom. The Laboratories. She needed to find Minnar.

Ilmar walked down many passageways until she found the new workshops. *This is it!* She moved inside.

There, an older woman sat at a worktable. As Ilmar advanced, she realized it was indeed, Minnar. She turned, and a bright smile lit her face when she recognized Ilmar. Minnar was older than Ilmar by at least nine or ten plantings and a lovely woman; an Empath, like Ilmar's mother.

"Ilmar!" Minnar called out, surprised. "So wonderful to see you." Minnar rose slowly from her chair. That's when Ilmar noticed it. With Minnar one of the first women with the charge of visiting the surface, Ilmar observed the hugeness of her, the roundness.

Mystifying. She is very pregnant! Even the words held a strangeness in her head. "Minnar," Ilmar breathed, "you are magnificent!"

"Thank you, my dear." Minnar laughed. "But I do not feel it. Just moving has become a chore." She took Ilmar by the hand and closed her eyes. "Hummmm, but you did not come here to bask in my enormity." Minnar brought Ilmar to the table. "I must sit. Do you mind?" Ilmar shook her head, and they both sat. "I feel your pain, Ilmar."

"I do not know what I am thinking lately." Ilmar couldn't keep the distress from her voice.

"Love rarely involves much thought."

"Me?" Ilmar asked. "In love?"

"Do you doubt it?" Minnar asked. Ilmar shrugged her shoulders. "So," Minnar continued. "This insane need to see this man again and again, even though you shall eventually kill him, does not mean you are in love with him?"

"How can you be sure? How can *I* be sure?"

"Ilmar, I have been inside your heart. Believe me when I tell you, you are in love with Danny."

Ilmar sighed. "What am I to do? I was hoping you might have something to help me."

"I have what you need. I made it myself. I had to." Minnar opened a drawer under the table and pulled out a very small box. "Being an Empath, I was overwhelmed by what we had to do on the surface; the pain that I caused others. My device is how I fixed the problem, I hope." She opened a small package and revealed a tiny gem on a curved post.

"What is it?" Ilmar asked, taking the thing and examining it.

"It is a replica of something I saw in the human world. The surfacers call it a belly piercing."

"Piercing, as in through the skin?"

Minnar pointed to the spot on Ilmar's abdomen. "Right there!" She took the gem from Ilmar. "Are you ready?"

"Now?"

"Yes."

Ilmar held her breath. "All right."

Minnar pinched the skin above Ilmar's naval, and then swiftly pushed the post through her flesh. "Ouch!" Ilmar whined. "It hurts."

Minnar took the ball and screwed it into place. She grabbed Ilmar's hands, gently laying them on top of the new wound. "Now, close your eyes and think about having no more pain."

Ilmar did as Minnar told her. Slowly, a slightly pale yellow glow covered her belly. She stared up at Minnar, her eyes wide in disbelief. "There is... no more pain!"

"Of course not, Ilmar. You are Healer!"

"I did not know how to do it. No one has ever shown me."

"Well, now you do."

Ilmar's grateful smile beamed. "How will this piercing help me?"

"Pinch the ball once, and it activates the gem, which is a powerful magnet. It generates a magnetic field around you, like a second skin," Minnar explained. "You shall be able to touch a human, without coming into contact with them. I have learned a lot about their technology from the man with whom I spent my time."

Elated, Ilmar jumped into Minnar's arms and hugged her tightly. They both took on the yellow glow of Healing. Worried, Ilmar moved away from Minnar quickly. "Oh, no! I am so sorry for touching you."

Minnar smiled. "You did not hurt me."

"I do not know what affect the Healing power would have on the child within you," Ilmar fretted.

Minnar placed Ilmar's hand on her large belly. "You could only give me the Healing Blessings from the Goddess herself." Both women stood motionless, enveloped in the warmth of the radiance of Ilmar's Abilities. When the light receded, each of them basked in contentment and jubilation. A sense of inner peace.

"Thank you, Minnar. I will never forget this." Ilmar left the Labs feeling hopeful for the first time in days.

***

Alkara sat on her Throne. She requested Azewrath's presence during Lacara's audience. Lacara stood below the dais, her head down in supplication, attempting to remain calm.

Azewrath spoke to Alkara. "My Queen, we are in the midst of a terrible undoing."

The Queen addressed Lacara. "My daughter has said you are not centered, Lacara. What say you of this?"

Lacara glanced absentmindedly at her sovereign. "I have done my duty in the name of my Queen."

"Yes," Alkara agreed. "I have consulted with the Mage'es, and they have found you to have indeed conceived. My only issue with this is if you are six weeks along in your term, why have you continued to go back to the surface? Once we have confirmation of implantation, there is no longer any need to return."

The weight of the Queen's words hung heavily on Lacara. *I shall never again see my Jeff. No! I must stop thinking...* "I understand, my Queen," Lacara responded out loud.

Azewrath studied Lacara. He narrowed his eyes, walking toward her and circled, deep in concentration. He tilted his head as he walked. Studying her, he stopped dead in his tracks.

"Oh, my Goddess!" He grabbed Lacara by the arm. "Stupid girl, what have you done!"

Lacara broke down and cried. "I am sorry... So sorry. I tried to stop, but I fell in love!"

"Azewrath, what is this about?" the Queen asked.

"I believe we need to call in Chancellor Torg, your Eminence. I sense we have a serious problem here."

"Then do so," Alkara ordered.

Azewrath went to the Chancellor's Council seat and placed his open palm on a panel on the long table. It glowed briefly. "He is coming."

"I am sorry," Lacara kept repeating. She dropped to her knees, still sobbing.

"LACARA!" Alkara raised her voice.

"I think she has passed coherency, my Queen," Azewrath relayed.

The Throne Room doors opened, and Chancellor Torg glided into the Hall. "Torg," Alkara addressed her Chancellor, "I need your assistance."

"I know," he answered flatly.

Torg moved to the huddled wreck of Lacara and raised one hand toward her. He closed his eyes, breathing deeply. He amplified his Telepathy to allow both Alkara and Azewrath to experience in their heads, all that Lacara had seen and done. Within seconds, both witnessed the damage she had brought to the human, all of his injuries, his slow pain, and how he suffered by her contact with him. Until his ultimate death, culminating with her anonymous call to the authorities.

Azewrath exploded. "I knew something was amiss. Mingling our two species could only lead to disaster." He turned to Alkara. "Your daughter is involved in this, somehow. I have not the proof you need as of yet, but I can *feel* it!"

"Ilmar?" the Queen questioned him. "I think you are mistaken, Azewrath." She stood. "Torg, I need to broadcast to the people."

"Yes, my Queen." He mounted the steps to the Queen's throne and grasped her forearm. She reached out and did the same back to him. Torg amplified her thoughts throughout the kingdom.

"My people," Alkara began, her words vibrated in the minds of her entire kingdom. *"My people,"* she repeated. *"We have come to a crossroads. Our very existence could be in great jeopardy. Effective immediately, any and all visits to the surface are forbidden! I command all Council Leaders and the entire envoy of women who have been to the surface, to appear before me in the Throne Room at once!"*

Everyone jumped as a thunderous crash pulled their attention to the giant Throne Room doors. They flew open and expelled an extremely angry Prince Pikkar. His emotional state spoke to everyone through the strobe effect that controlled the lighting inside the Throne Room. Alkara sat on her throne feeling hopeless for the first time in days.

***

Ilmartutar reached her quarters when her mother's words touched her. *No!* She begged. *No, not now! Not when I am so close.* She snatched an empty bag, filling it with all her human clothes. Slipping from her room, she made her way to the Reaction Lift.

When Ilmar arrived at the Lift, she opened the access door reserved for the Igniter. *I can figure this out,* she told herself.

She studied the room, puzzled. Nothing in the room gave her an idea of how to remotely start the Lift. The space held two round lights, one green, one red, about eye level. With no other objects in the room, she stood stumped.

I give up! She peeked out of the cubby, making sure no one had entered the hall. *All is still clear.*

Ilmar picked up her bag and opened the Lift doors, stepping inside. When they silently closed behind her, she pressed the button that made the Reaction Lift rise, usually. Nothing happened.

Well, I figured it would not work. Now, what do I do?

Everyone would be meeting in the Throne Room, and she would be found missing. Panic gripped her, but she needed to remain calm to figure out the Lift. Ilmar took a deep breath. She closed her eyes and let her mind find her center. She watched her father control the illumination of all the lighting in Akkadia many times.

How hard could it be? I can do this! She pledged.

Ilmar moved to the back corner of the conveyor. She placed each hand on a different wall, then concentrated. A slight white light spread from her fingertips across the wall, filling the entire room. A small quaking shuddered under her feet that grew and became a stronger rumble. Her body heated up, and sweat escaped her pores. Ilmar's body shook, as the Lift began its ascent to the surface. She screamed out in pain with the stress and concentration it took to control the Reaction Lift.

VII

The Betrayal

A crowd of people filled the Throne Hall. Council tables lined to the right, and the left of the Royal dais were aflutter with speculation. Each member of the Guilds in an uproar about the meeting. The noise level reached a deafening volume, but Alkara needed to restore order.

After Pikkar had stormed in, he grumbled and demanded to know what was going on, Alkara attempted to ease his anger. Now, he sat on the Queen's left side and stewed in his outrage, infuriated but silent. She noticed the smaller chair on her right – empty.

Ilmar… Alkara sighed, shaking her head.

From the highest seat of honor on the right far side Council table, Azewrath sat quietly. His elbows rested on the flat surface of the table, thumbs and fingers touched together in the form of a triangle, tented. His demeanor, in sharp contrast to the kinetic energy of the rest of the Hall – until he bolted straight up as if jolted.

Azewrath slammed his palms down against the tabletop. "QUIET! SILENCE!" he demanded. He stood, and captured the rooms attention quickly. "My Queen, Prince Pikkar… Ilmartutar is heading to the surface."

"What?!" Pikkar roared.

"How?" Alkara asked. As if in answer to her question, the Reaction Lift alarm blared.

Prince Pikkar immediately jumped from his throne. He descended the stairs, standing in front of Dinnac, the Igniter Council Leader, and Pikkar's brother. "The order was no more trips to the surface!" Pikkar confronted his brother. "Who is helping her run the Lift?"

Dinnac glared wide-eyed at his older sibling. "I can assure you, Pikkar, no one is!"

"Then you need to gather your people and bring the Lift back down before she reaches the upper realm."

"There is not enough time, brother."

Chancellor Torg stood. "It is Ilmartutar, herself, my Prince. She is controlling the Lift."

"How could this be? She has never been schooled in the arts of the Igniter Ability?" Pikkar demanded.

"Nonetheless, it is her," Torg reiterated.

"We must stop her!" Pikkar ordered. "Torg, call more Telepaths. Together, your combined strength shall pull the Reaction Lift back to Akkadia."

"I shall try."

Torg spread his arms open wide, creating a bond between himself and all the Telepaths in the kingdom. He searched them out, one at a time. Each person, answered his call to aid him and added their mental strand to entwine with Torg's dynamic stream of kinetic energy.

A colorful physical manifestation of their combined power came together and gave extra power to Torg's Ability. Every person in the sovereignty experienced its growth as it gathered in strength. It reached outward and upward, making its way to the Lift.

***

Ilmartutar worked feverishly to control the Reaction Lift, but she grew fatigued. Her body sweat profusely and shook violently. The exertion strained her Ability almost to capacity.

The trip is taking so long! She thought.

She tried to judge how much longer she could keep up the strain, against how much longer it would take to get to the surface and her freedom. Her palms slid down the walls with the moisture from her sweat, so she adjusted her stance over and again. With her robes soaked to the skin, she gritted her teeth tightly, causing her jaw to ache.

She cried, her pain hit her so intensely. *I have to be close.* She hoped. As she reached her breaking point, the Lift jumped and stopped its ascent. *I have made it!*

Ilmar opened the doors, taking her first sight of the sky and the trees. Laughing through her sobs, she fell to her knees. She wiped her face to dry her tears of joy and the sweat from her exertion, grabbing her clothes. Getting to her feet, she wrapped her arms around her bundle.

As she went to step out, the Reaction Lift shook violently, knocking her off her feet, and she fell to the floor. *Oh no!* She worried.

Deep in her heart, she panicked at the ramifications of the Reaction Lift's shaking and squeezed her eyes shut. The air around her filled with an electric charge. Ilmar opened one eye, hoping she was wrong. Crackling tendrils of energy reached up, winding themselves throughout the Lift doors, walls, and ceiling. There was so much electricity in the Lift with her, all the hair on her body stood up on end.

My parents have commanded the Telepaths to bring the Lift back down.

An undeniable fact. Slowly, the room moved, pulled down by the sheer will of the people of Akkadia. Ilmar observed the land in front of her rise, taking away her last hope of escape.

"Oh, no! You will not take me!" She yelled, propelling herself out of the receding opening. She reached back inside and barely got her pack out before the open door slid down below the surface. Ilmar rolled through the sand and watched as the lifeline to her world sank into the darkness, gone to her for good.

Ilmar wasted no time. She sprung to her feet, gathered up her robes and tied them up in a knot in front of her to give her more maneuverability. She threw her bag over her shoulder and took off at a run. Considering a real possibility someone might come after her, she had no intentions of being there when they did.

***

The Chancellor lowered his arms, shook his head and addressed the monarchy. "The Lift is safely on its way down, but I regret to inform you that your daughter is no longer inside." His declaration caused all the Council Leaders to speak at once.

"Enough!" Alkara commanded. "I have had enough insanity for one day."

Apparently, the Prince had not. The entire Hall glowed so brightly, the light temporarily blinded everyone. "Someone must go up after her, right now! Otherwise, we shall lose her." Pikkar ordered.

"I shall go and bring her back," Azewrath promised.

"You shall need a Telepath," Alkara added before regarding her Chancellor. "Torg, summon your daughter, Reeglar. If anyone can help us find Ilmar, it shall be her. She is Ilmartutar's best friend, and I am sure she knows something that can help us."

I am sorry, Ilmar. You have forced my hand, and I have no choice, the Queen thought to herself.

Chancellor Torg turned to Alkara but continued their conversation via their Telepathic link, in private so no one else could hear. *"I have called Reeglar. We shall do everything in our power to find her and keep her safe in the process, my Queen."*

"Thank you again, Torg, for sending Reeglar."

"She shall be a great asset to Azewrath," Torg thought back to her.

"Then hopefully she can temper his anger as well," Alkara continued her thoughts to him. *"He is, after all, Pikkar's best friend; cut from the same cloth."*

Reeglar came into the Throne Hall dressed in her human clothes. "I am ready, Azewrath. We must hurry, let us go!"

Pikkar approached them both. "Bring her back, Azewrath, by any means necessary." He said it to Azewrath but glared directly at Reeglar.

"We shall, Prince Pikkar!" she answered, sarcastically.

Prince Pikkar snapped his fingers at Phlynoc, the young Second of the Igniter Council under Dinnac – a worrisome and fragile young man. "Phlynoc, take your position and send them up, NOW." The last word was an order.

Azewrath and Reeglar took the fifteen-mile ride in the Lift to the surface. The doors opened, and they both stepped out. Azewrath immediately squinted his eyes against the light of the sun before gazing at her inquisitively.

"Do you have any inkling on where to start our search for Ilmar?" he asked her.

"The first thing we should do is get you some new clothes."

"Will this attire not do?" He gestured to his white tunic.

"Oh, it will work, all right. If you want humans to think you are the ice cream man." She giggled.

Azewrath's expression held one of puzzlement. "Who?"

"Oh, never mind!"

"Unfortunately, you girls have picked up too much of this barbaric language from your travels to the surface. It offends my ears."

Reeglar hit him with it full force, using all the contractions she could. "Yeah, I know! Come on, let's go, we're burning daylight."

***

Ilmartutar ran through the power lines until she hit the streets. She dropped her bag, bent over, and rested her hands on her thighs, catching her breath. They were at least fifteen minutes behind her. Aware of her father's behavior, she needed to push forward. The Prince would send a retrieval squad.

They will be here soon. I must force myself to keep going.

She motivated herself into action. With the street lightly traveled, procuring a car before she reached the main road would prove difficult. Ilmar picked up her pack and set out at a slow jog. As luck would have it, a car drove past. It pulled over and stopped just ahead of her. Pleased, Ilmar ran over to the car as the driver rolled down the window.

"Do you need a ride, sweetie?" said the tiny voice from within the car.

Ilmar almost laughed. She glanced into the window at the smallest, wrinkled, little woman. *This poor person can not even see over the steering wheel,* Ilmar thought.

"I am going far," Ilmar answered her.

"Well, where are you headed?" the old woman inquired.

"To Sutters School of Aviation, in East Quogue?" Ilmar hoped she said it correctly.

"Okay, honey, I know where that is, get in. I'll take you there."

"Really?" Ilmar asked. "You don't mind?" The old woman shook her head. Ilmar threw her pack in the back before sliding into the passenger seat.

"Of course I don't mind. I'm just out for a drive on a beautiful day! Doesn't matter to me where I end up. Plus, that bag looked heavy."

"It was... is, I mean. Thank you." Ilmar explained, nervously.

"Put your seat-belt on, dear."

"Oh, all right." It took her a second to figure it out, but she finally snapped one piece of steel into the other piece of steel.

"Hold on!" The old woman put her foot on the accelerator and Ilmar jerked back into the headrest.

Oh, my! Ilmar grabbed onto the door handle for stability.

As they chatted politely, Ilmar learned the old woman, Mabel, was an ex-WAC, whatever that was, and spent her life working for the Coast Guard. Ilmar guessed it was some form of human military. With the pleasant chatter, the ride didn't take that long at all. When the car stopped, she snatched her pack out of the back and jumped out.

"Thanks, Mabel!"

"You take care, Lilly. Don't let anyone tell you what to do, or how to live!"

"I won't!" Ilmar promised. As the car roared off into the distance, Ilmar was left to choke on the road dust.

Ilmar trekked down the long driveway to Danny's house. She knocked on the door and waited, but no one answered. Dropping her bag of clothes on the porch, she wandered over to the plane hangar.

Although the enclosure was gigantic and clean, all three planes filled the hanger lined up in a row, spaced perfectly apart. *Such wondrous things,* Ilmar marveled.

Human flight was such a strange concept to grasp. She witnessed the Telepaths levitate many times before, but planes in flight were different. The number of miles those crafts traveled could keep her hidden from any and all who searched for her.

Something I would like to do right now.

Ilmar thought something moved just out of the corner of her eye, by, or inside the last plane farthest from her. It wasn't the biggest plane in the fleet. She moved closer, as her curiosity drove her bravado. It was Danny's house, after all.

What could happen?

Danny had told her about the plane – a Dova D-1 Skyhawk. Patrick's aircraft, also his hobby. He loved it like it was his baby. Pat spent all his free time either tinkering with her or flying her. The Dova was not a school instruction plane. The Dova was Patrick's little girl – his only love.

Ilmar walked right up to the plane, but as she reached out to touch its smooth surface, the canopy window slid back, and Patrick popped up.

"Yikes!" Ilmar yelled, startled.

"Whoa!" Patrick almost lost his balance.

"Sorry!" Ilmar apologized. "I didn't mean to scare you."

"Oh, it's okay, Lilly, right? Just wasn't expecting you. I thought I was alone. Once I start working on the Dova, I get lost." Patrick stepped onto the wing and jumped to the ground. "What a pleasant surprise, but I'm afraid Danny's not here. I don't know where he is."

"I see." Ilmar pretended to be disappointed. "I really need his help."

"Let's go up to the house," Patrick offered. "Maybe there's something I can do to help you?"

"This is going to sound terrible," she apologized, as they walked. "But I need a place to stay. I sort of ran away from home." Patrick's eyebrows shot up when he saw her pack by the door. Ilmar understood his reaction and tried to explain. "Oh, not *here*," she clarified. "I just thought you might know of a place I could stay." Patrick's silence spoke to deep thought. "Since Danny's not here, maybe it would be a better idea if we didn't tell him about this, yet. It is, after all, my problem. We could just keep it between the two of us, okay?"

Patrick didn't know Lilly that well, didn't know her home life and didn't want to get caught up in it. But Danny was very fond of her, and by the look on her face, she was pretty broken up about running away. They entered the house, and Patrick opened the refrigerator to offer her a beverage.

"Want a beer?" He presented one, and she nodded. He cracked open the cap off a Miller Lite and handed it to her. "Look, I probably shouldn't get involved. Could things be that bad to make you want to leave your home, a place where people love you? Maybe you should rethink this, Lilly."

Ilmar took a sip of her beer, leaned back against the sink, and sighed. "It's just for a little while, Patrick," she promised. "Until I can figure out what to do. I've gotten to the age where what I want, and what my parents want for me, don't fit together." She gazed at him. "You know what I mean?"

The chances of my people finding Patrick are slim, but I am certain they will eventually find Danny. I can not let him know where I will be staying.

Patrick expelled a lungful of air as he thought. "Okay, look, there is a small outbuilding at the end of our property. We used to rent it out to our mechanic before Danny was old enough to work on the planes himself. No one's occupied it in years, but I guess you can stay there while you figure things out."

"Oh, Patrick, thank you!" She put down her beer and hugged him.

"O-K, O-K." He broke away from her. "Let's get you over to your new place, and maybe you could get yourself cleaned up. What the hell are you wearing, anyway?"

Ilmar glanced down at her soiled white Akkadian robes and gave him a crooked smile. "Don't ask."

Pat led her out the door and slid into the quad. He used the four-wheeler to take him places within the small airfield. She pushed open the door, picked up her bag, and jumped into the machine with Patrick.

***

Azewrath and Reeglar headed to the heart of town when they reached Montauk Highway. "Are you sure we have time for this?" Azewrath asked.

Reeglar used logic. "I do not know where Ilmartutar is, do you? Do you sense anything yet? Have you had a vision?" He gave her a sidewards glare before shaking his head no. "All right, then we get you clothes first. After that, I have an idea of where to start."

They walked about three-quarters of a mile, and she marveled at the insane amount of traffic at the intersection. A "diner" stood at the crossroads, so she explained to Azewrath the building was where humans met and ate their meals together, like in the Grand Hall. Reeglar glanced down the major highway as far as her eye could see, but only witnessed numerous cars. Miles and miles of them.

Where are they all coming from, and where are they going? She wondered, unaware it was a regular occurrence for a

Saturday afternoon in the Hamptons during the summer season.

"These cars will collide with each other. I have Seen it." Azewrath stated. "Many will die. So unnecessary."

"It is how the humans travel."

"Foolish!" he bellowed.

After another three-quarter of a mile through the heart of town, Reeglar took a right turn. She walked over to the waste receptacle on the street corner, reached in and pulled out a sheet of newsprint paper. She ripped off rectangular sections of 5-inch pieces, folded all six of them, and put them into her pocket. She yanked Azewrath into a man's clothing store. Carl and Bob's.

Reeglar quickly picked out a pair of jeans and held them up against Azewrath, checking that they were the correct size. She grabbed one dress shirt, a couple of nice T-shirts, and a sweatshirt zipped hoodie, completing the pile. Afterward, she pulled him to the checkout counter.

"Okay, let's go," she said.

"Why will I need so many pieces of clothing?"

"You never know."

She went to the register, and the store owner rang up the total. It came to $125.94 plus tax, which brought it to $136.80. Azewrath watched as Reeglar took out two of the six pieces of newsprint from the garbage. She stared at the shop owner and held out the two pieces of paper.

"This piece of paper is $200," she thought directly into his brain. The owner took the papers, put them in his cash register, and gave her $63.20 back.

"Thank you," she replied. Taking the bag, she dragged Azewrath by his arm and ran out the door.

She walked swiftly down the block and tried to usher Azewrath along, but he stopped and scanned the area. "I sense something… A connection, somewhere."

Reeglar nodded and pointed. "That is Frampton's over there," she instructed him, as they moved past. "And right there, where those men are laying down passed out on the cement? That is where we shall go later tonight. We may even see Ilmartutar."

"I doubt she will be that easy to track down. She is not a fool, Reeglar. I am sure she knows we shall be searching for her and using our Abilities."

"Yes, but does she know it shall be a Telepath and a Seer who search for her?" Reeglar offered, continuing onward.

"Where are we going now?" Azewrath wondered as he followed her.

"Back to the diner, so you can change your clothes, and we can eat. We do not want to go to Frampton's on an empty stomach."

"Wonderful," Azewrath moaned sarcastically.

Danny and Aaron were sprawled out on the sidewalk in front of Frampton's when Brad, the owner, pulled up. He got out of his car, stood above them, giving Danny a slight kick with his foot.

"Ugh..." Danny managed, as he peered upward, but had to squint because of the sunlight. "Brad... is that... you?"

"Yeah, what the *hell*, Danny?! You didn't come in last night 'cuz you were sick. And today, I find you drunk as a skunk laying on the sidewalk, and you gotta be to work in..." Brad looked at his watch. "Three hours. It's four o'clock already."

Danny sat up and leaned on his arms. "I'm okay, really. I'll be here on time. I promise, Brad."

"You do know you're already here, right? Whatever." Brad shook his head, turned around and walked into his bar.

Danny focused his eyes in Aaron's direction. Still passed out, he snored loudly with his mouth open. Danny reached over and tapped Aaron on his cheek with his hand. "Hey, wake up, beautiful."

"Hmmm..." Aaron managed to roll over and open his eyes. "How long have we been sleeping in the sun on the pavement?"

"Oh, I don't know, at least two hours? Well, at least that's what Brad told me."

"Aw, shit!" Aaron grumbled, rubbing his head with his hands. "I've got such a headache. Why did we drink so much?"

"I don't want to think about it." Danny changed the subject. "I need major coffee. Do you think we can make it to the 7-11?"

"Danny, it's only two buildings over," Aaron stated flatly.

"Yeah and...?" Danny asked again. "Can *you* make it?"

Aaron tried to get up but failed miserably. "You're right; I don't think I can." He collapsed back onto the pavement.

A black Ford Escape hybrid pulled into the parking lot. When Aaron spotted it, his guilt surfaced. "Uh-oh, we're in trouble now." He guided Danny's attention to the woman who exited the SUV.

"The cavalry!" Danny shouted out when Sarah approached them.

Sarah glared down at the two men. "More like the war party! I'm not even going to ask."

"How did you find us?" Aaron asked, still woozy.

Sarah reached down and helped them both to their feet, walking them to the car. "Brad called. He said you guys were littering his sidewalk, and someone needed to come and get ya before ya went out with today's trash."

"Hey Sarah," Danny began as he got into the back of the SUV, "can we stop at Sev's? We need major brewage!"

"UGH!" Sarah moaned, rolling her eyes. Nodding her head, she spat at him. "Of course!"

Afterward, Sarah dropped Danny off at his house. He ran inside, took a quick shower, and got redressed for work. With his stomach grumbling, Danny rummaged through the fridge for something to eat. He stood with the refrigerator door open and ate leftover KFC extra crispy chicken straight from the bucket.

I wouldn't be surprised if I threw up tonight at this rate. Danny stuffed his face as Patrick entered the kitchen.

"Oh, shit!" Patrick jumped, startled. "I didn't expect to see you there!"

Danny smiled, his cheeks full of chewed chicken, so Pat could hardly understand him. "Sooorwy 'bout dis morning. Thr was ssht goin' down... Serioss ssht!" Danny chewed and then swallowed. He cleared his throat and tried again. "Really Pat, I'm sorry. I'll work all weekend to make it up to you, I swear." He returned the bucket to the refrigerator and closed the door.

"Yeah yeah, I've heard that before."

"How were things here today? Everything okay?"

"Why?" Guilt spread through Pat, so he answered Danny too quickly. "What you mean? I'm fine, nothing happened."

"O-K! Fine! Look, I've got to get to work. I think by the time I get home tonight, I'll sleep like the dead."

"Just don't forget you've got to get back to work on that piston tomorrow. I gotta fly on Monday."

"Promise." Danny used his index finger to make a cross over

his heart. Picking up his coffee cup from before, he headed from the house.

VIII

What's Love Got
To Do With It?

By seven o'clock, Danny stood at the front door of Frampton's, just as he said he would. Hot, tired, and his head throbbed, making him feel like crap. But, it wasn't the first time he worked hung over, and it probably wouldn't be the last time, either. Only one way to push through his discomfort; get a few drinks under his belt, and he would be good to go.

With the bar packed, and the forecast for the weekend 80° and fabulous, Danny let the throng of people inside. It's what he loved about the summer, so many people out there. Happy people. Everyone smiled, sang, danced, and carried on into the wee hours of the morning. It made him happy too. He was doing his job, checking IDs when his cell phone rang.

Shit! Danny swore to himself. With his attention otherwise occupied, he gazed down at the screen quickly but didn't answer. *What does Aaron want now?*

As if in response to his question, he got a text message. Again, he glanced down at his cell phone. The screen said: "CALL ME!" In capitals with an exclamation point after it.

Can't be good. Danny worried.

Danny searched for some help. José, the bar back kid, walked by, so Danny grabbed him. "Stay here for a minute and check IDs, okay?" Danny held up the license, tapped on it, and brought it up to José's face. "Look! Get it?" He pointed to José's eyes and the license again. The young man nodded, but he had a panicked expression.

"Yes!" José said, smiling.

"Great!"

Danny left José at the front door and made his way deep into the bar. Walking out the back, he pulled out his phone, hit Aaron's number and waited for him to pick up. As Danny prepared, he checked out the night sky. As darkness fell, and the stars appeared in the twilight heavens, all was right with the world.

Finally, Aaron picked up his phone. "Jesus Danny, more weird shit," he announced.

Danny had him on speaker. "Well, hello to you, too!"

"Not really!"

"What else is new? Where's Sarah? And how much trouble are you in?" Danny laughed.

"She's in the shower, so I don't have much time. I'm so grounded. I feel like a kid."

"You're so whipped!"

"Okay, I know. Listen to this," Aaron continued. "Sarah talked about the case, about Jeff. Both the forensic pathologist and the CDC have run every test on him... on the body."

"And?"

"And, they don't think this stuff is contagious."

"Really? Cool!" Danny was okay with that.

"Y-e-a-h..." Aaron dragged out the word. "No! If it's not contagious, then what the hell is it, or what *was* it?"

"What'd Sarah have to say?"

"They don't know! They're still running tests. I just wanted to let you know."

"This is good news, right?" Danny asked.

"Danny, I had it, you had it, and Jeff had it. If it's not contagious, THEN WHAT THE HELL DID WE HAVE? You get it?" Aaron pounded the implications home.

"I don't know, bro. I'm not good at filling in the blanks."

"Yeah, I know," Aaron agreed. "That's why you keep me around."

"Hey, I gotta go. I left José at the door."

"Oh, no!" Aaron laughed. "Good luck with *that!* See ya!"

"Later, bud!" Danny turned off his phone, put it back in his pocket and made his way to relieve José at the door.

Reeglar and Azewrath stood in line at Frampton's, waiting to get inside. A short-statured young man took ID cards scrutinizing them. He held them up to people's faces, in hopes they matched.

Azewrath, uncomfortable in his human clothes, fidgeted, trying to remove the material from his rear end. "These jeans are so tight; they are sneaking into places I would rather wish they did not."

Reeglar giggled. "Well, they make your bottom look good."

"I am not sure I like the idea of people looking at my bottom."

"Loosen up, Rath," Reeglar instructed him as they entered the pub. They walked right up to the bar, pulled out two stools, and took a seat.

Azewrath scanned the environment. "There shall be some trouble coming."

"I do not read that from anyone at this point," Reeglar stated. "But we are in a bar, anything is possible." She caught the bartender's attention. "We'd like two drafts." She paid the tab with her real money; the change she got from the clothing store owner. Azewrath questioned her with his eyes, so she explained. "We might be here for some time. I do not wish to call attention to our phony money while we remain."

Instead of answering her, Azewrath eyes glazed as stillness took over. He sat that way for a few seconds. Reeglar witnessed his behavior before.

"I have just Seen something acutely disturbing."

She pushed the giant mug in front of him. "Then drink your beer, and you shall forget all about it."

He took a sip. "Not bad... Yet... Reeglar, we should talk about this."

Before he could continue, a young man sat next to Reeglar. "Hi," he said. "Can I buy you a drink?"

Reeglar barely turned to him. "No thank you." She pointed to her drink. "I already have one."

"Are you sure?" He moved closer and put his arm around her.

"She is with me, little person." Azewrath stood and approached the other man, menacingly.

"Wait, wait, it's okay!" Reeglar pushed Azewrath back into his seat.

While they were busy with each other, the other man took the opportunity to drop a few green and yellow pills into Reeglar's beer. "Hey," the intruder said, backing up, "I don't want any trouble. It's cool."

The young man returned to his friend and whispered to him. "I just juiced her up with some X. Let's see how unfriendly she'll be to me after the Green Turtles and the Louis Vuittons kick in." They both laughed and sat back to watch what would unfold.

"Was that the trouble you were talking about?" Reeglar asked Azewrath.

Azewrath looked almost embarrassed. "Hardly! Just forget about it. Do not give it another thought. I need to concentrate and so should you!"

Reeglar brought her mug to her lips. She took a large swig and swallowed. *Hum, this tastes different,* she thought. She tried it again. *No, I need something else.*

She handed her mug to Azewrath. "You can have this. I'd like something else, something sweeter, perhaps." She ordered a White Russian. The bartender placed it in front of her, and she took a sip. "Ummm! This drink is much better!" She watched as Azewrath finished his beer and grabbed the one she gave him.

Danny returned to the front door to relieve José. "Hey, thanks for watching the door."

José held up two licenses. "Yes," he said.

Danny took them. "Great... Okay, you go back and help Terri behind the bar." He studied the ID cards in his hand. "And I'll go find these poor people and give them back their license." He made a quick sweep of the bar, found the people, returned the IDs and apologized. He went back to the door when Reeglar glimpsed him.

"Azewrath?" She touched his shoulder gently. "I think I have found something... or rather someone."

Azewrath marked her hand on his shoulder, but the warmth of her touch went through his shirt, which oddly thrilled him. "What?" He jolted back to reality.

"Just let me do what I do," she told him. Reeglar reached out with her mind to touch Danny's. She searched and probed. *So many thoughts of Ilmartutar.*

Reeglar could "See" all the time Danny and Ilmar spent together. His emotions for Ilmar were genuine. As she walked through the phases of their love, his capability for tenderness toward her best friend warmed her heart.

He does not know anything about her whereabouts at all. He does not even know she is missing! Reeglar observed Danny scratch his head, and then tap at his temples, so she pulled out of his mind.

Reeglar turned back to Azewrath. "Dead end," she informed

him. "Our best lead seems to know nothing! Literally."

"Now what?" Azewrath finished Reeglar's beer and put the mug down on the bar.

Reeglar downed the rest of her White Russian. "We have two choices. We go back to Akkadia and return tomorrow, or we follow that man home and see if he eventually leads us to Ilmar." Reeglar pointed to Danny, who stood at the door, checking IDs.

"Who is he?" Azewrath asked.

Reeglar hesitated. "Well... He is, um... He is the reason Ilmartutar ran away."

Azewrath laughed. "THAT?" he bellowed. "*That* is the reason I have had to come to the surface?" He swung his bar stool around, observing the human. "He is a buffoon, Reeglar. What is *wrong* with that woman?"

"She fell in love, Azewrath."

"BAH!" Holding up his hand, he stopped her before she could say anything else. "Love is for the simple-minded. If it happens between two people over time, so much the better, but it is by no means, important to any equation."

Confused, Reeglar pressed him. "So, you do not love Ilmar?"

"Absolutely not!" he explained.

"Then why... Why...?" Reeglar honestly didn't understand.

"She is pleasing to look at, exceptional in bed, my mental equivalent, for the most part, and essentially, she shall be the Queen. So what if she is a little hard to control. It is to be expected. She is spoiled but destined for greatness."

"I see," Reeglar replied curtly.

"I suppose this means we are staying here all night?" Azewrath worried. "What human time cycle is it now?"

Reeglar searched the bar for a clock and found one. "It's 10:00 PM. Their cycles track chronologically in increments of hours, but the bar stays open until 4:00 AM."

"Goddess! I must sit here another six-hour term?"

"Ilmar might still come in tonight."

"Doubtful."

"We could play pool to pass the time?" Reeglar suggested.

"What is that?"

"It is a game of skill. You hit numerous balls on the table with a stick, forcing them into holes."

"Wonderful," Azewrath said sarcastically, standing. "I can not wait to learn."

Reeglar ordered each of them another drink and led him to the pool tables at the back of the bar. Their location concerned Azewrath. "If Ilmar does show up tonight, we are too far away to watch the front door."

"I have a link to Danny's mind, right now. If he sees her, I shall know immediately. Come on; we are stuck here, let us have some fun!"

At the back of the bar, two large pool tables took up most of the space. Two couples occupied one. They laughed with each other and were obviously having a good time. Reeglar collected all the balls on the next table and placed them in the triangle rack. She proceeded to explain the game to him.

"There are fifteen balls altogether, plus a white cue ball. That makes seven solid balls and seven striped balls. There is also a black eight ball." Reeglar placed the rack and the balls near the end of the table. "I set them up here, and then gently remove the rack, so the balls stay in place." She went to the wall and removed two cue sticks. She handed one to Azewrath, who accepted it. He studied it closely.

"How do I hit the ball with this stick?" Azewrath asked.

"Do not do anything yet. Just watch me. I take the white cue ball and put it on this mark, right here." She showed him the point on the table. Reeglar placed the cue stick down on the table and took the position. She bent over, but Azewrath was too close, and she bumped into him. "Step back a little; you are in my way."

"Sorry," he replied, moving to lean against the wall. He watched Reeglar make her break shot scatter the balls. For some reason, he couldn't take his eyes off her rear end.

So round and firm looking, he observed.

"See!" She turned to face him, grinning. "Now, I did not get a ball into any holes." She pointed to all six of the holes. "So, now it is your turn. Just position yourself behind the white ball and aim for a pocket."

Azewrath lifted his stick and tried to mimic Reeglar's form. He took his shot but missed the cue ball completely. "Arg!" he complained.

"It is all right, let me help you." Reeglar got behind him and brought her arms around his shoulders, laughing. He was too broad for her reach. She couldn't get her arms around him. From their position, her breasts pressed into his back as she tried to help him with his form. All he could think about was her nipples rubbing against him, back and forth.

"This is not working," he stated, flustered.

"I can not reach around you well enough." She backed up a bit and grabbed his right arm. "Loosen up," she instructed. "Let the shoulder remain still and swing the forearm from the elbow." She put her hands on him and tried to get him to relax.

"I am fine," he attempted to convince her. "Just... go stand over there." He pointed with his cue stick. "And let me try to shoot again." *Goddess! What is wrong with me?*

He shook his head, trying to clear his thoughts of her lean, muscular body. He gauged the table and studied the position of the balls. Aiming, he let the stick fly. The shot dropped two solid colored balls into the holes.

"You did it!" Reeglar jumped up and down, clapping her hands for him. Azewrath laughed as he watched Reeglar. "You must go again, but now you can only hit the solid colored balls into the pockets," she warned him.

Azewrath studied the setup and chose his shot. He missed. "Uga!" he exclaimed. "I missed! Your turn."

Reeglar picked up her cue stick and placed it on the table. A hypnotic song played, causing her to swing her hips back and forth in rhythm with it. Mesmerized by those swinging hips, Azewrath succumbed to fantasy.

In his mind, she wasn't standing in front of the pool table. She danced, spinning around slowly – a dance full of desire, of longing. She swayed gracefully around an empty room, empty except for her, whirling, her movements so sensual, so enticing. He shook his head again, attempting to clear it. She took her shot and missed, bringing him back to reality.

"Oh!" She turned toward him. "I could cheat, you know." Reeglar concentrated on the table, and a striped ball rolled into a nearby pocket. She faced Azewrath again and giggled.

"Reeglar!" Azewrath warned her. "Someone might see you."

She took a sip of her drink, smiling – her eyes twinkled over the rim of her glass. "The only person watching me right now is you." He gave her an innocent look. "Do not think you can fool me, Azewrath? I can tell. You can not hide anything from a Telepath."

She put her drink down, walked over to him, and deliberately swayed her pelvis as she walked. She moved slowly and came closer until she was inches away from him. Almost as tall as he, she blew her warm breath on his neck, caressing his skin. She tilted her head up and locked his gaze. Azewrath returned Reeglar's stare, and an overwhelming urge to take her overpowered him. They stood there for what seemed like an eternity... Waiting.

"Hey, we have the winner of the next game on this table."

Startled, they both turned to see who spoke. It was the same young man who wanted to buy Reeglar a drink before. "I'm Dave, and this is Bob," he introduced himself and his friend.

Reeglar addressed them. "We're not playing to win or lose. We're just having some fun." She made sure she used human contractions.

"That's cool with us," Dave said. "We can play partners for fun."

Azewrath took a swig of his beer and shook his head. "Not now."

"Hey, it's the bar's rules, dude," Bob told him.

Reeglar spoke to Azewrath quietly. "It's all right, Rath. It'll pass the time." She shifted her attention back to the boys. "Set us up, boys."

***

Ilmartutar spent the whole day cleaning the outbuilding. It was a mess. She found someone's old thong under-panties – dirt covered and crusty. She picked it up with a forgotten screwdriver she found lying around and put it in the black garbage bag Patrick left her.

Earlier, Patrick turned on the breakers to the cottage and found the electricity and running water still working. He came back with some food, a couple of towels, bed sheets and the blanket. He promised to be quiet about where she was so that Danny wouldn't know. It would be their little secret.

She finished up the cleaning and jumped into the shower. The water was warm but very wet. Something which she was unaccustomed, but she needed the relaxing sensation. She washed away the sweat of her escape, her old life, and the day's work. After the strain of bringing the Lift to the surface, and afterward cleaning, she needed to rest. The Princess never worked so hard.

Ilmar stepped out of the shower onto the tile floor, her bare feet cold against the clay tiles underneath her toes. She quickly grabbed a towel, wrapped it around her, and tiptoed into the other room. After she had dried herself off, she retrieved her bag and put on her human clothes.

A plane landing, or taking off at the military airport in the distance, caught her attention, so she peeked out her open window. It was late, the stars already twinkled in the sky, causing her eyes to play tricks on her.

Such a strange sight, she mused as a warm breeze blew through her window, stirring strands of her flaxen hair.

She made up the bed, settled down and let the softness caress her tired body. She drifted off to sleep. Her last thought was to sneak down to the house and surprise Danny when he came home.

***

With Reeglar's normal ability impaired, it was difficult to concentrate on what she was doing. Something was very wrong inside her. At almost 4:00 AM, closing time, she wasn't at all tired. She had had a busy day, yet she was wide-awake and full of energy. Azewrath had too much fun beating the tar out of Dave and Bob in the game of pool.

All right, so I am helping him a bit. Reeglar smiled at that thought.

She received weird intentions from Dave's thoughts, about things she didn't understand. He was up to no good, but every time she tried to explore his mind, it was like coming to the edge of a cliff. His thoughts were not cohesive, almost addled brained at times. He waited for some payout, however. She was sure of it.

Azewrath won a fair amount of money on the game from the

two boys. The wad bulged in his back pocket. With Danny leaving, it was time for them to get outside. If all went as she planned, they would follow him home. To accomplish that task, she needed to rely on her Telepathy.

Azewrath put the eight ball into the back pocket of the table. "Yes!" he said, triumphantly. Anger consumed Dave and Bob. They each slapped a $20 bill onto the edge of the table. "You boys should have quit while you were ahead." The Akkadian boasted.

"Azewrath, we should go..." Reeglar pulled him by the arm while he put all his money together.

"Thanks for the memories!" Dave called after them before whispering to Bob. "Let's follow them out."

Once outside, Reeglar studied the parking lot. "Danny drives a Camaro. We need to find it and keep watch."

Azewrath still smiled at his accomplishment. "How are we going to track him?"

"I have an idea. The two men whose money you have just taken?" she explained, and he nodded. "We are going to take their SUV."

"Their what?"

Reeglar surveyed the lot until she found Dave's car. *There it is.* "I found it, come on," she declared to Azewrath as they approached the Jeep.

Dave and Bob left Frampton's and headed straight for their truck. "Hey honey," Dave called out to Reeglar when he saw her standing by his car. "What's the matter? Couldn't get enough of me?"

Reeglar advanced toward both boys. She smiled and put her hand out. To their surprise, she brought her arms together in one sweeping clap. All at once they collapsed to the pavement from the shock wave of her force blast. She called out to Azewrath.

"Help me drag them into the bushes. Oh, and grab the keys." Azewrath joined her and stuffed them into the low brush. "They shall sleep it off and wake up refreshed. Do not look so worried."

"I am not worried about them. I hope you are driving. I am feeling a bit strange... Almost hyper-alive."

"Yes, I shall drive. I have seen it done, and I have peeked into Dave's mind for a more technical application." She unlocked the door to the Grand Cherokee. "Get in." Reeglar put the key in the ignition and turned over the engine.

They didn't have to wait long for Danny to leave work and walk to his car. Reeglar put the Jeep into gear and followed the Camaro. She pulled out of the parking lot, but bucked and jumped the Jeep as she shifted. Azewrath fought the urge to lose his dinner. After a few minutes and a couple of stop lights later, she had the whole driving thing under control.

As Reeglar drove, her entire head throbbed, disconcerting her. Her inner voice told her she still wasn't right. She experienced a tingle throughout her body, and her heart beat faster than usual. Azewrath picked that moment to place his hand on her thigh, stroking it with interest.

She jumped at his touch. *What is going on with him?* She wondered. He touched the leg she pressed against the gas pedal and made it more difficult for her to control the speed. *But his caresses feel so good,* she thought.

Azewrath slid his hand higher on her leg, his fingers tracing the silkiness of her skin. She didn't dare look at him. It took all her concentration to follow the Camaro. She tried to stifle a slight moan, but he heard her and brought his hand higher between her thighs. Her foot pressed the accelerator harder than she wanted and the Jeep sped up.

"Do not get too close!" Azewrath warned.

Reeglar gritted her teeth. "I was doing just fine… before…"

She slowed the vehicle down, leaving a more significant space between their truck and Danny's car. The dark road held treacherous curves, difficult to see with the lack of streetlights. It didn't help that she actually enjoyed, and even craved Azewrath's advances, which preoccupied her attention.

Danny made a right turn, so she made a right. The road took them through endless potato fields. They pulled up to a stop sign and watched as Danny's car made a left and then a quick right down a long driveway.

"You are going to lose him," Azewrath told her.

"No," Reeglar answered. "This is where he is going. It must be his house."

She found the switch that turned off the headlights and slowly followed him into the driveway entrance. Danny exited his car and went into the house. The outside light went out after a few moments, so Reeglar pulled the Jeep closer to the house, but stopped by the hangar. She turned off the engine and waited.

"Now what?" Azewrath asked impatiently.

"Let me open my link with him."

She sat back in the driver seat, closed her eyes and reached out to Danny's mind. Even engrossed in her preparations, she was astonishingly aware of Azewrath unbuttoning her blouse. She couldn't believe it and tried to pay no attention to his manhandling.

"Danny is getting something to eat, chicken I think. And there is no sign of Ilmar." As he listened to her oratory, he slid his hand into her shirt and wrapped his fingers around her breast. She bit the inside of her cheek, tamping down her angst and then continued to relay Danny's movement. "He brushed his teeth and is now going to bed. I am sorry, Azewrath, he is thinking about Ilmar, but she is nowhere around, as far as I can tell."

Reeglar opened her eyes and thought directly into his mind. *"STOP!"* she demanded.

The power of Reeglar mind slammed Azewrath's body into the passenger seat and pinned him there. She didn't even touch him. He sat, frozen in place as if something held him down, curtailing his ability to move.

Reeglar turned right to study him. "How are you feeling right now, hum?" she asked. "Can you not move?" She pushed herself onto her knees to get a closer look at him. "You were extremely liberal with your movements before." Reeglar leaned over the center console to get even closer, and she put her hand to her ear.

"What did you say? Nothing? Oh, that is right, you can not speak either at this term." She leaned back and laughed out loud. "How about I let you in on the little secret, Azewrath." She moved in again, closer to him. "I am a Telepath, remember? No one does anything to me unless I want it done. Do you understand?" She released her Telekinetic hold on him.

Azewrath took a huge breath. "Reeglar, I apologize. I am obviously not myself tonight. I do not know what has come over me."

"Oh, shut up!" she growled, surprising him and herself. Without further thought, she launched herself at him and pressed her lips to his forcefully. She deftly jumped over the console into the passenger seat and practically crawled on top of him. His shock evident by his outstretched hands, but it quickly turned to desire. His appetite for her was all-consuming.

Ferocious in their encounter, the kiss deepened. Reeglar bit Azewrath's lip and pulled it into her mouth. He wrapped his arms around her and crushed her body to his. He moved his lips down her neck to the sweet spot above her breasts – his warm exhalation causing sensual bumps to rise on her skin. She grabbed his head in return and brought him deep into her bust line.

"I want you to take me, Azewrath. Right now," she whispered longingly, her breath, rapid and profound.

He gazed at her warily and wondered at her behavior. "What about Ilmar?"

"I do not want to think about Ilmar at this moment. Do you? Really?"

Azewrath had to admit, at that moment he didn't. "No... No..."

She jumped into the back of the Jeep and brought the seats down, making a large area for their use. Azewrath peered into the back seat, observing her behavior. Reeglar unbuttoned her blouse, shrugged it off her shoulders, and unhooked her bra. She undid her jeans, pushing her fingers into the waistband and slid them down her thighs. Sitting back on her rear end, she slowly, purposefully, yanked her jeans all the way off and threw them to the side.

Her actions became an open invitation. Azewrath followed her into the back and helped pull off the last of her clothes. Her thong landed by her jeans. Azewrath wasted no time and joined her naked state. She fascinated at his well-trimmed abs as he pulled off his shirt.

So defined, Reeglar thought as she reached for the zipper of his pants. She pulled it down, and they both removed the denim along with his briefs. His body betrayed his readiness for her.

Azewrath pulled her close and gently lay her down on the truck's carpet. So hard – he had to have her. He raised himself above her, but she stopped him.

"Wait!" She held him off as he hung above her.

"What? Have you changed your mind?"

"No." Reeglar smiled. She reached up to place her fingers on his temples. "I am going to make this experience the best sex you have ever had," she promised him. "Make love to me, Azewrath, *now*." Sliding over to get under him, she allowed him to give her what she wanted. He took his entire length and entered her moistness. She reached out with her mind and entered him as well.

Immediately, her feelings and sensations assaulted him. Aware of his manhood as it filled her, he experienced what he felt like inside her. The actual awareness of penetration by himself and the ecstasy he gave her with each thrust of his throbbing shaft, fascinated him.

My Goddess!

Azewrath, overwhelmed by the tactile sensation he processed, in both his body and in his psyche, almost reached his peak. Individuality disappeared – her hands were his, and vice-versa. Lips and limbs entwined and shared pleasure. He throbbed and pulsed around his fullness. Entering and entered, giving and accepting at the same time.

Consumed with her excitement and ecstasy and at his own, his mind whirled. Closer to her now than he had ever been to anyone in his entire life – and closer to himself.

He attacked her with everything he had. He gave himself to her. He kissed her deeply, and meaningfully. She pushed him over, and he rolled, allowing her to take the top position. She continued to move with him. He grabbed her braid and untied it, letting her long, silky, mahogany hair cascade across his chest. She braced herself against him and enjoyed all of his measure. The new position led him deeper and deeper. As an enchantress, he would worship her forever – his mind, full of love and eternal devotion.

Pleased with Azewrath's acceptance, Reeglar's heart swelled. He opened to all the wonders she had given him and would give him again and again in the future. A familiar sensation crept in – just a tickle in the back of her mind. She realized the culprit of the intrusion. Ilmartutar. She was out there, somewhere… Somewhere close.

***

Ilmartutar hoped Danny's house didn't have an alarm. She waited until the lights of his car came down the driveway and took the long walk to his home from the cottage. Although, she moved in more of a skip than a stroll.

She snuck toward the house, pulled on the screen door, and it gave a little squeak. She stopped, in hopes no one heard. After a few deep breaths, she tried it again. It opened without any further noise, so she grabbed for the large doorknob. She turned it and bit her lip.

He did not lock it! She beamed. Ilmar pushed inward and quietly stepped inside. The glowing lights on the appliances allowed her to find her way through the house.

Thank the Goddess for human technology.

Gentle orbs of green and yellow lights lit everything. They accentuated the coffee pot, the microwave, the telephone, and television. Ilmar could continue naming objects with so many dancing lights. Their little world was never completely dark.

Ilmar tip-toed to Danny's room. She touched her belly ring, and the warm glow of the magnetic energy spread over every inch of her body. She smiled at the thought and the knowledge that she could protect him against her Abilities.

His room was dark except for the alarm clock; its face shined the time at 4:30 AM. His cell phone on the nightstand also glowed with the battery level in charge mode.

She walked to the bed and undressed, slipping in next to him. Crawling under the sheets, Ilmar settled down with her head on his chest, laying her arm across him. He moved slightly but didn't wake up. Comfortable and at peace with the strength of his presence, she drifted off to sleep in Danny's arms.

IX

Deceptive Truths

Aaron spent yesterday, well into the night, and most of the morning accommodating whatever pleased Sarah. He groveled, in the doghouse for getting stupid drunk in the middle of the day. Having Sarah retrieve Danny and himself made his punishment much worse. So Aaron stepped and fetched for his lady in an attempt to make it up to her.

He poured her a cup of coffee and placed it on the tray with the breakfast he made for her. Sarah was in a 36 hour "off" shift, and Aaron spent the night to play servant, slave, maid, cook, and gigolo in the bedroom last evening. He did his very best and gave her 110%, even though he had to take a break once to throw up.

He walked into her room, tray in hand, his next step in "I apologize," as he brought her breakfast in bed. Sarah slept, still under the covers when Aaron came into the room. With her red hair sprawled out on the pillow, she looked peaceful in her slumber.

So beautiful, when she's sleeping, anyway, Aaron thought. Sarah witnessed too much pain and death when awake. It always left her with a furrowed brow, but he loved her just the same.

"Good morning, Sleeping Beauty," Aaron greeted her, placing the tray on the edge of the bed next to her.

Sarah stirred, yawned and stretched. Rolling over, she smiled at him. "Oooooh! So much food!" she cooed. Sitting up in bed, she pulled the covers up and tucked them under her arms because she was naked.

"Nothing but the best for my girl!" he said.

"Why the Royal treatment?" she asked before remembering she was still mad at him and scowled. "Oh yeah! That's right! You've been a very bad boy!"

"But I made you eggs, and pancakes, and sausage. I even have strawberry syrup. Your favorite."

"I don't care!" she lectured him. "You and Danny, stone cold drunk in the middle of the day. Passed out on the sidewalk?!" She picked up a sausage with her fingers and chomped on it while she scolded him. "I mean, really Aaron. What could be that bad, that the two of you had to go drown your sorrows?"

Guilt spread across his face as he cut her a piece of pancake. He dipped it in the fruit sauce and held it up for her to eat. She narrowed her eyes to slits. "You think I'm going to accept all this pampering and just forget that I want an answer? I don't think so, mister! So, start talking!" Using her lips, she took the piece of pancake off the fork. Chewing, she savored the sweet taste. The flavor made her smile.

Aaron wrestled with what he was about to say. He needed some answers too, and he wasn't going to get anywhere with Danny as his ally. *I love ya bro, but a rocket scientist, you're not,* Aaron thought. He cleared his throat. "First, I'd like to ask you a question, and I want full disclosure."

"You making demands? I don't know…" Sarah told him, but Aaron expression turned serious. Sarah thought it over. She cut a small section of sausage and mixed it with the egg, swished it around in the ketchup before bringing it to her mouth. "Okay," she replied with her mouthful. "One question, then *I* want the truth outta you."

"Fair enough, I guess," Aaron promised. "The investigation into Jeff's death. Is there any further information on what killed him?"

He's really taking Jeff's death hard. I don't understand it. Sarah worried.

She picked up the breakfast tray and moved it to the other side of the bed. "Hey, this is really bothering you? I know you were friends with Jeff back in high school, but that was a long time ago. You two didn't even travel in the same circles anymore. You're a professional, and he was a volunteer firefighter. So, you hung at the same bars. So does everyone in this town." She wrapped the sheet tighter around her as she slid next to him on the side of the bed. "Well, I'm no doctor, but they said, all the cells in his body were dried out, or empty. Like all the life was drained out of 'em. Weird right?"

"That's not good," Aaron added, reluctantly.

"I don't understand the problem. It's just a big mystery. You and Jeff didn't even hang out. You two had nothing in common anymore, right?" His questions raised her suspicions.

"More than you know, Sarah." He sighed. Struggling to tell her his secret, he chewed his lip. "Danny and I had the same strange bruise marks all over. Just like the ones that were on Jeff, only not as bad."

"What? What are you saying? When?"

"A couple of weeks ago. I had only a few, but Danny said he had them all over. After talking to you, we were sure it must be something contagious. Then you told us the CDC said they didn't believe it was, so –"

"Aaron, why didn't you tell me?" She wrapped the sheet all the way around her and sprung from the bed. "This is important! And terribly frightening! The CDC didn't have all this information." Sarah grabbed clothes from her drawers. She dressed as quickly as she could on her way to the bathroom, yelling from there. "Both you *and* Danny? Shit, Aaron.

Running water splashed in the sink that signaled Sarah washed up. "But you said they believed it wasn't a transmittable disease," he hollered back at her.

"It didn't seem that way because Jeff was the only one affected. They didn't know anyone else had the symptoms."

Aaron jumped off the bed and went to stand in the doorway of the bathroom, as Sarah put on her jeans. "Calm down, Sarah," Aaron warned her. "You can't tell anyone, please! I promised Danny I wouldn't tell." He held her by her shoulders. "I couldn't figure this out by myself and having Danny as a sounding board... Well, you know how helpful he is in that department. I need someone smart like you to help me."

"We've got to tell them," she insisted. "I'm a police officer. I'll be obstructing the investigation if I don't report this."

"NO!" He left the bathroom and returned to sit on the bed genuinely depressed.

Sarah came out and sat next to him. "Okay, look, we'll try to figure it out together." He smiled at her. "But, I'm giving us one week only. If we still haven't found out what caused these bruises, we're going straight to the CDC. You got it?" Aaron nodded. "Good, now go get dressed.

"Why? Where are we going?"

"Danny's. We're putting our heads together on this."

"G-R-E-A-T!" Aaron drew the word out sarcastically. *He's*

going to kill me. "Maybe you should finish eating first. Give him a little more time to sleep. He did work last night, and he might not be alone."

"So, we'll just make sure we bring extra coffee." She took another bite of food. "You two spend so much time together; I sometimes think you'd be happier if it were just the two of you, spending your nights alone together rather than staying with me."

"Well," he paused, adding something just to tease her. "At least he doesn't snore."

Sarah made a face, dropped her jaw and jumped on him. Her action spilled the coffee onto the food tray, which caused them both to laugh.

***

Reeglar awoke with the first slivers of sunlight to illuminate the eastern horizon. It was still dark, but she observed her surroundings well enough.

I have a big choice to make. Reeglar contemplated her options. *I know what I am going to do, so why am I conflicted?*

Aware she would be unable to suppress what she knew about Ilmartutar from her father, Reeglar needed to compartmentalize her knowledge. Her only hope was to cloud the issues and try to hide the act of laying with Azewrath, along with the whereabouts of Ilmar. Their interaction last night, as well as Ilmar's hiding place, must remain a secret.

In the end, she would not give Azewrath up to keep Ilmar's location hidden. Sacrifices were necessary. She touched Azewrath gently and entered his mind with a "good morning" Telepathic endorphin rush. He opened his eyes and smiled at her.

"I can not remember ever being this happy." It was his first thought of the day. He pulled her down to him for an affectionate kiss.

She broke away from him. "We better get this truck back into town, before those guys wake up." Reeglar encouraged, as she dressed.

Azewrath placed his hand on her arm. "We need to talk, Reeglar."

Instead, she thought to him. Her projections filled with love, devotion, longing, and desire. Suddenly, her spoken words were not as important as the emotions she gave him through their bond.

"Soon, there shall be no need for words between us. Now hurry."

Eventually, he would find she was aware of Ilmar's presence. She could tell him now, but she didn't want to. While selfish, she would face that day to inform him, when it came, with no regrets. She jumped into the driver seat and started the Jeep.

"We shall have to come back and continue looking for Ilmar," he stated, trying to redress the best he could. He laughed out loud. "Why is it always easier to get undressed in tight quarters, than it is to get dressed again?"

***

A heavy weight on Danny's chest woke him. Groggy, he let his eyes adjust to the low light of the early morning to focus on what pressed against his chest.

An arm? Panic welled up inside him. He sent his gaze further. *A person? A woman? Who... Lilly!* He stroked her hair, studying her face as she slept – his anxiety lessening. *Holding her tight is what love must feel like,* he thought to himself and smiled. *I can't imagine being without her.* A thought crossed his mind. *How'd she get here?*

"Lilly," he whispered. "Lilly honey, wake up."

"Hmmmmm?" She woke up slowly. To him, her voice was a song. "Hi," she answered him sleepily, as a big grin spread across her face.

"Where'd you come from?"

"You would be surprised," she teased, kissing his chest. "Does it really matter? I'm here now."

"Okay, I like where this is going, but we have to make this a quickie. I have a lot of work to do today. Ever since I've met you, I've slacked off on my work. Don't want to piss off the boss, even though he is my brother. That would make it hard to live here, too! Working today is my punishment." His body responded, and he grew as she kissed him all over.

"Um-hum," she mumbled, without paying heed to his words.

She moved over to straddle him but just hovered over him for a moment. "So, you got punished as well? No one will tell me what to do." Ilmar leaned forward, slowly lowering herself onto him. She slid her hips back and forth. Gyrating, she continued with her conversation as if she went about everyday business. "I ran away from home yesterday."

Danny grabbed her hips and stopped her. "What? Are you okay? What are you saying? What happened?"

"Shhhhhh…" She placed her finger on his lips. "One question at a time." She moved on top of him again. "But later…"

He had to agree with her. "Okay, I give in, now you give in!" He smiled a meaningful sort of smile and thrust up to meet her. As the room brightened with the rise of the sun, he noticed her belly piercing. "You've got a new belly ring. Another rebellion from you?" She nodded to him. "HOT!"

She leaned over and kissed him full on the mouth, acknowledging greater pleasure in their bed play knowing she wasn't killing him. Ilmar savored it and more. She ran her hands all over his body while his muscles tensed and flexed as he worked her. They enjoyed each other. They moved, and thrust kissed and laughed.

During their lovemaking, a noise drew Ilmar's scrutiny to the window. She stopped and listened, worrying over a consistent bang. Glancing up from her position for a second, she puzzled over its absence anymore. Danny demanded her full attention, pulling her down to him, and they kissed, but the knock came again.

"There's someone here," she whispered to Danny. "I heard a knock or a bang."

"It's just the pounding of my beating heart, lusting after you," he replied back.

"No, really! You need to listen to me."

"I didn't hear anything."

He held her tighter and tried to regain her interest in his pulsing need, but her attention focused elsewhere. A distinct knock on the window repeated above her head. She stretched up, as far as she could toward the pane, but only as far as she could and remain on top of Danny.

"I'm telling you," she assured him. "There is something right out there." Ilmar finally reached the window shade and pulled it open just enough to peer out. "AHHHHHHH!" she screamed, coming face-to-face with Aaron. She swiftly jumped off of Danny, grabbing the covers from his bed to wrap around her torso.

"What's wrong?"

Ilmar snatched her clothes, threw down his covers, and redressed in a hurry. "There is someone out there!" She pointed. "He was looking at me right *through* the window."

"Okay, I'll get dressed and take a look," he offered. "I'm sure you just woke Pat up anyway."

"Oh!" She placed both her hands over her mouth. "That was not my intention."

Danny threw on a pair of shorts and a white wife-beater and headed from the room. "I'll be right back."

"Wait!" Ilmar cried.

She followed him out but held onto his shirt and clung to him for dear life. She shuffled behind him every step of the way. When they reached the back door, Danny opened it. Both Aaron and Sarah stood there. They smiled and waved meekly.

"Morning!" Aaron gave a crooked smile.

"Aaron, Sarah? What the *hell* are you guys doing up so early?" Danny asked. Ilmar finally pried her fingers off of his shirt.

"Sorry to wake you…" Aaron stated.

"Oh, we weren't sleeping," Ilmar reverted to her contractions.

"Uh, they know that, Lilly," Danny informed her.

"We brought coffee!" Sarah offered. "Can we come in?"

"Oh, sure, sorry." Danny opened the door to let them inside, and then they all sat at the kitchen table. "Sarah, this is Lilly." He introduced them. They exchanged hellos. "Aaron, I don't think you've officially met Lilly, either."

Ilmar blushed a little. "Only through the window."

"Yeah, sorry about that," Aaron apologized. "If it makes you feel any better, I didn't see anything."

"Aaron!" Sarah elbowed him in the ribs.

"Ouch, hey!" he complained.

"Well, I feel better knowing you didn't see anything," Danny stated.

Sarah handed Ilmar a cup of coffee. "We didn't know how you took it, so we just added one spoonful of sugar and a little bit of milk."

"Thank you. I've never had coffee," Ilmar disclosed.

"What? Never?" Danny asked Ilmar.

She shook her head. "No."

"More of a tea drinker, are ya?" Sarah asked, suspiciously.

Ilmar shrugged. "I'd like to try it, though." She brought it to her lips and took a sip. "Oh!" The hot liquid burned. "That does taste good."

Sarah glared at Danny with a severe tight lip. "Danny, Aaron I talked this morning... And he told me everything."

Danny swigged his coffee. "I don't know what you're talking about. What do you mean, everything? Everything what?"

She turned to Aaron, a questioning attitude crossing her features as if to say, "is he really that stupid?" Then she thought it. *Is he really that stupid?*

Aaron read the expression on Sarah's face and agreed with her thoughts. He stared Danny right in the eyes. "She knows, Danny. I told her everything," Aaron admitted. "All about the bruise marks, like on Jeff. That we both have had them."

Danny almost spit his coffee. He moved his gaze back and forth from Aaron to Sarah, and then to Ilmar. She glanced down at her lap. The last thing she wanted was to be part of the conversation. In fact, at that moment, she just wanted to run away.

Danny sighed. "You don't know everything," he confessed. "I did have them, but it was more than that, I was covered in them, and I was so delirious; I could hardly move." He turned to Ilmar, took her hand in his and squeezed it tenderly. "If it wasn't for the cream I used, I might be as dead as Jeff right now."

Aaron and Sarah regarded Danny. "Cream?" Sarah asked him.

"Hey!" Patrick greeted them when he showed up in the kitchen. Everyone jumped. "What's all this commotion on a Sunday morning?"

Stunned, no one answered, but Danny recovered first. "We have coffee!" He handed his brother a 7-11 cup.

Sarah chimed in. "It was such a beautiful day, Aaron and I thought we'd grab Danny and Lilly for a day at the beach."

Danny cleared his throat. "But I told them I had way too much work to make up for this morning," Danny explained to keep Pat from suspicion.

"So, we're just having coffee instead," Aaron added.

"O-K..." Patrick judged. "You guys are acting really weird. More so than usual." He turned to Ilmar with restrained alarm. "What are you doing here, Lilly?"

"She ran away from home, Pat," Danny told him.

"Really?!" Patrick forced himself to act surprised.

"Yes," Ilmar confirmed. "But I did manage to find a place to stay for a while." *Oh, this is becoming too complicated.*

"Well, that's great!" Pat exclaimed.

Danny put his hand on Ilmar's arm. "You found a place to stay already?"

"I was lucky," she told him a half-truth. "I was in the right place at the right term, uh, time." Then she smiled at him. "And, it's not too far away, so I walked here."

Sarah had a hard time with the small talk. "So, what are you doing today, Pat?"

"I have a date," he replied.

"Really?" Danny asked. "How did *that* happen?"

"I'm not dead, bro, just choosy. Present company excepted, no offense girls."

"What's she like?" Sarah prodded him.

"Oh no!" Pat avoided the question. "This is my little secret. I'm not sharing her until I'm ready. She doesn't need to meet this motley crew, not yet."

They all laughed. Patrick turned to Danny. "You are going to get to that piston today, right? I've got to use that plane for a lesson tomorrow at 3:30."

"I swear, Pat!" Danny promised. "I'm going to get on it, soon. The Cutlass will be in the air with no problems tomorrow. I'll take her up myself first if you want."

"I'm holding you to that. Now, if you'll excuse me, I'm hitting the shower. Nice to see you again, Lilly."

"You too, Patrick." *He kept my secret!* Happiness filled her.

When Patrick left, the heaviness returned to the room. Sarah leaned forward over the table towards Danny. "Now, where were we?"

116

Danny interrupted her. "I'm sorry guys, but we really have to move this party to the shop. I gotta go."

"I'm going to get going, as well," Ilmar told him. "You've got work to do. Will I see you later?"

Danny got up, moved her away from the others, and opened the door for her, disappointed at her departure. "I've got to work at Frampton's tonight, but this is it for the week."

"I could sneak into your room again tonight like I did last night."

"Okay. Sounds like a plan." Danny kissed her on the cheek, and she waved as she walked away. When Danny turned around, Aaron accosted him.

"We need to talk about this stuff, Danny."

"I know, I know, but I gotta work, so come out to the shop with me."

Aaron turned to Sarah. "It's the only way we're going to get anything accomplished today, honey."

Sarah rolled her eyes but agreed. "Okay, but I don't know how Danny will be able to work and talk, all at the same time."

"Ha, Ha!" Danny's comeback fell flat. "I love you, too!"

Both Aaron and Sarah followed Danny into the shop. Danny opened his toolbox and pulled the canvas off the Cessna's piston. "Say goodbye to my clean hands." Aaron and Sarah glared at him like he was out of his mind. *"What?"* Danny asked them. "We're all fine now, no one died. Why so serious?"

Sarah tried to get Danny involved in their serious conversation. He loved to talk about himself, so she prompted him. "So Danny, you were so sick, you were close to death?" She feigned interest. "What happened?"

"I had to lay in bed all day. I was almost too weak to make it to the bathroom. But I did it."

"You are an amazing individual!" She encouraged but rolled her eyes again. "To find out how you got those marks, we have to figure out what all of you have in common." Thinking out loud, she took a seat on a stool. "It's not your jobs, although all of you come into contact with toxins in the environment."

"If that were the case," Aaron conjectured, "wouldn't there be more people affected?"

"Yes," she agreed. "So, for a start let's narrow the possibilities down to just the three of you." Sarah postulated out loud. "What do Aaron, Danny, and Jeff have in common?"

Danny answered right away. "We all hang out at Frampton's." He wore that idea like a badge.

"Oh, Jesus!" Aaron swore.

"No, wait, Aaron," Sarah agreed. "That might just be our link."

"Wouldn't there still be other people sick?" Aaron asked. "A lot of people go to that bar."

"Maybe we got into something there," Danny suggested. "You know, poison or something."

"How have you managed to live this long?" Sarah wondered. "Your brother must really love you."

"Of course he does, Sarah. What does that got to do with anything?"

Sarah sighed, changing tactics. "Has anything different happened there lately? Did Brad change chefs or food suppliers, or has there been different clientele, maybe?"

Danny thought hard. He found it troublesome to concentrate on the Cessna's piston as well. Every time he spoke, he needed to stop his work. "Hey Sarah, just so you know, you were right." He paused. "It is hard to work and think about our problem at the same time."

"That's why I love ya, bro." Aaron slapped Danny on the back.

"Yes, his list of talents abound," Sarah commented, sarcastically.

"Hey! There has been something different at the bar!" Danny announced. "We've been hanging out with Lilly and her friends, remember?" Right after he spoke, he knew he messed up.

The expression on Aaron's face made it seem like he just swallowed his tongue, but he hadn't. "Yeah... Yeah... You're right." He spoke as if someone dragged the words out of his mouth against his will.

"Lilly *and* her friends?" Sarah asked. "How many friends does she have?"

"I don't know," Danny answered cautiously. "They all come as a group."

"What do you know about Lilly, Danny? Do you know her

last name, maybe, or where she comes from originally? How to get in touch with her if you need to? How long have you actually known her?"

"Hey!" Danny put down his tools and the piston. "How did this all of a sudden become about Lilly?"

"Think about it for a second, Danny." Sarah walked over to him. "She shows up, says she ran away from home and is staying… where exactly?"

"I don't know," Danny admitted. "I'll ask her tonight when I see her here after I get home from work."

"She doesn't come to the bar anymore to see you? Why do you think that is? Maybe she doesn't want her friends to find her with you. Maybe they don't want her to hang around with you all the time," she added. "Just a thought."

"Sarah," Aaron interjected. "You're making Lilly and her friends out to be co-conspirators to... *What?* Biological terrorism?"

"I don't know," she maintained, exasperated. "I haven't figured that out, yet."

Sarah grabbed the stool and sat again. Aaron could see she was thinking. *I have no one to blame for this, but myself. I asked her to help. Why does she have to be so smart?*

She jumped off the stool like a light bulb went on over her head. "Where's this cream you talked about?" she demanded.

"The cream!" Danny stressed. "I'll go get it. Be right back." He took a rag to wipe his hands and then ran up to the house.

"Do you really think Lilly has something to do with all this?" Aaron asked Sarah.

"It's not a coincidence, honey." She put her hand on his arm. "I've been doing this for too many years, and there's a connection here, trust me."

Aaron felt sick to his stomach. *My little world is going to come crashing down right on top of me,* he thought in a panic.

Danny returned and handed the jar to Sarah. She took it and moved closer to the light to study it. Aaron pulled Danny aside. "Dude, what are you... *Crazy?* What are you thinking telling Sarah about the girls? You promised!"

"Oh man, I'm sorry," Danny apologized. "Sarah made it sound like a quiz; I just wanted to give her the right answers. It's the only time I've actually *had* the right answer."

"This could be the end for me." Aaron worried. They watched Sarah open the jar. She dipped her index finger to check out a dollop of cream. She rubbed it on her arm and waited but experienced nothing.

"Well?" Aaron asked her.

"I can't tell if anything is happening. I'm taking this," Sarah told Danny, as she held up the cream jar. "We have to have this analyzed."

"By who?" Danny asked. "And that belongs to me." He went to take it back, but she pulled it out of his reach. "What if I need it again?"

"Well, then I guess you're shit outta luck, buddy," Sarah told him. "This is an investigation, and I told Aaron I'd give us one week to figure this out. If not, then I'll turn all my information over to the authorities. So it's in your best interest to get this done now."

Danny had to agree. "Okay, do it."

"We'll let you know what we find out," Aaron told him. "Now, get back to work, or Patrick's gonna kill you."

"Yep," Danny agreed, as Aaron and Sarah left him in the shop. He watched, as they got into Sarah's Escape and drove away.

***

Reeglar and Azewrath returned the Jeep to Frampton's parking lot and observed the two boys from the night before, still unconscious. She dropped the keys by Dave's body.

"Thanks," she said to him, turning to catch up with Azewrath.

He retrieved his pack of clothes they bought where he left it under the bushes. They headed back to the park in silence, each acutely aware of the presence of the other.

When they reached the sandy trails, Azewrath surprised Reeglar by picking her up to carry her the rest of the way.

She laughed. "What is this all about?"

"Your footwear does not lend itself to walking through this deep sand," he instructed her. "Besides, I wanted to have you close for as long as possible." Once they returned to Akkadia, their special time together would be over.

So unfair, Reeglar thought.

She wrapped her arms around him tightly, placing her head in the crook of his shoulder and neck. She let herself feel the comfort and adulation of Azewrath's words.

They entered the Lift and held each other close all the way down. Reeglar touched their bond. *"Azewrath, I want you to know this,"* she thought to him. *"Even though we can not be together, I shall be with you in this way... always."*

Azewrath thought back to her. *"You must not allow yourself to be found out. If our bond puts you in jeopardy, I shall not have any of it!"*

"All shall be well," she assured him. *"I am not yet my father's master, but I can confound him with bullshit!"*

Azewrath's confusion found her through their link, but he understood her meaning. *"Ah, never mind. I see it is a human colloquialism."* Reeglar sent him back amusement.

As the Lift neared Akkadia, they broke away from each other. When the Lift alarm sounded, Reeglar expected to be met by her people when they reached the bottom. When the doors opened, she could not have been more surprised to find Prince Pikkar standing in front of her.

"What news have you?" Pikkar's spoke words even before he allowed them to exit the Reaction Lift.

"My Prince and friend," Azewrath greeted him first in hopes to keep him calm by changing the direction of his thoughts.

"I shall give a detailed report in the Throne Room, as soon as I have had some time to rest," Reeglar informed him as she walked passed.

Pikkar grabbed her by the arm. "You shall do it, *now,* Reeglar! Just to me, not before the entire Council."

It was all Azewrath could do to keep his composure as he watched Pikkar manhandle Reeglar roughly. She, on the other hand, smiled gratefully. It was easier to fool Pikkar than her father.

"As you wish, my Prince." She raised one hand and touched his temple to send all the information she wanted him to know. The information she gave him relayed they did not find Ilmar, but she would try again without Azewrath.

"Disappointing," the Prince groused after she finished.

"Ilmartutar is extremely skilled at concealing her whereabouts and her intentions," Azewrath told Pikkar. "I had not one single prophetic episode about her while we were on the surface."

"Then it is decided," Pikkar stated. "Reeglar shall return tonight. You remain behind, Azewrath. One may go places two might not. We shall convene in the Throne Room after the last meal." Pikkar turned and strode away.

Azewrath and Reeglar exchanged glances as they both tried to stifle smiles. He cleared his throat. "I had an interesting time with you, to say the least," he stressed.

"And I did as well." *"Hopefully, it will not be our last."* She imparted to him. As they parted ways, both traveled down the corridor in opposite directions.

When Reeglar arrived at her quarters, she stripped down to nothing and sprawled out on the bed. Hungry, happy, and exhausted, all at the same time, she put her feelings aside to ready her mind for later. Just in case her father decided to take a peek into her brain. Again, she promised herself she would take a nap, but she had a lot of work to do right now and needed Ilmar's help.

Reeglar turned onto her back, closed her eyes and breathed deeply. All personal memories of Azewrath and the possibility of Ilmar's location must be locked up in an unreachable part of her mind. A place her father could search for, but not find. A difficult task, as she could not expose any trace of what she did on the surface. Her vault of memories must remain safe. Her biggest challenge was to fool her father. She decided that presented an impossibility, so she chose a different tactic.

Reeglar locked it all away. The guardian of her mind, she had the key to her private place. She made many such places and put her regular mundane memories inside. The more secret places she created, the harder it would be for her father to check them all. He would try... Even though she apprised Prince Pikkar of the situation, her father might want to see, first hand, representations of what transpired.

Dizzy from the circles she ran inside her mind, Reeglar stumbled and then fell. She rested on the floor of her synapses. Her eyes closed, but she popped them open again, fighting to stay awake. She failed, succumbing to exhaustion and her eyes closed again. They fluttered, and she struggled against it, but time worked against her, and she slept.

Reeglar awoke refreshed, quickly showered, braided her hair and redressed in human clothes. It might be unseemly at the Council meeting, but she was in a hurry to get back topside. She made sure she had all her money before remembering Azewrath had some too.

I shall grab that from him before I go. The thought brought a warmth to Reeglar, which spread over her body, and she giggled. Her pulse quickened with memories of their lovemaking. Overwhelmed with happiness, she resisted the urge to reach out and touch them. Too many other minds around.

With her hunger paramount, Reeglar sprinted to the Grand Hall. She hadn't eaten all day, and her mouth watered as she entered. When the aroma of the food met her nostrils, her stomach rumbled. She sat down at her family's table to eat, acknowledging her mother and father, who watched her attack her plate.

Her late arrival caused the food to turn cold, but she didn't care. Everything tasted wonderful going down, nonetheless. Azewrath sat with the Queen and the Prince at the Royal table, with Ilmar's chair empty beside him.

The resounding gong announced the Council meeting in the Throne Room. It rang loud and constant in its call. The High Council members – her father and Azewrath included, rose and excused themselves from the Grand Hall. Her father kissed her mother and peered over at Reeglar. She smiled back at him and stuffed a few more pieces of her meal into her mouth. When she finished chewing, she jumped up, kissed her mother as well, but ran passed her father to the Throne Room.

The Council members settled into their seats as Reeglar entered the room. She walked through the center with all the Council Leaders to the left and the right of her. When she reached the Royal dais, she stopped and gave a slight bow.

The Queen spoke. "Reeglar, Prince Pikkar has explained you were unsuccessful in finding my daughter, Ilmartutar."

"He is correct, my Queen. The Prince has charged me to try again tonight. I am prepared to leave as soon as this audience has your dismissal."

"Very well," Alkara granted her leave. "I give you one more day, Reeglar."

The Guardian Council leader stood up and spoke. "There is something a few of us would like to address, your Highness."

"We recognize General Nutrion, of the Guardian Council. You may speak," Alkara commanded.

"My concern is for the safety of our world. With your daughter running around loose on the surface, who is to say how much information concerning Akkadia she shared with the humans."

"You make Ilmartutar out to be a saboteur of her world, Nutrion?" Prince Pikkar asked menacingly.

"Not intentionally, my Prince." Nutrion corrected himself quickly.

"You have something in mind, General?" Alkara asked. "A way, perhaps, to retrieve Ilmar before she does any damage?"

"I do not, as yet, my Queen. But I believe we must address the problem. Give me some time to assemble an operating plan."

"We can not set the Guardians loose in the human world, General," Alkara continued. "I am sure you could modify any plan with that in mind." When General Nutrion caught Prince Pikkar's gaze, a shared nod passed between them.

Reeglar stood in the midst of the combative atmosphere when she felt her father's tendrils reach out to tickle the edges of her mind. Each strand searched the locked places inside. He found many and opened numerous doors, but his confusion as to the many compartments humored her. For a split second, his admiration surrounded her mind. She turned to glance at him in his place at the Council table. He sported a beaten smile on his lips.

"We have heard enough for this meeting," the Queen announced. "This Council is dismissed."

Reeglar wasted no time, she bowed, turned on her heels, and exited the Throne Room.

X

Subterranean Revelations

Sarah and Aaron headed west. Traveling along County Road 104, she drove faster than the speed limit. She could do so as it was a small highway. Aaron watched the scenery pass by from the passenger window. As he counted the pine trees that went by, he dreaded the moment when Sarah would say something. Ever since Danny spilled the beans about the girls, he waited for retribution, but she hadn't said a word yet.

She'll kill me later, he thought.

Sarah's mind moved a mile a minute. Her neurons arced and sparked while she worked on the "possible" murder mystery. She made solving Jeff's death her priority, no matter what. Her hypothesis involved foul play. It ranked high on her theories. Even if she found it wasn't out-and-out murder, someone was responsible for his death. Breaking the case would show the lieutenant she was ready for a promotion. She concentrated on that one thought because if she didn't, she'd have to think about Aaron.

And that's just not going to happen, she thought. *I'm just not going to think about that, right now.* The Escape reached the traffic circle, and Sarah drove into the heart of Riverhead.

Aaron couldn't keep quiet any longer. "Where are we going?"

"We're going to your lab in Atlantis," she stated flatly. "You're gonna find out what's in this jar!"

It was a bad idea to argue with her in her present frame of mind. "Okay, but you know I'm only a marine biologist, right? You people think I have all this incredible medical knowledge and training."

"You should be thrilled we put that much *faith* in you," Sarah offered.

Was that sarcasm? Aaron wondered, but he just let it go.

Atlantis Marine World – open to the public every day, year-round (except Christmas Day), from 10:00 AM - 5:00 PM. As their assistant Marine biologist, Aaron worked the weekday schedule, Monday through Friday. Occasionally, he pulled a few weekends when sick or injured animals washed ashore, or if they needed him to go along on a rescue.

Sunday was a busy tourist day, and the attraction carried a full staff of employees, except for the biologists. After they pulled into the parking lot, Aaron couldn't believe how many cars filled the area. With his lab empty, they headed there.

Aaron entered through the employee entrance and met a few people he knew. As he passed, he received a couple of "good morning, Dr. Remington," so he nodded and exchange pleasantries back to them. Keeping his cool, he and Sarah made their way to the labs.

His office, part of a typical research lab, housed tools, electronics, and computers. Although, the differences with his position and others involved a marine quality. The lab held large tanks filled with water. All were empty but carried the ability to accommodate a significantly sized shark if they had to.

Aaron went directly to his analysis machine and held his hand out for Sarah to give him the jar. She did, and he unscrewed the top. He took a tiny sample with a sterile tool and placed it in the vector machine for analysis. The equipment hummed.

Aaron sat in his rolling chair. "Now, we wait," he told Sarah. The silence in the room spoke volumes. His fear kept him from saying something to her. He truly loved Sarah and his night with Lilly's friend was just what guys did. The guilt got to him.

"Sarah," Aaron started. "I think you know I love you, right?"

Sarah inhaled deeply, as if to speak, but was interrupted when the door to the lab burst open. One of the animal handlers, Jennifer, he thought it was, ran into the room with a panicked expression.

"Oh, thank God you're here, Dr. Remington!" She tried to catch her breath.

Aaron jumped off his chair. "What's the matter? Jen, right?"

"Yes sir," she said. "Daria was feeding Grey Beauty, and well, her cataracts are so bad that she couldn't tell where the fish ended, and Dari's hand began. And well, she's bleeding!"

"How bad?" he asked, grabbing his medical bag.

"Don' kno," Jen answered. "Stitches, maybe?"

"Let's go," Aaron announced.

"I'm coming too! Who's Grey Beauty?" Sarah added. She

followed them out but pocketed the jar of cream.

Aaron explained. "She's a gray seal in one of our exhibits."

Aaron witnessed a crowd of employees gathered at the seal tank. In the center of the commotion, Daria held her right hand, wrapped with a rag as a makeshift bandage.

The director of Atlantis, Nathan Lutz, turned to greet Aaron. "Sorry to bother you, Aaron, but when this happened, one of the girls mentioned she saw you come in, and that you still might be here. I don't think it's bad enough to call an ambulance."

"No problem, Nathan." *I bet you didn't want the publicity, either,* Aaron thought, but he just let it go. "What happened?"

"Just a slight misunderstanding. Beauty bit the girl's hand by accident while she was feeding her. Beauty doesn't see very well, you know."

"How bad is it?" Aaron prompted him.

Nathan shrugged. "I'm not a doctor, but I think it could use a few stitches."

Aaron bent over to examine the wound. Daria's index finger was torn open, but it wasn't bad. She was lucky. Aaron helped Daria to stand. "Well, you won't die from it, but we should get a stitch or something there, and maybe a tetanus shot? Can we use your office, Nathan?"

"Sure, let's go," Nathan agreed. When they entered the director's office, Aaron sat Daria on the couch. "If you've got this," Nathan told Aaron, "I'll get back to the seal tank and try to restore order."

"Yes, thanks, Nathan," Aaron answered him. He unwrapped Daria's hand. "I'll be right back. I'm going to get my bag." He got up and went over to the desk. Sarah utilized Aaron's absence, by peeking at Daria's wound herself.

Daria met her gaze. "I'm such an idiot!"

"These things happen, dear," Sarah assured her, to hide an ulterior motive. "Before Dr. Remington comes back, how about putting some of this special cream on it. It helps with seal bites."

"Yeah? Okay," Daria agreed.

Sarah opened the jar, scooped out a small amount of the white gel, and spread it on the injury. Immediately, it glowed with a slightly yellowish light. Aaron turned around in time to see Sarah apply the cream. He almost soiled his shorts at the sight of what she attempted. All blood drained from his face.

"Hey!" Daria cried. "This feels great!" She stared at her finger. "And it's healed already! It closed all by itself." She held her finger up in the air to show both Sarah and Aaron. Aaron glared at Sarah like he was going to kill her.

Thinking fast on his feet, Aaron explained. "It's surgical glue, Daria. One made especially for marine animal bites. Looks like you're good as new." He helped Daria up again before walking her to the door. "I'm sure you're glad you didn't need stitches."

"Or a tetanus shot!" Daria smiled at him. "Thanks, Dr. R!" She ran from the room and went back to work.

Aaron grabbed Sarah's arm. "Come on!" He pulled her out of the office and dragged her back to the lab. He turned on her as soon as he slammed the door. "What the HELL? Are you *crazy* or something?" he screamed.

"Relax Aaron; I knew nothing bad would happen."

"Really? How?"

"Danny used it, and he was all right. I figured she would be too."

"You don't even know what *it* is, or what's in it," Aaron reminded her. "Something terrible could have happened to that young girl, and I would've felt responsible."

"I get it; I'm sorry," Sarah apologize. "But did you see that shit?" She laughed excitedly. "It healed! The injury actually *healed*, Aaron." She tried to get him to stop pacing back and forth, but he held his head in his hands and moaned. "What did the analyst readout say?"

Aaron stopped pacing. "Oh, shit, I forgot." He checked the print out on the screen of the computer, turned around with a truly puzzled look on his face, confused. "This doesn't make any sense. It's just Argol."

Sarah shared Aaron's confusion for another reason. "What is Argol?"

"It's an old Earth organic compound," he explained. "A crude, unpurified form of potassium bitartrate. Nothing special and certainly not capable of creating the effect we saw on Daria."

"So, we still have no idea what it is?" She held up the jar and studied it.

"Nope, afraid not."

Sarah shook her head and tried to think. She opened a jar, brought it to the sink and placed it on the edge. Bewildered, Aaron wondered what Sarah contemplated. She reached for a scalpel and brought it to her left forearm, but before he could stop her, she sliced a three-inch gash, deep into her arm.

"Sarah, *no!*" He ran over to her.

She held the wound to stop the bleeding. "Shit! Get the cream, quick!"

"What the hell are you thinking?" Blood spewed everywhere.

"GET THE CREAM!" Sarah screamed.

Aaron swiped three fingers into the jar and slathered it on Sarah's arm. A yellow glow enveloped her arm and overwhelmed her with incredible strength and life-affirming energy. She became renewed; rejuvenated.

Aaron held her in his arms. "Jesus! You've gone over the deep end, honey. Are you okay?"

"My God, Aaron! I've never felt better!" She beamed. "This stuff is fabulous!" She looked directly into his eyes. "Where did Danny say he got this cream?"

Aaron tried to remember. "I don't recall him saying anything about it."

"We need that information!"

"I know, babe," Aaron began. "But can't it wait 'till tonight? We'll meet him at Frampton's or something. Right now, I'd like to get you home to rest and get you out of those bloody clothes. Okay?"

"I give up. Whatever," Sarah said. "Let's just go." He helped her up, and they made their way to the Ford Escape. Sarah started the car, and they drove away in silence, unspoken words between them hung heavily in the air.

***

Finishing his chore for the day, Danny put the Cessna Cutlass engine back together. When he left the shop, he spotted Ilmar walking up the driveway. After his day, Danny presented a filthy mess, full of grease and sweating like mad. He hoped he wouldn't offend her.

Oh great! Danny thought. *I'm sure I probably smell, too!* Still happy to see her, he approached. She smiled back and waved as she continued.

"Hi!" Danny yelled, smiling that smile, that full tooth flash kind of smile which radiated charm. "Don't come any closer," he warned her, holding his hand out to stop her. "I'm disgusting!"

"I don't care, silly," she yelled back. "Clean, dirty... I'll take you either way."

She walked up to him and gently touched her lips to his, making sure not to let her body contact him anywhere else. Sweat beaded on his upper lip moistened hers, but she didn't mind at all.

"I thought you were going to come by tonight?" Danny stated.

"I became impatient." She smiled knowingly.

"You're still coming here later after I get off work, right?"

She nodded. "Plus, I didn't have anything to do."

"What do you mean?" he asked again. "Don't you have a job?" He laughed. "Or are you independently wealthy?"

"No." She laughed as well. "I'm not wealthy, and I don't have a job. I guess I'll need to work on that."

"I've gotta go get ready. Want to come up to the house?"

"Sure," Ilmar said, accompanying him for the walk.

"Is there something special you'd like to do?" Danny inquired. "It easy to find a job out here in the summertime."

"I haven't really thought about it."

As they entered the house, his first act was to get himself a beer and offer one to Ilmar. "You want a beer? Wait. You're not driving, are you?"

"No, not driving. And yes, a beer would be great, thank you!" She took the open bottle from him.

Danny tipped his Miller Lite up and drained the whole thing in one gulp. "Ahhhh..." he hissed taking a breath. "Refreshing!"

Ilmar watched him; her eyes widened in disbelief. "How did you do that?"

"Years of practice!" He laughed. "I've got to get into the shower. Do you mind waiting?"

"No, it's fine," Ilmar told him.

"Okay, see ya in a few." Danny headed to the bathroom.

As Ilmar sipped her beer as the sound of water pelting the porcelain tub reached her. She imagined Danny undressing, stepping in, and surrendering to the warm water. She pictured his rippling muscles as he let the water flow over him – his hands moving across his chest, then down towards his abdomen. She couldn't take it anymore.

Ilmar tiptoed down the hall and opened the door to the bathroom slowly. Hoping it wouldn't squeak, announcing her presence, she bit her lip. Stepping inside, Ilmar closed the door gently; grateful Danny hummed a song that covered the noise she made.

Removing her clothing, she dropped them one by one to the floor. She stepped out of her jeans and entered the tub one foot at a time. Touching her belly ring to activate the magnetic field, she found Danny's back facing her. His latissimus dorsi, so pronounced, his gluteus maximus, so round and firm, she couldn't help but reach out and wrap her arms around him.

Danny jumped sky high and screamed like a little girl. He whipped around but realized it was only Ilmar. He pulled her close to him and laughed out loud with relief. They stood there facing each other as the warm water washed over them.

"I didn't mean to scare you," Ilmar teased.

"I wasn't expecting you to jump in. Nice surprise."

Danny kissed her full on the lips. She let herself melt into his arms, returning his kisses in-kind. He wasted no time and picked her up to lean her against the wall. The tiles, cold against her back, braced her as Danny supported her weight. She wrapped her legs around his waist and slid down onto his massive, throbbing pleasure. Ilmar clung to him as he hammered her against the wall – his strong glutes working his lance deep inside her.

She accepted his fullness, wanted it, in fact, Using her thigh muscles to pull him towards her, she helped his thrust penetrate deeper. She engulfed him, surrounded him, and became a part of him.

"Faster Danny," she whispered to him. Her lips and warm breath pressed close to his ear. "Harder... Deeper..."

Her words, like a spark, ignited a fire that grew within him. It took all his concentration not to reach his release point. He continued instead to satisfy her. He did, however, resume their lovemaking with renewed passion.

Danny assaulted Ilmar until she cried out. "Is this what you wanted?" he asked her, slamming her into the wall over and again. Danny's mind drifted as his body pushed through a workout. *Thank God I'm in the shower. I'm sweating like a pig.*

Ilmar's breathing increased and came shallow. The water in the shower turned colder as it ran out of the stored hot water. Her muscles shook with her release as she reached her climax. She tightened, creating pressure against his shaft. Thankfully, he let himself go as well.

Ilmar slid down the wall until she could touch the bottom of the tub with her feet. Her legs, a bit wobbly at first, barely supported her weight. She smiled at him, laying her head against his chest while his strong arms encircled her. They stood there with the water droplets running over their bodies, refreshed and satisfied.

"I'm having trouble making myself want to move from this spot," Ilmar cooed.

"I'm just having trouble moving," Danny laughed. "My legs feel like I ran a marathon."

She pulled away from him, searching his eyes. "Can I trust you, Danny?"

Even the warm water couldn't keep the shiver from his bones at her question. "What do you mean? Of course, you can trust me! What kinda question is that?"

"An honest one," Ilmar answered. "I don't know you... Know your heart." She placed her hand on his wet chest.

Danny stepped out of the running water. "Hey, what's gotten into you?"

Ilmar embraced Danny tightly before placing her head on his shoulder. "I just need to believe..."

"Believe in what?"

"In truth and honesty."

Danny laughed and turned off the water. "You want honesty? We're wasting hot water, and Patrick is tight with his money." Reaching for a towel, he handed one to Ilmar, and then took another for himself.

Ilmar changed the subject. "I'm going to go to my cottage and take a nap. I'm sorry you have to go to work."

"Yeah, me too!" Danny said as he covered himself with a towel. "You're wearing me out, girl." He slapped her on the rear end.

"Hey!" She protested but giggled while she redressed.

Danny walked from the bathroom to his bedroom. Ilmar followed and attempted to put on her shoes as she walked. She managed to hop from one foot to the other without losing her balance.

"You sure you're going to come back here when I get home?" Danny asked again as he finished dressing for work.

Ilmar watched his wonderfully naked body get covered by his clothing. *Such a shame*. "You're beautiful..." she informed him.

"You can't call a man beautiful," he told her. "It's a girly word."

"I don't mean just the way you look, but you, with the whole person. The way you move, think, and well, what makes you, you."

"Hmm..." Danny contemplated. "I'm still not comfortable with being called beautiful."

"Okay," she sighed. "Truthfully, if we were just talking about beautiful, your brother has got you beat!"

Danny pulled on his shirt. "Oh really? Now that's depressing," he whined, grabbing her and picked her up in his arms. They laughed as he carried her through the house. He snatched his keys off the kitchen counter while taking her the rest of the way outside. Descending the stairs carefully, he put her down on the ground.

"Do you want me to drop you off at your house?" Danny asked.

"No, thanks. I'd rather walk. It's not far."

"Okay. I'll see you later?" He slid inside his Camaro. Ilmar leaned into his window and rested her arms on the door.

She nodded before kissing him."Um-hum. Have a good night!"

"Bye." Danny started the engine and backed the car out of the driveway.

***

Ilmar practically skipped down the driveway on the way back to her new home. The cottage. She couldn't have been happier.

My new life is good, she thought and smiled to herself.

As she neared the outbuilding, her attention fell to someone that sat in front of her house. Ilmar squinted to focus better. It was Reeglar. Warning bells went off in her head, and she thought about running, but it was Reeglar, after all. She would just find her again.

"How did you find me?" Ilmar asked when they were face-to-face.

"Really?" Reeglar spoke directly to Ilmar's mind. The thought wasn't just a word, but a feeling she imparted to Ilmar that she was easy to find. *"All this would be much easier if I explained it the quicker way."*

Reeglar touched Ilmar's temples and conveyed to her, (almost) all that had transpired since she ran away. How angry Ilmar's father was, the chaos in the Council, and how she and Azewrath had come to the surface find her. Reeglar explained how she hid the fact that she did, in fact, know where to find Ilmar.

"Why did you not tell them where I was?" Ilmar asked.

Reeglar sighed and touched her again, giving her a brief synopsis of her feelings for Azewrath. *"That is why."*

Ilmar jumped away from her, shocked. She didn't quite know what to say. She attempted to speak, stopped, opened her mouth again, and then, wholly baffled, she cocked her head and shook it.

Reeglar laughed and touched Ilmar's arm. *"You are allowed to feel possessive,"* she offered. Ilmar's emotions revealed an easing of her mind though, and not a bit of jealousy.

"What?" Ilmar thought back to Reeglar. *"No. Please, you can have him."*

"Thank you, my friend. Now, how do we convince your father this is a good idea? It is why I am here. I need your help on this."

"Let us go inside, Reeglar," Ilmar said out loud. "We will come up with something, all right?" Reeglar breathed a sigh of relief. She stood, nodded and followed Ilmar inside. Ilmar continued, insisting. "I am sorry you are suffering for my actions, but I am not going back down."

"The Prince shall not accept no for an answer. He shall do something drastic if you do not return."

Ilmar tossed her hand in the air dismissively. "The Council

will never let him jeopardize our secrecy."

"Well," Reeglar warned her, "some Council Leaders believe you have done so already. And, they want you back. *Soon.*"

"I am *not* leaving!" Ilmar stressed again and stomped her foot. "I like my little home here."

"Hum." Reeglar took in her surroundings. "Opulent, really."

"I will not be here forever."

"What is your plan, Ilmar?"

"I have not gotten that far, yet." Ilmar went to her tiny refrigerator. "Can I get you something to drink? Beer, maybe?"

"Sure." Reeglar sighed, accepting the beer. They sat and drank the last two Patrick had given her.

"So, let us talk," Ilmar started. "And I think you should consider staying the night."

"I do not want to get in your way at all."

"I am not going to be here tonight; I will be sleeping at Danny's. So you will have this place all to yourself."

"All right," Reeglar agreed. "Now let us put our heads together and come up with a way to make the situation work for both of us."

***

At Frampton's, Danny checked the clock every ten minutes. *These next hours are going to be the longest of my life.*

As busy as the bar was, time should have sped by. In fact, it hadn't. All the incredibly drunk people that didn't have enough fun at the Boardy Barn when it closed at 8:00 PM, stumbled their way the two miles to Frampton's.

The locals called the phenomenon, "the walking dead." Groups of people trekked the whole way, so they didn't drive and get a DWI. The smarter drunks and the ones with money took the taxi buses. No matter their mode of transportation, Sunday nights were always crazy. It was also Watermelon night at Frampton's. The bartenders cut watermelons in half, making melon balls from the sweet pink inner meat. Next, they hollowed out the fruit, soaked the spheres in Frampton's unique vodka mix, and then put them back in the watermelon shells. They served the mixture in paper cups. A favorite Sunday signature drink offered to everyone.

At midnight, Danny's eyes caught Aaron and Sarah walking to the door. He smiled as they approached, but neither one of them looked happy. Sarah's sour expression worried Danny, but she glared at him that way often. On the other hand, Aaron seemed nervous and pensive.

"Take a break?" Aaron asked, but it didn't sound like a question.

"Sure," Danny replied, bewildered. They headed to a table in the back to sit as far away from the crowd as possible.

Sarah wasted no time. She held up the jar to Danny. "Where did you get this?"

Guilty, Danny lied. "I... I don't remember."

Sarah leered at him, raising an eyebrow. She opened the jar and placed it on the table. Ominously, she held her hand over the flame of the candle that burned in the center of the table. She sucked air into her lungs to fight the pain of her crisping skin.

"Damn it, Sarah!" Aaron scolded her, trying to pull her arm away from the fire.

"What are you doing?!" Danny asked her in a panic.

Finally, Sarah took her hand away, and the smell of burnt flesh permeated the air. Her pain was evident on her face. She applied the cream to her palm, allowing the yellow glow of Healing to spread across her hand and travel deep into her being. As she held her hand up for Danny to see, not even a scar remained.

Sarah stared directly into Danny's eyes and spoke deliberately. "Where - did - you - get - this - cream?"

"Holy shit!" Danny yelled. "How'd you do that?"

"You didn't know it could heal a wound?" Aaron asked him, incredulously.

"Hell no... Well, it made me feel better than I've ever felt before, sure, but that... that's just wild!" He laughed, shaking his head in disbelief.

"Let's just say it has the power to do more than what we just showed you," Sarah explained. She reached across the table and grabbed Danny by the collar of his T-shirt. "This stuff is not conventional medicine. You got this from Lilly, right? That's why you didn't want to tell us."

"Yeah... Yeah, okay," Danny admitted and pulled away from

her. "She gave it to me, so what?"

Sarah screwed the lid back on the jar and took it back. "You don't get it? The whole thing fits together." Danny shook his head again, so Sarah continued. "The girls, the bruises, Jeff's death, and this cream! Get it yet?"

"No, I don't," Danny said. "You're nuts."

In an attempt to defuse the whole volatile situation, Aaron jumped up. "I need a drink! Anybody else?" He stood, pointed to both of them like he was checking a list. "You? You? No?" No one answered him. "Okay, I'll just guess."

Sarah continued to interrogate Danny. "Who *is* she, Danny?"

"What you mean by that? She's just a girl."

"I don't believe that, and neither should you."

"Alright Sarah," Danny inquired. "Who do *you* think she is? Hum? Why don't you tell me."

Sarah appeared conflicted. "I wish I knew. I need some more information. Some *actual* facts." She leaned back in her chair. "I think it's time we confront her."

"Okay," Aaron interrupted them. "Everyone, calm down. Have a drink and just relax."

Danny grabbed the glass from Aaron and drank his drink. "Fine! She'll be at the house when I get off work."

"Then we're coming with you!" Sarah informed him.

"Whatever!" Danny growled. Slamming his glass on the table, he left them to go back to the door.

"You had to piss him off?" Aaron declared.

"Yes, I had to," she answered. "But what's new? I always piss him off."

XI

The Loss

Ilmartutar snuck over to Danny's house for the second night in a row, hoping the door was open. She tried the handle. *It is!* She beamed, pleased.

Slipping in, she slowly inched her way through the dark house. As she entered the kitchen, she thought she heard a noise coming from the living room. She stopped, barely able to breathe.

Was that a giggle? She wondered.

With the high back of the couch in her line of sight, she couldn't make out anyone in the room. A light, perhaps a flame from a candle, flickered in the living room. Something moved. A head popped up from behind the couch back, and Ilmar recognized Patrick. She flattened herself against the wall in an attempt to remain unseen, but she could tell he wasn't alone.

That was a woman laughing. Oh, my! Patrick brought his date home after all.

Ilmar quietly tiptoed down the hall and hugged the wall until she got to Danny's bedroom. It was late, or early, depending on how you looked at it. Carefully, she climbed on his bed, gazing out the window to wait for him to come home. Before long, headlights came down the driveway, making her smile. Unexpectedly, another set of lights followed Danny's.

Two cars? She worried.

She decided to watch out the window until she understood the circumstances. After Danny got out of his car, she witnessed Aaron and Sarah exited the second. Ilmar surmised they were in an argument, so she wasn't sure what to do. In the end, she decided she'd better get outside.

Ilmar peered out from the bedroom door. Patrick and his female company were still otherwise involved. She crept out through the kitchen, reached the back door, heading outside as quickly and quietly as possible.

Sarah witnessed Ilmar emerge from the house and pointed at her. "Speaking of the devil!"

Ilmar approached them. "Danny, what's wrong?"

He took her hand in his. "There are things we don't understand about you, Lilly. We need to ask you some questions, and we need some honest answers."

"I don't think this is a good time to discuss anything," Ilmar warned them. "Patrick is inside, and he's *not* alone!"

"What?" Danny smiled. "That dog..."

"Focus, Danny!" Sarah reminded him and snapped her fingers in front of his face. She held up the jar for Ilmar to see. "How about you start by telling us what this is."

For Ilmar to say something about the Healing cream would place herself in a sensitive position. "You've already made up your mind about me, Sarah. Why should I tell you anything?"

"Can you blame me?" Sarah asked. "If you cared about Danny at all, you'd never put him in danger, right?"

Ilmar unlocked her fingers from Danny's hand and leaned against the car. "I would not."

Aaron had to agree with Sarah, so he pressed her. "We really need some answers, Lilly."

"None of you are open-minded enough to hear this," Ilmar stated.

"Don't worry about us, Lilly, we've already seen how the cream inside the jar works. Let's say we're curious," Sarah said.

"You don't sound curious. You sound like a lynch mob." Ilmar sighed. "So, you know you're holding a Healing cream."

"It Healed me," Danny agreed. "And made me feel like a new man."

"Yes," Ilmar told them. "It will Heal any and all wounds."

"Like Danny's bruises?" Sarah asked.

"The bruising is an unfortunate side effect of prolonged physical contact with us," Ilmar explained.

"US?" Sarah repeated. "Who the hell is *us*?"

"People like me," Ilmar answered. "And my friends."

"Like you?" Confused, Sarah pushed her. "I don't understand. What's so special about people like you?"

Aaron thought he put it together. "You and all your friends...What are you, carriers?"

"There is nothing wrong with us, and there's nothing wrong with you. We're just not compatible with a long-term physical contact relationship."

"Not compatible? That's putting it mildly." Sarah freaked out. "You almost killed Danny! And what about Jeff? Hum?" She turned to Aaron. "And you! You had them on your body, too!"

The final trap closed on Aaron. "Sarah, it's not what you think."

"Not what I think. *Really?*" She leaned toward him. "So, you didn't sleep with one of them? 'Cuz, *that's* what I think." Sarah pushed him away. "Damn it, Aaron!"

Danny acted surprised. "Sarah, I swear… I had no idea."

Sarah glared at Danny. "Oh, shut up, Danny. You're a real ass, sometimes!"

Danny eyed Ilmar. "I got sick because of you?"

Ilmar couldn't meet his gaze. "Yes. Our physiology is so much stronger than you humans. When we touch you, our positive ions actually pull out your energy. Your very life-force."

"Huh?" At that point, Danny moved farther away from her.

Ilmar continued. "It is not a problem for us to make physical contact once. The adverse effects wear off in a few days, with only slight bruising. I warned you! I didn't mean for you to get hurt, Danny. "

"I just can't believe it's your fault I got so sick! What happened to honesty?" Danny repeated.

"I was honest! I am honest! I ran away from home for you, I fell in love with you," Ilmar admitted to him. "I care about you more than anything, and I want to find a way for us to be together. There is my honesty."

Danny backed away from her. "Are you an alien?" he asked her, fear in his voice.

"If what I've just heard wasn't so insane, that would be a funny question," Aaron stated flatly, as he paced. "Of course they're aliens!"

"I am not an alien. I am from the same Earth as you, just lower."

"Lower? Like where? The Hollow Earth Theory? Inside the Earth? How is that even possible?" Sarah asked. "Who are you people?"

"Does it matter?" Danny asked Sarah. As his fear escalated, their voices grew louder. "This is crazy shit!"

"You must keep the noise level down!" Ilmar begged.

As if in direct response to her statement, the door to Danny's house opened and Patrick turned on the outside light. He stood at the door and hollered at them. "What's all the noise about? You guys know what time it is?"

"Pat, go back inside!" Danny told him through gritted teeth.

"I think everyone should come inside, or go home. Thank God we don't have any neighbors."

"We can't let her leave!" Sarah screamed. "I'm calling this into the station. We've got to get the police involved to set things straight, here."

"What?" Pat asked, bewildered. "The police? Someone needs to tell me what the hell's going on out here!"

Ilmar realized her night was not going the way she planned. Danny was afraid of her, Patrick was losing his patients, and Sarah was going to get her phone and call the police. She closed her eyes in a failed attempt to bring herself back to center. Ilmar called out to Reeglar in her mind. She would help.

"Reeglar, I need you here now! I know you have been listening. All this is out of hand."

Ilmar thought all the details to her friend back in her cottage while watching as Sarah went back to her Ford Escape, opening the door so she could get her cell phone.

Within seconds, Reeglar answered her. *"I am here, Ilmar."*

When Reeglar came out of the shadows from behind Danny's house, all eyes focused on her. Aaron recognized her immediately. The guilt on his face told Sarah the new woman was Aaron's indiscretion. Angrily, she reached for her cell phone more determined than ever to end the madness.

Reeglar raised her hands as she emerged into the light. She brought her hands together with a sonic bang, and the shock wave knocked everyone down, sending them into unconsciousness. Danny, Aaron, and Sarah, all lay on the ground, while Patrick collapsed in the doorway.

Ilmar ran to her. "We need to erase their memories. I have made a mess of this. My father was right."

"We shall take care of this, Ilmar," Reeglar promised her. "They will wake tomorrow and remember absolutely nothing."

Ilmar looked into Reeglar's eyes. "He will not remember me at all?" she asked. "There is nothing you can do to change that?"

"I am sorry, Ilmar. Some things are just what they are. We can not change it. Let us get to work. We shall return to Akkadia in the morning."

Ilmar knelt next to Danny and bent down to kiss his cheek. She stroked his brow, lovingly. Reeglar sensed the loss Ilmar experienced; a pain both women shared. As Reeglar leaned over to help Ilmar lift Danny, she put her fingers to his temples, just for a second, pushing a thought into his mind. Just one thought. As both girls worked together, they struggled with Danny's dead weight but managed to carry him toward the house."

Reeglar scanned the scene. "This might take us all night."

"Let us get it over with," Ilmar said, sadly.

***

Danny woke Monday morning in his clothes from the night before. *What the hell?* His first thought of the day made him laugh to himself. *I must have had one drunk fest of a night last night.*

He examined his bed and found he was alone – no woman passed out next to him. *I must have been REALLY drunk.* He checked his cell phone on the nightstand. The time read 10:30 AM. *Crap! I better get my shit together. Gotta test fly the Cutlass this morning for Pat.*

Danny sat, and waves of dizziness came over him. *Hangover?* He thought. *I'm okay with that.* He got undressed from his soiled clothes and redressed in clean attire, slowly. He headed to the kitchen for a cup of coffee and found Patrick forgot to make some. *Strange?*

It was odd for Pat not to make a pot of coffee as soon as he woke up in the morning. By the time Danny got up and had his cup, the stuff was already old, but he drank it anyway. With no work involved, it was free and easy. Today, he had to make the coffee if he wanted it. And he did. He needed it. Surprising himself, Danny found all the necessary ingredients in the kitchen.

Mesmerized by the drip, drip, drip, of the coffee as it brewed in the pot, Danny was unprepared for the sight of Patrick strolling into the kitchen, still in his boxer shorts. He sported a severe case of bed head, and he stumbled a bit while rubbing his eyes at the bridge of his nose.

Danny nodded at Patrick. "Morning, bro. You a victim of too much alcohol last night, too?" He pointed to the pot. "I made coffee!" Danny said it with a sense of accomplishment.

Impressed, Patrick managed a slight nod but couldn't muster up the effort to show anything more. "Will it be ready soon?" It was all he could say as he dropped into a chair at the kitchen table. "I feel like I've just come out of anesthesia." Pat slowly gazed up at Danny. "Dopey, you know what I mean?"

"Boy, do I! " Danny laughed. "This is how I feel when I wake up most Mondays."

"Yeah, I know. That must suck!" Patrick turned his thought to a more serious topic. "But, I didn't think I drank that much last night. Well, at least not enough to make me black out. It was our first date. I just wouldn't do that."

"You blacked out?" Danny asked as he poured a cup of coffee and handed it to Patrick. "Dude, that's terrible! Been there many times. Not a lot of fun anymore. I think I'm done with that kind of behavior."

Pat took the cup from Danny. Once again, amazed at his brother's thoughtfulness. "Thanks."

Danny sat next to Patrick. "So," Danny began, "what do you think happened to you last night? Got any ideas?"

"No," Pat answered. "I decided to bring Trish back here after our date –"

Danny interrupted him. " 'Cuz you knew I wouldn't be home. Oh! You *dog*, you!"

"It wasn't like that; at least, I don't think so." Pat shook his head. "I just can't remember what happened. If we – you know." He shrugged his shoulders, lifting both arms in a gesture inferring something else might have happened. "I don't know if we did..."

"Did she say anything?" Danny asked.

"Trust me," Pat assured him. "She looked so surprised, if not more so than me when we woke up together in bed. I just called her a cab. I can't drive anywhere right now. My eyes are still crossed. She's in the bedroom getting dressed. Some first date, huh!" Pat sipped his coffee. "Ahhhh! Good job, Danny. This coffee tastes wonderful!"

Sheepishly, Trish walked into the kitchen, her purse in hand.

"Taxi's here," she told Patrick. "Will you walk me out?"

"Sure." Patrick introduced her to Danny. "Trish, this is my little brother, Danny."

"Nice to meet you," Danny said.

"You too!" Trish responded.

Patrick stood but realized he was undressed. "Shit! I don't have any pants on."

"That's okay, Pat," Trish told him. She kissed him on the cheek. "I think I had a good time last night. You can call me again if you want."

"Really?" Pat asked, amazed. "Okay, I will."

"Bye!" Trish waved. She walked out and closed the door behind her.

Danny teased Patrick, as he watched her leave. "She's, uh... kinda hot, bro!"

"She is, isn't she," Pat agreed. "God, I'm such a mess. Good thing I don't have a lesson until 3:30."

"No worries, Pat. I'm out to test fly the Cutlass." Danny got up, put his coffee in the sink, and filled the glass with water.

"I'll be out in the shop as soon as I wash up," Patrick informed him.

Danny stopped at the door. "Take your time, bro. You're a wreck."

Suddenly, Danny felt the dizziness return. He grabbed hold of the door handle for support when he was immediately assaulted with flashes in his mind, of lights, shapes, and shadows. The whole experience was familiar, yet just out of the reach of his memory. As swiftly as it hit him, it was gone.

Patrick jumped to his side in no time. "Hey! You okay?"

Danny took a deep breath. "Yeah... Yeah. I'm fine. I think I just need more sleep on the weekends."

"I can't let you fly the Cessna right now. Not in this condition."

"Really, Pat. I'm fine." Danny went back to the refrigerator and took out a piece of cold pizza. "I just need something to eat." He bit into it. "Low blood sugar and all," he said, with his mouth full as he chewed. "I'm going. I'm going!"

Pat waved him off, shaking his head. "Go, go. But if you crash that plane..." Pat didn't finish the sentence.

***

When Sarah opened her eyes, the sun shined brightly into her room. As she stretched, she found Aaron laying next to her. As if hit by a truck, her brain woke up. She spun and grabbed the alarm clock. 10:00 AM.

SHIT! Her mind screamed at her. She missed the beginning of her shift by three hours.

Jumping out of bed, she reached for her cell phone. She had thirteen messages from her Captain. *Shit, shit, shit, shit, shit!* She thought as she threw on her clothes as quickly as possible. "Aaron!" she hollered. "Aaron, wake up. Damn it!"

Confused, Aaron jumped up and threw off the covers, as he sprang from the bed. "WHAT?!" He stumbled around until he realized he was still in his clothes – dressed from the previous night, he whistled. Aaron watched Sarah frantically run around with a brush to her hair in one hand and a brush to her teeth in the other.

"Did we have a good night last night?" Aaron asked her, eyes wide in disbelief. Sarah gawked at him. "W-H-A-T?" Aaron asked again, as he dragged the word out. He thought his question was a valid one, motioning to her the fact he still wore his clothes while in bed. "Just saying… We must have been hammered!"

Sarah spat into the bathroom sink. "Ya think?! We sure must have been. And I'm so late!"

She tossed her old clothes in the hamper, and a jar dropped out of her pocket to the floor. She picked it up and placed it on the bathroom sink countertop. As she did, she was overwhelmed with a dizzy feeling and a flash of bright light burned behind her eyes. She braced herself against the vanity until the feeling passed.

I've got no time to stop for food this morning, she thought.

"What time is it?!" Aaron checked the alarm clock. "WOW! I've got to get to work, too!" He ran toward the door but planted a goodbye kiss on her on his way out.

Sarah wasn't far behind him. Strapping on her pistol holster, she grabbed her keys and sprinted out the door.

***

Ilmartutar walked around Akkadia as if in a trance. She did as she was supposed to and ate when she was supposed to. She made time for Azewrath to please her mother and father, like she was supposed to, but made sure to hand him off to Reeglar. She kept their secret. She didn't want him, never did, in fact. She didn't want anything anymore.

She hardly slept. She just lay there in bed for most of the cycles she should be slumbering. Ilmar's will to die burned inside her. At some point, either her not eating or her not sleeping, would do it for her – slowly. It was as good a plan as any.

Ilmar lay in bed and stared at the ceiling of her bedchambers. With no light in her room during their sleep term, she couldn't see anything. Her eyes were open, yet they gazed at nothing. Mirroring what was in her heart – nothing.

Without warning, the day's illumination brightened her room. Just a bit at a time, which allowed her body to adjust to the artificial circadian rhythms it followed since ancient times. The light indicated her father and mother were now awake as well.

Ilmar turned to a sitting position in bed. She eyed her robes, hanging on the wall and remembered a time when she would have thrown a tantrum at the sight of them. Not anymore. That required her to care, and she didn't care about anything. Ilmar slipped from the bed, stumbling through her morning routine without emotion. After she washed and dressed, she walked out the door.

Ilmar ended up at the Grand Hall. She entered and sat next to her mother and Azewrath. He placed his hand on hers, but she didn't look at him. Alkara observed her daughter's behavior. Ilmar's condition faded. She lost weight, dark circles appeared under her eyes, and her skin seemed to be unhealthy and gray.

A Level 2 Telepath placed the meal in front of her, but she didn't bother to look at it. Frustrated, Prince Pikkar watched his daughter's absent expressions. He sat beside his wife and crossed his arms. He refused to eat either, and his patience about the issue wore thin.

Alkara soothed him with a gentle caress on his arm. His stern gaze relayed his intent, but she shook her head ever so slightly, to dissuade him from speaking. As a determined man of action, it did no good.

"I have had enough of evading the issue, here!" Pikkar announced.

"It shall be handled today, my love," Alkara informed him. "Now, eat your food." She managed to get Ilmar's attention. "You also, my dear. You need to eat something. All right?"

Ilmar picked up her utensil, stabbed her food, brought it to her mouth and nibbled. Reeglar caught her glance from across the Hall.

"Ilmar!" Reeglar called out to her mind. *"Please, come back from wherever you are."*

She read nothing in Ilmar's mind; she was a shell, hollow and empty. Only Ilmar's body had come back to Akkadia. The rest of her, of her soul, remained above on the surface with Danny.

With the meal over, Ilmar might have eaten a few bites. Alkara stood, helped her daughter up by her shoulders and escorted her to the Healing Ward. Reeglar followed, resolved to be a part of whatever was going to happen. The Queen brought her directly to Mage' Rom.

Rom met the women and bowed. "My Queen," he acknowledged.

"ROM!" Alkara greeted cheerfully. She hugged him, brushing his cheek with her lips. "You have known me from birth. I am Alkara to you, Mage'."

"Do not remind an old man of his lost youth," he teased.

Reeglar helped Ilmar to sit on the exam table. The Telepath smiled at Rom also. "Mage'."

Ilmar focused on the back wall, and a lone tear ran down her cheek. Concerned, Mage' Rom put a finger to his lips. "Has she been like this all week?"

"Yes," Alkara answered. "I am distressed. I believe she has lost the will to live. And I shall not sit by another day and watch her slip further into the abyss."

Reeglar added her observations and experience as well. "More importantly, there is nothing inside her mind. I can not find Ilmar when I enter."

"That is extremely serious!" Rom declared. "I shall try to do what I can." He turned to Reeglar. "I might need you to put a cap on her memories if I succeed in bringing her back. Do you agree to try?"

"Anything I can do, I shall!" Reeglar agreed.

Rom took Alkara's hand in his. "This could take some time, my dear."

Alkara understood what the Mage' meant. "I shall await your summons." She turned to leave, and then put a hand on Reeglar's shoulder, giving her a weak smile. "You are different... Changed?"

"I am not sure what you mean, my Queen." The statement confused Reeglar.

"You are not the same now that you have returned, as you were before you left." Alkara smiled at her. "It shall all be well."

The Mage' took Ilmar in his arms to lay her down on the table. Reeglar sat in the nearest chair and waited until needed. Rom closed Ilmar's eyes. He positioned his hands on her. One on her forehead to Heal her mind, the other on her chest over her aching heart.

His hands became a yellow light of Healing, spreading outward along her body. The glare brilliant, so much like the sun's auroral blaze, encompassing the whole room. So bright was the light; Reeglar had to rely on her Telepathic "sight" to keep track of Rom's progress. The glow, accompanied by intense heat, raised the temperature in the room, creating sweat beads that covered her skin.

"The process is taking too long," Reeglar thought to Rom, sensing his strength waning. He leaned on Ilmar, instead of giving her his energy, his yellow glow dimmed, diminishing until nothing remained except silence.

The stillness and calm only lasted for a few seconds. Reeglar took Mage' Rom by his shoulders and helped him to the chair that she vacated, but Ilmar chose that instant to let out a bloodcurdling scream. It was an outcry of devastating loss, of a lamented sadness, so powerful; it knocked Reeglar to the floor before she could hold on to something. The pain Reeglar experienced through her connection to Ilmar almost crippled her.

Dragging her body, she grabbed the edge of the table, pulling herself upright. All the while she struggled to make contact with Ilmar psyche. She wrapped her fingers around Ilmar's head and held her down as best she could. Reeglar tried to quiet Ilmar, but

Ilmar's body thrashed with all the misery she experienced in her mind and her heart.

Rom cried out to Reeglar. "You are not strong enough! You need to call your father."

"No!" Reeglar demanded, peering over at him. "I can do this!" She turned back to Ilmar, determined to give her friend her full attention. "I just need more time." *I can do this!*

Reeglar jumped back into Ilmar's mind, prepared to search for what she sought. Everywhere she examined, memories of Danny surfaced. She encountered a large black cloud which swirled around in the stark white of Ilmar's frontal lobe. The darkness appeared heavy and cumbersome, dragging Reeglar down further and further. Fighting the sorrow, she reached out and collected all she could.

Creating a massive wall, she compressed the swirling mist and pushed it behind her memory cap. After she used her mind to close it, so there were no openings. Her thoughts ignited, burned, and cauterized synaptic tissue like a welding torch. Reeglar noticed something out of the corner of her eye. The only shiny thing to stand out from all the darkness. The brightness was the memory of Ilmar's and Danny's first meeting.

Reeglar took it gently in her hands. She turned it around and checked the darkness, confident it was still walled off, locked tightly away. Pleased with the seal, she held Ilmar's last glimmer of happiness in her hands, a glowing ray of hope. Reeglar squeezed it together until it shrunk to the size of a fingernail. She placed it down and softly gave it a push, sending it on an endless journey in Ilmar's mind. Watching it roll away, she breathed a sigh of relief. Someday, Ilmar would find this tiny piece of happiness again.

Afterward, all was stillness in the Healing Ward. Ilmar lay quietly on the table, and Reeglar watched her intently, waiting for her to wake. Recovered, Mage' Rom joined her. He stood next to the table and took Reeglar's hand while they remained together. When Ilmar opened her eyes, she took a large inhaled breath, her eyes staring wide. She let out an exhale and gazed up at Reeglar.

"Hi," Reeglar whispered.

"Hi," Ilmar repeated. "What... Hum... What happened? What

am I doing here?"

"You were not feeling well," Reeglar explained.

Rom held Ilmar's hand. "You are much better now, my Prime."

"I shall inform the Queen she is awake," Reeglar reported to the Mage'. "I shall be right back," she promised Ilmar. Moving away, she closed her eyes and contacted the Queen. After Reeglar had made contact, she returned to her friend's side. "Your mother is on her way. She shall be pleased to see you."

"How are you feeling, Ilmar?" Rom asked her.

Ilmar pushed herself into a seated position and smiled. "I am starving!"

Rom laughed at her. "We shall have something brought in for you. You had eaten so little this past week. Do you have any preferences?"

"No," Ilmar answered. "Just have them bring a little of *everything*."

Rom smiled at her again. "All right." He turned to leave but placed a hand on Reeglar's arm on his way. "Watch her and –" He stopped in mid-thought.

"What is wrong, Mage'?" Reeglar inquired, distressed by the expression on his face.

Rom put both his hands on her; his concerned glance slowly changed to a giant knowing grin. "Reeglar, my lovely young woman," he began, "you are with child. You are pregnant."

XII

Unity and Healing

The whole world stopped turning for Reeglar. She stood there, unable to think for probably the first time in her life. Rom continued to speak, so she refocused on his words.

"Are you all right? I need to stay with Ilmar. Reeglar?" The Mage' asked her as he tried to get her attention.

"Yes!" she assured him. "I am sorry. It was just the shock. I am all right, truly."

"You are one week along, little mother, but there is still no doubt."

"One week?" Reeglar repeated. "Are you sure?"

"Yes. Five to seven days; give or take."

"That is impossible!"

Alkara picked that moment to walk into the Ward, followed by Prince Pikkar. "Mage' Rom!" She greeted him again. "Ilmar is?"

"She is here, my Queen." He ushered her along and brought her next to the exam table.

"Ilmartutar!" Alkara reached for her daughter's hand, squeezing it tight.

"What happened to me, Mother?" Ilmar asked.

"We are still not quite sure, my dear. Yet, you are better now. I can tell."

"Why do you insist on making us worry?" Pikkar asked her.

"I will not be happy until I am responsible for all your gray hairs, Father," Ilmar teased him.

"I have your meal." Rom came through the door with a tray and put it down on Ilmar's lap.

"Thank you!" Ilmar moved to devour everything on her plate.

Reeglar took Mage' Rom away from the others to corner him on the other side of the room. "Rom, I can not be one week along." She repeated to him.

"I am very precise with my time-lines, Reeglar."

"Mage'…" Reeglar confessed. "I must tell you something. I was on the surface seven days ago, but I have not been with a human male in twelve days."

"What are you trying to tell me, Reeglar?" Suspicion colored his eyes.

"I have only lain with Azewrath in the last seven days."

Rom's eyebrows shot upward. He hesitated, stunned, unsure of what to say, so he sighed instead. *Oh, this is not good!* "Are you sure about this?"

Reeglar gave him a look. "What do you think? I need to know how this can be?"

"I am afraid I am completely dumbfounded. I shall have to examine Azewrath," Rom told her. "Does Ilmar know?"

"Yes. Well, Ilmar *did*. Oh, my Goddess!" She realized she was going to have to tell Azewrath. "This is going to be quite the mess, so I would appreciate it if you would keep this just between us."

Rom nodded absentmindedly but gave a warning. "I have no wish to be in the center of this! You do realize that it is quite difficult to keep a secret in Akkadia."

"I have done fine, so far. I just need to stop people from touching me. I must go." Reeglar squeezed in between the Queen and the Prince to get over to Ilmar. "I am glad you are feeling better, but I must attend to some... things. You are in good hands." She leaned over and kissed Ilmar on the cheek, and then ran from the room.

"Where is she going in such a hurry?" Ilmar asked the Mage'.

"I am sure I have no idea," Rom replied.

Queen Alkara gave Rom a sidewards glance. "Hmm," she hummed, unconvinced.

***

Reeglar moved so quickly; it was as if she flew through the corridors on her way to Azewrath's quarters. Reminding herself not to think, she tried to count floor tiles, scuff marks on the walls, anything, to keep her mind occupied with trivial things. She was about to put her hand on Azewrath's door, but he opened it before she could do so.

"That is very unnerving, you know," she teased him, entering his rooms. She spun quickly to face him.

"And what you do is commonplace, I suppose?"

All smiles, Reeglar exploded. "Ah, I am who I am, my love." She fell into his arms, resting her head on his chest. "I have news. Ilmar is better, finally awake and near to normal again."

"Really? Then, I am happy for her."

"There is more," she taunted. "But, we must keep this very quiet, just between the two of us for right now."

"Is that why I have not felt you in my mind all day?"

"Oh yes," she whispered. "This is too sensitive to Telepathically project. As a matter of fact, I think I need to keep all my projecting to a bare minimum at this time. Too many prying minds.

"Sounds intriguing." He kissed her neck, and she moaned with pleasure.

Reeglar almost sent him the news through their bond before quickly pushing it out of her mind. It was such an automatic response. *No! No! No!* She demanded of herself. *Speak it out loud!*

Unable to hold the information in any longer, the words burst from her lips. "I am with child!" She spat it out like an exploding volcano. Azewrath, taken aback, released her. His reaction was not what she expected.

Confused, she confronted him. "I thought you would be pleased."

"I am pleased... for you." He forced out the words. "I would think now you should be wed."

"Well, of course!"

Azewrath sat in his chair. "Has your father picked out a husband for you?"

"I am not to be Queen. The decision to marry, and to whom shall be mine alone." She went to him. "I shall be with you, Azewrath. I see no reason we should not wed."

"I must be joined with Ilmar, Reeglar. You know this," he stated.

"I hoped that our time together changed your mind," she replied sadly.

"It is not something I can simply undo."

"Or, is it something you do not *wish* to undo. Have I just been a willing plaything for you?"

Azewrath took her hand in his and brought them to his heart.

"You have been, and shall always be, the most wonderful thing I have ever had in my life. If only for this short time. I once told you love was a folly; I regret ever saying such a thing." He put his lips on her palms. "I shall love you, always. Remember that."

Tears sprung to Reeglar's eyes and try as she might, she was unable to stop them. She cried in frustration. Since it was easier to explain through their bond than with words, she showed him. Reeglar reached up, cupped his head in her hands, and brought her forehead up to meet his. She opened her mind to him, revealing all of her feelings, all of her hopes and dreams. Including the new unique life they now shared.

When she finished, he pulled away from her and stared intensely into her eyes. Slowly, a smile spread across his face and moved all the way to his eyes. He jumped to his feet and pulled her up with him. Lifting her off the floor, he swung her around, ending with a giant bear hug.

When he released her, and her feet were once again on the ground, she put her finger to his lips and shushed him. "You must not think about this too hard," she warned him. "Push it down, cover it up and only take it out to peek at it. Do you understand me?"

"I am trying, Reeglar. Truly I am! Yet, my heart burns. It burns as the Abyss of Fire!" He kissed her like he never kissed anyone before.

***

Ilmartutar stuffed herself with food until she couldn't move. Mage' Rom cleared her to return to her daily routines, but the Prince wasn't sure. He called Chancellor Torg into the Healing Ward to make sure Ilmar was ready.

Ilmar sat on the exam table and fidgeted. The act of joining with a Telepath would leave a person either feeling renewed or drained. Depending on the treatment. Rejuvenated and refreshed, she was ready to get going.

Torg entered, bowing low to being summoned by his monarchy. "I have come as you commanded, my Prince."

Pikkar motioned to Ilmar. "Your daughter, Reeglar, has done

157

what she can for my daughter. She appears to be well enough, yet it will give me peace of mind to have you tell me she is better." Torg raised an eyebrow, slightly. Pikkar corrected himself. "I am sure Reeglar is an admirable Telepath, but why have the student do something when you can have the master?"

"Hum," Torg began. "I shall do as you ask, only to prove that Reeglar is capable, if not more so than myself." He strode over to Ilmar. "Good morning, my dear."

"Chancellor," Ilmar replied.

"I shall be quick."

"It is all right, go ahead." Ilmar permitted him to touch her.

Torg placed two fingers on Ilmar's temple and entered her mind. He witnessed all of Ilmar's memories, from early childhood onward as they passed by at great speeds, inconsequential to his search. They brought him to the wall of darkness. He checked the memory prison Reeglar created, pleased with the results. She had done an excellent job in protecting her friend.

The confinement shall hold for quite some time, Torg decided. He released his hold on Ilmar. "She is healthy, and from what I saw, happy as well."

"I am happy," she informed him. "Now, may I please go?" she asked her father.

"Yes," Pikkar agreed. "Go... Do whatever it is you do."

Ilmar jumped off the table, kissed her mother and father as she sped away, waving her goodbyes.

Pikkar turned to Torg. "Are you truly pleased with the hold on the memory cap?"

"I am," Torg announced proudly. "Reeglar accomplished her task. The memory cap shall hold for quite some time unless she comes into contact with someone or something that can set off a memory."

"What should we do?" the Queen asked.

"Be careful with your words and the words of others," Torg warned. "Also, I would never let her return to the surface."

***

Ilmar trotted down the halls and after a few minutes before

realizing she didn't know where she was going. *I was so intent on leaving the Healing Ward.* She laughed to herself. *Where to go... What to do? I know, I will find Reeglar!*

Ilmar made a right turn and followed the maze of circular corridors until she came to the living quarters of the House of Torg. She knocked on the door, waited, but it seemed no one was home.

Hmmm... Where is she? Ilmar wondered. As she walked on, her thoughts moved to Azewrath. *I suppose I should go to his quarters and apologize for being sick.*

She didn't remember what had gone on for the past couple of days. Feverish and unable to respond, she couldn't have been good company. She changed direction and put herself on a course to Azewrath's quarters.

***

Azewrath held Reeglar in his arms, his kisses, more passionate, more demanding. His wants moved Reeglar to understand. Their bond left no questions unanswered, no desires unfulfilled.

She entered his mind as she undressed. Untying her robes, she dropped them to the floor and came toward him. He grabbed her by the hips to pull her to him. Azewrath brought his lips to her belly and kissed it lovingly.

"I love you both," he whispered to her soft skin.

Reeglar smiled as she cradled his head between her breasts. "And life does grow..."

He opened his trousers, pushing them down to expose his manhood, ready for her. He sat a throbbing and engorged symbol of his desire. She moved onto him, wantonly.

"This child shall be a merging of a Telepath and a Seer. He shall be a very dynamic leader."

"What do you mean, he?" Reeglar asked as she slowly rode him tenderly, rocking back and forth.

"You shall birth me a son," he stated proudly.

"Really?" she asked. "You have Seen this?"

"Indeed," he replied. "Truly. He shall be powerful, and we shall make him Chancellor to the Queen after your father has stepped down with age."

She bent down to kiss him. "Well, we better start grooming him for the position now!" She took his hands in hers and moved them down to her abdomen. "Did you hear your Father? You shall be an important man. Yet, no pressure, little one." She laughed.

Azewrath stopped in mid thrust. As soon as he knew a thought, so did Reeglar. She saw what he saw. She jumped from his lap and gathered her robes to redress. He fastened his trousers just in time. Ilmar was on her way.

"What shall you tell her?" he asked.

"Me?!" Reeglar wondered. "Why am I in charge of this?"

"She is your friend."

"And she is your intended!" Reeglar shouted indignantly and then sighed at the futility. She shook her head and laughed.

"Why are you laughing?" Azewrath wondered, panicked.

"I just remembered; I told her about us already."

"Did you not wipe her memories of her time on the surface?" he questioned.

"Yes, and no," she explained. "I took some of her specific memories from her time above, not all of them. She should remember this!" *I hope. Now, I am not sure.* "We need to be cautious about what we say to her when we refer to her time up there."

Ilmar reached Azewrath's door, and for the first time, it did not open before she knocked. She realized that this was where Reeglar must be.

She should be here. Why would she be here?

Ilmar's head ached. She leaned against the wall for a moment, rubbing her temples. As she stood there, the door opened.

Reeglar peeked out and smiled at Ilmar. "Ilmar! I am happy to see you up and around so soon."

"I knew you would be here," Ilmar told her. "Although, I'm not quite sure how?" She went through the door into Azewrath's rooms. "This is still a secret from everyone, correct? You two, I mean." She pointed back and forth from Azewrath to Reeglar. "I am sorry, some things are still a bit jumbled up in my mind." Ilmar put her fingers to her temples again. The pain was back.

"You need not apologize to me," Azewrath said. "It is I who

owe you the greatest debt of gratitude."

"Oh, Azewrath," Ilmar started. "I do not think I have ever heard you beholding to someone else." She smiled at him. "I think I am going to like the new you."

Reeglar got Ilmar's attention. "Did you need help with something? I noticed you were resting against the outside walls."

"No, I am all right. Just a slight headache," Ilmar reported.

Concerned, Reeglar pressed her. "Perhaps you should take the rest of the day to relax and get some real sleep?"

"True," Ilmar agreed. "I have not been sleeping well, and I have had a very rough week, or so I have been told."

Reeglar walked her to the door and kissed her on the cheek. "Be well, my dear friend." She whispered to her. "And thank you for Azewrath."

"Love is blind, Reeglar," Ilmar told her. "And I saw way too much in Azewrath that would never make me happy. Good luck to you!" Ilmar turned and walked out.

***

In the Healing Ward, Queen Alkara decided while she had both Chancellor Torg and Mage' Rom in the same place, she would confront them and broach the subject of their new predicament.

"Gentlemen, I need some advice," she began. "Instead of calling a full Council meeting, I would rather come up with a solution with all of you here."

"It would seem we need another plan," Torg agreed. "The mingling of our race with the humans created unforeseeable consequences."

Alkara turned to Rom. "How many impregnated females have we after this nine-month experiment?"

"Only two, my Queen," Rom answered. "Minnar and Lacara." Experiencing slight guilt at the small lie, Rom justified his thoughts in his mind. He needed to be free of doubt in the company of the Chancellor. If he was to be honest, only two women were impregnated with the human/Akkadian hybrid children.

"Ah!" Pikkar uttered in disgust in reference to Lacara. "That woman!"

"She has caused her fair share of trouble," the Chancellor mentioned.

"Indeed," Alkara agreed. "But this woman must be treated as a treasure. She is carrying our very future."

"Minnar is close to term," Rom announced.

"How is she progressing?" the Queen asked.

"She is well," Rom offered. "All is ready, as I wish to be prepared for an early birth, just in case. We have no idea what to expect."

"We need to send our hopes for the future in a new direction?" Alkara questioned.

Rom wanted to let her know there might be a new mitigating circumstance. Azewrath's seed might be motile. But, he was still unsure. For the time, Rom suggested something else.

"I have been told by some of the women who have gone above about places called sperm banks." They exchanged glances, confused, so Rom went on. "It is a bizarre tradition for the humans. They keep viable male sperm in containers, in freezing conditions for later use. I have concluded from this information that the humans must have fertility issues as well."

"Would this mean no more trips to the surface for our women?" Chancellor Torg asked.

"Yes," Pikkar answered. "No more trips."

Rom added. "You might be able to get inside one of these places with a competent Telepath and confiscate some samples. The visit might help our cause."

Pikkar wished to engage the Chancellor. "We shall need your opinion on your best Telepath."

"I shall work on that, my Prince," Torg replied.

"Good. Our business has concluded." Alkara turned to go, and then added one more comment. "I want to thank both of you for Ilmar's return to health. Pikkar?" He held out his arm, and she wrapped her hand in the crook of his elbow as they attempted to walk out of the Healing Ward.

A young woman who the Queen recognized, ran by Alkara and Pikkar, straight into Mage' Rom. "Mage'! It is Minnar! She is in need of a Healer. She is in labor!"

The Queen immediately turned around. "Let us retrieve her,

Torg!"

XIII

Something Old, Something New

Sarah stepped from the shower after a grueling four-day, 16-hour shift schedule at the police department. Her captain let her know that the CDC Director of the Vector-Borne Disease branch signed off on the Jeff Donaldson case. Lyle Peterson, and his colleague, John Roehrig, along with the Director of the Special Pathogens branch, Stuart Nichol, all closed the book on the incident.

Satisfied it was an isolated episode they released his body for burial. Sarah even went to the funeral, closing the case. In her mind, there was more to this case than they knew, although, she couldn't find evidence to the contrary.

I'm not going to think about this now. I'm going to have a good time, Sarah told herself. The rough week took its toll on her, and she wasn't at the top of her game. She suffered from dizzy spells. *Working too hard,* she thought. Her excitement grew, as she planned the evening in her head.

Going out with Aaron and Danny, meant an evening with men behaving like four-year-old children. When the two of them got together, trouble followed. At least she'd be there to stop something before it escalated.

After drying her hair, she put on minimal makeup and attempted to choose a body lotion. As she reached for the bottle, she noticed a jar she didn't recognize.

What's this?

Sarah opened the jar. Inside, she found an odorless, milky white, thick textured cream. She tried some. Rubbing her hands together, she applied it to her skin. Unhappy with its texture, she put it away and opted for the larger bottle of lotion.

Without warning, her eyesight blurred, and she missed the bottle completely, overtaken by dizziness. Sitting on the toilet, she waited until she regained her focus. With her strength returned, she applied the lotion. She rose slowly, shuffling to her bedroom as the front door open and Aaron walked in.

"It's just me!" he yelled.

"Hey, babe!" Sarah shouted back. "I'm in the bedroom, getting dressed."

"No! No, wait!" Aaron pleaded. He ran to her room to stop her.

Still in a towel, Sarah examined her clothes laid out on the bed. Aaron slid up to her and wrapped his arms around her. He kissed her hard on the mouth, pressing himself against her body.

Sarah pulled back. "I'm trying to get ready!"

"Um-hum." He kissed her neck, moving his mouth lower and lower. "I'm helping."

Aaron untied the towel from around Sarah's chest and dropped it to the floor. He caressed one of her breasts and then leaned lower to bring her erect nipple into his mouth. He nipped it with his teeth and tickled it with his tongue.

Sarah moaned with pleasure as her hands grasped his head. "Stop... we need to go..." She halfheartedly tried to stop him as he slid his other hand between her thighs in search of her moistness. He found its glistening, warm opening and pushed his fingers deep inside her. "Oh, Aaron..." she whispered.

He took her leg and wrapped it around his elbow, forcing his hand further into her. She moaned again, excited by his touch. Aaron pressed against her, and he grew hard inside his jeans.

Oh, we can't do this right now! Sarah forced herself to stop him and pushed him away. "Not now!"

"Hey," he sulked. "Look what you're leaving me with." He grabbed the bulge in his pants.

"I didn't start anything. It was all you," Sarah scolded him. "Why don't you make yourself useful and give Danny a call. See if he's ready."

"All right." Aaron pulled out his cell phone. "Thought I *was* making myself useful. Just not fair... I got this thing going on here, now... What am I supposed to do with it? Hang suits on it... SHIT!"

He attempted to maneuver his piece of meat into a more comfortable position inside his pants as he walked into the living room to call Danny.

***

The whole week held amazing possibilities for Danny.

Something came over him that changed his entire outlook on life. He quit his bouncing job at Frampton's and put all his efforts into the family operation. So much so, Patrick changed the name of the business to Sutters Brother's School of Aviation.

Danny spent the week handing out fliers, business cards, and going to places frequented by the summer tourist. Danny added at least 40 new clients/students to their lessons. The numbers so great, Patrick created a new kind of teaching – a group tour where the students received a brief half-hour lesson on the ground. The group would go up in the Cessna, taking turns at the flight controls. No one earned a license, but the new income Danny helped generate more than made up for the rise in fuel costs.

In fact, Patrick was able to buy a new car with the extra profit. As the tow truck company carted away his 1974 Mustang, Pat waved goodbye without any nostalgia.

They went to Jeff Donaldson's wake, and funeral after the CDC released the body, with a big to do at the J. Ronald Scott Funeral Parlor on Ponquogue Avenue. Police and firefighters alike lined both sides of the streets with siren cars and fire trucks, in reverence and respect for a fallen comrade. The extension ladders lengthened over the road in honor at their full expanse. Danny, Patrick, Aaron, and Sarah, attended and were not surprised to find it wouldn't be an open casket.

Another Saturday night found Danny finishing up in the shop for the day. For the first time in five years, he headed to Frampton's as a customer. He put the last of his tools away and grabbed a rag for his hands, as always.

If he could only stop the weird dreams he had when he was asleep, and even when he was awake. Add to that the headaches and the dizzy spells, it all took a toll on him. He popped over-the-counter painkillers like tic-tacs.

It's just too much workload. I've gone from being a bum to having all this responsibility.

He hoped it had to be something like that. The other alternative meant something was wrong with his brain, and that wouldn't be good.

As he closed the door to the shop on his way out, he caught a glimpse of Patrick out of the corner of his eye. His brother pulled out of the driveway in his new charcoal gray Acura Advanced.

Danny flagged him down and yelled. "You out, bro?"

Patrick let the car roll down the window automatically. "Yep, gonna get Trish and go out for dinner. You?"

"Tonight will be my first night as a customer at Frampton's."

"Well, good luck with that! Have a good weekend."

"You're not coming home?" Danny asked.

"With any luck, I might not!" Pat answered, laughing and winked. He shot Danny a wave and drove away.

Danny waved back and walked into the house. He stripped for a shower, letting the water run. Pulling his shirt over his head, he unbuttoned his jeans and slid them down. Hopping from one foot to the other, he pulled his legs out. Shedding the last stitch of apparel, he dropped everything in the clothes hamper.

As Danny jumped into the running water, he washed swiftly. Once finished, he reached for the towel and wrapped it around his waist. Stepping out, he searched for his razor.

Wiping the fog off the mirror, he plugged in the electric razor to shave. While attending to his unruly stubble, something besides the buzz of his shaver got his attention. A far away noise. He turned the razor off and cocked his head to listen. From his bedroom, his cell phone rang again and again. It alerted him to an incoming call. He ran to his bedroom, answering it right before his voice message engaged.

" 'Lo?"

"Hey, man!" Aaron murmured into the receiver.

"Sup, bro!"

"Sarah and I are on our way. You gonna meet us there, right?"

"You bet. Getting dressed, and then I'm gone."

"We're gonna have a blast!" Aaron promised.

"Oh, yeah. Bring on the drinking and the women!"

"I thought you'd gone all grown up on us now?" Aaron teased him.

"Hey, I might have gotten more respectable, but a man still has needs." Danny laughed.

"Alright, dude. See ya in a few. Later!"

"Yep, bye." Danny hung up, dropped the phone on the bed, and continued dressing for the night out.

***

The height of summer and Frampton's was packed, with a line that formed out the door into the parking lot. With nowhere to park, Danny put his Camaro at the train station on Good Ground Road and walked to the bar. When he got to the strip mall, Aaron's Ram truck pulled in and stole a space right as another car pulled out. Danny spotted them as Aaron and Sarah got out of the vehicle.

"Dude!" Danny called out as he approached them. "Why did you drive? I wanted to get shit faced with you tonight!"

Aaron pointed to Sarah. "No problem. I brought a designated driver. The old ball and chain." He smiled, but Sarah punched him in the arm on the way to the bar. "Ow!"

"Aren't you going to have a drink or two with us, Sarah?" Danny asked.

"I sure as hell am!" Sarah affirmed. "You think the police are going to pull me over? NOT!"

When they got to the door, Danny laughed out loud. Standing there, checking IDs, was Darren. The twenty-three-year-old was all muscle, about the same age as Danny when he gained employment, bouncing at Frampton's. Darren was their part-time bouncer.

Guess he got a promotion! Danny surmised.

"Danny!" Darren hailed, greeting his mentor. "It's an honor, man. Go right in."

"Oh, we're in the presence of royalty," Aaron teased.

"Yeah, royal pain in the ass!" Sarah shot.

"Shut up," Danny responded in his defense. The three sat at the bar, and Danny caught the bartender's attention. "Hi, Lisa."

"Danny!" Lisa smiled at him. "Gonna miss you around here, big guy." Lisa held a small crush on him. She poured a draft beer, placing it in front of him. "This one's on me."

"Thanks, Lisa, but I'm a customer tonight," Danny informed her. "I should pay."

"Your money's no good here, darling," Lisa insisted again.

"O-K." Danny gave up. "But, let me at least get Aaron's and Sarah's drinks. Gang?"

"Just a draft for me, Lisa. Thanks," Aaron told her, so she

poured another.

"I'm in the mood for a frozen margarita, please." Sarah placed her order.

"No problem," Lisa replied. "I'll be right back."

The boys took their first gulps of beer which prompted Aaron to bang his fist on the bar. Yelling in rhythm with the pounding, he voiced his desires. "Shots, shots, shots! Shots, shots, shots!"

Danny laughed. "Don't worry, Aaron. I'm not pacing myself tonight!"

"Can I, at least, get my drink before we start doing shots?!" Sarah asked. "I hadn't planned on getting sloppy."

Lisa came back with Sarah's drink. She put a bar napkin under it, and a couple of salt crystals fell onto the paper. "Thanks," Sarah said, licking her finger. She brought it down on the errant grains of salt, which stuck to her wet skin. Finally, she delivered it to her lips and sucked it off with a moan of pleasure.

Aaron watched closely. "Nice form!" he offered. "Got some of that for me?"

"Later..." she teased and winked.

"I heard we need shots over here?" Lisa questioned. "Of...?"

Danny and Aaron said at the same time. "Not Jack!" They both exchanged glances and laughed.

"Southern Comfort?" Danny suggested.

"Oh, yeah!" Aaron agreed.

"Set us up, Lisa," Danny ordered. Lisa spilled the bottle into three shot glasses. They raised them, clicked the small drinks together and downed the golden liquid.

"First of many!" Aaron promised, banging his shot glass on the bar.

Lisa raised an eyebrow at Danny. "Just leave the bottle?" she asked, but knew the answer would be yes.

"Yes, great idea!" Danny agreed, throwing out a compliment. "You're the best and most beautiful bartender around."

"Hold that thought, sweetheart!" Lisa interrupted. "I got other customers to please. Be right back."

"Is no one safe?" Sarah asked. "I think this is a new all-time low for you."

"What?" Danny questioned her indignantly. "Lisa's single, I don't know why, though."

"She probably has morals and high standards," Aaron added.

"Not if she's attracted to Danny." Sarah laughed.

"Hey!" Danny took offense. "There's nothing wrong with me!" he told her. "I just know what I want, and I take it."

"You have no idea what you want, Danny," Sarah informed him. "That's why you do the things you do."

"What do you mean by that?" Danny asked her, pouring another shot. He drank it swiftly, attempting to keep his calm. Sarah always got his hackles up.

"Hey guys," Aaron broke in, something he had to do every time the two of them were together. "Let's just calm down and have another round." He tipped the bottle into everyone's shot glasses.

"Hum," Sarah continued, a little more subdued. "In all the years I've known you, and we go back about seven, I don't think I've ever seen you in love. Not once."

"So," Danny argued. "There is no crime against that. I'm still young... having some fun. There's still plenty of time for love."

"Ya think?" Sarah asked him. "Have you looked in the mirror lately? Do you like what you see... The person you are?"

"Sarah," Aaron stopped her. "Shut up and drink your drink. We're here to have a good time. We're here for a celebration, remember?"

Sarah turned to Aaron, stunned. "Whatever," she answered. "Let's celebrate. Woo-Hoo!" She downed her shot, gulping her margarita down she got brain freeze.

Lisa returned. "Need another drink, Sarah?"

"Oh yeah," Sarah affirmed, gesturing with her hand. "Keep 'em coming. I'd like to get to the point where I black out tonight. Maybe, if I'm lucky, I'll forget all this."

Lisa took her glass and brought back a fresh one. "Anything else, for anyone?" she asked, as her eyes met Danny's slyly.

Danny rested his elbow on the bar, leaning in toward Lisa. "I'm sure I can come up with something you can give me."

"I don't know, Romeo," Lisa remarked. "Where is that real pretty girl you've been hanging out with every weekend? I don't want to start any trouble between the two of you."

Danny gave Lisa the once-over as is she was crazy. "I'm not seeing anyone. What are you talking about?"

Aaron turned to Danny questioningly. "Bro, you hiding a girl on us?"

"News to me?" Sarah added.

Confused, Lisa continued. "Uh, she hung out with you guys too."

Sarah shook her head. "I don't think so, Lisa. We'd remember Danny with a steady girl."

"I have pictures," Lisa told them. "For the Summer collage of the patron board? You know, all the pictures we post on the wall?" She pulled out her cell phone. "I'll show you."

"Okay," Danny requested. "I'd like to see that!"

"Me too!" Sarah agreed, disbelieving her.

Lisa flipped through some photos and finally brought up a specific picture. She tapped the screen to enlarge it and then handed the cell phone to Danny. "See? I'm not lying, *or* crazy."

Upon inspection of the pictures on the phone, Danny almost choked. There they were there. Himself, Aaron and Sarah, glasses raised, all smiles. And someone else was with them. Another woman he didn't know, but he had his arm around her in a very possessive posture. She was young, blonde, hot, and smiled as well. She seemed happy nestled in his embrace, and so did he.

What the hell? He wondered, handing the phone to Aaron. Danny eyed Lisa. "Okay, very funny. Where's Brad?" He glanced around. "You guys are fucking with me for quitting, right? I get it; it's funny." Lisa shook her head, no. Danny continued. "Look, I've been punked. O-K, you guys got me. I've gotten really drunk here, many times, but I've never been so shit faced that I'd ever forget dating that chick, *ever*."

She did seem familiar, however. Aaron wondered. *How do I know her? Why can't I remember this? And why does it feel like I have seen her before?* Aaron shrugged, shook his head, handing the phone to Sarah. She studied it closely.

Danny reached for the bottle of Comfort, pouring three more shots. "And away we go!" He raised his glass and threw his head back. *What the hell is going on?* His brain hurt.

Sarah handed Lisa back the phone. "I'm stumped. You're sure you're not pulling a joke on us?"

Lisa swore. "I'm telling the truth." She went to Danny. "Look,

I like you; I can't help myself – even though I know who you are, and how you treat your women. I don't know why I'm saying this, but I'm not going to break up a couple, you know?"

"Sorry Lisa," Danny told her. "I have no intentions of being a couple with anyone, but thanks for the offer."

"Sure Danny, no problem." Embarrassed, Lisa walked away.

"You do know you just made Lisa feel like shit, right?" Sarah told Danny. He shrugged, unable to worry about that. Sarah contemplated the picture. "That's got to be a trick of some kind. Photoshop, you know? It can do that," she added. "If not, then we're all crazy, or need to check ourselves into rehab."

Aaron couldn't get passed it. "There's no way she's real. Well, at least, the picture isn't, right?"

"There's a problem with that logic," Danny stated.

"What?" Aaron asked.

"She's the woman of my dreams."

"Oh, brother!" Sarah remarked.

"She was beautiful enough," Aaron added. "But you could do better."

"No," Danny corrected him. "You don't understand. I've been dreaming of this girl. Literally." He poured himself another shot and downed it quickly. "When I'm sleeping, and when I'm awake!"

"How can you have a dream when you're awake?" Aaron doubted.

"It can happen. It's like I'm in a trance. I don't know; I'm sure I've just been working too hard, that's all."

Sarah leaned back on her bar stool, arms crossed. "Well, why can't we all remember her?" She admitted something to them. "Look, I've had dizzy spells, and it seems my mind is playing tricks on me lately." She drew closer to both of them. "I think something is going on with all of us. This mystery is only the tip of the iceberg."

"Honey," Aaron started, "you see a conspiracy around every corner, truthfully."

"Okay, have either of you felt dazed or lightheaded at all recently?" Sarah asked Aaron.

"Sarah, I miss meals all the time," Aaron admitted. "Sometimes, I get a little hazy, but I just need to feed the head, is all. Food always makes me feel better."

"You guys can spend all night arguing about this," Danny offered. "But I'm going to drink myself silly! I don't care about any of it. My head hurts, and none of it makes any sense."

"You don't care that none of us have any idea who the woman in the picture is?" Sarah challenged him.

"Nope, well, yes… Well, I don't know," Danny stuttered. "Relax and drink your drink, Sarah. I came out tonight get drunk and have a good time, and right now, all I'm getting is a huge headache!" He poured another shot, drank another shot, and slammed the glass on the bar.

"I don't get you," Sarah told him.

"You don't have to," Danny said. "I'm not your boyfriend, your brother, or your friend, thank God! Aaron, I'm submitting you for sainthood."

Aaron never heard Danny speak to Sarah that way. He never spoke to anyone, that way. "What's going on here? Slow down, gang. I'm getting tired of being a referee for the two of you!"

"You know what?" Danny turned to them. "I'm tired of the two of *you!* This mystery woman? Just another chick I don't remember. Nothing new."

Danny stood and grabbed his beer, scanning the room. There was a pretty, tight bodied girl who watched him from one of the tables. "Look, there's another one I won't remember tomorrow." He held up his glass in a toasting gesture to Aaron and Sarah. "See ya!"

He walked over to the young woman, sat next to her, and poured on the charm. He leaned on his elbow while he made small talk and laughed. Placing his arm around her, she slid closer to him. Ten seconds later, he had his tongue in her mouth.

Stunned by Danny's display, Aaron's jaw went slack. *How does he do that?* Always amazed at Danny's ability to pick up total strangers, he smiled, irking Sarah.

Sarah sighed and shook her head. "He's such a pig!"

"He's not a pig," Aaron said, still astonished. "He's a GOD!"

Frustrated, Sarah spun on him so quickly, she almost fell off the bar stool. "If you really believe that, then I don't know you at all!"

"Come on, babe…" Aaron apologized. "I'm just playing.

Lighten up, please?" He leaned over to kiss her, but she put her hand up, so he kissed her palm, instead. He snatched her hand in his. "See, I can't even get my own girlfriend to kiss me, and he's swapping spit with strangers."

"Yeah... Well, he's going to catch a terrible disease, someday. Mark my words," she offered.

Seconds later, Danny came back, took his seat next to Aaron, sliding his beer across the table. "What the –?" Aaron managed to gather his thoughts. "What the hell just happened? You were sucking face with that chick two seconds ago."

"Yep," Danny agreed. "She just wasn't that interesting." He poured himself another shot, drank it, and then finished his beer. He pushed the empty beer mug forward and placed his coaster on top of the glass.

"You leavin'?" Aaron asked.

"Yep." Danny addressed the both of them. "I'm going to find that girl in the picture if it's the last thing I do." He turned and walked away. Leaving the bar and his two friends confused.

"Some night out," Sarah complained. "You know he's crazy, right? He's not going to find anyone."

"Maybe, maybe not, but I've never seen him so determined."

***

Minnar sat at her worktable and breathed deeply – a puddle of water beneath her. Astonished to witness the Queen, Prince Pikkar, and Chancellor Torg stroll in, she sucked in another breath. Minnar tried to bow, but Alkara moved to Minnar's side swiftly, curtailing her attempt.

"My Queen." Minnar leaned over.

"Please Minnar," the Queen pleaded with her. "Do not try to do that." The Queen motioned Torg over. "Torg, please... We need to bring her to the Healing Ward immediately."

Torg approached Minnar and closed his eyes. He extended his arms to lift Minnar gently without his touch, levitating her with his mind. She rose from the chair; her body pushed into a prone position. She lay in midair with her robes draped. They hung to the ground, and her head and legs hovered in line with the floor.

Linock, Minnar's husband, ran into the room just in time to

hold her hand for the trip to the Ward. "I am here, my love," he assured as Torg sailed her down the corridor.

The Queen and Prince followed behind. Mage' Rom, remained in the Ward preparing everything for the birth. Minnar floated by led in by the Chancellor.

Rom turned to the waiting crowd. "I know this is important to everyone, yet I must ask you all to stay here and wait until I have finished, or if, Goddess forbid, I need anyone's help."

Torg released Minnar to the exam table. He let her down gently, placing his hand on the Linock's shoulder. "Good luck!" He offered to the new father and walked out, meeting the crowd of onlookers, including the Queen.

"She is in good hands," Torg informed the Queen.

"I am aware, Torg," she agreed. "I also believe this is a good time to send someone to the surface. You have a candidate for us yet?"

"My opinion is Reeglar should ascend once again," he suggested. "She is the most familiar with their customs."

"I am in agreement with you." She turned to her husband. "Do you agree, Pikkar?"

"Yes," he said. "It should be done swiftly, as Reeglar has frequently gone above. One more trip should suffice."

"I shall inform her," Torg replied.

"We shall be here. I shall stay for as long as this takes. Minnar's birth is crucial." Alkara sat on the waiting room bench. "You are dismissed, Chancellor."

"Yes, my Queen." Torg bowed, exiting the Ward and headed to his family's quarters. He reached out to his daughter, surprised she shut down her mind at first. Then, little by little, she crept into his consciousness. He relayed curiosity to her, as well as her new instructions. No matter what, she would assist him in any way, whenever he needed her. She met him at their door, already dressed for her journey topside.

Reeglar barely kissed his cheek, letting him experience her excitement about Minnar's coming child. When Torg went to hug her, she stepped back. "Goodbye, Father. I love you and shall return soon." She escaped down the hallway. As she hurried, she recited in her head the entire Royal line of Monarchs from the beginning of time, leaving Torg quite mystified.

XIV

Memories

As Reeglar ascended to the surface with her small case draped over her shoulder, she quickly scanned the thoughts of random minds floating in the air. She searched for something or someone who held the answers about the objects she sought, even if the information remained locked in their subconscious. Through the whispers of many people, she tried to pick and choose the pertinent information from the rest of the nonsense.

Finally finding one that told of the medical building she wished, Reeglar used her mental ability to stop a car that approached. She opened its door and entered. "Take me to 180 W. Montauk Highway," she told the driver, as he pulled back out into traffic and drove away.

It wasn't long before the car stopped again. She leaned forward to touch her fingers to his temples. Closing her eyes, she thought something directly to his mind. *Forget...* She exited the car, making sure the driver was unaware of her presence.

Reeglar entered the Lab Annex. An information desk sat in the entryway, so she began her inquiry there. *"Where shall I find frozen stores of sperm?"* she thought to the woman behind the desk.

"Fertility Lab," the woman projected back to her with a smile.

Reeglar erased the woman's memory of the visit. She walked through the halls and attempted to read the signs on the doors as she went. It wasn't long before she stood in front of the door she prized. She tried the handle, opening it with ease.

Sneaking inside, she swiftly surveyed the area. A large refrigeration unit in the back of the room seemed to hold promise. She searched it, but the tubes were not in there. She continued to investigate the place until she found a large cylindrical container resting on a large table. Carefully opening the clamps, she lifted its thick lid. Immediately, a steam cloud of liquid nitrogen escaped from the cylinder.

I found it!

Reeglar closed her eyes, lifting the samples out with her

thoughts. She opened her small case and carefully sent them in one at a time. She counted twelve tubes in all, not an overly numerous amount, but it was a start. She put everything back the way she found it, walked out the door of the lab and then casually continued out of the Annex itself.

Out in the sunlight, she shielded her eyes from the brightness. *One job down, one to go.* She needed to do something else before returning to Akkadia. *Now, how do I get there? Oh well,* she thought to herself, as she flagged down another car.

***

Sunday morning, 9:45 AM. Already, the relentless sun heated Danny's bedroom to unbearable temperatures. Awake, but unable to get out of bed without a reason to get up, he sulked like a child. What went on last night at Frampton's with Aaron, Sarah, *and* Lisa upset his apple cart. Add the whole dizziness thing, the headaches, the dreams that disturb his sleep; it made him want to give it all up.

Danny pushed himself up and tossed the sheets away, laughing at his condition. It didn't matter how bad his one head felt; the other one was always ready to go. He grabbed his tool and massaged it.

Wanna go for a run this morning, buddy? Danny thought. *Well, all right then.* He made sure to take a handful of tissues off the nightstand.

Laying back down in bed, Danny used the pressure of his fingers around his shaft skillfully. Try as he might, he couldn't get the image of that girl from Lisa's picture out of his thoughts. Going with it, he fantasized a scenario of how they would meet and their first lovemaking...

***

Alone on the beach with no one around, Danny scanned the horizon of dunes as the seagulls squawked over the sound of the rolling waves, covering the shore. The seafront was not as deserted as he first thought. She lay in the sun, but she her skin wasn't tan. Her generous sized breasts called to him from where he stood, so he decided to get a closer look.

As he approached her, she picked her head up off the towel and shaded her eyes from the sun. Sensing her silence as an invitation, he bent down next to her and she, in turn, reached up to pull him to her.

They kissed as he maneuvered over her to feel her full bust crush against his chest. He extended his hands and seized the strings of her bikini until they released, rendering her topless. Danny caressed her breast, searching out her nipples with his lips and tongue. She moaned with pleasure as he continued downward, on his way to her bikini bottoms, also connected with strings. He untied them, worked past her navel and brought his tongue to her mound, tasting her moistness.

Sliding off his shorts, he lowered himself on her and kissed her purposefully. His manhood throbbed hard, and he worried he might burst as soon as he entered her, but true to form, his lance remained rigid and firm. He hammered her as she raked his back with her fingernails.

Danny kissed her hungrily, as waves from the tide crashed over them up the shore, bringing with it, its salty coolness. But the ocean was no match for their desire. The streaming surge of water could not quell the lust in his loins for her. They reached their release, as the rolling sea washed away his seed.

***

Danny cleaned up his chest with the tissues and tossed them in the garbage pail on his way to the shower. Jumping in, he let the water run over him, hoping it motivated him. As Danny soaped up, he went through a list of what he needed to do to find this mystery girl of his dreams. He made a big statement last night to Aaron and Sarah about his plans. Especially considering he didn't have a plan at all.

I'll show them! All he needed was a positive attitude; that, and a little luck.

Danny toweled himself off, then returned to his room, dressing casually. It was Sunday, after all, and he didn't have to work either job. Grabbing a pair of khaki shorts and a new white wife-beater tank top, he entered the kitchen to make a pot of coffee. A chore he finally mastered.

Danny took his full mug out the back door to the patio and made himself comfortable on the outdoor furniture. As the sun rose higher in the sky, it gave the illusion of a quiet and peaceful morning. With no engine noise from the airbase behind the house, no neighbor mowing the lawn, just the chirping of birds, he relaxed.

He leaned back in the chaise lounge and let the sun's rays warm his body. Taking in the fresh air with a couple of deep breaths, he exhaled slowly, enjoying the moment.

Danny closed his eyes and sipped his coffee. Clasping his mug in both hands, he rested it on his lap. As comfortable as he was something nagged at the back of his mind. Something called his name, so he opened his eyes and searched the yard. Its emptiness mocked him false. He sat back again and took another mouthful of coffee.

"Danny?"

The assumption of a voice calling his name came again. *Okay, I'm losing it!* He thought as he stood.

"Danny?"

Came the call for the third time. But it wasn't someone calling him – the word was in Danny's head. He heard it without really hearing it. It touched and tickled his brain.

"I hear you," Danny announced out loud. He frantically searched the yard with his eyes, attempting to glimpse a physical person. "Where are you?"

"I am everywhere." Came the response.

And I am going crazy! He considered to himself.

"No," Reeglar told him. *"You are far from crazy, yet you are also far from a calm state of being. Will you promise not to make a judgment and give me an opportunity to talk with you?"*

"You call this talking?" He glanced toward the house but found nothing.

"Will you accept our communication, then?"

"Do I have a choice?" Danny felt her laughter and genuine amusement inside his head.

"Yes, I find you amusing," Reeglar told him.

"Damn, she can hear everything I think?"

"Yes again. And there is no need to panic."

Reeglar entered the backyard through the side gate passageway. He found her strikingly tall, good-looking, and oddly familiar in some way.

"Indeed," she answered him again. *"You have seen me before."*

"Look," Danny spoke out loud. "This is really freaking me out. Can you speak to me instead?"

"I can speak," Reeglar told him.

"Oh, thank God!" He dropped to the chaise and rubbed his forehead.

"I would like to help you," Reeglar said.

"You want to help me?" he repeated. "I didn't know I needed any."

"Well, you do. And in aiding you, we shall both benefit."

"Really!" He doubted her words.

"I am not lying to you."

"Of course not, why would you?" Danny was a little more than annoyed it was too early for a bottle of beer.

"I see you have put your mind to applying yourself to your business, instead of simply living for self-gratification," Reeglar informed him.

"How do you even know that?"

"I can see it in your mind, and I also helped you along in that area, the last time I saw you," she explained.

"Look, honey, I know I've never seen you before, no matter what you say."

"Yes, you have," Reeglar told him. "I just took away that particular memory."

"You took away my memories?" Danny's nerves plummeted in a downward spiral.

Reeglar felt his escalating panic and calmed him down. When he visibly relaxed, she continued. "Will you let me explain?"

"By all means." He offered her a seat, and she excepted it.

"I am here to give you back something you lost."

"What," Danny asked. "Like a watch?"

"No," she corrected him. "Not something material. Something spiritual... Love."

Danny laughed. "Now I know you're crazy. I never lost love, 'cuz I've never had it."

"I think you already know that statement is not true."

"Are you talking about the girl I can't seem to recall? The one I saw in my friend's pictures?"

Oh, my Goddess! Someone recorded proof she was here? Move on, Reeglar, she told herself. "Indeed I am."

"So, I can't remember her because...?" He leaned in close. "You took those thoughts I had of her out of my consciousness?"

"Both your conscious and your unconscious," she added. "Although, I did leave a trace of her presence inside you so that you wouldn't forget her entirely."

"I feel like a puppet."

"Do not..." Reeglar stood, walked over to him and knelt beside him. "With your permission, I would like to give your memories back to you." She raised her arm, but he grabbed it.

"Am I going to freak out?"

"I promise to keep your fear under control, to give you time to process all this knowledge, intelligently." She smiled at him.

When Danny let go of her, she placed her fingertips against his temple. Reeglar kept all of Ilmartutar's experiences with Danny in her head. Scrolling through the chronology of their relationship, she left nothing out as she replaced his memories.

His mental vision put them together as they made love over and over again. He recapped the night he almost died. She showed him Jeff's death, as well as the media circus that ensued afterward. Aaron and Reeglar, and Sarah's subsequent reaction to that news, and, of course, the Healing cream.

Next, she flowed memories of their discovery that Ilmar was not human, down to the moment Reeglar took away their cognizance of those events.

Reeglar let him go but kept a tight hold of his emotions, sensing his need for her to calm him. The amount of information caused Danny to hold his head with both hands. Not in pain, but as a way to discern and control the flow. Unsurprised, Reeglar witnessed the understanding spread across his face.

"I remember everything..." Danny stated. Slowly, Reeglar let him have his emotions back, and his eyes filled with love and tenderness.

"Where is she... Ilmar, I mean?" he asked her, unsure of the name.

"Yes, that is how you pronounce it. Ilmartutar is home, where we live," Reeglar answered.

"I need to see her right *now!*" Danny rose and pulled Reeglar to her feet in one swift motion.

"No! No, you can not," she insisted, shaking her head.

"But why not?" He pleaded with her.

"I shall show you; it will be quicker this way." Reeglar touched him again and showed him the history of Akkadia inside his mind.

"From the beginning of our time, the first Akkadians lived on the surface of the planet as the humans do today, on the continent of Pangaea. During the great volcanic age, the people separated. Some traveled East, and others, West. The Eastern travelers ended their roaming on the continent of North America. The massive amounts of volcanic activity spewed sulfur in the atmosphere and created dangerous conditions. So, those Akkadians went underground. Yet, seismic activity underground was much more powerful; they needed to burrow deeper and deeper into the Earth's crust.

"As the eons rolled by, both sects of Akkadians developed differently, and eventually, the continent broke apart. The Akkadians that remained in the open air on the surface became the humans of today, who in turn, are actually the descendants of all Akkadians. Without the suns powers, the subterranean people relied on the earth's geothermal energy, making their lives as prosperous and healthy as the surface dwellers. During this time, something else took place inside their bodies. Over generations, the proximity of the people to the core of the planet changed their DNA. The earth itself bonded to their bodies. From years of living underground, the dense iron accumulated in all Akkadian's bodies gave the people great powers. Powers that made their lives under the crust of the earth easier. These Abilities manifested themselves in each differently.

"Many of our people would seem strange to you humans. We lived peacefully, but when the earth became toxic, we suffered a devastating blow. Our birth rate dropped, and our greatest Healers worked a solution to our new problem. We ran genetic compatibility tests, and our shared ancestry left our two species

with practically nothing in common. Yet, we were able to mate successfully with each other. Unfortunately, that didn't go as planned, as you well know, and Akkadia is on lockdown. We are no longer allowed to return to the surface. We have caused enough trouble, bringing our land extremely close to exposure. We can not let that happen."

Reeglar took her hand away from his temple. "So, now you know everything. The reason we came here in the first place. Yet, now I need to leave and go back home. I just thought it would be better if you understood. I could not leave you in the semi-state of confusion."

"It's not better!" Danny told her. "I've got to go down with you and bring her back. I can't live without her. I *need* her. And I've never needed *anything*. EVER!"

"I am sorry." Reeglar held him by his shoulders. "You have to go on without her. You have no other choice."

"I don't understand. Then, why did you bring my memories back?"

"I left a spark in you, a part of Ilmar," she explained. "It leached out into your consciousness. I did not wish to leave you like that."

"Reeglar," Danny begged, "let me be with her!"

"Oh, Danny…" Reeglar took his hand in hers. "Ilmar is to be Queen of Akkadia. She can not leave."

"So, let me come down with you right now, and we'll be together down there," he insisted.

"And how would you get back to the surface?" she asked.

"I would stay for her," Danny announced.

Reeglar laughed out loud. "I am sorry. I do not mean to seem callous, but you do not know her father. He would kill you before you took two breaths of Akkadian air."

"You're a very powerful Telepath, so I know you can hide me," Danny suggested. "You've been inside my mind, but I've also seen inside yours. What did you say before, mutually beneficial?"

Reeglar opened her mouth to protest. Instead, she pondered his words. *I truly must be ill…* She thought to herself. *Yet, it shall free Azewrath. He will need to spend no more time with her.* Reeglar decided.

"What the hell..." Reeglar used the human curse word. "I am hiding numerous things right now, from my Father and the rest of the Akkadian Council... What is one more crazy thing? I know I shall more than likely take the heat for this, but it would be preferable if someone else could take the heat as well. I just need to warn you, Ilmar will not remember you, as I have capped her memories of you."

"Can you reverse it?"

"Yes, all shall be as it was, in time." Reeglar thought of something else. "What about your brother?"

"Wow! I didn't even think about him. When they say 'love is blind,' they really mean it. Some brother I am. Leaving him, after he changed the name in the business just for me." He shook his head at Reeglar. "What should I do?" She tossed her hands up in indecision. "I know. I'll leave Pat a note, telling him not to worry, but I've gone away for a while. Yeah... That'll work." He disappeared inside but poked his head out the door again. "Will I need anything?"

She shook her head. "Doubtful."

"K, be right back." Danny found a piece of paper and a pen, then started writing on it. "... Remember, I love you, and I'll be okay..." He spoke out loud as he wrote the last words. "There!" He tagged the paper on the fridge.

Danny went to his room and changed into a pair of jeans. Surveying the kitchen, he grabbed his car keys, but at the last second, he opened the refrigerator and snagged a bottle of beer.

"Let's go!" He yelled as he ran out the door full of excitement. He grabbed Reeglar by the hand and pulled her into the front yard before pushing her into his Camaro. As he jumped into the driver seat, he popped open the beer. He held it up as if to announce a great proclamation. "My last Miller Lite."

"We do have intoxicants in Akkadia, you know," Reeglar informed him.

"It won't be the same," Danny said, drinking it down. Swigging his beer like a sailor, he cranked over the engine and drove off on a new adventure.

He spun the wheels, pulling a holeshot out of the driveway. Loose pebbles sprayed in all directions as the back end of his

Camaro swerved and skidded along the tractionless sand.

***

After hiding the Camaro in the park's wooded area, Danny found his cell phone in his pocket, pulled it out, and showed it to Reeglar. "Oh, shit, I don't suppose you have cell towers in Akkadia."

Reeglar shook her head. "You will not need it as it will not work."

Danny opened the glove compartment and tossed the phone inside. "Damn, there goes my link to the outside world."

It would run out of battery life eventually, so he figured he didn't need it anymore. As he left his old life behind, they walked through the long trail, finally reaching the deserted baseball clearing.

Reeglar stopped him. "You are going to see things that might be overwhelming. Do you need me to dampen your emotions, or can you handle it?"

"I'm good!" he promised, a little too eagerly.

Reeglar picked up a rock and turned it over. On the bottom was a switch. When she flicked it, the ground rumbled and rose in front of Danny's face.

"WOW!" he hollered, jumping back. "Now I get ya!"

They entered the Reaction Lift, and Reeglar pushed the button that told the Igniter in Akkadia to bring them down. "We are descending fifteen miles down into the Earth's crust. You might start to feel strange. I am just making you aware." She closed her eyes and raised her arms to the ceiling of the Lift. Creating sounds of creaking metal as she opened a hatch, her plan was clear.

"You wanted me to hide you, right? Well, we are going to start now." She pointed to the hole in the ceiling. "I am going to put you up there."

He looked at her strangely. "How?"

"Just be ready," she added. Reeglar closed her eyes again and concentrated on lifting him through the hole. Danny's feet left the floor, surprising him.

"Whoa!" he huffed, vexed, struggling to keep his balance as

Reeglar slowly sent him toward the ceiling. He made it through the opening and turned to look back down at Reeglar. "Now what?"

"You are going to be very quiet. And I am going to try to make sure we are not met by the entire Kingdom of Akkadia. The alarm announces the Lift's arrival."

"Will you come get me?"

"As soon as I can. Now, be *quiet!*" She shut the hatch on him. "Oh! Humans…"

Reeglar needed to do the job right, but she had to do it carefully as well. She must reach Azewrath – searching deep inside their bond she tried to contact him. She was still miles away from Akkadia and out of Telepathic range, but she prayed to the Goddess she might be able to touch his mind.

"Azewrath, I am in trouble. I need you to meet me at the Lift. Make sure no one else is there! Azewrath?!" She focused all her attention on the special bond that joined them together in their link. She could just about brush against it. Then, she connected.

"Where are you? You feel far off. And is this form of communication safe between us?"

"I have no choice and no time to explain!" She thought urgency to him. *"You must make sure no one meets the Lift except yourself."*

"I am sorry Reeglar, but Mage' Rom shall be there. He is already on the way. I can not stop him now."

"All right, I have an idea. You need to be there as well. Quickly, my love." She turned her attention to her human charge above the Lift. *"Are you still all right up there, Danny?"*

"Yes, it's just very dark."

"You will be fine, trust me."

"I will, only 'cuz I don't have another choice right now," Danny thought back to her.

Reeglar took a deep breath and leaned against the wall. She needed to prepare her mind for the upcoming task. Diving inward, she attempted to gain control of her Abilities. With her arrival in Akkadia imminent, there were too many unknown variables that could send her plan astray.

What was I thinking? Reeglar searched the bottom of the shaft and eventually "Saw" Mage' Rom in the corridor, but not

Azewrath. The Lift stopped as it reached the bottom of the shaft. She waited impatiently for the doors to open when Azewrath's essence entered her mind. *"Oh, thank the Goddess!"*

Azewrath thought back to her. *"I can tell you are not alone, so trouble must be with you."* It was not a question.

"I shall explain later," she tried to shush him.

As the doors yawned open, Reeglar witnessed Mage' Rom in conversation with Azewrath. The Mage' turned his attention to Reeglar as she stood in the doorway.

"Reeglar," Rom asked, "was your trip a success?"

"Yes, indeed Mage'," she replied. "I have the samples right here in this bag." She removed the strap from her shoulder and handed the small case to him.

Reeglar tried to engage the Mage'. "Why are you here? Did Minnar have her baby already?"

"No," Rom answered. "She is still in labor. Seven hours so far, but I believe we shall see her little one soon! I am headed right back as I left Seeleem in charge." He brought the conversation back to her. "And how are you feeling, my dear? I was just discussing with Azewrath, that he needs to come in for a checkup."

Yes! Reeglar was thrilled. *It worked, just as I had hoped.*

The plan was to get Rom away from her, so she could stay here and sneak Danny into Azewrath's quarters, unnoticed. And for that, she needed Rom to be busy with someone else. Azewrath.

"I think that is a good idea," Reeglar stated. "You should go now. We need some answers. And time to figure out what to do and what to say; how to explain this to the Queen and Prince Pikkar. Never mind how to break the news to Ilmar."

Rom laughed. "Oh, I would not worry about Prime," he said, using Ilmar's nickname. "She is resilient."

Disturbed, Azewrath disagreed. "I do not think to be Pikkar's best friend shall save me from his displeasure and temper." He turned to Rom. "I shall go with you now and get this done and over with."

Rom contemplated that idea. "I should have enough time before Minnar delivers. Let us go, Azewrath."

Reeglar quickly touched Azewrath's mind. *"After you have*

finished in the Healing Ward, get to your residence as fast as you can. Trouble does await!" "Good luck," Reeglar called to him out loud as they disappeared down the corridor.

A young man exited the side door next to the Lift, startling Reeglar. It was Phlynoc, the Igniter. She didn't expect to see anyone so soon. With all the deception, she forgot the Igniter would be there. He nodded to her and walked away down the hall.

What did he hear? She wondered. *How much did we unknowingly reveal? And does anything we said have any bearing on his life? Would he even bother deciphering the information he just heard?* Unable to answer her own questions, she decided to get back to Danny. *"Danny? Are you still up there?"*

"Where else would I be, silly woman! Oh, sorry, I forgot you could hear everything I think."

"It is of no consequence. Yet you should treat me with more respect. I could expose your presence here and then where you would be?"

"I apologize for being a jerk, okay? Now, get me outta here. It's dark and oppressive."

Reeglar's mind pulled open the hatch and lowered Danny through the opening until his feet touched the floor. The bright light in the corridor made him squint.

"Hold on to my arm and stay shadow close," Reeglar instructed him. "I will make anyone that might pass us see me and not you."

"Will I be invisible?"

"No, you will just seem invisible. Now be quiet, as invisible people do not speak."

Reeglar walked quickly, but not so fast as to attract unwanted suspicion. They traveled down many halls and passageways. With its stark white walls and grayish floor tiles, Danny perceived it as a very sterile looking place.

"Akkadia is more than these walls," Reeglar thought him. *"I do not know if you shall live to see any more of it, yet let us hope so.*

As they drew near to Azewrath's quarters, more people passed them. Reeglar kept her cool, nodding to passersby. By the time she noticed General Nutrion heading toward her, it was too late for her to change direction. She could not believe her bad luck – he would most assuredly stop her to chat. She could tell the man had an interest in her.

He smiled at her as he approached. She smiled in return but kept her brisk stride. "Reeglar?" the General called out to her.

Pushing Danny behind her, she turned to face him, addressing him formally. "Yes, Guardian?"

"Reeglar, will you not call me Nutrion?"

"That would be too personal and inappropriate, Guardian," she reminded him. "As First Guardian Council Leader your role is as the protecting force of Akkadia. Your attentiveness is greatly appreciated." She wanted no part of Nutrion. While still in top physical condition, he was over twice Reeglar's age, going gray, and too much like Prince Pikkar.

"I want you to be more personal with me, Reeglar," Nutrion told her. "I am sure your father would agree."

"That might be, Guardian, yet my father does not get to make that choice for me. Now, if you will excuse me..." Reeglar trailed off, attempting to go past him.

Nutrion stopped her by grabbing her arm. "I was not finished talking to you, my dear,"

Danny didn't like this guy. He took liberties where none were welcome. Taking advantage of his temporary invisibility, he pulled back his right fist and let it fly. His knuckles connected with Nutrion's jaw and sent the man back into the wall.

Nutrion glared up at Reeglar as he rubbed his bruised mandible. "Who was that?" he demanded. "I saw someone behind you."

"There is no one here, General," she spat at him. "Perhaps you shall think twice before you touch a Telepath without permission again." She turned and ran, pushing an invisible Danny along, until they reached Azewrath's room safely.

**

Assaulted by a woman's screams, Azewrath and Mage' Rom shared a panicked look before running toward the Healing Ward with haste.

"Not through the front way, Azewrath," Rom began. "The Queen and Prince are there. I would rather not have to explain the reason you are here at this time. We shall use the other entrance." Azewrath nodded, following him around to the other side of the Ward.

Entering through the rear door brought them directly to the exam rooms. The other Mage' that Rom left in charge stood next to the table, holding both hands over her ears. Linock, Minnar's husband, slumped in the corner of the room. He also covered his head. On the exam table, Minnar thrashed, shrieking her head off. Rom shook the Mage' to get her attention.

"Seeleem!" Rom demanded. "What is going on here? Why is Minnar in pain? Is there something wrong with the baby?" She shook her head, indicating no. "Then, put your hands on her, right now!"

"She will not let me, Rom. *Look* at me!"

He did. Seeleem's hair twisted in every direction – a matted mess. Scratches laced her face, and a red welt on her cheek would turn into a bruise if it didn't get a Healing hand on it soon.

"Do you believe I did this to myself?" Seeleem motioned to her disheveled state. "Linock bled from his nose, but he let me Heal him."

Azewrath bent down to Linock, who pushed his hand outward, waving the Seer off. "Do something for Minnar, please!" he begged.

The old Mage' approached Minnar. Her labor pains increased, which played havoc with her mind. She flailed about on the table. Rom went to lay his hands on her, but she fought him back fiercely. Her hands flew. She slapped and batted Rom away, over and over again.

"NO!" She screamed. "I need to feel every minute of this... this incredible agony."

"Minnar," Rom warned. "We do not know if this pain is normal for the mingling of the two species. Let me help you through this."

"I made a promise to myself, Mage'," she told him. "I would do this, this way, to fully experience the pain, for my human. It was what he wished for his wife someday, I felt it from him. Natural childbirth is what he called it."

"Let me at least check and make sure you have dilated, and the child is still in the correct position."

Minnar gazed deeply into Ron's eyes, hoping he spoke the truth. In labor, her Abilities faltered. Exhausted, covered in sweat, she finally nodded at him, giving in. Rom swiftly wrapped his fingers around each arm and thigh. The Healing yellow glow spread outward from him to her entire body, curtailing her immense pain. She sobbed at his interference.

Rom tried to comfort her. "I am just calming you down, my dear. I shall allow you to feel your torment if you wish, just not all the pain. It is for your and the youngling's own good."

Azewrath helped Linock to his feet. He rejoined his wife, now controlled by Rom's Ability. "How is she?" Linock asked.

"She is almost there," Ron answered. He pulled Seeleem aside. "Part of our task is to control the situation. It is all about how you talk to people, Seeleem. We are Healers, but we must also be liars at times." He put his hand on her shoulder. "Have you seen Calantra?"

Seeleem nodded. "She stopped by, yet it was not her cycle shift, and I had everything under control, at that time."

"Hum. I shall check on Calantra later, I suppose. Now, I need step away for a short time. Can you keep her in this peaceful state until I return?"

"Yes, Rom. I apologize everything got out of hand." Seeleem returned to Minnar and continued to string yellow rays of Healing light to the pregnant woman.

"Azewrath," Rom called, "let us use this room." They left the others in relative quiet as they slipped into another exam room. "No need to get on the table, Azewrath. Just sit in this chair." Rom motion to it with his hand.

Azewrath took the seat. "How long shall this take?"

"Not long, I would assume." Rom placed his hands on Azewrath's shoulders. "I am not an Empath, so I might not find anything." Rom searched deep inside Azewrath's body, attempting to judge his fertility levels. "This is amazing!" Rom announced. "You are completely Healed. It is a miracle!"

"How did this happen, Mage'?" Azewrath asked. "I am thrilled it did mind you, but this has created an extremely complicated problem."

"I can only guess, yet I am unfamiliar with a large number of chemicals circulating through your system. None are natural; they seem synthetic. It must be human in origin." He took his hands away. "I assess that your sperm is viable, healthy, and potent."

"I believe I already know that!" Azewrath stated flippantly.

"If we could find what did this to you, our race could be saved."

"I wish I could tell you, yet I have no idea," Azewrath swore to him.

"Hum..." Rom wondered. "Perhaps a very powerful Telepath could tell us."

Azewrath sat up straight. "I would like to keep this information away from all Telepaths at this point in time."

"Yes... Well, I agree. Maybe at a later time interval." A long, drawn-out moan, escaped from the other room. "You are cleared to go, Azewrath. I have a very pressing appointment with history now." He grabbed Azewrath's forearm in a handshake of sorts. "The first hybrid to be born!"

"Good luck to you and all of us as well." Azewrath left the Healing Ward via the back door, freeing Rom to return to Minnar's side.

Mage' Seeleem spoke to Ron. "It is time."

"All right, Minnar," Rom encouraged. "The next time you feel a contraction, you need to bear down and push. Can you do that?" Minnar nodded to him. "Good."

As the waves came over her, Minnar squeezed Linock's hand. She sensed his concern for her and tried to make him relax. Using her Empathic Abilities, Minnar attempted to calm her husband.

Rom stopped her. "Enough of that! You must concentrate on the baby, Minnar. Linock is old enough to take care of himself."

"All right, I shall. Let us just get this over with, please!" Minnar managed to breathe out between contractions.

"Get ready to push," Rom reported, estimating it was time. "Now!" Minnar pushed with all her strength. "I see the head coming!"

Unable to wait any longer, Alkara and Ilmar peeked their heads into the room to watch. The birth was going to be the most wonderful happening in the entire Kingdom, perhaps ever in

Akkadia.

How could Rom expect me not to watch! Ilmar thought, sharing this moment with her mother.

"You can do this, my love," Linock urged Minnar. She pushed again as Rom helped by guiding the infant free.

"Keep pushing, Minnar!" Rom encouraged again.

Minnar gave a last push and roared. "Rawerrrrrrr!!" The child slid into Rom's arms.

"It's a girl!" Rom announced. The infant cried as the Mage' set the child on her mother.

The entire Healing Ward cheered. The Prince walked up to both his wife and his daughter as they stood in the doorway. Watching mother and child share their first intimate moment together, Alkara beamed.

"Congratulations Minnar! To both you and Linock," Alkara announced. "You have done well. We are all proud."

Pikkar put his arm around the Queen. Smiling, she reached up and covered his hand with hers, a sign of her love for him. "This is new territory, Pikkar."

"Yes," Pikkar agreed. "And who knows what this hybrid shall be capable of doing with her new Abilities." His mind began to form plans upon plans.

XV

Trespassing

After Reeglar had made Danny comfortable at Azewrath's, they sat and waited for him to return. A prolonged time of awkward silence ensued, prompting Reeglar to make conversation.

"When Azewrath gets here, just let me do all the talking, all right?"

"Sure, I don't have anything to talk about to this guy."

"Oh..." Reeglar laughed. "I think you have more in common than you know. Azewrath is Ilmartutar's intended husband. They are betrothed."

"What?" Danny said, confused. "I don't understand."

"It has gotten complicated. Azewrath is Ilmar's father's best friend, promised to Ilmar by Prince Pikkar himself."

"That's just gross." Danny made a disgusted face.

Reeglar laughed again. "He really is quite the prize, but beauty is in the eye of the beholder, correct?"

As they spoke, the door opened, and Azewrath entered his house. Spying Reeglar, he smiled and came toward her until he noticed Danny sitting on his lounge.

"GREAT GODDESS! What is *THAT* doing here in Akkadia? Have you lost your mind, Reeglar?"

"Ease your heart, Rath." She joined him at the door and embraced him, surrounding him with her love. She kissed him gently on the lips. "I have missed you."

"Excuse me," Danny interrupted. "Now I really don't get it. I thought you said he was Ilmar's husband to be?"

"I am," Azewrath bellowed.

"He *was*," Reeglar corrected him. "Like I said before... Complicated."

"I do not understand why you brought him here?" Azewrath wondered.

"He is here for Ilmartutar," Reeglar told him.

"I thought you were a smart woman, Reeglar. Your behavior is foolish! Pikkar shall kill him and punish you severely." He questioned her motives. "Why would you take all this risk and why did I not See you were going to do this?'"

"I hid my thoughts and intentions about this from you," she offered. "And Danny *loves* her."

"So?" Azewrath didn't care.

"She loves him as well."

"You do this simply for your feelings of guilt about us; that is all."

"I have been inside them both," Reeglar stated. "I have seen what I have seen. I need to do this."

"We shall all be cast out," he warned. "I am Seeing this now. There shall be a terrible end to this scenario, my love. If you go down this path, we shall *all* suffer."

"What's he talking about?" Danny asked.

"Azewrath can See into all possible futures," Reeglar explained. "He can tell ahead of time what will happen, good or bad."

"Something bad shall happen. It already has."

"Enough!" Reeglar ordered. Azewrath stopped, raised an eyebrow and then smiled at her as she continued. "You both shall wait here. I am going to bring Ilmar back with me."

"Well... If you refuse to be smart, be careful," Azewrath warned her.

"I shall be fine. Both the Queen and the Prince are busy with Minnar's new hybrid."

"Maybe so," he admitted. "But, I was more concerned about your father. You can not keep him at arm's length forever."

"I am going to run into him?" she asked, hesitantly.

"It is... uncertain." Azewrath shrugged.

"You are right, as usual, my love!" She kissed him again before addressing Danny. "Play nicely together. I will return with Ilmar, I promise." Heading to the door, she turned to take a final look back, hoping there would be no trouble. Reeglar hesitated and then walked out.

The two men said nothing, but they gazed at each other, sizing the other one up. Azewrath walked around the room, never taking his eyes off Danny. He fixed a statue, touched this little trinket, or straightened a vase, all the while he kept Danny under scrutiny.

"So," Danny began, breaking the silence, "you're engaged to

Ilmar, but you're sleeping with Reeglar? Is that how things work down here?"

"I do not need to explain myself to you, HUMAN," Azewrath responded, condescendingly.

"No, you're right." Danny corrected himself. "I guess there's no need to explain. I kinda understand where you're coming from. Back home, I've slept with about seven hundred women without care. I feel ya!"

Azewrath regarded Danny, incredulously. "Seven hundred women? Hum... I am sure. Your boast seems outrageous."

"Well, give or take," Danny guessed. "When you get that high, it's hard to keep track."

More admiration for Danny slipped into Azewrath's mind then he would have liked to admit to himself. "Then, your human women must be desperate... or addle-brained."

"You're insulting me." Danny's statement was not a question. "Too bad Azewrath, I thought we were going to be friends."

"You have had a thought... Amazing." Azewrath went on. "How long do you think you can hide here? Akkadia is a place filled with Telepaths. You can not conceal your thoughts from them forever. What was your plan? Did you even have a plan? Did you think you could just come here, rescue Ilmar, and take her away to the surface where she would live the life of a slave? No, of course not. Wait... perhaps you planned on staying here, to become her Prince and sit next to her on the throne!" He laughed out loud.

"Yeah!" Danny challenged. "Why not? What's wrong with me?"

"You are an *idiot!*" Azewrath attacked him with words. "We have younglings who hold more intelligence than you. Do you have any idea the danger you placed upon Reeglar in convincing her to bring you down here? And now, we shall all be conspirators." He sat in his favorite chair. "I think I shall enjoy watching Pikkar kill you with his bare hands."

"Great," Danny said flippantly. "Something to look forward to."

Azewrath stared off into space, watching their future unfold. And it wasn't good.

**

Ilmar spent the rest of the day in the Gardens, one of her favorite places to escape. After witnessing Minnar's birthing, the expectations from her mother and father weighed her down. She needed some time alone. Something about the beauty of this place, along with the heavenly scents of the flora, always brought her back to center when the pressures of life arose. Here, she could put aside all the trappings of her future so neatly laid out for her in advance.

Ilmar lay there, between all the buds and blooms, satisfied the Cultivators were far away and tended to their field of colors. She was deep in her thoughts of loneliness. It never occurred to her that she spent a considerable amount of time with Azewrath. She was well aware now that she had too much time on her hands.

You know your life is boring when you think, 'what do I have to do today?' And your answer is – nothing.

Ilmar stared up at the cavern ceiling and studied the stalactites of limestone hangings. Every so often, the calcium carbonate laden water droplets plummeted down to build stalagmites but not here. The Cultivators made sure to remove all ground forming columns, so the shrubs and the grama; the equivalent of the grasses on the surface of the planet, could grow unimpeded. A wet splash that fell on her cheek informed her of the calcium carbonate's assault. She giggled, wiping away the moisture.

"Ilmar, are you in the Gardens?" The warmth of Reeglar's mental touch entered Ilmar's mind.

"Yes," Ilmar answered her in her head. *"I was just enjoying the beauty and the solitude."*

"Then I am sorry for disturbing you, dear, but you are going to want to come with me." Reeglar sent heartwarming emotions to her.

Ilmar pushed herself up and searched through the rows and rows of flowers, trying to locate Reeglar. When they spotted each other, Ilmar went to stand.

"Sit back down, Ilmar. I shall come to you."

While the request was strange, Ilmar returned to her seated position. Reeglar found her friend and knelt down next to her, taking Ilmar's hand in hers.

Reeglar searched out Ilmar's eyes and connected their gaze. "You know I would do anything for you, right?"

Worried at Reeglar's cryptic opening, Ilmar panicked. "What is wrong? I felt good things from you, not bad."

"I need to go back inside your mind."

"Is there something wrong with me, again?" Ilmar asked.

"No," Reeglar said. "And yes." She sighed. "Just trust me," Reeglar asked, so Ilmar nodded, allowing the touch to her temple. Reeglar inserted herself directly into her friend's brain. *"This way is just more natural."*

Inside Ilmar, Reeglar found the darkness, a swirling mass of gloom behind a Telepathic wall. She spotted the marble-sized shiny brightness. Picking it up in her hands, she held it high to study it. Smashing it down against the floor of Ilmar's mind, it broke and emitted a huge glow, temporarily blinding Reeglar when the wall shattered.

As the light overpowered the darkness, all memories of Danny came flooding back to Ilmar. Revelations opened up to her, knowledge of Danny's presence in Akkadia, and something else. Sharing a bond allowed information to pass both ways. Ilmar realized Reeglar was… pregnant?

Reeglar backed out of Ilmar, and the two women faced each other. Both smiling, they embraced. Ilmar beamed. "I am so happy; I do not know where to start! For me! For you!"

"Ease your mind," Reeglar warned. "What I have done just proves that I have obviously lost my mind and have gone absolutely insane. My hormones are to blame to be sure. If we get caught with Danny here –"

Ilmar cut her off. "My father will kill him, I know." She finished Reeglar's sentence. "Where is he?"

"I have him at Azewrath's," Reeglar informed her.

Ilmar giggled and then placed her hands on her lips to try to stop. "Oh, I hope he is still in one piece when we get there." She grew quiet, turning to serious conversation. "Reeglar, I have seen. How did you... Um... How long have you been... You know." Ilmar pointed to Reeglar's belly before she stood, helping Reeglar to her feet.

"Only seven days. The Mage' has given me no further information." Reeglar held her belly. "But, we need to block all of these things from our minds. If my father, or your father, got an idea of any of this, we would be in dire straits!"

"Why?"

"Complications. Please, leave it at that."

Ilmar nodded many times, trying to concentrate on the threads in her robes as they made their way back to Azewrath's. After many twists and turns through the corridors, the women arrived at Azewrath's quarters without incident. He had opened the door before they knocked, as usual, prompting Reeglar to usher Ilmar inside. When Ilmar entered, Danny got up to meet her. Ilmar smiled at him happily but put her hand up to stop him.

"Wait! Do not touch me yet," Ilmar warned him. She reached into her robes and squeezed the ball on her belly ring. "I have spent all week wondering why I had this piercing. Now I remember." She held both her arms out to Danny, and he gladly encircled his own around her. Azewrath rolled his eyes.

Danny gave him a dirty look. "Do you mind?"

"This is my living space, human," Azewrath growled.

"Azewrath!" Reeglar scolded. "I have a wonderful idea. It is time for our evening meal. Let us go eat something and give Ilmar and Danny some time."

"And leave them alone in *my* dwelling?!" he asked her. "I am not comfortable with that."

"Come on, darling." Reeglar pulled him out by his arm. "I will try to bring back some food," she yelled to Ilmar as Reeglar and Azewrath left.

Danny turned Ilmar's face back towards him. "Hey, I've missed you... And I love you! I'm not waiting one more second to tell you."

"Still?" she asked. "After all this?" She motioned a circle with her hand. "For you, my heart burns as the Abyss of Fire."

"I hope that's a good thing. So..." Danny paused, kissing her neck. "You're not quite human."

"Perhaps it is you who are not quite Akkadian."

"Okay, maybe I don't care right now." He moved to untie her robes.

"We can not do this here!" She refused him.

"Come on... You know he thinks we're going to do it here anyway." Danny picked her up and threw her on the lounge couch.

"Danny, no!" Ilmar protested halfheartedly, giggling all the way.

Danny returned to untying Ilmar's robes. Opening them, he found she was naked underneath. "Jackpot..." he whispered. "I like the whole 'not a lot under the robes' thing you got going on." He talked while he ran his lips and tongue between her breasts.

"Mmmmm..." She moaned. "A little less talking and little more lovemaking, sir. I have missed you so."

Pulling off his shirt, Danny rose to his knees ready for her waiting, warm moistness. Resting his hand on her thigh, he gently rubbed her enticing slit with his thumb. Her body called to him, and his manhood throbbed, growing hard for her.

He never assumed he could feel this way about someone. Danny leaned back down to meet Ilmar, and with one swift move penetrated her. She sucked in her breath as he entered, exhaling right before he brought his lips down to her lips.

"I love you, Danny," she told him after he let her draw another breath. He kissed her hard, thrusting himself far into her beckoning darkness simultaneously. She wrapped her legs around him, pulling him even deeper. "I want to be with you, forever."

"I don't care where we are; I'm not leaving you," Danny promised.

"It is not the place that matters. You will always live in my heart."

Danny brought his lips to her ear. "A little less talking and a little more lovemaking, miss!"

***

Reeglar and Azewrath split up. He went straight to the Grand Hall, and she went home to freshen up before the meal. As he entered the Hall, one of his Seer peers met him.

"I wish to talk to you," Damon confronted him.

"Right now, Damon?" Azewrath noticed Pikkar watching.

"Yes." Damon pointed to the hallway, so Azewrath followed him out. "I have Seen disconcerting things and wanted to know if you have had a similar experience."

"What have you Seen?" Azewrath asked, hoping it was

nothing.

"An invasion!" Damon stressed.

"By whom?"

"That part was shrouded in darkness. I am assuming, humans."

"Hum..." Azewrath contemplated the statement. "There are a few holes in this theory. How would they descend into Akkadia? By the Lift? No, I have not had any inclination of this sort. Have you discussed this with any other Seers? Your Father, perhaps?"

"No. Not as yet," Damon informed him. "As First Council Seer, I wanted to check with you first."

"Then, I shall leave this up to you." Azewrath charged him with the task. "Talk amongst the others. Glean what you can."

"As you wish, Council Leader." Damon went to the Hall and back to his table.

Concerned, Azewrath knew better than to delve deep into his thoughts. There were too many Telepaths and prying eyes. He followed Damon back into the Hall, making his way to the Royal table.

As Azewrath joined them, Pikkar addressed him. "What did Damon seek? You seemed distressed."

"Damon had a vision and inquired if anyone else had the same. I told him, I had not."

"Are not all Seers capable of 'hive' prophecy?"

"It is so," Azewrath answered. "That is why Damon checked with me. If something catastrophic were imminent, then we all should experience the same premonition."

"Indeed..." Pikkar changed the subject. "Where is Illy, and why has she not joined us? I have not seen her since earlier, at the Healing Ward."

"She was feeling quite fatigued and decided to skip this meal. I told her I understood." Pleased he was not speaking to Chancellor Torg, Azewrath let out a sigh, unable to hold his breath any longer.

Alkara added her own thoughts. "She has been through a lot, recently. I am sure she shall renew after some sleep."

"I am sure as well," Azewrath agreed, a little too sarcastically. He raised his eyes and caught sight of Reeglar running to her family's table. He fought the urge to smile at her, trying hard to concentrate on his meal. Instead, he forced himself to think thoughts only of Ilmar.

Reeglar slid in next to her mother. She focused on counting all the people in the Grand Hall in her head. "Pleasant tidings, everyone," she greeted them. "Has anyone stopped in to see Minnar yet?"

Reeglar's mother, Solara, answered. "I did! Such a miracle, truly!"

Reeglar loved her mother's tender heart. Solara was a calm, reserved woman. She was of the Scholar Guild, one of many in Akkadia, with plenty of experience at patience. She had the same beautiful long dark hair as her daughter. Only Solara wore it free-flowing, tied back from the sides at the base of her skull. She adorned it with a colorful flower, picked daily from the Greenhouse Gardens.

"I have not visited, as yet, Reeglar," her father told her. "I shall make it a point for tomorrow, I promise." Reeglar's father entered her mind, probing for some inclination about her odd behavior of late.

"Why have you become so obsessed with counting recently?" Torg asked her.

"Why can I not have a little privacy in my own mind? I have seen twenty-three plantings, Father. You should trust me by now."

"You should not hide things from me. Then, I could trust you."

"I am not hiding anything," Reeglar blatantly lied.

"You have become very good at disguising your thoughts, but you have not yet learned to cloak them. I am your Father; I know you are concealing something."

"I have nothing to tell you."

Solara interrupted their internal communication. "Are the two of you having a conversation without me again?"

"No mother," Reeglar told her. "That would be rude. Would it not, Father?"

"Humph!"

They ate in silence until Reeglar excused herself. She didn't even kiss them goodbye. She didn't dare. She grabbed her plate, piling more food on top and walked away from the table. Azewrath watched her go and made an excuse to the Queen and

Prince, explaining his departure.

How shall we ever explain this? He thought to himself, as he rose to leave. *How do I explain I wish, instead, to marry Reeglar?*

Chancellor Torg's head shot up. *Someone is thinking about Reeglar!* He snapped his gaze around, studying the mass of diners. *Where did that thought originate?*

Torg gently picked apart people's thoughts. He went into their minds. A scratch at the edge of one here, a nudge of another there, but try as he might, he could not find the origin of the thought.

"Something is going on here," Torg said to Solara.

"What are you talking about?"

"Someone here, in this room, was just thinking about Reeglar."

"What is wrong with that? Hopefully, it is some handsome, young man, wishing to take her away." She chuckled.

"That is not what I meant!" Torg admitted. "Why must you frustrate me? It was a thought concerning her, and, I am almost certain, there was an inference about the surface as well."

"You are making too much of this, Torg," Solara scolded him.

"I am not! Ever since we have gone to the surface, there has been nothing but discord in Akkadia. I assure you, unrest is coming to our world."

"And I thought only Seers were prophets of doom!" Solara teased, returning to her meal. Torg sighed, as General Nutrion approach the table.

"Chancellor, may take this time to speak with you? Without disturbing your meal?" the General asked.

Torg smiled pleasantly at Nutrion. "Of course, General."

Solara stood. "Please, take my seat, Nutrion. I have finished and have other things to attend." She bent down to kiss Torg. "I shall see you later, darling." Solara walked out of the Grand Hall.

"I have meant to talk to you for some time," the General began.

"Indeed?" Torg inquired. "What can I do for you, Nutrion?"

"I know I am not a young man," Nutrion stated. "Yet, I have a lot to offer the right woman."

Torg did not like how the conversation turned. "I think I know what you are going to say, General. And let me first tell you that my daughter is the judge and jury of her own heart. Reeglar makes her own decisions." *Was he the one thinking about Reeglar?*

"That is what I expected you to say, Torg." Nutrion tried another angle. "All I ask is that you have a talk with Reeglar, and perhaps guide her in the right direction."

"The right direction would be toward you, I assume?" the Chancellor asked, sarcastically.

"I realize I am thirty-plus plantings older than she, yet I have a genuine affection for her, as things stand right now."

"Nutrion," Torg stated, "you do remember you are talking to a Telepath."

"Hum, indeed," Nutrion replied. "I am but an open book, Torg."

Torg stood to leave. "I shall take all this into consideration."

"Thank you, Chancellor." Nutrion also stood, then turned on his heels and walked out of the Grand Hall.

***

Reeglar left the Grand Hall, making her way back to Azewrath's; a plateful of food in her hands. She traveled at a walking pace, but in her mind, she ran for her life. When she knocked on the door, Ilmar opened it. She smiled at Reeglar, who handed her the plate, sliding inside swiftly.

"Oooooh!" Ilmar cooed. She pulled the napkin off to expose the wonderfully aromatic food and then brought it over to Danny. "Smells good! I am so hungry."

Danny gazed down at the food. There was something white and flaky. *It could be fish, of some sort,* he thought. Next, a tube-like, root vegetable looking substance. Also, slices of a sweet smelling red fruit? *Hard to tell, but I'm just so hungry.* Danny realized.

Ilmar used a utensil to cut off a piece of the fish, holding it up to feed it to Danny. He accepted the food, chewed it and swallowed. His expression turned to pleasure while he savored the taste.

"This is good!" Danny said.

Reeglar laughed. "Why are you so surprised? Did you not think we ate well down here?"

"Honestly, no," Danny admitted. "I would never have imagined…" He trailed off but took a sampling of the side entrée. Ilmar joined him. They took turns feeding each other. "I mean, there ain't no sunshine down here."

Reeglar explained. "We do not need the sun. We have everything we need with our geothermal energy and our Cultivator Ability. The Guild can grow anything." She sat in the chair opposite Danny and Ilmar. "We need to figure out what we're going to do with you, Danny. You can not stay with me, as I still live with my family."

"With me, either!" Ilmar added. "I can not have you getting close to my parents at all!"

Reeglar had a suggestion. "I think you are going to have to stay here with Azewrath."

"Oh, no way!" Danny said, refusing.

"There is nowhere else, my love," Ilmar stated. "He is the only other person who knows you are here, and he will keep it private, as he has too much to lose."

Unnoticed, Azewrath stood in his doorway, they were so busy discussing Danny's fate, no one saw him come into the room. "I should have a say in this!"

"Of course, Rath," Reeglar assured him. "Yet, think clearly, he can not stay with me –"

Azewrath cut her off. "Absolutely NOT!"

"Yes, you see?" Reeglar went on. "And he can not stay with Ilmar."

"I fail to see why he has to stay *at all?*" Azewrath whined.

Ilmar left Danny's side to confront Azewrath. She gently placed her hand on his arm. He wasn't expecting that. "I need you to do this for me," she spoke to him softly. "It is the least you can do, Azewrath. I have graciously stepped aside so you and Reeglar can be together."

"What makes you think I shall not still marry you and keep Reeglar on the side?"

"UH! I hear you!" Reeglar yelled. "I am standing right here!"

Danny stood up, menacingly. " 'Cuz, I'll kick your ass."

"Gentlemen, please!" Ilmar ordered, jumping between them.

"My life might not be the way I like it, Azewrath, but I will be the first to my Father's side to let him know how you have betrayed me!"

"You would not dare!" Azewrath seethed at her.

"Watch me!" Ilmar threatened him.

"YOU!" Azewrath pointed to Danny. "All this is your fault!"

He blew by Ilmar and charged Danny, but Danny was quicker and landed a punch to Azewrath's jaw. The blow sent him sailing across the room. Azewrath hadn't time to get to his feet when Danny dove onto him, poking him with another punch. This time Azewrath grabbed Danny, managed a backward somersault, which propelled Danny. Furniture broke, scattering about the room around Danny's sprawled body. When both men got up, Reeglar threw her arms out to put an end to their fighting, but Ilmar stopped her in mid-movement.

"Leave it be, Reeglar," Ilmar said. "Let them work it out for themselves. Please."

"All right, but then I am soundproofing this room," Reeglar warned her. She closed her eyes, raised her hands and pushed outward, creating an invisible barrier that surrounded all four walls.

The two men punched, kicked and threw each other around the room. After a short time, both men bled; Azewrath, from his lip, and Danny, from a slash on his forehead. Reeglar and Ilmar moved out of the way a couple of times to avoid being knocked over. The fight seemed as if would never end. As one would have the advantage, he would lose it, and the other would take control. Ilmar worried about the outcome, although Danny's offensive created more contact against Azewrath. But, Azewrath's swift recovery allowed him to throw Danny about with ease.

As time wore on the confrontation ran out of steam. Danny threw his right fist and missed. Azewrath charged Danny and push him instead of tossing him around. Finally, the punches came less in number and the recovery time lasted longer. Eventually exhausted, they stopped moving. Both men sat on the floor, each breathing deeply, sweaty, bloody, and weak. They couldn't even expend the energy to look up at each other.

"Are we finished?" Ilmar asked them. Danny laughed, rubbing his beaten body. They couldn't even muster enough muscle to respond to her.

Reeglar scolded them. "You both should be ashamed of yourselves. I do not think I have ever seen such an unsightly, disgusting display of brutality in my life!"

Ilmar knelt next to Danny's bleeding body. He met her sight and smiled through the blood running down his face. She shook her head. "*Children!* You both are acting like children, truly!"

"Ilmar," Reeglar called, worried. "Come here and Heal Azewrath, quickly. I think he might have a broken rib."

"I am sorry, Reeglar. I do not know how to do it," Ilmar apologized.

"Just think about Healing his bones and all his injuries. Hurry!" Reeglar grabbed Ilmar by the hand and brought her to Azewrath. She placed both of Ilmar hands on him. "Now, just think!"

Ilmar tried to work her Healing magic, but nothing happened. "It is not working." Anguish covered her face.

"Try harder!" Reeglar stressed.

Ilmar concentrated again as hard as she could, and still, nothing happened. She stared at Reeglar with helplessness in her eyes. "I can not do this!"

"Yes, you can," Reeglar encouraged her.

Ilmar sighed before she realized something. "Wait!" she exclaimed. "I need to turn off the force field."

"Of course," Azewrath managed sarcastically.

Ilmar pressed the ball attached to her belly ring, and her hands immediately glowed with the yellow light. She placed her hands back on Azewrath, fixating on his wounds, both exterior and interior. The radiance spread all around him. Covered in the glimmer of saffron, Azewrath Healed. It wasn't long before the light faded, and she released him.

"This is much better. Thank you, Ilmar," Azewrath acknowledged her skill, rubbing his sore arms and body. "You are a very talented Healer for someone who is untrained."

Reeglar retrieved a wet cloth to wipe away the blood that crusted over on Azewrath's lip. He took it from her and gave her a disgusted expression. Limping toward his lavatory, Azewrath used the cloth to clean himself up the rest of the way.

Ilmar returned her attention to Danny. Reeglar handed her

another damp cloth, and Ilmar gave it to him so that he could clean his wounds.

"I do not know what this will feel like, so I am just warning you, all right?"

"Just do it! I'm aching all over. I'm sure something's broken, too!" He tried to joke with her.

"Big baby!" she teased, laying her hands on him.

Again, the golden glow of her Healing powers spread out from her fingers across Danny's body, just as it did with Azewrath. The reaction with Danny involved dark bruises that popped up on his arm. They quickly disappeared, then reappeared again but soon faded and were gone. This pattern repeated itself over and over.

Ilmartutar finally let Danny go. "Please, tell me you feel better," she said with concern.

"I feel great!" He jumped to his feet.

"It is getting late," Reeglar reminded them. "What have we decided?"

Azewrath strode out, fresh, clean and changed. "I shall share my space, but I shall *not* like it."

"He will need something else to wear," Ilmar told Azewrath. "Can you lend him one of your tunics?"

"Will this torment ever end?" Azewrath lamented. He left the living area again, disappearing into his bedchambers and returned. "I left something on the bed. Go change if you wish, you will sleep out here on the lounge."

Ilmar took Danny by the hand, leading him to the bedchamber. "We will be right back."

Azewrath folded his arms across his chest. "I do believe even at his young age; he is old enough to dress himself."

"Leave it be, Azewrath!" Ilmar hissed.

"Make it swift!" Azewrath ordered.

Ilmar and Danny disappeared behind the bedchamber door. She grinned like the Cheshire cat as she leaned against the door to close it, all the while biting her bottom lip.

"You're thinking naughty thoughts... I like that about you," Danny teased her, pulling off his dirty, ripped shirt.

Ilmar approached him. She moved purposefully, swaying her hips, enticingly. She touched his abdomen, and ran her hand upward, letting her fingers feel every muscle. She caressed his chest, sliding her hand up to his neck and placed one thumb on his jugular vein. His strong heart pumped his blood throughout his body and pulsed under her touch.

"You're going to get me going, and were supposed to be quick." Danny's lance grew inside his pants.

"We can be quick," she suggested.

"Oh, you're so tempting!"

Danny grabbed her, wrapping his arms around her in a lustful embrace. She leaned up to kiss him, and he met her hard, crushing her lips to his. He pushed his tongue deep into her mouth, searching for her's. Ilmar reached for the button on his pants and unzipped them. She slid her hand down into his open jeans and seized his engorged, throbbing manhood.

The bedchamber door opened and Azewrath cleared his throat, addressing them. "The door stays open." They jumped away from each other. "Get dressed," Azewrath said, leaving the doorway.

"Well, are you going to change?" Ilmar asked him.

"Waiting for the big boy to go back to sleep, if you know what I mean." He pointed to his crotch.

Danny sat on the bed and took a deep breath. He couldn't finish taking off his jeans because he still sporting a generous rod. He waited until it wasn't obvious.

Ilmar giggled. "What a waste!"

"We'll just save it for another time," he promised her, pulling off his sneakers and dropping his jeans to the floor. He put on the white tunic trousers and sandals Azewrath gave him, observing their fit. "They're a little long, but thank God for the drawstring!" He grabbed the shirt and pulled it on but left it unbuttoned.

Ilmar looked at him. "Now you can pass for one of us."

Danny picked up his clothes as they walked from the bedchamber. "What should I do with my old clothes?"

"Burn them," Azewrath stated. "I do not know how you can wear those jeans. They are far too confining."

"Just give them to me," Ilmar answered. "I will wash the jeans, but this shirt has got to go." She picked it up with her index finger and her thumb and brought it to the incinerator. She opened the hatch and dropped the shirt in as the stench of something burning permeated the room.

"That smells bad," Danny said.

"Burning it usually does," Azewrath replied.

"All right, boys!" Reeglar began. "I think I have had enough fun for one day." She hugged Azewrath, kissing him deeply.

Ilmar also wrapped herself around Danny's muscular body. She gazed up at him with love. "I shall see you tomorrow, my love and will bring you breakfast." She offered one more piece of advice in a whispered voice. "Do not let Azewrath make you angry. He can be extremely good at it."

"And," Reeglar added, "keep your thoughts to yourself. Try not to think about anything. We do not want someone to pick up your alien images."

"Okay, by all accounts, girls!" Danny kissed Ilmar again, and then both women left Azewrath and Danny to share each others company for the night.

Azewrath removed himself from the living area, returning with a cover for Danny. He threw it on the lounge. "I hope you shall be able to get comfortable." With no more circumstance, he withdrew to his bedchambers.

Danny took off his shirt and draped it over the chase arm; he wasn't going to sleep in it. He sat on the lounge, but there was still light everywhere, so it was impossible for him to tell what time it was. He gazed down at his watch, and it read 11:56 PM.

Wow! Long fuckin' day! He thought. *Oh, that's right, no thinking!*

He lay down and tried to clear his mind as best he could. Covering himself with the blanket, he glanced up at the ceiling, deciding to count ceiling tiles. He hoped it would put him to sleep.

After a few minutes, all the lights in the room went out. Danny was in complete darkness. *Maybe the lights go out at midnight. Oh, shit! I'm thinking again.* He resolved himself to stop. Eventually, after a hectic day, sleep found him.

XVI

In Plain Sight

Patrick returned to the house late Sunday night and noticed Danny's car wasn't home yet.

Dirty stay out!

Laughing to himself, he parked his car, walked into the house and deftly made it to his bedroom through the darkness. Undressing for bed, he never bothered to give his brother's whereabouts another thought.

When Patrick woke Monday morning, he jumped straight into the shower, hoping to beat Danny. After he had finished, he reached for a towel. Drying off, Pat wrapped it around his waist and made a pot of coffee in the kitchen. He got the canister and the filter, filled the glass canter with water, and poured it into the coffee maker. He opened the cabinet, took out two mugs before setting them out by the brewing pot.

Pat reached for the handle of the refrigerator to get the milk, but a note hanging on the door caught his eye. He jerked the paper out from under the magnet, reading the page. He mumbled to himself as he scanned Danny's letter.

"He left?" Patrick said out loud, sprinting to Danny's room and opening the door. He found the room empty and his bed perfectly made. "Damn him!" Patrick yelled before punching the wall.

***

As the lights came on at Azewrath's, Danny woke up immediately. "What? Huh?" He sat up quickly, unsure where he was. Gazing around the room, he slowly remembered where spent the night. His watch face read 6:00 AM.

Why the hell do they gotta get up so early?

Danny decided to snoop around Azewrath's place. Sparsely decorated, with the essentials plus a few statues and tapestries, it held no secrets. He found nothing to listen to like a radio, or watch like a television, or talk on like a phone.

What the hell do these people do down here?

As he explored, he encountered some thin rock-like tablets with runes on them. More like letters, almost Latin in origin, he guessed. He picked them up and studied each flat stone closely.

Well, I guess it looks like they read here. Danny had his hands full of tablets when Azewrath came into the room.

"Do you always touch other people's property without their permission?" Azewrath asked.

"Just trying to keep busy and learn everything down here. I can't read 'em, anyway," Danny told him, placing the slates back where they belonged.

"Hum," Azewrath hummed, assuring him. "Of course you can not. It is in the ancient text." Azewrath made sure his clothes were all in order and headed toward the door. "I shall be taking my breakfast. I implore you to have a bathing while I am out. You stink of alien smells." He stopped at the door, turning to Danny. "One more thing."

Danny stared back at him and made a questioning gesture with his head. "Yes?"

"Do not attempt to leave. That would not be a well thought out idea." Azewrath exited, closing the door behind him.

"Do not attempt to leave..." Danny repeated, emulating Azewrath. "What an ass!"

Danny took Azewrath's advice to have a shower, hoping the level of complication remained low. *Although, it seems these people don't have any technology down here, at all! Shit! I'm doing it again.* He found it difficult not to free think. Instead, he concentrated on his actual actions.

Danny entered the bathroom surprised to find it was not at all what he expected. As a large rectangular room, with no discerning features, he wondered how they could call it a bathroom. Examining the walls, Danny searched for a button to press, or a hatch to pull with no luck.

Going back to the doorway, he turned around and faced inward, glancing to the right, a depression in the shape of the handprint caught his attention. The room magically transformed when he placed his hand on the impression. Spigots extended out from the walls; hooks and racks appeared as well. A rectangular shape rose from the floor with a doughnut-shaped covering.

That must be the toilet. Danny hoped. He took off his perfectly white tunic shirt, hanging it on one of the hooks, and then did the same with his pants.

Danny walked over to the toilet to relieve himself. When he finished, he stepped back to find a flush handle. As soon as he moved away from it, the commode sunk back into the floor. When it rose again, it was empty and clean.

Impressive! No technology my ass. Now, for a shower.

At the far end of the bathroom, twenty nozzles protruded from all three walls, including the ceiling. Taking a chance, he stepped under the ones from above and instantly warm liquid caressed him. It must have been water, but Danny was unfamiliar with its texture; soft on his skin with a swift evaporation property. It wet his hair, and then he would dry, only to experience a wetness again. With no accumulation of excess water, there was no reason for a drain either. And there was none.

His body responded to the titillating, tactile phenomenon he experienced, prompting a fantasy about Ilmar. Remembering he wasn't supposed to do that, he rinsed off one last time.

Danny stepped away from the cascading water, and it stopped flowing. He couldn't believe it, but he was completely dry. No need for a towel.

So cool! Now, if I could just figure out how to shave.

With no mirror in the room, he focused on redressing. The Akkadian clothes were different but very comfortable. Danny left the bathroom and entered the living area. Deciding to fold the cover Azewrath gave him, he hoped to waste a bit more time.

"Now what?" he said out loud to no one before checking his watch. 7:15 AM. *I wonder what Patrick's doing right now?* He worried. *Probably cursing me out.* "Damn!" He slapped his thigh for thinking again. *Not thinking is harder than I thought.* "Oh, I give up!" He sat on the lounge and sulked.

***

Ilmartutar went to first meal in a wonderful mood. She kissed and hugged her parents, and after sat with a big smile on her face. "Mother. Father," she greeted them both cheerfully.

Alkara smiled back at her daughter. "It is so nice to see you in a pleasant mood." She patted Ilmar's hand, finding her mood genuine.

"There is just so much to be happy about," Ilmar told her.

"Really?" Pikkar asked. "Is it something of which we should be made aware?"

"No. Just the beauty of life, and the promise of what each day might bring."

"All right. Your moods certainly do fluctuate Illy," he said, leaving it at that.

Azewrath joined them at the Royal table. Ilmar kissed him, placing her hand on top of his before squeezing it. She even winked at him.

Crazy woman! He thought but smiled back at her as best he could. *We are all just one big happy family. Yet... Not quite.*

He searched for Reeglar but found the Chancellor casting a glance directly back at him. Azewrath quickly put a block on his thoughts, but smiled and nodded to Torg, in acknowledgment of his gaze. Reeglar picked that moment to join her family. He swiftly directed his attention to Ilmar with thoughts of their lovemaking, hoping to cover what he really wanted. Reeglar.

Reeglar forewent a greeting to her father that included touch. She sat next to her mother again, giving her a welcoming kiss. She deemed it likely her father might take offense to the fact she snubbed him on a kiss as well, but her mother couldn't tell she was pregnant with one touch. Her father could. She took a great chance allowing him in her proximity at all. As Reeglar ate, she realized she was hungry, so she attacked her food.

These feelings will only get worse, she thought, laughing to herself inside her head. She took a deep breath in shock. Dropping her head, she realized she dispensed an errant thought. *Any moment now...*

"Reeglar," Torg began a conversation, as expected. "I may be predictable, yet you are as well."

"It has been a challenge growing up in his family. Can you understand that?" she informed him.

"Let us not argue at the table," Solara began. "Or, have a private mental chat that excludes me."

"I love you, Mother." Reeglar smiled.

"Of course you do, dear." Solara squeezed her hand. "That is because I never know what you are thinking."

"I love you because you are a wonderful mother," Reeglar told her.

"I have a request for you, Reeglar," Torg continued, ignoring his wife's intrusion.

"A request? For what?" she asked.

"For your hand," he stated. "It was a casual request, not a formal one."

"I do not care if it was a written one," she spat. "You do not actually believe it wise for me to marry Nutrion, do you?"

"You could do worse," Torg answered positively.

"Father, please! Tell me you are joking. Nutrion is older than you are!"

"Torg," Solara questioned him. "You are not serious, dear."

"I am merely suggesting an option as it was presented to me." Torg finalized his end of the discussion.

"Well, then it is a good thing we do not arrange marriages at this time!" Reeglar fumed. "Thank the Goddess I can still make my own choices!"

"I shall never bring this up again," the Chancellor promised. "Yet, I have been receiving very peculiar impressions from Azewrath. About you, Reeglar. Has something happened between the both of you since Ilmar's return?"

It took all of Reeglar's years of training not to respond in a movement of body, nor mind, to her father's words. He tried to rattle her, but she kept her cool. Steady breathing, slow heartbeat, nonreactive on every level. She was sure she mastered any perceptive nuance that her father might observe.

"I am sure I do not know what you mean," she insisted. "Perhaps I have been spending too much time with Ilmar."

"Hum..." Torg added. "Then, perhaps you should give them some space."

"All right, Father. I shall." She placed more food on her plate. "But I think I shall retire, as I am suddenly feeling unwell."

"Are you ill?" Solara asked.

"I shall be fine, Mother," Reeglar assured her. Standing to depart, and immediately overcome by a spell of dizziness, accompanied by a little bit of nausea, she spoke through gritted teeth. "I must go." She hurried from the Grand Hall with the plate of food in her hands.

Torg raised an eyebrow at his wife. "She shall be fine, Solara."

"I am not a Telepath, and even *I* know that is not true!"

At the same time, Ilmar rose from her chair, taking a full plate with her as well. Azewrath took her by the hand before she left. "I have a Seers meeting to attend. I shall see you after."

Ilmar understood. "All right, I shall wait for you in your quarters." She didn't lie. Turning to her parents, she flashed a huge smile. "Goodbye, my loving family." Ilmar practically skipped out of the Hall.

Pikkar regarded Azewrath. "Whatever you are doing, Azewrath, must be working. I have never seen Illy so happy. Thank you." Pikkar clapped him on the shoulder.

"My pleasure, my friend," Azewrath answered, excusing himself. "My Queen and Prince." He stood, bowing slightly and exited the Hall. *This charade gets more difficult with every spoken word!* He thought as he made his way to this Seers meeting. Azewrath had no idea his day was about to get worse.

***

Reeglar and Ilmartutar ran into each other after they left the Grand Hall. Both women held plates of food. Ilmar laughed when she saw Reeglar and motioned with her plate to show they had the same idea.

"It would seem we are both overly hungry today. What did you have?" Ilmar noticed Reeglar didn't look well. "What is wrong?"

"Quite a bit, I should tell you!" Reeglar answered before picking up her pace. "I have to get to Azewrath's quickly. I believe I am going to throw up." Reeglar's expression showed her discomfort and Ilmar found it painful to watch. They ran down the corridor until they reached Azewrath's rooms. She knocked on the door with such insistence, Danny jumped up and sprinted to open it.

"Open up!" Reeglar demanded from the other side. "It is Reeglar!" Danny released the lock and Reeglar raced in like she was on fire, heading straight to the lavatory.

"She is feeling sick," Ilmar informed him, now holding both plates of food. "Hungry?" She passed him one tray.

"Very!" He accepted it and returned to the lounge. They attempted to ignore Reeglar losing her morning meal.

"Well, maybe not so much anymore," Danny offered. Reeglar retched again, loudly. "Oh well..." He put the food down for the moment. "Morning sickness, huh?" He guessed. "I hear it can be brutal."

"This is awful! To be sick because you are pregnant?" Ilmar shook her head. "No thank you."

"What's all this 'no thank you' you're talking?" Danny teased her. "You were trying to make a baby with me, remember?"

"Yes," she admitted. "But, that was before."

"What do you mean?" He sounded hurt. "Before you knew me? I'm not good enough for you anymore?"

"No silly!" Ilmar smacked him on the arm. "A lot is going on now. It is not a good time. I have no desire to become pregnant with the uncertainty."

Reeglar finally joined them. She wiped her mouth with the back of her hand. Ilmar thought she still appeared piqued but feeling better. Reeglar sat in one of Azewrath's comfortable chairs, seeming to melt into it.

"Are you okay?" Danny asked her.

Reeglar nodded. "I believe I am now."

He addressed both girls. "Okay, what am I eating today?"

Ilmar pointed to the lumpy, white stuff, first. "That is a grain meal, like your oatmeal. And these," she motioned to the small red, marble-like objects. "Are Aquaroe. Like your fish eggs." She picked up a long, thin, rolled object and fed it to him. "This is akin to your fruit crapes."

He ate it all and savored the taste of everything. "This is great! You girls are spoiling me."

"Only because I love you!" Ilmar wiped food from the corner of his mouth and kissed him gently.

Reeglar got up and walked away. She backed up and held her hand out. "I might be feeling much better, but I can still smell all that food. I think I shall be better off over here. I am done with eating for the day!"

"Sorry, Reeglar," Ilmar sympathized. "Oh, Azewrath wanted

me to tell you he had a Seers meeting but would meet you here later."

"Good," Reeglar said. "That shall give me time to visit Minnar and her new baby."

"Oh," Ilmar remarked. "That sounds like fun!"

"No way! I don't think so," Danny told her. "You better spend the day with *me*, Ilmar."

"Ilmar WILL stay with you, Danny," Reeglar promised.

"Of course, my love," Ilmar assured him. "I have plans for you today."

Reeglar continued. "My Father believes you and me, Ilmar, are spending too much time with each other. I might be keeping you away from Azewrath." She gave Ilmar a meaningful look. "He is not a stupid man."

"This is getting complicated." Ilmar worried.

"We shall figure it out together," Reeglar encouraged her.

"You sure you don't want any of this breakfast you brought?" Danny asked Reeglar.

"NO! No thank you," Reeglar added. She put her hands up and backed away even farther. "I have had enough, truly I have."

"Cool," Danny said, smiling. "More for me!" He dove back into the plate of food.

Reeglar made a face. "All right, I think I shall leave you two alone for a while. If Azewrath gets here before I get back, just let him know I will return."

Reeglar went to the door, and Ilmar met her there to see her off. "Be careful, and take care of yourself. I will be worrying until I see you again."

"I shall be fine, Ilmar. Nausea is normal for some women." She put her hand on Ilmar's arm. "You take care of him and be extra cautious, please."

"I shall. Do not worry." Ilmar smiled at her.

"I wish I would not, but I have been feeling strange vibrations churning up complex sentiments inside our people." Reeglar's serious expression as she closed the door behind her.

"What was all that doom and gloom from Reeglar?" Danny asked.

"She must be sensing dark emotions." Ilmar sat next to him. "There has been great tension in Akkadia since Lacara's terrible mistake. And, I am afraid we have made it *worse*."

"Why? What have we done?"

She put her hand on his face and cradled his chin. "Oh, my love, do you not see? This conspiracy of ours to keep you here is what is putting us all in jeopardy."

"I thought everyone said the worst that could happen was your father would kill me." Danny laughed.

"You are not taking this seriously," Ilmar warned him. "I am sure my father would literally, kill you. As in dead! No longer breathing! Then, he would probably send your body back to the surface to let the animal scavengers eat your bones before anyone found you."

"That's quite a scenario! A charming picture! Extremely graphic." Danny's nervous laugh echoed. "What will happen to you?"

"We will be *punished*," she explained. "To what extent, I can not know. Although, Azewrath and Reeglar would incur a hefty sentence, to be sure."

"I shouldn't be at the center of all this drama," Danny stated, unhappily.

"Let us not worry ahead of time," Ilmar offered. "We will suffer the consequences of our actions in the proper order of time."

"Okay, I'm stuffed. Now, what are we doing?" He put the plate down and pushed it away from him.

"I am taking you on a tour of the kingdom," Ilmar told him.

"Is that safe?" Danny asked her.

"Safer out there where there are fewer people than here, closer to everyone's dwellings."

"When? Now?"

"Yes, now!" She hurried him up with her hands. "Just keep your mind on nothing, and follow me."

"That was a lot easier when I had nothing to think about," Danny replied, following her out the door.

***

Patrick's anger and concern about Danny's sudden disappearance, caused him to make a call to Aaron. While he waited for the young man to answer, the cell phone played its greeting.

"Please enjoy the music, while your party is reached..." Then Stone Temple Pilots, Plush, assaulted Patrick's ears. After a few bars, Aaron picked up the phone and answered.

"Hello? Patrick, is that you?" Aaron asked.

"Yes, Aaron," Patrick started. "I'm sorry to bother you this early in the morning, but I didn't know who else to call."

Worried about Patrick's tone Aaron pressed him. "What's wrong?" Sarah stood at the front door with it halfway open, waiting for Aaron to leave the house.

"It's Danny. He's gone," Pat reported.

"What? Gone? Gone where?"

"I don't know."

Sarah punched Aaron in the arm to get his attention. "What's happening?"

"Danny's gone," Aaron told Sarah.

"I know! I just told you." Aaron's side conversation with Sarah confused Patrick.

"No," Aaron said over the phone. "I'm sorry, Patrick, I was telling Sarah."

Pat continued. "I was hoping you could tell me what might have happened. He left a note telling me not to worry."

"I bet he went to look for that girl." Sarah nodded to Aaron.

"Oh, right. Wow, ya think?" Aaron questioned her.

"What?" Pat asked. "Do you have any idea where he is?"

"Not really, Pat," Aaron began. "It's a long story... Kinda."

"Give me the short version, Aaron," Pat demanded.

"All right." Aaron took a deep breath. "There was this girl —"

"Of course," Pat interrupted.

"Well, long story short... He went to go find her."

"What? How?"

"I don't know. It was the last thing Danny said to us Saturday night. He walked out of Frampton's all pissed off."

"And, you didn't think to tell me?" Pat raised his voice.

"Well," Aaron insisted, "we sure didn't think he was leaving town. How long has he been gone?"

Patrick walked into Danny's room, glancing at the surroundings. He touched everything. He picked up clothes; he opened the closet – anything to give him some idea.

"I'm not sure. I got home late last night and didn't look around; I just went straight to bed. But, his car is gone. Look, he didn't take anything. All his clothes are still here, and so are all the suitcases. So, where did he go?"

"I'm stumped, Pat. Really."

"What should I do?"

"Hold on." Aaron turned to Sarah. "What should he do?"

"Tell him, I'll see what I can accomplish down at the station, but it's not a missing person's case yet," Sarah offered.

"Okay," Aaron replied to Sarah, then he spoke into the cell phone. "Sarah said she'll see what she can do. I think you're just gonna have to wait for him to show back up. Sorry, Pat."

"Yeah," Pat agreed. "I think so too. Thanks, Aaron. I'll let you know if he comes home."

"Same here," Aaron added. "If I see him first."

"Okay, bye."

"Bye, Patrick."

Aaron hung up. Placing the phone in his pocket, he ushered Sarah out and closed the front door to her apartment. "I just don't know what's gotten into Danny. He doesn't use his head sometimes."

"Oh, he's using his head, all right," Sarah confirmed as she opened her SUV's driver side door, "just not the right one."

Aaron laughed and kissed Sarah. "I'll see you later? I have to hurry and get to a rescue. There's a beached humpback whale in East Hampton again."

"Oh, sorry to hear that, but no good for tonight, babe. I'm on late shift."

"I'll call you later, then." Aaron got into his Dodge Ram truck.

"Yep. Love you, honey!" Sarah called out as she drove away.

***

Azewrath sat at the head of the small table, against the wall of the meeting suite. As a large room, it accommodated all sixty Seers. They ranged in age, from thirteen to over seven-hundred plantings. With the tension in the room palpable, Azewrath curtailed his conversation to the pertinent.

Something is brewing, He thought, worried. When he was sure the space was full, and everyone had arrived, he banged the granite gravel, demanding order.

"As the Seer Council Leader, I call this meeting open. Drakar, as my Second, do you say yay?"

"Yay, Council Leader," Drakar said. "If it pleases, Azewrath, I would like to address the people, first."

"As you wish." Azewrath abstained.

Older than Azewrath by more than fifteen plantings, Drakar was Damon's father, a skilled Seer himself, but Azewrath dreaded what he was about to say. And it wouldn't bode well.

"My son, Damon, has spoken to most of you sitting here today," Drakar began. "As I understand it, no one experienced a shared vision, but we are all in agreement a war is coming." This statement brought a loud commotion, spreading throughout the crowd of clairvoyants.

Azewrath quickly took over. "I know this war seems imminent." He had to raise his voice over the noise of the crowd. "It sounds atrocious when it is spoken out loud, but we must all keep our heads and cipher what to report to the Queen."

Damon stood from within the ranks of Seers. "Azewrath, may I speak?"

"You have the floor, Damon."

"Thank you, Council Leader." Damon addressed the confluence of people. "In my investigation, I have put together the pieces of information you have given me. We are all in harmony with the facts, and no matter what the other details, it culminates in war between Akkadia and we assume, the human world. And the humans were not alone in culpability."

The entire multitude burst into loud shouting as they concurred. It was over for Azewrath. *The direction of sentiment is ruinous!* He thought as people around him screamed for him to take action.

Someone yelled from within the crowd. "I have Seen a Telepath involved."

"And I have Seen an Igniter!" Came another.

Drakar stood up next to Azewrath, dropping a bomb on his people. "And I have Seen a Seer who did side with the humans!" The people cried in denial.

"Not one of our own?" Another anonymous person screamed.

Azewrath turned to Drakar. "What have you Seen?" He studied the older man's eyes.

"I have Seen Akkadians siding with the humans."

"Are you sure? I have Seen no such thing." *What does he know?* Azewrath needed to glean the truth.

"How many times have you been wrong about your prophecy?" Drakar asked him.

"Point taken. I am rarely wrong."

"As am I!" Drakar informed him.

Azewrath addressed the room of Seers. "Everyone! Quiet, please! I shall call for a Council meeting with the Queen. I shall leave here and go directly to her chambers. We will stop this before it happens."

Great cheers came from the people in the room. Drakar put his hand on Azewrath's arm turning him toward him. "I shall go with you."

"That is unnecessary, Drakar."

"Oh, but it is, Azewrath." Drakar faced the crowd. "We will be strong, and we will be triumphant!" Again the cheers went out, as Drakar and Azewrath left the meeting. The other Seers patted them on the back and shoulders as they passed. Trouble brewed for Azewrath as Drakar acted more like a custodian, not a comrade.

I need to get away as soon as possible. Azewrath plotted. *Although, it could just be my own guilt, causing me read signs where none exist.* The two men made their way through the maze of corridors to see the Queen.

***

Reeglar met Mage' Calantra at the entry of the Healing Ward. "Please, tell me I am allowed to see Minnar."

Calantra smiled. "Of course!" She walked Reeglar into Minnar's room. "I shall send Seeleem in to take the baby and give her a bath."

"Oh," Reeglar moaned, disappointed. "I wanted to hold the baby first."

"Well, be quick about it!" Calantra told her before stepping out to fetch Seeleem.

"You can hold her, Reeglar," Minnar offered, beaming, happy to see her. Minnar handed her daughter to Reeglar, and in the process touched her. Surprised, by what she sensed, she scrutinized Reeglar.

Reeglar's gigantic smile spread as she studied the infant. "Oh, my Goddess! She is perfect! What did you name her?"

"Linock has decided on Peony," Minnar told her. "I love it!"

Seeleem walked into Minnar's room. "All right. Bath time!" Reeglar handed Peony off to Seeleem. "I promise I shall bring her back when she is all clean." Seeleem sailed out with Peony, leaving the two women alone.

"You must be so happy," Reeglar guessed.

"I am," Minnar told her. "And, what about you?"

"I am perfectly fine," Reeglar replied, seemingly confused. "Why?"

"Reeglar," Minnar scolded, "you can not fool me. I know you are pregnant."

"Shhhhh!" Reeglar put her fingers to her lips. "Do you want to get me in trouble?"

"No one knows? How is that possible?"

"Mage' Rom knows," Reeglar explained. "And... Some others..." she insinuated, vaguely.

"This is something to celebrate!" Minnar whispered. "Not to be kept quiet."

"Hum..." Reeglar sighed. "Very complicated."

"All right. I shall let you keep your secret. You shall let me know when you are ready."

"Thank you." Reeglar changed the subject. "So, when do you get to take her home with you?"

"I believe I have at least two more days here in the Healing Ward. The Mage' wants to make sure everything is perfect with Peony being the first hybrid. I am not sure I like that word." Minnar made a face.

"Well, Peony is perfect!"

"I would have to agree!" Minnar boasted. They chatted about the promise of motherhood and their expectations but were interrupted when a baby's cry wailed from the empty cradle. "Did you hear that?" Minnar asked.

"Yes," Reeglar agreed. "I did." She got up to peek into the tiny crib. "Oh, my Goddess!" she exclaimed, reaching inside. When she withdrew her arms, a wet, naked Peony filled them. "How in the world –?"

Minnar held her arms out for Reeglar to hand her the infant. She did so. "I do not know?! Unbelievable."

Within seconds, Seeleem entered, annoyance covering her features. "I was going to bring her back, Minnar *after* she was dried and dressed. You did not have to send Reeglar in to steal her."

"We did not fetch her, Seeleem," Minnar said.

"She just appeared in her bassinet," Reeglar explained.

"Oh, she did, did she?" Seeleem asked, disbelievingly. She took the infant back from Minnar. "I shall bring her right back." Seeleem walked out of the room again with Peony.

"She did not believe us," Reeglar remarked.

"Would you?" Minnar asked. "I do not know what just happened." She couldn't help but giggle.

"I am not quite sure myself," Reeglar declared. Just then, another cry emerged from the cradle. "Not again." Reeglar checked the baby's crib. Reaching in, she withdrew Peony for the second time and then handed her off to Minnar. "We might have a new Ability, here?"

"A Teleporter?" Minnar caressed her little girl.

"The unknown added human element," Reeglar offered, smiling. "Uh, oh, here comes Seeleem."

The younger Mage' stormed in with her hands on her hips. "Minnar and Reeglar, *truly!*"

"Seeleem, Peony did this all by herself," Minnar swore up and down.

"I am sure!" she spat sarcastically.

"Reeglar," Minnar asked. "Will you take Peony back to the bathing room?" She handed the baby to Reeglar. "Seeleem, stand here and watch the cradle." Reeglar left the room this time. Less than a few minutes later, Seeleem witnessed Peony materialize in the crib right before her eyes.

"My Goddess!" Seeleem breathed, picking up Peony and giving her back to her mother. "Your arms are where she wants to be obviously. Far be it from me to fight with a day-old infant! I have had enough."

Reeglar returned, laughing. "The new Ability is exciting news!"

Minnar laughed, as well. "My life just got more complicated." She smiled, rocking her new baby, the Teleporter.

***

Ilmartutar casually strolled through the corridors with Danny, with no one giving them a second look. He made sure to follow her and think about absolutely nothing. It was easy for him, with white walls, almost colorless floor tiles, and the stark white light from above. In his mind, Akkadia was bland.

As they exited the halls, they entered the world of the Cultivators and the Artisans. He received his first glimpse of the people who actually ran the kingdom and created everything the Akkadians used.

Ilmar reminded him to clear his mind. "You can look around, yet please try not to wonder about the beauty. No thinking, Danny. You must try!"

"Okay!" He said back, trying to keep his astonishment under wraps. An extremely difficult as incredible commerce took place right in front of him. Services for hire, with wonderous objects for sale. *Do they even have money?* He quickly put the brakes on that thought.

"Can I talk to you? I think that might help keep my mind from wandering."

"All right," Ilmar replied. "I am sure you can see we are in the heart of the Commonwealth. Anything you might want to have or to experience is here for the asking."

"But..." Danny got to ask his question at last. "Do you use money or not?"

"No. Not paper money as your people do on the surface," Ilmar described. "We *barter*. If I want an outfit made for me, I just go to the Artisan I admire. They do the job and ask for something in return."

"What would you do for them? Give me an example."

Embarrassed, Ilmar had no answer. "Well, perhaps I might not be the best example." She smiled at him. "My parents usually take care of my bartering tabs."

"I see." He smiled back at her.

"Other people might... Oh, I don't know, trade food from the Cultivators stores, or plantings from the Gardens or an Igniter might run the lights in a shop for the shop owner. Do you understand how it works now?"

"Yes, I get it." Danny shook his head. "But trading money is easier. Either you have it and buy something, or you're broke, and you don't."

"I think it just depends on what you are used to doing," Ilmar suggested.

They walked past the shops and headed out to the less populated area of the Gardens, with two distinct sections. One for leisure, the other for agriculture.

"The first caverns are our Agronomic Greenhouses."

"Is this where your food comes from?" Danny asked, amazed.

"Yes," she answered. "It is amazing, is it not?" It was almost like she read his mind.

"Uh, yeah," Danny agreed. "How'd you get things to grow down here without any sunlight?"

"That is a Cultivator's Ability. They just have to touch something, and it will grow into a full, well-developed fruit or vegetable; ripe and delicious!" Ilmar pushed him along with her hands to keep him moving.

The next caverns consisted of a succession of connecting tunnels. *What a beautiful place,* Danny thought. "I'm sorry, I can't help but think this is absolutely breathtaking."

"That's all right," Ilmar replied. "I believe we have left the numerous Telepaths behind. The Conservatory Greenhouses are some of my most favorite places to visit. If I can not be found, they search for me here. I have spent many occasions here, just laying in the grama, feeling its leafy coolness on my skin. It is my place of peace. I keep it close to my heart, bringing no one here. You are the first."

"Not even Azewrath?" Danny inquired.

"Ha! No, I come here to *escape* Azewrath!" She smiled and took him by the hand, escorting him into the parkland. "I have been other places with him, but this sanctuary belongs to me."

"I feel privileged." Serious, Danny raised her hand he held, up to his lips, kissing her knuckles. "Am I allowed to do that here?"

"We are more than likely alone, plus or minus a few Cultivators. Not very many Akkadians come here during a busy day of toiling."

Rows and rows of flowers all colors and shapes, exotic and strange to Danny, filled his vision. The scents, so tempting to his nostrils, brought a huge smile to his face.

"Everything smells wonderful," Danny declared. "I can see why you come here. Time sorta stops."

"Yes it does," Ilmar explained. "I come here when I need to get away from the pressure everyone puts on me."

"Well, I can understand that." Danny stopped her. "You're going to be the next Queen, or so I've been told. That's a huge responsibility."

"Humm," she murmured, skipping away from him playfully, which made him follow her. "I do not want to think about that right now." Ilmar spun around and around in the grama grass until Danny caught up with her.

He embraced her tightly in his arms. As he brought his hands up to her face, he held her there and kissed her tenderly. "My Queen," he whispered.

"Danny, do not..." Ilmar's reply, laced with sadness, hit home. "Being the Queen would mean we could no longer be together." She sprinted away, laughing and shouting at him over her shoulder. "And, I said I do not want to think about *that!* I have somewhere else to take you! Catch me if you can!" She ran ahead of him.

"You little cheater!" Danny chased after her.

Ilmar ran through a tunnel, but Danny closed the gap between them. She laughed and giggled when he seized her. They both caught their breath after the quick sprint. While they leaned against the wall of the cave, deep breathing replaced giggling.

Ilmar held out her hand for Danny to hold. Taking it, he entwined his fingers with hers. She motioned with her other hand to exit the tunnel. When they came to the end of the cave, Danny witnessed something that would stay with him for the rest of his life.

"Oh, my God!" he exclaimed, awestruck. "This is incredible. *Incredible!*" he repeated. As he laid eyes on the endless underground lake, his heart filled with wonderment. He turned to gaze at Ilmar. "Thank you," he whispered to her.

"For what?" Ilmar asked him.

"For allowing me to witness all this. Never in a million years, would I have guessed any of this existed." He made a significant sweeping motion with his arm in the direction of the lake.

"Lake Lunar is beautiful!" Ilmar agreed.

"Beautiful? Illy, there are no words. Really!"

She retook his hand and tugged him along. "There is more to show you. Come."

Danny and Ilmar walked along the edge of the water line, their feet making crunching sounds on the small, pebble-sized rocks that made up the shore. They strolled for a while in silence, as Danny took the enormous size of the cavern into the scope of things.

If it weren't for the fact that the color above him was a light shade of bronze, he could imagine a blue sky overhead. The boats and docks set up in the distance, made him stop.

Ilmar noticed him staring off. "Our version of fishermen. It is their job to feed all of Akkadia with the 'fish' they catch."

As she guided him into another cave-like opening, they kept to one side, making sure they didn't fall into the water that rushed by them. They moved along the ledge above the churning torrent that fed the lake with fresh water.

"Where's the water coming from?" Danny asked her as he noticed the swift current flowing past them. The sound of crashing water came from up ahead.

"You will soon see." She smiled, slyly.

As they accessed the next cavern, he could barely make out light at the end of the tunnel. When they entered, Danny was again, overwhelmed by what he witnessed.

Cascading waterfalls dove from every corner of the subterranean cave. The multitude of bioluminescent moss, or algae, sparkled across the falling water, creating a mobile kaleidoscope of psychedelic colors that danced on the cavern walls.

Ilmar moved away from Danny and disrobed. She dropped her coverings to the ground and stepped into the pool of water. Wading deeper until only her shoulders showed, she turned and beckoned him in.

"Well, what are you waiting for?" she teased.

He smiled, tossed his clothing next to hers, and entered the water. "Hey!" he exclaimed. "It's warm!"

"Geothermal energy springs," she told him. Parting the water with her hands, she created tiny whirlpools. "Is it not wonderful?"

Danny waded in deeper until he reached her. They embraced each other, tenderly, slowly circling in the buoyancy as the water swept across their naked skin.

"I don't think you've ever looked so beautiful," Danny complemented her. He meant every word. With the light in the cave reflecting off the water droplets on her skin, she glistened. "I'm such an idiot! I should have brought my camera phone down here to take pictures of all this."

"Is not a mental picture good enough?" She breathed in his ear. "This place... just you and I... here alone. Branded into your memory, forever." She kissed his neck, gaining back his attention. Her soft, warm, moistened lips called to him in the romantic setting.

His lips and tongue searched for her in the dim light, finding their mark. They breathed in each other's essence, holding each other tight. Her arms reached around his shoulders with his moving around her waist. His growing manhood demanded her as he pressed against her abdomen; desire building to an urgency they could not ignore.

Danny lifted her easily with the buoyancy of the water giving her near weightlessness. He brought his head down to her breasts, capturing her erect nipples. He drew them in and nipped each of them, making her gasp as he lowered her onto his rigid pillar of pleasure.

Her muscles tightened around him as the hilt of his thighs stopped her descent. With his hands on her hips, he lifted her effortlessly, only to pull her down onto him again. Using her legs to grip him around his torso, she rose in the water and then sank back down to him. Over and over again, she moaned with gratification as he parted her, plunging deeper.

Danny gently swam them over to the deep side of the pool, near a less powerful waterfall. He placed them both underneath its cool running torrent as the water cascaded over them, causing his hold on her to slip. As their lovemaking became tricky, Danny picked her up and placed her on a ledge behind the waterfall, joining her there.

Ilmar lay down, inviting him to continue. He moved above and mounted her once more. The dark and quiet in the small space behind the veil of the falling water allowed the sound of breathing to fill their ears. It took some time for their eyes to adjust, but he finally saw her smile up at him.

Bending down, Danny kissed her – his tongue and manhood thrusting simultaneously. He sent himself into her tenderly, so as not to grate her bottom on the sharp, jagged rocks beneath her. They made love and enjoyed each other, exploring every inch of the other's body.

Danny held her tightly and rolled over, switching their positions; himself on the bottom and Ilmar on top. She adjusted her position, enabling him to penetrate deeper. She moved back and forth with her palms resting on his chest for leverage. He grabbed her hips and pulled her faster, rocking her against him, heaving up to meet her.

He dug his fingers into her generous hips, causing a frenzy inside him as his release closed in on him. She ground her hips against him while her muscles squeezed his shaft. Danny couldn't hold back any longer, exploding inside Ilmar, filling her with his love. She climaxed as well, drawing his essence into her as her muscles contracted.

Spent, Ilmar glanced down at Danny. "Do I tell you enough how much I love you?"

"Yes," Danny acknowledged. "And every time I make love to you, it only gets better," he said lovingly, touching her face.

"It can only be good for us, my love."

"You're amazing," he stated. "This place is amazing." He hesitated, changing the subject. "But, I want to go swimming. And I'm starving!" He slipped out from under her, diving through the opening of the cave through the waterfall into the pool. "WOO-HOO!" he yelled, as he jumped.

Ilmar shook her head and laughed, following him out into the giant pool of water. When she surfaced, Danny floated freestyle and backstroked around the waterfall. As she swam closer to him, he maneuvered around her and dove down. Grabbing her by her leg, he pulled her under the water.

He swam away quickly as she surfaced and tried to catch her breath. He laughed, and Ilmar giggled, wiping her eyes free of the water. "Oh, is that how it is going to be?" she asked him. "You are not going to get away with that!" She dove under, giving chase.

He sped away as fast as he could through the small spring, but she pounced on him and pushed him under, laughing the whole time. He came back up, spitting water. "Okay, I give up!" He captured her in his arms, and they kissed again. "Time to go?"

Ilmar sighed. "Yes, we should. I am hungry as well. Although, I could stay here with you all day."

They walked from the pool, picked up their clothes and redressed. Danny shook his fingers through his hair to knock the water from it, letting it air dry. Ilmar spun her hair with both hands as she wrung the water out. Bending over, she threw her hair over her head, slapping it against the warm, drying air. After righting herself, Danny wondered at the unkempt look she sported.

"Sexy!" he told her.

"Hum, thank you. I am sure." She laughed. "Always at my best." She took his arm, and they began their trek back to civilization. Danny stopped suddenly, turning around. Ilmar worried as he stared at the waterfall. "What is the matter?"

"Just taking that mental picture you spoke about." He placed his hand on hers that lay in the crook of his elbow, and they headed back the way they came.

XVII

The Judas Kiss

Exhausted after a desperate rescue, Aaron sat in the cab of his truck and rested before he set out. The fishing boats managed to drag the baby humpback whale out to sea where it belonged, ending a stressful day for all involved, including the whale.

With the sun setting on the summer Monday, he exchanged "good work" and "goodbyes" with all the volunteers, as he started his truck. While struggling to tie the ropes around the whale, he cut his left forearm. It wasn't a deep gash, but it stung like hell and forced him to favor it.

All the God damn bacteria floating around, gonna give me an infection, he thought.

Aaron remembered he told Sarah he'd call her, so he hit his Bluetooth on the steering wheel. "Call Sarah," he said, and the car dialed Sarah's cell phone number. He threw the Ram into gear and drove home from Easthampton.

When Sarah answered the call, her voice came out of the Ram's radio speakers. "Hey, honey. You just get done?"

"Yeah," Aaron told her, making a left turn as he pulled onto Montauk Highway, heading west. "But happily, we saved her."

"Are you going home, or to my place?" Sarah asked him.

"I should go home; I'm beat." He counted to three, expecting her to talk him into coming over to her apartment.

"Oh, I'll be home in less than three hours," she coerced. "You could just as easily fall asleep in my bed, and then I'll crawl in right next to you when I get home."

Aaron laughed. Her smile was practically audible on the phone. "Sometimes, I wonder why I even have my own place."

"Is that an offer, Mister?" she teased.

A tingling panic rose in the back of Aaron's mind, and he stuttered. "Uh, uh..." It was all he could muster in answer.

Sarah cut him off. "Don't get so worried. I'm just fine with our present situation, silly." Still silence from Aaron. "Okay, so I'll see you later, right?"

"Yeah," he gave in, having no willpower. "I'll be there, and you can snuggle with your teddy bear when you get home."

"Thanks, hon! I love ya!" Sarah hung up.

Aaron shook his head as he watched the sun pull the last of its rays behind the horizon line. *At least it's more comfortable to drive, now.* The beauty of the sunset lost to him.

Hours later, Sarah did what Aaron said she would. She got undressed and crawled under the covers. She nuzzled Aaron, spooning with him. When she wrapped her arms around him, she woke him up.

"Ummm," he managed to verbalize his pleasure, rolling over to face her.

"Hi, big guy!" Sarah moved closer, kissing him, but she leaned on his left arm, the one he hurt earlier, causing him to cry out.

"Ouch!" Aaron backed away from her.

"What's wrong?"

"I hurt my arm today. You just rolled over on it."

"Sorry, honey, let me see."

The full moon shined high in the night sky through the window that made it easier to see in the dark room. Sarah took Aaron's arm, examining it. A thin black line ran up his forearm from the wound.

"It doesn't look serious, but it doesn't look good, either," she offered.

"It's not," he agreed. "It's just sore from the salt water making it all tight. Probably has some of that nasty whale bacteria in it, I'm sure."

Sarah reached for the nightstand lamp, turning it on to get a better look. Squinting his eyes, Aaron attempted to adjust to the sudden light. "Let's go to the bathroom and look for something to eased the pain, you big baby!" she added, getting back out of bed.

Aaron followed Sarah to the bathroom and watched her rummage around in the medicine cabinet for something. As she stood on her tiptoes reaching upward, the hem of her nightshirt crept above the bottom of her tush cheeks.

"Umm, umm," Aaron hummed, checking Sarah out. "You've got an awesome butt, honey."

With her concentration broken, she turned around. "PIG! You could be helping me, you know." She returned to her search.

"All right," he griped, checking the shelf next to him. Aaron picked up a jar with no label and opened it. "Found something."

Sarah turned around again. "Where?" she asked, scrutinizing the cream in the container. "Oh, I don't know where that came from. It doesn't have a nice fragrance, though."

"Who cares." He stuck his fingers in and pulled out a dollop. "As long as it stops the pulling and the itching."

"You sure you don't want some antiseptic stuff instead?" she offered as he rubbed the cream on his arm. Their simultaneously stunned reactions held their jaws agape when the yellow glow of the Healing cream spread across his arm. As it dissipated, where there was once a gash on his arm, nothing remained, not even a scar to show any prior damage to the area.

"What the fuck –?" Aaron exclaimed.

"Exactly, what just happened?" Sarah grabbed the jar out of Aaron's hands, studying it. "I used this cream Saturday night to get ready, and nothing happened to me."

"Where did you get it? There's no label on it."

"I don't remember." She concentrated so hard she experienced vertigo. "Well!" She sat on the toilet for support.

"You okay?" Aaron asked.

"Yeah, just dizzy. Again!" She snapped. Poking her finger in the jar, she pulled out a healthy size of the cream, determined to rub it on her arm.

"Wait!" Aaron yelled, seizing her by the wrist before she made contact.

"What?" she barked at him.

"I don't know," he answered. "What if something bad happens?"

"Oh, you're such a wuss!" Sarah scolded him, spreading the cream on her arm with no reaction.

"I'm having a déjà vu moment," Aaron announced. "We must have done this before."

"Humm..." Sarah hummed, disappointed at the results. "I think so, too." She checked Aaron's body for other wounds. "Did you hurt yourself anywhere else today?"

"I've got some cuts on my feet, but nothing bad. Why?" Aaron asked, suspiciously.

"Sit down." Sarah stood and then pushed him down on the

toilet bowl. Inspecting one of his feet, she found a small scratch-like cut. "Give me the jar." Handing it to her, she applied some to the wound on his heel. Immediately, the glowing light covered his foot before vanishing. The cut disappeared as well. "Son of a bitch!" Sarah released Aaron's foot, dropping it hard to the floor.

"Hey! Ouch!" he whined, but she wasn't listening.

She held the jar like it was an heirloom; made of gold. Gazing at the medicine cabinet, she reached for the hair cutting scissors. "I wanna see something."

"Oh no!" Aaron jumped up, taking the scissors out of her hand before she stabbed herself. "All right, now I'm SURE we've done this before."

"How is any of this possible?" Sarah wondered, mesmerized by the possibilities.

"How the hell should I know?" Defeated, Aaron sighed.

"It has something to do with Danny's mystery girl," she guessed. "It has to. I know it!" Her mind worked on the puzzle. "What time is it?" She ran from the bathroom to the bedroom, checking the alarm clock.

"Why?" Aaron followed her. "What do you plan on doing, now? It's 12:42 in the morning, for Christ sakes!"

"We've got to get the stuff tested," she stressed. "We can take it to your lab in Atlantis."

Aaron gripped Sarah firmly, cutting her off. "Honey, stop this. All of it can wait until tomorrow." He sat her on the bed. "It's not a matter of life and death."

"Really?" she asked. "This stuff just might be able to cure the most horrible diseases in the world! I'd say that was a matter of life or death."

Aaron laughed. "That's why I love you." He kissed her forehead. "You never give in, and you always think big." He sat next to her. "That's also why I hang around. You're gonna make it big someday, and I wanna ride those coattails! But – this crazy train ends now, for tonight. Okay?"

Sarah pouted but put her arm around him and teased. "Ah, where'd all the love go?"

Aaron leaned closer, kissing Sarah. He ran his hand up her thigh and under her tee-shirt, slowly pushing her down on the bed. As he made progress with her amorous response, Aaron's cell phone rang. Perturbed, he sprang away from Sarah, picked it up off the nightstand, checking the screen.

"Who the hell would be calling me at this hour from the Hampton Hamlet Inn?"

***

On the walk to the Queen's quarters, Azewrath weighed the pros and cons of contacting Reeglar via their bond. In the end, Drakar's uncomfortable silence made up his mind for him.

"Reeglar, this is a matter of great urgency and importance!" He practically yelled at her in his head.

"All right, you do not need to shout!" She thought back. *"This contact must be important for you to risk this form of communication."*

"I believe we are about to experience some trouble."

"Do not waste time telling me, just let me see it in your thoughts."

Azewrath gave her the events of the Seers Council meeting, letting her know who he was with at that very moment, where they were now, and where they were going.

"I need to know if Drakar suspects me of anything. Can you read his mind?"

"Yes. I shall."

Carefully, Reeglar approached Drakar's mind; her thought tendrils dancing on the outskirts of his thoughts. She barely touched his unconscious, picking the desired information she sought.

"Drakar is very suspicious of you, but could not imagine you would side with the humans."

"Neither can I!" He thought about saying "I told you so," but she heard him through their bond.

"I shall take the blame for this."

"Indeed. Yet, this is not the time for blame. We need a perfect plan."

"I have an idea. Can you meet me passed the Scholar's corridors in the Historian Section, after you confer with the Queen?"

"If I have made it out in one piece, yes."

"Then, unless I hear from you otherwise, I shall see you soon."

"You are extremely quiet Azewrath," Drakar stated, breaking Azewrath's thought link with Reeglar.

"Hum, indeed," Azewrath agreed. "I am keeping my mind clear for any visions."

"Of that, I am sure," Drakar affirmed.

After they reached the Queen's dwelling, the House Igniter greeted them. Azewrath addressed the man. "We are here to request an audience with the Queen and the Prince. Tell them, Seer Council Leaders, Azewrath, and Drakar are here."

The man bowed and slipped inside. Within moments, the Igniter returned to escort them in. He beckoned, and they followed. Being Pikkar's best friend, Azewrath visited the residence many times and was aware of their destination.

I shall mourn the loss of that friendship, he thought. Then, worried that the House Telepath might be close enough to pick up on that stray thought, he regained his concentration.

As the House Igniter led them through a large foyer into a smaller version of the Throne Hall, Azewrath held his breath. Inside, two modest thrones were the only furniture in an ornately designed room. Those thrones were not empty – both Queen Alkara and Prince Pikkar waited for them as they entered.

Azewrath and Drakar bowed low in reverence to their monarchs before rising without needing permission. Azewrath addressed their sovereign first.

"My Queen, my Prince," Azewrath said. "I am here officially, as First Council Leader of the Seers, and have brought the Second Council with me today. We have come to ask for a Council-wide assemblage.

"On what grounds, Azewrath?" Alkara asked.

Azewrath took a deep breath, eying Drakar. "The entire faction of Seers has had a cumulative vision."

"I have been waiting for this!" Pikkar hissed. "What is to be?"

"War!" Drakar interrupted. "Between Akkadia and the humans on the surface."

"Impossible!" Alkara doubted.

"It is as Drakar says," Azewrath reassured her, attempting to concentrate on their conversation only. "Yet, I believe on an infinitely smaller scale than Drakar does."

"Tell me when this shall happen," Pikkar demanded.

"It is... uncertain, my Prince," Azewrath offered.

"There has been no indication of the time frame," Drakar added. "Yet, there are more unsettling facts." Drakar gave Azewrath a sidewards glance.

"Speak them!" Pikkar ordered Drakar.

"It would seem..." Azewrath attempted to volunteer the information, hesitantly, "Akkadians *could* be involved."

"What are you saying, Azewrath?" Alkara asked. "Our own people shall turn against the kingdom? Are you making implications *against* any specific individuals?"

"No, my Queen," Azewrath admitted. "That information has yet to be revealed."

"What we do know," Drakar continued, "is that it could involve an Igniter, a Telepath..." He stopped, sighing before he added his next words. "It pains me to add this, a Seer."

"This is *outrageous!*" Pikkar screamed, jumping from his throne, facing down both men in anger.

Drakar spoke to Pikkar. "We need the Telepaths to gather. It is the only way to learn the truth."

"Then, we shall have a kingdom-wide assembly after the last meal," the Queen promised. "All Telepaths shall attend." She stood from her throne, joining Pikkar. "I am extremely disturbed by this meeting, gentleman." Alkara put her hand on Azewrath's shoulder. "We shall get to the bottom of this. I pledge it!"

***

Ilmartutar and Danny strolled back through the Gardens, arm in arm when Reeglar's warning slammed into Ilmar's head. *"Ilmar! We are all in danger! I need you and Danny to meet me in the Scholar's quarters near the Historian's rooms. Please hurry!"* Ilmar stopped in her tracks.

"What's the matter?" Danny asked. "Are you okay?"

"Yes," Ilmar told him. "Reeglar just told me to meet her somewhere. She said we are in danger."

"What's happening?" Danny panicked, trying not to lose it. All he could hear in his head was what everyone told him when he got there. *Ilmar's father will kill you, kill you, kill you.*

"I am not sure, my love." She took him by the hand. "Let us just go! Come with me." They took off running.

When they reached the Commonwealth of Akkadia, Ilmar released Danny's hand. Curious, he drew his eyebrows together, raising his hands.

"You need to lock up your thoughts again, Danny." She walked in front of him. "Shadow me, and follow my lead. No one will even notice you. Everyone follows me."

Ilmar and Danny found their way to Reeglar. She waited for them by the Historian sector. "Do not ask me why we are here, Ilmar," Reeglar uttered quickly. "I am sure you can guess."

"To see Gelfromm? Why?" Ilmar asked.

"We need him."

"Who is Gell-from?" Danny asked.

"Gelfromm," Ilmar corrected him. "Not now!" She waved him off, returning her attention to Reeglar. "Again, *why?*"

"We need the information in his head," Reeglar claimed. "And you need to convince him to give it to us."

Ilmar shrugged her shoulders but knocked on the door. "Gelfromm?"

"He already knows we are out here," Reeglar conveyed to her.

"So, why isn't he opening the door?" Danny questioned.

"It is personal," Ilmar answered.

Reeglar answer Danny's question. "Gelfromm has been in love with Ilmar since we were young. For at least twelve plantings."

"Gelfromm!" Ilmar called through the door again. "We need to talk to you right now. So, open this door!"

The door opened slightly, as an eye peered out of the slit hole. A soft, meek voice answered. "Only if Reeglar promises not to assault my mind."

Ilmar turned to Reeglar, raised her eyebrows, and opened her eyes wide encouraging her to speak up. "Reeglar?!"

Reeglar sighed. "In the interest of expediency, I promise to stay in my own head. All right, Gelfromm?"

"All right," Gelfromm agreed. "Come inside." He opened the door.

Gelfromm grew up with both girls, spending many years in study together. As a small young man with a very petite frame and bone structure, he stood the same height as Ilmartutar. And he was pretty. That was the only word to describe him, but his looks and physique had nothing to do with who he was. He was a Historian.

The Historian Council's hierarchy differentiated from all the other Akkadian Guilds. With no more than four Historians living at any given time, only two spent most of their lives together. When the two old Historians reached a great age, the kingdom made sure two more were born. When the young Historians reached the age of fifteen plantings, they participated in a Rite to assimilate all the memories of the old Historians. In turn, they took the anamnesis of all the Historians that lived before them.

Their memories went back to the beginning of Akkadian history. All the knowledge of every era that went before placed in the minds of the two most important people in the monarchy, besides the Queen and Prince. All that made Gelfromm an essential Akkadian. The people treated the Historians with special reverence. They were not to be touched by any Akkadian.

Danny regarded the little man. *Can I even call him that?* "He's going to help us?"

"Who is this?" Gelfromm asked, curiously studying Danny. As he walked around him, Danny spun, keeping his eyes on Gelfromm. "Hum... Human, in Akkadia?" Surprised, he glared at the girls. "No wonder you need me. What have you both done?"

"Way too much to explain, right now," Reeglar warned him. "We came here to receive your knowledge of our Histories."

"And, why should I help you? Your misdeeds shall more than likely be a punishable offense." Gelfromm gave Danny a sidewards look again. "You can not keep him here, in Akkadia, and you can not leave, either. Ever since your last episode, Ilmar, there is a Telepath holding the Reaction Lift in place at all times."

Reeglar sighed. "Yes, yes, Gelfromm, and we could have just saved all this time if you would just have let me enter your mind."

Gelfromm jumped away from her. "You promised! That is *never* going to happen. So, why do you still need me?"

"For an alternate way out of Akkadia. *NOW!*" The voice that spoke from the doorway was loud and authoritative. Azewrath stood at the door; his expression, less than happy.

"My Lord, Seer!" Gelfromm bowed low.

"Get up, boy!" Azewrath snapped. "We need your full attention, yet, I respect your fear. It is a more than an adequate motivational tool."

"What is happening?" Ilmar inquired of Azewrath.

"It seems, some of the Seers have had premonitions about an invasion, or war, which they believe involve the *humans*." Azewrath eyed Danny.

"What are you looking at me for?" Danny asked. "I'm not gonna start an invasion."

"We must get Danny back to the surface," Reeglar demanded.

"We must get all of us to the surface," Azewrath inform them.

"Why? What have you not told us?" Reeglar prodded.

Azewrath took a deep breath. "Drakar has Seen, and he has informed the Monarchy, that Akkadians are helping the humans. He was extremely specific, without giving any names." He motioned to each of them with his finger. "A Telepath, an Igniter, and," he put his hand on his own chest, "a Seer. I have just come from a meeting with the Queen and the Prince. There shall be a gathering, and the Telepaths are to be employed. There is no more time."

"Then, you are correct. We must leave as well," Reeglar decided.

"Can you do that?" Azewrath went to her. He took her hands in his. "Leave your home? Your Father and your Mother. Now that you are to become the mother of my child yourself?"

It was as if Azewrath had just dropped a bomb in the room. Ilmar new Reeglar was pregnant, but she had no idea the father was Azewrath. Confused, she stared at them.

"How… How –?" Was all Ilmar could get out.

Reeglar smiled. "It is a miracle! Perhaps I shall have time to tell you about it later." With her serious side returned, she cornered Gelfromm. "Right now, since you will not help us, you and me, Gelfromm, shall spend some quality time together!"

"Oh no, Reeglar!" Gelfromm protested. "You *promised!*"

"We are out of time, so I guess I lied." Reeglar raised her hands, approaching him.

***

Prince Pikkar made his way through the maze of corridors, crisscrossing the circular configuration of Akkadia until he came to the Guardian District. There the lodgement was much larger than in the typical quarters around the realm to accommodate the occupants greater height and size. The Prince had made the trip many times in the last few days since Ilmartutar's rebellious escape.

I know Illy better than Alkara ever will. The child is more like me than anyone would care to admit – which is why I must be prepared. Pikkar knocked on the door. He didn't have to wait long before it opened, revealing General Nutrion. The smaller man bade him enter.

"My Prince, right this way," the General offered.

The area inside was no living place, but a vast chamber, used primarily for training; the Guardian's military training. Three thousand years passed since the Guardians needed to protect Akkadia, but they worked daily to develop their skills in combat. The Akkadians born to the Guardian Guild learned discipline at an early age and were schooled to bring to bear any opponents demise. General Nutrion made sure that they were ready; his soldiers would always be at the ready.

The General led the Prince through the training area, where Pikkar witnessed Guardians twice their standard size. "Your warriors are always quite impressive, Nutrion," Pikkar offered.

"They are the best I have had in some time. We are fortunate."

"Let us hope we suffer not the same accident as our previous incident."

"Not to worry, my Prince," Nutrion assured him. "We have put that training on hold for the time being."

A soldier off to the right picked up a large boulder that could crush twenty opponents with one blow and flung it like it was a child's ball. It crashed into the walls of the training room, shattering into tiny pebbles.

Nutrion led Pikkar into a side cubicle with a large table and some abnormally thin paper-like schematic maps made from a material not of their world. They rested on the table as the General's first officer, Lieutenant Thorium, perused the maps. A giant of an Akkadian in his normal state, taller, even than Pikkar, who had to look up to the Lieutenant to reply to his subject's address.

"My Prince," Thorium began, bowing. "We have spent every waking moment on this plan for you."

"Thank you, Thorium," Pikkar answered. "You shall taste the blood of battle soon!" He clapped his hand on the taller man's shoulder before turning to Nutrion. "Now, General, show me where we stand in your grand plan."

***

Poor Gelfromm, Ilmartutar thought, gazing at his sleeping form laid out on his bed. *He does look at peace, however.*

Reeglar motioned them to the door. "He shall sleep through our escape. I did not want him up and around for the Council meeting."

"Will they not come look for him?" Azewrath asked.

"Most certainly, they might," Reeglar answered. "Yet, they shall just find him in a deep sleep, with no memory of this occurrence."

Ilmar put her hand on Reeglar's arm. "My father will use your father to invade Gelfromm's mind again."

"Yes, well," Reeglar laughed. "Let us see how long *that* takes him."

"What's wrong with the Historian?" Danny asked. "Why did he have such trouble with Reeglar entering his mind. It doesn't hurt." He followed them out of Gelfromm's, closing the door behind him. Danny made sure he locked it from the inside. "Just in case."

"The process of Telepathy does not hurt you, nor the rest of us," Ilmar told him. "A Historian harbors memories of all the Historians that have gone before, archived in their brain. We are talking about tens of thousands of generations of Historians. Reeglar had to weed through quite a bit of information and, she had to be quick."

"Oh man," Danny sympathized. "That sucks for him."

"He shall wake with quite a headache." Reeglar believed. "Now, we have some traveling and searching to do." She made sure to discuss her idea with all of them. "I need you all to follow me and do try to look less conspiratorial, please."

Ilmar corrected her. "You should all follow me. The people will never question a procession behind me."

"I believe it would be best if everyone followed me," Azewrath said. "There shall be dangers ahead."

"Someone start walking!" Danny stressed.

Ilmar huffed, taking the lead. Reeglar called after her. "Do you even know where you are going?"

"No! Nor do I care!" Ilmar yelled back over her shoulder. "You will tell me to turn sooner or later." Ilmar turned her head back to Reeglar and smiled. They all jogged to catch up with her.

"Head to the Repository," Reeglar thought to her. Ilmar visibly skipped a beat in her step, making a right turn to compensate. The Repository was near the Guardian's quarters, and she hated going there.

"I realize, Ilmar," Reeglar agreed with her. *"With our luck lately, we shall waltz right into Nutrion."*

They walked for a time without seeing a soul until Reeglar ran up to Ilmar and stopped her. She held out her arm, pinning Ilmar to the wall and placed her finger up to her lips. "Shhhhh." The procession held their position leaning against the wall, while Reeglar used her Telepathy to communicate to all of them at once. The clandestine action took quite an effort on her part.

"Everyone be still and do not move. Prince Pikkar is near. I think he is with General Nutrion."

Sickness overwhelmed Ilmar. *"Oh, no! He can not find us all here!"*

"Relax Ilmar," Reeglar attempted to keep the calm. *"I am hiding all of us from their sight and perception. Just wait until they pass. And they shall as – they are coming."*

The foursome became one with the corridor walls. Danny's heart beat loudly; he was sure everyone would hear it and give away their location. Three men marched through the halls, passing by the hidden conspirators. They continued as if nothing were amiss. Relieved he could breathe again, Danny let out a huge sigh.

Everyone visibly relaxed, so Danny spoke. "It's a good thing everyone here wears white. We blended right in with the walls."

Azewrath just shook his head. Taking the lead next, he made the first left turn to the Repository with the others following behind. He attempted to push the door open, but it didn't budge.

"Locked," Azewrath reported.

"Step aside." Reeglar touched the handle, and it clicked open. She cocked her head, smugly, motioning everyone inside.

The pitch blackness of the room made it difficult to see inside. "I have this," Ilmar spoke from somewhere in the darkness. Seconds later, the storage space glowed with the light of Igniter illumination. "Hey! I did it!" she stated proudly.

As Azewrath surveyed the room, shelves upon shelves of old, unused machinery, and discarded tools, lay in heaps. The Akkadians used them a few times eons ago but left them to decay.

"What are we looking for in here?" Azewrath asked Reeglar.

When Reeglar turned to him, her eyes sparkled. "The Crystal Dragon!"

Dismayed, Azewrath moaned. "The time grows short before they call the assembly and we are on a scavenger's mission to find a legendary, *imaginary* object?" He placed his palms over his eyes trying to alleviate the pain that settled there. "We have come all this way for nothing."

Reeglar reached up to grab Azewrath's hands in hers. "Gelfromm knows it is here. We just need to *find* it."

"We do not have the *time!*" he emphasized.

"We need to *make* the time!" Reeglar stressed back. "And it would be best if we start looking instead of wasting our time arguing."

Danny broke in. "What am I looking for? And don't say the Crystal Dragon. Describe it to me."

"It is big!" Ilmar told him. "It may take many men to hold it."

"Just two men, Ilmar," Reeglar corrected her. "It is about two meters wide and just as long. Circular, with corkscrew gimlets, encrusted with diamonds along its entire front edge." She put the picture in his mind.

"A giant drill head, huh. Gotcha!" Danny went to explore.

Reeglar approached Ilmar. "You shall need to run it."

"You need me to run the Dragon fifteen miles up to the surface? That shall take forever!" Ilmar exclaimed, depressed.

"No, Ilmar," Reeglar promised her. "We're going to find the Stairway to Niamuck."

Both Ilmar and Azewrath let out a sizeable, doubtful sigh. Azewrath pointed at Ilmar. "Why did you put her in charge of this escape?!"

"*I* did not!" Ilmar countered. "She was just the only one with a plan!"

"You two can stand here and argue," Reeglar informed him. "But I am going to look for the Crystal Dragon." She spun on her heels and scoured the shelves.

"We are all doomed!" Azewrath lamented.

"Oh, grow up and lend a hand." Ilmar ran off to join the search.

"I give up," Azewrath said out loud to no one in particular. "How shall I survive when I am surrounded by women... *and* their village idiot." Giving in, he went to inspect the relics.

At the top of one of the stacks, Danny searched through small, rusty parts of ancient gadgets. Azewrath wondered at his intelligence, so he called to him. "The Dragon is very heavy. Do you truly think you are going to find it way up there?"

"Do not be a bully, Rath," Reeglar yelled. "We all have to work together."

"Jerk!" Danny muttered under his breath, climbing down. He rummaged through the first bunch of discarded machinery, and to his surprise, he found it. *I'm sure this is it!* He yelled out at them. "I found it!"

"Are you *sure?*" Reeglar asked, first to respond.

"No," he replied. "But I think so. Take a look." He moved out of the way.

Reeglar inspected the mechanism and couldn't believe her eyes. "Oh, my Goddess..." she whispered. Ilmar and Azewrath reached Danny and Reeglar at the same time.

"I do not believe you," Azewrath countered. "Where?" Reeglar stood back to give Azewrath a better view. "This is truly unbelievable!" He turned to Reeglar with a big smile on his face. "You are an amazing woman. It *IS* the Crystal Dragon. You never gave up."

"Now what?" Danny asked. "We found it, now what are we gonna do with it?"

"We are taking it to the Stairway to Niamuck."

"And that means…?" Danny asked.

"It means," Azewrath answered him. "We shall all be caught trying to escape and spend countless years tortured at the hands of the Prince."

"Rath!" Reeglar scolded him "Do not say that to Danny. It is not true! You have not Seen it? Have you?"

"The Stairway to Niamuck is just mythology, Reeglar," Ilmar reminded her. "Stories and legends from our kindred line."

"It is *real!*" Reeglar swore. "I saw it in Gelfromm's mind. We found the Crystal Dragon, and you still do not trust me?"

"I trust you Reeglar," Danny assured her.

"Thank you, Danny," Reeglar said, sincerely. "You would think my *own* people would have as much faith!"

She moved everyone back, motioning with both arms toward the giant drill, raising her hands upward. The Crystal Dragon shook, broke away from the other artifacts, and slowly lifted off the shelf, hovering in midair. Reeglar held it there with the power of her mind.

"We need to leave, now. Azewrath, you shall lead this time. I shall carry the Crystal Dragon. Ilmar and Danny, you fall in behind me."

As they motivated, the drill took to the air. Azewrath opened the door and peered out slowly, checking both directions. "All is clear."

"Good," Reeglar suggested. "Now, as quickly as we can, head to the Provincial Zone."

Azewrath gawked at her again in shock. "The Provincial Zone is on the other side of Akkadia."

"Then we better hurry," Reeglar told him.

Azewrath shot her a glance one more time. He thought about saying something but changed his mind. Instead, he headed out the door. Reeglar sent the drill through sideways, following him. Ilmar exited the room, and Danny stepped out last, putting his hand on the door handle. Ilmar touched the door, making the lights go out inside the Repository. After closing the door, Danny followed Ilmar, bringing up the rear.

Leaving the old warehouse, they traveled in the opposite way from which they came. They hoped it would be a better idea not to follow in the same direction as the Prince and Nutrion. Although choosing the path that brought them toward the Telepath and Seers quarters would be just as dangerous.

Reeglar let them know what to do one last time. "We shall be passing by a susceptible section of Akkadia. I shall try to hide us as best I can, yet please, no stray thoughts." She directed that comment at Danny. "It could be a matter of life or death."

Danny couldn't help one last thought. *She sounds like a tour guide from a horror movie.* He laughed in his head.

"Danny!" Reeglar shouted back, scolding him with her thoughts.

"Sorry, couldn't help it. That's the last one I promise. I'll try not to do it again."

He put on a serious face, checking his wristwatch for the time. 2:10 PM. Hunger gnawed at him. They hadn't even brought anything to drink. *I could use a beer. Oh, shit!* He began counting floor tiles. They passed a few Akkadians, but no one seemed to notice them traipsing through the halls with the Crystal Dragon floating in the air.

Danny glanced at his watch for the second time. 2:39. They walked for a half hour. Danny's mind wandered once more. *I'm hungry!* He thought, again. *I wish I had some pizza, or fried chicken, or a juicy burger.* He pretended to eat something, enjoying it immensely, but his stomach growled.

Reeglar tried not to worry, but they were coming up to the Seer and the Telepath family housing. Azewrath turned his head, glancing back at her, his expression grim. She peeked around the Dragon, attempting to smile at him. She hoped he would sense she was not worried. Reeglar walked swiftly in silence. Struggling with the weight of the Dragon, she used all her energy, keeping the drill buoyant and moving. All the while, shielding them from unwanted prying eyes – and minds.

As the group came to the last side corridor leading to the Provincial Zone right before the Seers quarters, a door further down the hall opened. A tall man stepped out, his physique familiar, and Reeglar knew in her heart before she saw him; it was her father.

Chancellor Torg left his lodging and surveyed the corridor. They appeared empty to him. *So, why do I hear these alien words? Pizza, fried chicken, a juicy burger? All human words!* He realized.

Reeglar attempted to push the sudden rush of panic, deep down inside. She needed all her concentration. Leading, Azewrath spied Chancellor Torg, thankful Torg's back was to him. Making a quick right turn through the last side corridor, Azewrath vanished out onto the rocky terrain of the Provincial Zone.

Reeglar inhaled and sent the Crystal Dragon out after Azewrath. Wasting no time, she bolted after him. Mustering the last of her strength to keep the Crystal Dragon afloat, Reeglar ran over the rocks as fast as she could, but it was slow going.

Ilmar stopped just for a second, her eyes wide and mouth open. She grabbed Danny, pulling him around the corner in one swift motion. Once they were out of sight, they took off running. Torg wouldn't be far behind.

Chancellor Torg strode down the hallway with purpose. He passed the Seers quarters, searching the out hall to the Provincial Zone. Journeying to the very end of the Akkadian made construction, he gazed out upon the untamed expanse of the land beyond.

Nothing moved in the Zone. He spied only the hard rock landscape, giving way to the barren black rocks further out in the vast cavern. Unsettled by the mysterious encounter, he studied the horizon. Jarred from his mental continuity, he worried at his sudden desire for beer.

Danny watched the figure of Torg, silhouetted against the light of Akkadia, which shined from behind. Ilmar tugged at him hard, removing his attention from the Chancellor. Treacherous terrain covered the Zone region as boulders changed to jagged rocks. The careful climbing caused Ilmar to let go of Danny's hand. She needed both to keep herself from falling.

After a half a mile of traveling over the rocks, the ground surface evened out. As they entered a cave, the darkness closed in on them, creating an uncomfortable silence.

Reeglar had stopped before their sight was lost to the blackness and let the Dragon rest on the floor of the cave. "I think it is safe to rest a time, but that is all we can afford right now."

"Who was that guy?" Danny asked. "He was still standing at

the end of the hall, even when we entered this tunnel, watching. It was creepy."

"That was Chancellor Torg, Reeglar's father," Ilmar told him. "I am sure he is still there. Watching, waiting, reaching out with his mind as far as he can."

Azewrath went to Reeglar. She leaned against the wall of the cave, resting. "Are we far enough away from him? Are you all right?" he asked, noticing her fatigue.

"Yes, on both counts," Reeglar smiled weakly. "I do not believe his Telepathic reach is this far. Well, I am hoping it is not." She reached for his hand. "I am a little tired, so resting is a good thing, but we must move soon." Azewrath brought her hand to his lips and kissed it. "Ummm, that feels good," she cooed.

"It's kinda dark that way," Danny interrupted, pointing in the direction where they headed. "How'r we gonna see?"

"Ilmar shall be our guiding light," Reeglar told him. "You both will lead this time."

"The both of us?" Ilmar questioned. "There are no glow globes in the cave. I can not Ignite them to give us light."

"That is true, indeed," Reeglar started. "We can not use your Igniter Abilities here, as there is nothing Akkadian-made in the cave. Yet, if you turn off your force field and hold Danny's hand all the way through the darkness, you shall radiate your yellow glow of Healing, and we shall see."

Azewrath smiled. "You are a brilliant young woman."

"I see!" Ilmar understood.

"I don't!" Danny said.

Ilmar explained it to him. "When I touch you, you will need to be Healed so that the yellow light will shine and we will be able to see. Now, do you understand?"

"Oh..." He understood all right. The expression on his face went from dull confusion to regretful understanding. "I do see now. Your solution to our lighting problem is to torture me all the way to the end of the tunnel?"

"Everyone must do their part," Azewrath declared, sarcastically.

"Fine!" Danny agreed, grabbing Ilmar's hand, he held it tight. He raised it up above their heads, bringing Ilmar closer to him. Their kiss was heartfelt but brief. When she backed away from him, she smiled. Nodding to him as a warning, she touched her piercing and signaled Reeglar.

"Ready?" Ilmar asked Danny.

Danny acknowledged with his head. As they turned to go, his hand and arm immediately broke out in bruises. He cringed, but the Healing glow covered their arms and upper bodies, making them a luminous beacon of Healing brilliance.

Reeglar's Telekinesis lifted the Crystal Dragon again, sending it forward. "Let us go, swiftly," she ordered. "My hopes are we are not followed, yet I would not bet my life on it." They headed deeper into the tunnel and further away from Akkadia.

***

Chancellor Torg stood in the opening of the out corridor, glaring at the black rock of the Provincial Zone. He searched for something substantial with his thought tendrils, to no avail. Retreating, he walked back through the short hallway and returned to the corridor. As he made the right turn, he ran right into Drakar.

"Drakar!" Torg exclaimed, surprised.

"Torg," Drakar replied. "You seem startled to see me."

"Indeed," Torg said. "There are other things on my mind at present."

"Hum," Drakar wondered. "It is not often you are caught off guard. What has you so out of sorts?"

Torg sighed. "It is probably nothing." Drakar stared at Torg in disbelief. "All right," Torg continued. "I thought there was, well; there might have been someone in this corridor. Someone, who was not... Akkadian."

"Are you saying there is or was, a human here?"

"None other. I know the accusation makes me sound insane..." Torg admitted. "The Lift is under constant supervision."

"Indeed. Yet, I fear you could be right. How is this possible?" Drakar asked.

"I am not sure. I have picked up some very alien thoughts."

"About the coming invasion?" Drakar inquired.

"Invasion? Um, no." Torg shook his head. "These thoughts

were more about food than fighting. More a feeling of hunger than harm."

"You must inform the Queen at once!" Drakar ordered. "Azewrath and I have just held audience with our Monarchy. There is a war coming. Multiple Seers have had visions."

"Truly...?" Torg wondered, seemingly lost in his thoughts.

"There shall be a mandatory Council-wide meeting after the last meal," Drakar informed him.

"I see," Torg replied. "I think I shall go and speak with the Queen as you suggest."

XVIII

Up, Up, and Away

Ilmar's Ability emitted such a bright light; it blinded Danny. He sensed the tunnels grade rising sharply, making it difficult, like climbing a small hill. The incline went on forever. By his watch, they walked upward for two hours. Doing the calculations in his head, he figured how far they traveled.

Six miles? Now I'm ravenous. He broke the silence. "Hey, isn't anyone else hungry?"

Ilmar giggled. "*Men* – always thinking about their stomachs."

"Well..." He smiled at her. "I've had a lot of exercise today, even before we went on this walk from hell."

"Hush!" Ilmar scolded him.

Reeglar called out from behind them. "We should be nearing the exit soon. Do you see any indication of an opening?"

"It's hard to tell with all this light," Danny yelled back over his shoulder. "But, I see a faint reddish hue up ahead."

"All right," Reeglar acknowledged. "Just keep going."

Azewrath thought to Reeglar. He should not say his words out loud. *"I have been thinking... Torg was watching us for some time. Do you believe he knows you were there?"*

"On some subconscious level, perhaps. I am sure my father heard Danny."

"How do you know that?"

"I heard him. His thoughts centered around food. That is why my father followed us to the edge of the hall. I am sure he was wondering what a juicy burger was."

"Oh, my Goddess! The imbecile. *He shall get us all killed, eventually."*

"Relax, my love. Stay centered. We are safe for the moment."

With the end of the tunnel upon them, Ilmar released her hold on Danny. The glowing brilliance diminished, allowing their eyes to adjust to the low light of the next cavern.

Danny gazed out, amazed at the size and height of this space. "Wow..." he mumbled quietly.

"We are now in the Obsidian Zone," Ilmar informed him.

"I think we should rest again," Azewrath offered. "Before we attempt to scale this topography."

Reeglar shook her head. "No, no time. We must keep moving."

"I thought you said we were safe?" Azewrath asked her.

"For the moment," she answered. "The moment is fleeting. We must continue our escape. We still have a lot to do!"

"Okay." Danny stepped out onto the Obsidian Zone terrain – a dark place, full of sharp, protruding black rocks. Everywhere, the area shinned like polished glass.

If any of us take a spill out there, were done. As Danny walked, he watched the placement of every footfall. *Maneuvering would be easier with my sneakers. Hey! I forgot them!* He spoke to Ilmar. "I left my sneakers and jeans behind. Is that a problem?"

Her eyes went wide. "Oh... I do not know. I have your jeans in with my human clothes. That should not draw any attention. Where are your sneakers?"

"At Azewrath's, I think."

"That," Azewrath said, "could be a problem."

"Perhaps, if my father finds them, he will just think they belong to you?" Ilmar suggested. "You are both about the same size."

"Of course," Azewrath replied, sarcastically. "I always wear that awful footwear. Your father shall know in an instant."

Danny turned, shoving his finger in Azewrath's face. "You know, I've had enough of your bullshit, buddy. You want to go at it again? Maybe I can break a few more ribs."

Reeglar dropped the drill, crashing it to the ground. "We do not have time for this nonsense!" She marched as best she could to where the men faced off. "Why can not the both of you get along?"

"Mostly for the reasoning that he is an imbecile. Do you not see, Reeglar?" Azewrath countered. "All *this*..." He motioned with his hand to everyone. "This – is *his* fault!

"Now, wait just a *damn* minute!" Danny yelled.

Azewrath continued giving no heed to Danny's warning. "We are leaving our home without our dignity because you brought him down here!"

"So, by your logic, it is *my* fault. Do not blame Danny,"

Reeglar assured him. "I brought him down here; he did not force me. I need you to stop. Please!"

"We are wasting time with this bickering," Ilmar joined in the rebuking. "Do you both see that ahead? It is the Obsidian rocks." Ilmar pointed to the landscape. "It is a hazardous crossing, and we must do it quickly. I need promises from both of you that you can put your differences aside and work together." She faced her ex. "Azewrath, how long before they realize we are gone and may come after us? Did you say something about a war? Well, I am sure my father would use this as an excuse to flex his soldier muscles. Yet, we have chosen our side. I believe it is us against them from now on."

"Well said, dear," Danny admitted, trying to lighten the mood. He gave her a quick hug. "Okay, I feel like a fool, so... I'm all in. What's next?"

"Azewrath?" Reeglar asked.

"Yes, *yes!*" he answered without truly meaning it. "I promise to behave... for as long as I can. And *that* is as good as it gets!" He turned from them, attempting to climb the rocks.

"Well then, I suppose that must be good enough." Reeglar sighed, lifting the Crystal Dragon. "Everyone... be careful."

They followed Azewrath over the sharp rocks, picking their ways through blade-like formations. Ilmar tried to move slowly, but she slipped and cut her leg.

"Ouch!" Ilmar cried, as blood ran down her ankle.

"You okay? What happened?" Danny called over to her.

"I just cut myself on these nasty rocks." She reached down and Healed herself. "I am all right. Not to worry."

"Be careful!" he warned but watched Ilmar instead of his footing. His sandals made it more difficult to maneuver, and he lost his step. Skidding, he slid a few feet and gave himself a deep gash, losing blood. "Whoa!" he yelled, as he went down.

"Danny!" Ilmar screamed, making her way over to him as best she could. "Oh, my Goddess! You are losing a lot of blood." She thrust both hands on his wound, beginning the Healing process. With Danny's trouser leg torn open, he watched the large cut slowly disappear until only the red stain on his white pant leg remained.

Ilmar took her hands away from Danny, allowing him to

resume his trek, but he tripped forward and almost slit his throat on a knife-like, sharpened outcropping. As he inched away from the ebony blade, his eyes caught sight of something in the expanse of black. Something white. A skull. He stifled a scream.

"Hello!" he called out to everyone loudly. "There's a skeleton over here!" Azewrath glanced in Danny's direction. Taking a misstep, he stumbled, cutting himself.

"Watch where you step, and do not mind the bones," Ilmar offered to Danny before moving along to help Azewrath. She took three steps and cut herself again. "Oh, my Goddess. Again?" Ilmar had to Heal another deep gash across her calf muscle. She stopped and held her leg until the light faded before resuming her way over to Azewrath more cautiously.

"How bad is it?" Ilmar asked when she reached Azewrath.

"Not very," he explained. "Just messy." She held onto his thigh and Healed him, leaving a nice red blotch on his trousers. "Reeglar," Azewrath called over to her. "This is not going to work. We can not move fast enough. If Ilmar has to stop and Heal us every time we slice ourselves open on these rocks, we might as well be going backward."

"At least now I can understand why no one has tried to explore these Zones," Danny remarked.

"Oh, some have tried," Azewrath informed him. "But as you can see…" He pointed to where the skeleton lay. "Without a Healer along, they did not live very long."

"So," Danny asked. "What're we gonna do?"

Azewrath turned to Reeglar again. "I know you are tired, and we still have far to go, yet we shall not get through this without levitation."

Reeglar appeared dismayed and dropped her head. "I shall try." She took in the expanse of rocks over the horizon. "It is a long way to the next cave."

"I know you can do this," Azewrath assured her.

She nodded to him. "Get ready."

"Get ready for what? Whoa!" Danny's confusion led to clarity, as his feet left the ground.

Danny watched as the same thing happened to Azewrath and Ilmar. Reeglar spread out both arms, gritting her teeth against the strain of her exertion. With one hand she lifted the Crystal

Dragon, in the other, she levitated her three friends. Taking a deep breath, she floated herself upward, moving them onward, up and over the dangerous Obsidian Zone rocks.

"My God!" Danny gawked in amazement. "I'm flying without a plane."

Ilmar laughed. "I can not believe you fly WITH one."

Azewrath witnessed sweat break out on Reeglar's brow. "Are you all right? Can you do this?"

"I am not sure!" she admitted through the pain. "I do not believe I can hold all of you!"

"Then put me down!" Danny said. "You can come back for me later."

"I shall stay as well," Ilmar added. "Quickly now, Reeglar. Before something tragic happens to all of us."

Slowly, Reeglar let Danny down into the sharp quarry. Danny tried to keep some semblance of balance as he touched the rocks, but he sliced both his hands open. Blood ran everywhere.

"Damn!" He cursed, holding both palms high in an attempt to keep the blood loss to a minimum.

"Oh, no!" Ilmar screamed. "Hurry Reeglar put me down!" As soon as she slid into the sharp rocks, she worked her way over to Danny.

Hovering above them, Reeglar spoke directly to Ilmar. "I shall be right back. I swear." She sped away with Azewrath and the Crystal Dragon.

Ilmar moved too fast in her haste at reaching Danny. She cut herself many times, on her palms, wrist, shins, and thighs. As she closed the gap between them, something prevented her from moving forward.

What? She wondered, searching for the cause. Ilmar found her robes caught between two sharp rocks, hindering her ability to move any further.

"Danny," she announced. "I am stuck. My robes have caught." She pulled on them, trying to release her clothing from the jagged spires.

"Pull your robes along the sharp edges," Danny told her. "It should slice it right through."

"I shall try again," she responded. Ilmar took both bloody hands and grabbed her garment. She pulled and tugged, but the material wouldn't budge. "It is no good. It is not ripping." She checked on his status. "How are you doing? Are you still hemorrhaging?"

"Y-E-S..." he said slowly. "You can do it, Illy. Now, try it again and do it before I *bleed* to death!"

"Oooooh!" she lamented. "I *am* trying!" She wound her robes around her slippery wet fingers. The blood made everything sticky. Ilmar sawed her clothing back and forth over the Obsidian edge, hoping the serrated rock would cut through. She worked furiously, dragging her gown over the blade-like outcropping.

"Illy!" Danny called. "My clothes ripped easily. What's the holdup?" His white shirt turned red, soaked with his dripping blood.

"These are Royal robes, spun unlike any other clothing," she responded. "And I think I found the only rock with the blunt edge." Ilmar pulled with all her might. "Argggg!" she groaned, as the material finally let go. It ripped a small amount, so she pulled with more force. "It is coming!" she breathed heavily in response. Finally tearing a huge chunk of her skirting away, she exposed most of her legs. Now free, she maneuvered over to Danny.

"About time!" He tried to joke with her, as his consciousness faded from the loss of blood.

"I am so sorry that it took so long." She put her shredded hands on him. The Healing light sealed his wounds, giving him back his strength.

"Oh, man." Danny made a fist and stretched his fingers out again, flexing his muscles. "I wish I could do that. Should we head out?"

After Ilmar Healed herself, she held his face in her perfect hands. "We are going to sit right here and wait for Reeglar to get back."

"Yes, mother," he said, sarcastically.

"I will show you I am not your mother!" Ilmar wrapped her arms around him, bringing her lips close to his.

Nibbling his lips, she ran her tongue along them, teasing him. Danny's breath deepened as the desire built in him. He wanted her desperately. She kissed him, pushing her breasts against his chest and he held her close, grabbing handfuls of her hair. Pulling her head back, he ran his mouth and tongue down her neck.

Neither of them realized they were no longer in the rock mine but floating in midair. Reeglar had come back. She smiled at the sight of them in their oblivious embrace and brought them to the other side of the Obsidian Zone. They stayed in each other's arms, lost to their surroundings until Reeglar lowered them to the ground.

"I see everyone is safe," Azewrath observed, rolling his eyes.

"Thank God for Ilmar," Danny said, pulling Ilmar to her feet. "Or I'd have bled to death." He added a complement to Reeglar also. "Oh, and nice save, Reeglar! Thanks for the ride."

"I do not suppose you have ever traveled by levitation before, hum?" Reeglar giggled.

"Nope, but it's something I'd do again." He smiled at her.

"Hopefully, not anytime soon," Reeglar informed him. "I need to regain some strength for our final ascent."

Azewrath stepped in between her and Danny. "I am going to have to demand you stop and take a break, right now!"

"All right, all right!" Reeglar gave in. "I shall sit and relax for a few moments." She sat down on the nearest boulder. "See...?" She told Azewrath, spreading her arms in a "look at me" gesture. "This is me... resting."

Danny stared down the next tunnel. "This looks like a steep upward climb."

"It is," Reeglar answered. "But it is a short one. You should be able to see the other side."

"Yep." He could, but he didn't like what he witnessed. A slight heat wave hit him when he stood in front of the entrance. "I'm afraid to ask what's on the other side."

"Danger!" Ilmar mocked his question, running up to him and grabbing his arms. "We call it, the Abyss of Fire."

"That doesn't sound good," Danny worried.

"It is not," Azewrath added. "There are old stories, legends of crossings. Our people used to use this passageway eons ago," Azewrath explained. "Things have changed here."

"I have seen how to do this," Reeglar assured them. "There is so much in Gelfromm's mind, yet I was only able to take so much away."

"You still haven't told me what we'll find on the other side of this tunnel," Danny pushed her for the information.

"Just the fires of hell!" Ilmar remarked, dramatically.

"Oh, joy!" Danny moaned with sarcasm. "Sounds wonderful. I hate to say this, but why didn't we just steal the Reaction Lift? I think it would have been easier."

"It was too well guarded," Azewrath told him. "Pikkar had a Telepath and the Guardians patrolling the area. They would have caught us immediately. This way, at least we have a chance."

"Yeah," Danny agreed. "It also sounds like we have a chance of dying, too!"

"Some, more than others..." Azewrath smiled.

"I will not let anything happen to you, Danny," Ilmar swore. "Just stay close to me."

"Never further away than a scream!" Danny winked.

Walking over to examine the giant drill, Danny studied it closely. As a huge drill bit, equipt with 50 separate diamond heads that collectively spun when activated, it boggled the mind.

Activated by an Igniter, he thought, glancing back at Ilmar. *There's an incredible power in these people. And they're just so nonchalant about it.* "Can you really run this, Illy?"

"I should be able to." Ilmar joined him at the Dragon. "You see these Dragon claws on both sides?" She pointed to the grips of the Dragon. On each side, fixed protrusions shaped like Dragon talons adhered to the drill head. Each sculpted steel claw held a man's arm. "See, here and here," she said, as she pointed.

"Yes."

"An Igniter man –" Ilmar began.

Reeglar cut her off. "Two!"

Ilmar sighed at Reeglar's interruption, correcting herself. "*Two* Igniter men place their arms through the talons, then lift it to the rock, holding it like a shield. That is how our ancestors dug through all the rock."

"Just add power," Danny said, shaking his head in disbelief.

"We like to call them our Abilities," Reeglar interrupted again. "Even if we share the same Ability, each person has a different way to wield them. Not every Seer, Sees the same way, not every Telepath can levitate objects, not every Igniter can run all of Akkadia's lights."

Reeglar's statement brought memories of Ilmar's father. By the expression on Azewrath face, he reminisced as well.

Ilmar mused. *What will happen at the Council meeting? Or, is it happening right now? Will we get out before they come after us?*

Reeglar thought an apology to Ilmar. *"Sorry, Ilmar, I did not need to set your mind in a firestorm."*

"It is something we should not forget! It is not your fault I think about my Father." Ilmar smiled in her mind to Reeglar.

"So," Danny asked Reeglar, "What will your child's Abilities be? Do you know?"

"We can not be sure... until he is born," Reeglar answered.

"But," Azewrath added, "he shall be powerful. I have *Seen* it." He put his hand on her abdomen, bending down to kiss her. "Are we ready to continue?"

"Yes," Reeglar agreed. "I have rested long enough." She stood and motioned with her hand. The Crystal Dragon lifted, traveling through the entrance of the tunnel. She turned to Danny. "It should be bright enough in the tunnel for our journey through, with no need to torture you... *this* time."

"I'm all for no more torture, thanks," Danny declared, following Reeglar, Azewrath, and Ilmar into the red darkness.

The ascent into the tunnel held a steep gradient, causing Danny to grab handholds along the walls every so often. With the walkway narrow and rough, Reeglar sent the Dragon through sideways. Periodically, the metal would strike the side of the cave, sending sparks flying.

The further up they traveled, the heat increased. Sweat gathered on Danny's forehead, but his rising temperatures were more from watching Ilmar climb in front of him, then from the upcoming fires. With most of her hind end showing, he ogled the roundness of each cheek of her bottom as it moved back and forth with every step.

"You are a very naughty boy! With even naughtier thoughts" Reeglar thought to him.

"Hey!" Danny said out loud.

Ilmar turned around. "What is wrong?"

"Nothing, sorry – just thinking out loud." Danny flashed his pearly whites at her, so she smiled back.

Danny scolded Reeglar in his mind. *"Reeglar! No fair*

sneaking a peek!"

"I could not help it! You were screaming your desires! Quite interesting!"

"I'll work on whispering, instead. Now get out of my head!" She giggled inside his mind once and then he was alone in his own skull.

As the opening of the exit approached, he focused passed the bodies in front of him, attempting to view the next cavern. Uncomfortable with the increasing warmth, Danny took off his shirt, tossing it aside. With it soaked in his blood, it smelled, as his lost plasma mixed with sweat. He prepared himself for what he would experience when he exited the tunnel.

Danny watched Reeglar disappear after the Dragon, and then Azewrath. Ilmar stood at the exit. As a dark silhouette against a reddish background; her hair flowed, blown by a breeze. A thermal current of hot air blew a steady gust from the depths, swirling around her. She turned to face him, extending her hand. He took it and joined her on the outside.

The magnificence of the cavern astounded Danny. With extremely high walls, it gave the impression of an endless wasteland, continuing in all directions. Numerous catwalks connected stone walkways, like bridges from one place to another over the lava flow. Everything emitted a glowing red hue.

Noticing the lack of stalactites, he realized those formations required water. With temperatures as high as they were, it would be an impossible formation. The tremendous heat even pulled the sweat droplets off his skin.

As Danny stood on a giant ledge at least twenty feet long, the heat vapors rose in front of them. From his vantage point on the edge of the cliff, he observed long, dancing waves, streaming from the incredibly baked, dry atmosphere. It was the kind of air that rose from the pavement on a hot summer's day in the Hamptons.

"What's down there?" Danny pointed to the drop-off.

"Take a look," Azewrath dared. "If you're not afraid to lose your eyebrows."

"I'm not afraid!" Danny told him, walking toward the ledge's edge.

Ilmar grabbed him by his arm. "Do not let him taunt you into doing something stupid."

"You shall see more than you wish soon enough," Reeglar warned him. "Let us move on."

Reeglar sent the drill ahead and followed it across a good-sized catwalk. Attempting to contain his apprehension, Danny watched her braid flit back and forth with the updraft from the inferno below. Azewrath strode onto it next and walked without a care in the world, neither looking left nor right. Ilmar retook Danny's hand, and they walked across it side by side. He didn't need to go to the edge of the rock bridge to see what was going on beneath him. Red molten magma bubbled away below.

"Jesus…" Danny whispered. "Fires of Hell, for sure!" He took a deep breath. "It burns to breathe."

"Try not to talk," Reeglar instructed him. "And breathe shallowly."

Ilmar squeezed his hand, encouraging him. The first land bridge merged into a second, allowing them to climb higher, and then, another after that. Each crossing took them further up the cavern walls. By the time they were five hundred feet above the lava, the stifling heat had lessened, making it easier to breathe.

The trade-off on the other hand; the bridge crossings narrowed in width. Danny and Ilmar returned to walking single file, slowing down their pace for safety's sake. Studying their next level, they stood in front of a very thin extension.

Reeglar turned to warn everyone. "We have come to a place where we need to take great care."

"At least it's not that hot up here anymore," Danny said. "Thankfully."

"Yet, it is just as dangerous," Azewrath assured him.

"What difference does it make, Danny?" Ilmar stated. "If you fell into the lava flow at five feet or five hundred feet, you would still be dead. You understand?"

"I hear you!" Danny scrutinized the bridge. "It's kinda thin, and it doesn't seem that strong. Is it safe?"

"We shall find out." Reeglar took her first step very carefully.

The rock bridge they crossed was the thinnest one yet. Barely one foot wide, pieces crumbled and fell into the molten Abyss as they made their way across. Azewrath followed Reeglar and walked purposefully behind her. He slid one foot, and then the other, repeating the process. Ilmar joined the shuffle. She moved across the rocks, watching the pebbles plummet all the way down to oblivion.

Danny took a deep breath. "Great! Here goes nothing!" He exhaled, guiding a foot onto the crossing. After taking two steps, he stopped, listening. "Did any of you hear something?"

Halting their forward motion, they harkened. Azewrath cocked his head and glanced around at the surrounding cavern. "I do not hear anything, yet I have Seen something is coming."

Far off in the distance but still ominous in its presentation, a high pitched screech sounded. Long and drawn out, it echoed over and over, a blaring cry that bounced throughout the hollows of the cavern. Something was alive and coming their way.

Danny couldn't tell what it was or from which direction it came. "I thought there were no animals down here?"

"There are none," Azewrath assured him.

"Okay, so what was *that?*" Danny asked. "That was an animal! And not a friendly one." They listened to the scream again, closer this time. "I'm not hallucinating, right? Everyone else hears that?" Danny repeated, pointing straight upward and shaking his hand back and forth.

"There are more legends..." Ilmar began. "About flying creatures that hibernate for many plantings, only to awaken when an abundance of food became available."

"The dragottes?" Azewrath asked.

"Yes," Reeglar affirmed. "I saw them in Gelfromm's past Histories. They are real!"

"Why did you not warn us?" Azewrath asked her.

Reeglar shrugged. "I chose not to believe it."

"So..." Danny hesitated. "What?" His nerves took over. "Are you saying they consider us their 'abundance of food'? That they woke up because they smelled us?"

"We are!" Ilmar told him. "I thought the stories were told just to scare children."

"Aw, shit!" Danny swore.

Reeglar sprinted off the catwalk. "I think it best if we hurry." They joined Reeglar on the shaky ledge. She pointed to a deep cave-like hole, but to get there, they needed to cross another land bridge. This one was smaller than the last. "We need to get over there, now! We should be safe; only we must move quickly!" She landed the Dragon and headed to the next bridge, checking to see if they followed her. "Just go around the Dragon. I shall pick it up later."

Azewrath stepped carefully around the drill. The cries of the dragottes grew louder, which caused him to turn to spot the approaching beasts, but the cavern was empty. "Keep a sharp lookout!"

Danny slipped by the Dragon next. He regarded the long drop, as he peered down into the churning lava below. *One misstep and BARBECUE!*

Reaching over the Dragon, he picked Ilmar up, carrying her over it. Once on the other side, he put her down, and they both ran to follow the others.

The only way to cross the rock arch was to put one foot in front of the other, heel to toe. It wasn't even six inches wide and one foot deep in the center. Not thick enough to hold more than a few people. Cracks had spread throughout the shelf before they crossed.

Oh, boy, this looks safe. Not! What he said was different. "The girls should go across first."

"Agreed," Azewrath concurred.

Reeglar put one foot on the walkway. Holding her arms out for balance, she inched along one foot in front of the other. As she shuffled along, the dragottes appeared. The animals screamed, taking a quick pass at Reeglar's head. One flew by her swiftly with a great whooshing sound, and a strong passing of wind wake accompanied them. Reeglar ducked and lost her balance, slipping off the bridge.

"REEGLAR!" Azewrath yelled.

She didn't fall. Reeglar just hung there, suspended in mid-air next to the walkway. "No worries, Rath, I am all right." She levitated herself to the other side and crawled inside the small cave.

The dragottes came back. Flying at them one after the other, they swooped at Azewrath, shrieking. This time Danny got a good look at them. At two and a half meters, nose to tail, they resembled mythical dragons or bat-like creatures. With heads fashioned like a dragon, they had a mouth full of teeth, like an alligator, but their bodies were not scaly.

Equipped with membrane wings instead of forelimbs, they cut the air with ease leaving their strong back legs free to rip and shred. With their upper bodies covered in hair, they seemed mammalian while their bellies were smooth like a reptile. Their long, thick, dragon-like tail, whipped through the air, sporting a sharp barb at the tip.

"They're mini dragons!" Danny remarked. "Or, maybe large bats?"

"They are hungry carnivores," Azewrath reminded him. "Best you remember that."

"Oh, hungry…" Danny's stomach growled again. "I need food soon!"

"Do not think about food, lest you become food!" Azewrath turned to Ilmar. "Go, Ilmar. Cross *now*."

Ilmar removed her sandals and started across, heel to toe. A dragotte cried, diving in with its talons raised, heading straight for Ilmar. She took one giant jump and landed on the other side. Rolling over the rock, she covered herself with the loose dirt. Returning to her feet, she leaped into the cave, bruising and cutting up her skin. At the last second, Ilmar grabbed her footwear, bringing them into the cave with her. Relieved to see Ilmar, Reeglar hugged her in greeting.

Next, Azewrath approached the span of rock. Wasting no time in getting to the other side, he did not try to balance. He walked purposefully across as if he had done so a million times before. Joining Reeglar and Ilmar inside the cave, he waved to Danny.

"How did you do that?" Ilmar asked when he reached them.

"I knew it was not my time to die," Azewrath stated flatly.

Three dragottes flew by again, this time circling the cave entrance. They swooped in, trying to make a contact strike, but Ilmar and Reeglar recoiled as far back into the cave as they could, for Azewrath sake.

The largest of the dragottes propelled itself into the cave, catching Azewrath's forearm in a vice grip of its razor-sharp, spiked, slicing teeth. It beat its wings hard, attempting to pull him from the safety of the cave, but Ilmar grabbed Azewrath by his other arm, keeping him grounded inside.

Reeglar charged forward. "Not this man, you beast! You can

not have him." She threw her hands out sending a powerful blast wave of air past Azewrath, hitting the large dragotte. When the creature refused to release Azewrath, the blast sent the dragotte back pulling Azewrath out with it. Ilmar lost her grip on his arm and fell over onto her bottom.

"Owwww!" Ilmar cried.

"Let go, creature," Azewrath ordered, using the fingers on his other hand to pry the dragotte's mouth open. Its wings flapped hard in an attempt to get away with its meal, hitting Azewrath, making it hard for him to see. He gave up on beating it, finding it necessary to shield his face from the creature's claws. The other two dragottes flew in, each wanting to get their piece of Azewrath's flesh. They fought each other for prime space. Reeglar threw out a mind blast, repelling the animals.

"Eat molten lava, you monster!" Reeglar screamed. Her air blast knocked one of the dragottes out of mid-flight, sending it careening to the boiling magma below.

Danny tried to distract the remaining dragotte. "Hey, membrane wings! Over here!" He jumped up and down. Flagging the beast, he crisscrossed his arms over his head in a waving motion. After Danny had gained the creature's attention, the dragotte honed in on him. The dragotte gave a high-pitched screech before plummeting down on him.

"Oh, shit!" Danny cursed, and he dropped to his belly, hitting the ground hard.

The dragotte dove low, only missing Danny by inches. The small dragon rose high, shrieked loudly again, and set up for another pass. Danny scrambled out onto the bridge on all fours, crawling as fast as he could.

Azewrath and Ilmar beat the large dragotte, and it let go of its prize. "Let me see." Ilmar took his arm in her hands and Healed him. Azewrath's shirt – ripped and bloody, spoke to the ferocity of the beast, but that was all that remained of his attack.

Reeglar grabbed his shirt, unfastening its clasps and slid it off his shoulders. "I think we shall just get rid of this."

"Hey!" Danny shouted from the catwalk. "I could use a little *help* here!"

After he had called to them, they peaked out from the safety of the cave. Sprawled on the bridge, trying to duck the onslaught of the dragotte's attack, Danny grew alarmed. The larger one dove, and Danny flattened himself against the rocks, holding on for dear life. The dragotte missed him, but its flailing tail barb cut a gash in Danny's back as the creature passed. The second one came in for its assault, talons forward. He waved it off, but it grabbed deep into his back, its sharp claws drawing blood.

The dragotte attempted to lift Danny off the bridge which made him wrap his arms around the thin rock ledge tighter. He couldn't hold on much longer. The talons in his back caused excruciating pain, and the cut from the tail barb burned him from the inside out. In danger of losing his grip and his balance, Danny silently prayed.

Ilmar screamed. "Danny! *Hold* on!" She watched in horror as the rocks gave way, breaking apart underneath Danny. Small pebbles crumbled away at first, and then larger bolders plummeted into the lava.

The heat from the disturbed magma floated up, causing Danny to perspire. The beast still had its talons buried deep into his skin, making it hard to keep his grip. The moisture of his sweat created a slippery surface.

With the stress of the struggle, the catwalk could take no more punishment. The dragotte ripped its claws out of Danny's back as the bridge gave way. The beast flew high up in the air, but its barbed tail caught Danny in his side, fastening itself there. For the dragotte to escape, the animal had to pull away forcefully, leaving a piece of itself stuck inside Danny.

Reeglar threw her full force at the dragottes. As the force blast hit them dead on, they tumbled away, screaming. Danny sensed the stone under him crumble, and in the next moment, he fell. There was nothing he could do.

It can't end like this! Danny reflected.

Azewrath stood above him, and at the last second grabbed Danny by his forearm and held him there. Danny hung, dangling above the molten lava, wondering if Azewrath would help him up or let him go. The two men locked eyes.

"Give me your other hand," Azewrath ordered Danny, without emotion. Danny extended his other arm and grasped Azewrath's hand. Lifted by both Azewrath and Reeglar's Abilities, he breathed a sigh of relief.

When both his feet were back on solid ground, Danny turned to Azewrath and clapped him on the shoulder. "Thanks, man! I *owe* you big time."

"You might want to start keeping score," Azewrath said, sarcastically.

Ilmar crawled out of the cave, ran to Danny and embraced him. "Oh, thank the Goddess!" She mumbled into his chest. "You are a mess!" she huffed, examining him. "Oh, no!" Ilmar ran her hand across his back and pulled out the dragotte barb. She held it up to show it to everyone. She put her other hand on Danny, Healing his superficial wounds.

Azewrath took the barb from her. "This is *not* good."

"Why? And where did the dragottes disappear to?" Danny asked.

"I blasted them out of the air," Reeglar declared, smiling sadly. "We are almost to our goal."

"Okay..." Danny hesitated, watching everyone's reaction. "That's good, right? So, why all the serious faces?"

"You have been stung by the barb, twice. *AND* it embedded," Ilmar explained to him.

"I take it that's not a good thing," Danny remarked.

"It is the legend that the dragotte's tail barb possesses a deadly poison." Ilmar gazed up into his eyes, searching.

"There is no cure." Azewrath offered, grimly.

"So? Ilmar can just Heal me, right?" Danny suggested.

"The sting of the barb does not respond to Healing," Azewrath informed him. "You shall die, and it shall be ugly."

"You gotta be kidding me!" Danny hoped they were wrong. "All your Abilities and there's nothing you guys can do?"

"I am sorry, my love." Tears welled in Ilmar's eyes.

"How long?" Danny questioned.

Reeglar came over to him. "One, two of your hours at the maximum."

Danny glanced at his watch. It read 8:13 PM. *Okay, by 10:00 I'll be dead. Wonderful.*

He observed the Akkadians glaring back at him. "If we've got a new time limit, I guess we better find the Stairway to Niamuck and get you guys to the surface before I kick the bucket." Ilmar squeezed his hand.

Reeglar levitated the Crystal Dragon and drew it to her. "Let us go."

Azewrath stopped Danny from walking away with the girls. He held him by his bicep. "I am not good at finding a need for friends, but…" He hesitated, clearing his throat. "I have decided I can call you friend."

Danny stuck out his hand, and Azewrath took it. "Hey, thanks again, Azewrath. Look at the bright side. I'll never be that guy that asks you to help him move on a beautiful weekend." Danny winked before taking off to catch up with Ilmar. He put his arm around her, and she kissed his cheek. Azewrath stood there, watching him disappear and then shook his head in bewilderment.

They continued to climb higher and higher, scaling semi-vertical rocks. Danny asked one more question during their trek. "What will my symptoms be when I start to feel the effects?"

Ilmar answered. "It is a hemotoxic venom." But she couldn't go on. Ilmar placed her hand over her mouth to hold back her sobs.

Reeglar explained further. "It kills the tissue inside your body, slowly digesting it away. People find it hard to breathe as the first symptoms appear."

"Great, t-h-a-n-k-s!" Danny moaned as he climbed onward. "Something to look forward to." He took a deep breath while he still could.

When the cavern ended, and they reached the top, there was nowhere left for them to go. As far above the lava as they could get, miles up, Danny peered down and was hit with the feeling of vertigo. The maze of rock bridges far below brought back bad memories.

Reeglar held up her hand and pointed to a large opening in the ceiling of rock above them. "We have reached our destination." She was full of excitement as she sent the Dragon through the hole and watched it disappear. "I shall send you all up one at a time."

"Let me go first," Azewrath offered.

Reeglar nodded. She raised her hand, and Azewrath soared upward through the large aperture. Her gaze followed him up. "Is everything all right?" Reeglar yelled at him through the hole.

Azewrath peered down from the empty blackness. "All is clear. Send everyone up."

Reeglar did just that. Ilmar walked under the opening and slowly rose straight into Azewrath's arms. They held each other for an awkward moment, each unable to look at the other. They separated with haste. Danny came up next. Ilmar took both his hands and kissed his palms. He wrapped his arms around her and hugged her tight.

Reeglar levitated last. When she landed, she surveyed the area. "It looks like we have our work cut out for us."

"This is it?" Ilmar asked. "Have we found the Stairway to Niamuck?"

Reeglar pointed to a large piece of granite that could have been man-made. A long rectangle. A stair, under what appeared to be an endless amount of rubble of rock and stone.

"This?" Danny inquired. "There have to be at least a hundred thousand tons of rock, here." He went over to the sediment pile. "This is going to take us forever to clear up."

"It shall not take forever," Reeglar responded.

"Well," Danny assured her, "*longer* than I've got."

"Danny..." Ilmar joined him. "Do not think like that. Please."

"We are so close to the top, Danny," Reeglar pleaded.

"I know," Danny admitted. "I understand, and I'm sorry." He went to Reeglar and pulled her aside. "I need some alone time with Ilmar." He turned back to his woman. She sat on a large rock, bent over, her head in her hands. "You know what I mean, right?"

Reeglar nodded. She understood all too well. "I can lower the both of you back down for some privacy. Rath and I shall do a little bit of exploring around here. Is that all right with you?"

"Yes, thank you." Danny returned to Ilmar and explained his plan. Ilmar threw her arms around his neck and buried her head in his chest. With one hand, Reeglar picked them up and once again, put them down through the hole. She faced Azewrath and sighed.

***

Chancellor Torg stood outside the Royal quarters for the entire afternoon as the house Telepath would not let him in to see the Queen. Even though Torg was Tecma's Guild Leader, he would not allow the Queen to receive the Chancellor. Torg tried again.

"Tecma," Torg offered. "Read my mind. What I need to tell them is… very important!"

"I have looked, and it changes nothing," Tecma replied. "I have been charged not to disturb the Queen or Prince under any circumstances. Their order supersedes all else." He lowered his head in reverence to Torg. "You shall speak with them at the meeting."

"Agh!" Torg growled, throwing his hands up in frustration.

He tried, again, to make contact through the palace walls. He raised his hands towards the enclosure behind Tecma, who glared at him like he wasted his time. Torg could not break through as the special shielding would not let his mind penetrate the blockade.

The shield was set up by the ancients, his ancestors, to repel every Ability in the kingdom. This way, no Noble Houses could unite and ally with each other to overthrow the Monarchy.

Torg gave up, lowering his hands. He had to wait for them to come out to him. There was no alternative. Torg sat down on the bench and crossed his arms. He didn't have to wait long.

When Alkara opened the door and stepped out, surprise covered her countenance to see Chancellor Torg. Pikkar followed, and then the House Igniter closed the door behind the Prince.

"Chancellor Torg, what are you doing here?" Alkara asked.

"There is no time to explain." Torg lifted his left and right hand to their temples. He relayed all he knew and all he suspected through their mind link.

Pikkar broke away, his hands in fists. "Enough!" he yelled. "How could all this be going on without your knowledge?"

"I do not know. Drakar must be correct in assuming the humans have Akkadian help."

"I sensed the impression from your link you believe Ilmartutar has something to do with this?" Alkara inquired.

"I am afraid I do, my Queen," Torg spoke the truth as he knew it.

"Where is the proof, Torg? Produce it!" Pikkar said through

gritted teeth.

"You heard the voice in my head, my Prince," the Chancellor reminded him. "It was not Akkadian, and it was... here."

"Was here, but not here any longer?" Pikkar wondered.

"No," Torg replied. "They escaped toward the Obsidian Zone."

"Fools!" Pikkar laughed. "Then their fate is sealed."

"I think not," Torg disagreed. "I sensed a definite plan."

Amazed, Alkara tapped her finger to her lips. "I knew it was necessary to keep Ilmartutar under control, but I had no idea the resolve of this human male. That it would be so strong as to gain him access here."

"What are we to do, my Queen?" Torg asked.

"We are going to this Council meeting. NOW!" Pikkar ordered, pointing in the direction of the Throne Hall. He turned and strode off yelling over his shoulder. "This is the beginning of a new Age. The Age of Akkadia!" The Queen and the Chancellor followed Pikkar, quickly. Exasperated, Alkara threw her eyes up to the ceiling and shook her head.

Prince Pikkar burst open the doors to the Throne Room and strode up to his dais, pushing his fellow Council Leaders out of the way. Alkara and Torg entered after the Prince. She glided to her place of renown in the center throne while Torg took his Council seat.

As the Councilors found their chairs, a strange quiet spread throughout the large room. Alkara surveyed the Council tables. Drakar, the Second Seer, sat in his seat, but Azewrath's chair was empty, and Drakar did not appear happy. The Queen noticed only Leona in attendance at the Historian seats. Her Second, Gelfromm was missing as well. The other Council Firsts and Seconds were all seated, and unusually silent.

The only indication anything was amiss, was the constant flickering of the lights above which blinked with the rhythm of Prince Pikkar's heaving chest. He breathed deep, on the edge of losing control. Alkara gazed to her right at the empty throne belonging to Ilmar; also among the vacant.

Oh, my daughter... What have you done, now? She thought sadly. Alkara beckoned her House Telepath, Tecma, over and whispered in his ear. Tecma nodded, walking out of the Throne

Room.

When the Queen stood, she spoke with a heavy heart. "I called this meeting today to discuss a distressing possibility. I now believe there is nothing to discuss with you any longer. The time for discussion has passed. We must look to the future – to all of our futures. Now is a time for action! And if action is needed, there is none better than our Prince, my husband, Pikkar." Extending her left hand, Pikkar took it and stood next to her as his towering height commanded everyone's attention.

"Councilors," Pikkar began, calmly, "we can see the empty chairs of people we know and love. These Akkadians are the betrayers, the *conspirators*, for which we called this meeting. The Seers say war is coming." The Council tables whispered to each other, a reaction of disbelief all around. "Well, I am here to tell you that it is already here! I shall take the Telepaths, the Guardians, and the Igniters, and lead them in a war against the humans! Together, we shall take back what we have lost." He slapped his fist on his chest.

With cries of "Hear! Hear!" and, "Indeed!" from the crowd, Pikkar continued, spurred on by their calls. "We shall bring our people home, and we shall make the surface dwellers pay!" His speech met with cheers around the room and bolstered his already inflated confidence.

The Council Leader of the Empaths stood amid the celebratory calls. All eyes turned to the table on the Queen's right. "My Prince, we have managed to stay at peace with these modern humans for over five thousand plantings. Why now?"

"Because, Barrious," Pikkar answered, "we have proof a human has been hiding here... in Akkadia." The noise level in the room went off the scale.

Some Council Leaders banged their fists on the table tops before they pointed at each other, arguing over the empty seats. The emotions in the room overwhelmed Alkara. She waved her hand to get Torg's attention and pantomimed a signal for him to restore order.

Chancellor Torg understood. Standing, he closed his eyes, reaching out with his arms and his mind. *"ENOUGH!"* He ordered. As always with a mind command, the Councilors grew quiet immediately. Even Pikkar was stunned into silence.

The Queen spoke again. "As you all know, I am an Empath. All this talk of war is extremely distasteful to me. Yet, with the evidence we have, I must agree with the Prince. We shall go up to the surface and bring them *back*."

When the grand doors to the Throne Room opened, the Queen stopped speaking and motioned Tecma to come forward. He strode to the front of the dais.

"My Queen and Prince," the Telepath greeted her.

"Speak, Tecma," Alkara commanded. He hesitated. "Speak, man. Out loud for the entire Council to hear."

"Yes, my Queen," he replied. "Ilmartutar is not in her rooms, in fact, she is not in Akkadia at all."

Prince Pikkar acted as if he was about to suffer a massive heart attack. "*WHAT?!*"

Alkara held her hand up to stop his temper. "Center yourself..." She returned her attention to Tecma. When she spoke again, her voice sounded strained. "Continue."

Tecma cleared his throat. "The Seer, Azewrath, is not in his quarters nor anywhere in Akkadia, either."

"This makes no sense!" Pikkar growled.

"Pikkar!" The Queen gave him a sharp glance before nodding to Tecma again.

"We have found Gelfromm. Someone placed him into a Telepathic sleep, and we have brought him to the Healing Ward. The Mage's, Seeleem and Calantra have found traces of thought tendrils that match House Torg."

The entire Council trained their eyes on the Chancellor. "Surely, no one thinks it could be Reeglar or me?" Torg asked.

"Yes," Tecma answered. "The Mage's believe it was Reeglar."

Mage' Rom addressed the Queen. "My Queen, may have leave to return to the Ward and aid Seeleem and Calantra?"

"Please do," Alkara excused him, motioning him to the door. "My Council Leaders," Alkara began, trying a new angle. "I believe I have found a connection to all this madness." She put it all together. "All this appears to be about Ilmartutar and the human she spent time with on the surface." The Councilors remained silent, not understanding, so she went on. "Do you not see? Azewrath and Reeglar are just helping the human and my daughter. I do not condone this, but it is no reason to go to war."

The Councilors began to murmur. "This is about one human, not the entire human race. It is not about war, but about love. I plead with you all..." She turned to Pikkar. "Please, my husband, do not do this! It shall be a mistake. Send a small party out to bring them back."

Drakar broke in. "I disagree, my Queen. We have Seen this – And in this, I shall not waver. It is our course of action."

"That does not make it the right course," Alkara pleaded with him.

Pikkar crossed in front of her, blocking her off from the crowd. "This changes nothing! We have decided! We shall go to WAR!"

Cheers throughout the Hall came crashing down on Alkara. She dropped back to her throne as the Throne Hall emptied. She sensed defeat before any Akkadians even left their home.

Pikkar's emotions, whipped by the crowd, caused him to breathe like a wild man. He sucked in so much air lightheadedness threatened. He paced back and forth staring at Ilmar's empty throne. Alkara realized he neared his breaking point – his anger deepening with every pass.

General Nutrion, Seer Drakar, and Pikkar's brother, Dinnac, stood at the left-hand Council table, watching the Prince's anger level escalate. Pikkar stopped marching, but his breathing remained deep and quick. He caught sight of Azewrath's empty Council seat.

My friend! He growled in his head.

Pikkar lost it.

He descended the stairs from the dais and strode over to the vacant seat, huffing, and puffing. It made him think about friendship, about betrayal and lies. Pikkar glared down at it, gritting his teeth. He watched the three men, only moving his eyes. He never raised his head which made him look insane. To them, he did seem a madman. The men jumped back at that expression as they had all seen it before and knew what it meant.

The lights in the Throne Hall went into strobe mode, in sync with Pikkar's very mood. They turned off and on and then off and on in sequence. As Pikkar reached out with both hands, the brightness of the room rose to a blinding level. He grabbed Azewrath's chair, picked it up over his head and brought it crashing down onto the table, screaming with his exertion. The stone chair shattered into a million pieces, scattering small pebbles flying throughout the room.

***

Danny took Ilmar by the hand and brought her to a niche in the cavern wall. They sat together on the crumbling floor. She wasted none of their precious time and ran her fingers through his hair, pushing it back around his ears. She kept her hand on his face, stroking his cheek with her thumb. When he gazed at her, and their eyes met, only love shined from Ilmar. That and a few tears glistened her cheeks.

"I want you to know something before... before..." Danny stumbled over his words.

"Shhhhh...." she urged, putting her index finger to his lips.

"No... *No!*" He grabbed her hand and pulled it away, but held onto it. "This is serious." He turned away. "I don't know if I'll ever get this chance again..." He trailed off. Ilmar squeezed his hand, prompting him to turn back and face her, so he continued. "These last two days have been the happiest ones I have ever had in my entire life. I just wanted you to know; you gave that to me." He repositioned his hand to hold her face in his large palms. "You have given my life meaning." He shook his head. "I've never had anything in my life that has meant so much to me. I've lived selfishly. I was narcissistic *and* hedonistic, but you saved me from all of that." He smiled sadly. "I just wanted you to know that I *love* you."

Ilmar cried, unable to hold back the tears. "I love you, too. So much more than life!" She breathed quietly, bringing her lips to his. "I love you," she whispered again, kissing him on his neck. "I will love you forever." They kissed each other everywhere. They held each other tight, and she ran her hands up his back until she reached his shoulders, caressing him through her sobs of sorrow. "My heart burns, as —"

"I know. As the Abyss of Fire. I get it."

Danny untied what was left of her robes, sliding them off her shoulders. He leaned on his knees and undid his trousers, pushing them down until he pulled them off. She gazed up at him through sparkling, tear-welling eyes. He flashed his famous smile, and she tried to do her best to smile back at him as he lay her down.

Hovering over her, he came down and kissed her forehead; after he tenderly kissed her mouth. It was a slow, deep, meaningful kiss, filled with love and regretted unfulfilled desire. Of heartache and loss. He entered her like it was the first time – like it was the last time – and they made love. A sorrowful union of grief and a joining of sadness.

Danny made sure he worshiped every inch of her body, explored every curve and experienced every incredible sensation. They move together as one. Ilmar never wanted to let him go. Tears streamed down her cheeks and pooled in her ears. She held him tighter and brought her legs around his waist, squeezing him close to her. Her desire for him spurred him deeper, sending the last bit of his devotion, of his masculinity, of his love, inside her.

Danny took a deep breath of air and lay down on Ilmar's chest. Resting his head on her breast, he listened to her heartbeat. *So, this is what love feels like, this connection to another person,* he thought, so full of appreciation of life at that moment.

Ilmar stroked his head, as she held him gently, kissing his mop of golden hair. After all, he had been through, he was at peace with the end of his life.

"How do you feel?" Ilmar asked him quietly.

Danny picked his head up and stared into her eyes. "You mean, besides euphoric?" He smiled. "Oddly enough, I don't feel that bad. Both cuts still burn like they're on fire, you know? Maybe you could just try to Heal me."

"The legend says it will not work."

"On Akkadians. Healing doesn't work on Akkadians." He sat up excited at the thought. "That's it! I'm *human*. We're slightly different. Maybe the sting of the dragottes isn't fatal for me." He pulled her up, so she could sit next to him.

"I will do anything within my power to try to keep you alive," Ilmar promised, holding little faith. She placed her hands directly on his back and his side. Her thinking was, the closer her hands to the wounds, the better it might help. The warm yellow light spread out from her to Danny. She watched in amazement, as the gashes left by the barb closed as if they responded to the Healing.

"Hey... It's *hot!*" Danny told her.

"Oh, my Goddess, Danny. It could be working!" She dared to hope.

Without warning, the yellow light changed, corrupting itself into an ominous brown hue, swirling like so much pus. The infected light repelled itself away from Danny's wounds, taking refuge inside Ilmar. Petrified, the Healing light ran away from the dragotte's poison. She let her hands fall.

"I can not understand what I just experienced," Ilmar murmured in disbelief.

"What?" Danny wondered, turning around to look at his back. "What happened?"

"You began to Heal," Ilmar explained. "The wounds are not as pronounced, yet it was like the venom sent its poison against my Healing light." She glanced down at her hands. "It retreated into me as if it were running scared." She watched him get back into his pants. "I can not explain it. I'm sorry, Danny."

"Don't be." He winked at her, tying his trousers. "You might have bought me some more time." He checked his watch. "Speaking of time… it's 9:30. We better hustle." He clapped his hands together. "Come on, get dressed. Chop, chop!" Danny walked to the opening in the ceiling of the cavern, hailing Reeglar. "Hey, Reeglar. Come pick us up."

Almost immediately, he soared upward away from Ilmar. "Whoa!" he said, unsteady in his ascent, trying to balance himself with his arms, failing miserably.

Ilmar slid into her ruined robes just in time. Giggling, she placed her fingers on her lips as he floated out of sight.

"Next"

Ilmar sensed Reeglar in her mind. *"I am ready!"* Ilmar thought back, lifting into the air. Once topside, she made a perfect landing without breaking her stride.

"I am impressed!" Reeglar thought. Ilmar just smiled at her. *"Ah, I see."* Reeglar understood what just happened. She walked over to Danny and examined his injuries. "Your wounds do look better."

"Yes." Ilmar joined them. "But he is not fully Healed."

"Let's worry about that later," Danny encouraged. "Now, we got work to do." Earlier, Reeglar and Azewrath moved a substantial amount of boulders while Danny and Ilmar made their farewells. "Wow! You two have gotten a lot done."

"Tedious, menial labor," Azewrath complained. "I was not born for this."

"You might not have been born to it," Danny laughed, "but you better get used to it. People have to work hard most of their lives."

"Well, I shall *not*. If I have anything to say about it, at least," Azewrath answered smugly.

"Right!" Danny agreed and pointed a finger at Azewrath like he was shooting a gun. "Okay, so… Let's do this thing."

Reeglar touched all three of them, giving them the mental picture of how to run the Crystal Dragon. "Does everyone understand?"

They nodded. Reeglar levitated the drill and sent it as high as she could until it reached the rubble line she and Azewrath cleared. Danny and Azewrath walked up the man-made stairs, each of them sliding their arms through the Dragon's claws. Danny took the left side, and Azewrath took the right. Ilmar managed to squeeze between the two of them, placing her hands on both the left and right claws.

"Are we ready?" Ilmar asked.

"Yes." Azewrath braced himself.

"Hit it, Illy!" Danny told her.

Ilmartutar closed her eyes, concentrating on the diamond heads. In her mind, she pictured them spinning, rotating quickly and cutting deep into the rock. The Crystal Dragon came to life, humming and glowing with a muted white light. The slight vibration in the drill shook them as the many heads turned.

Danny flexed his right arm muscles and took a firm footing. As the drill launched into the wall rock, it spit gravel and pebbles everywhere. Reeglar made sure she remained close enough to use the drill's large size to shield her from flying debris. The diamond drill heads cut the bedrock like butter, allowing Danny and Azewrath to simply walk up the Stairway to Niamuck as they drilled through to the surface.

Oh, the noise! Danny thought.

They worked for hours, and Danny tired, but he was still alive and grateful for that fact. No one would hear him over the grinding of the rock, or he would have said so out loud.

"Yes, it is loud," Reeglar thought back to him. *"We should be getting close to the surface. It will not be long, now. How are you feeling?"*

"I'm getting tired."

"I can tell." Reeglar used as much of her levitation ability as she could to make it easier for him. *"We will be there soon, Danny,"* she assured him.

"Great, thanks!"

He turned his head to check on Ilmar. Soaked in sweat, the moisture from her hands rubbed off on him. Her eyes closed as she climbed each step, dream-walking.

All at once, the Dragon had a mind of its own. Reeglar, sensing their fatigue, pushed it upward through the piles of the old boulders, creating a tunnel around the stairway. The song, Stairway to Heaven, by Led Zeppelin, played in Danny's head.

"La, la, la, buying a stairway to… Niamuck." He sang along with his memory and faintly heard Reeglar laughing in his head.

They charged ahead with the drill vibrating, straining their muscles to the maximum. As they forced the Dragon closer and closer to the surface, sweat was Ilmar's constant companion. The hum and lights of the Dragon faded and faltered. Ilmar had not joined them on the next step up. Instead, she stretched forward as far as she could to keep both hands on the claws, but she was out of strength.

"I can not go on," Ilmar managed to get out. "I just can not…"

"You must!" Reeglar informed her. "We are close."

Danny released his right arm from the grips of the drill to aid Ilmar. With his departure, the Crystal Dragon wobbled before it tilted, leaving Azewrath alone to hold it. He struggled with its weight, but Reeglar instantly compensated, using her mind to bring it back to level.

"Thank you!" Azewrath thought to her.

"You are welcome, my love," she projected back to him.

Danny put his arms around Ilmar and helped her to sit on the stairs. "Take a few minutes."

Ilmar breathed deeply, trying to regain her center. She crossed her arms in front of her chest, holding onto her opposite shoulders. Her Healing yellow light surrounded her, wrapping her in a cocoon of radiant brilliance. With so much light, Danny couldn't see her. As the glow faded, her eyes opened, and she smiled, taking another deep breath. The first thing she observed was Danny – a worried expression on his face.

"You okay?"

"Oh, yes. Now I am," Ilmar replied, bounding up.

"Are we ready to continue?" Azewrath inquired.

"Yes, sorry," Ilmar apologized, smiling. "I am not used to working so hard."

"We are very close, now. It shall not be much longer," Reeglar informed them.

Danny draped his arm around Ilmar, walking her up the stairs to the waiting Dragon. He set himself inside the claw grip again, nodding to Azewrath.

"Ready, hon?" Danny asked Ilmar.

Ilmar put her left and right hand on the claw handles. She closed her eyes and set the Dragon to spinning its diamond heads again. As they continued, the sound of grinding rock eventually gave way to clay, and then to dirt, before finally to sand. The sandy layer created a hissing sound as the drill passed through. With one final push, silence greeted them. Just the whirr of the spinning heads met their ears.

Reeglar came up behind them, retaking control of the entire Dragon. "Take your arms out, boys and I shall lift it out of our way."

"Are we there, yet?" Danny asked, making a joke no one understood, nor answered. He and Azewrath removed their arms, and the Dragon flew from the hole to reveal a beautifully clear, starry night above. Danny gazed up and thought he never witnessed anything so wonderful.

"Didn't think I'd miss it this much," he said out loud.

"It is lovely," Reeglar agreed.

"Let's get the hell outta this hole, huh!" Danny begged, feeling the stress of his exertion in his condition. He checked his watch. 12:32 AM. *Shit! It's late.*

"Everyone, get ready," Reeglar warned, sending them out one at a time. Danny first, and then Ilmar, lastly Azewrath. Reeglar herself floated up and out afterward, landing softly on the dewy wet grass. She picked up the Crystal Dragon, Telepathically, and put it back down into the hole they just created, making sure she sent it very deep into the stairway.

Danny sat in the empty field. *Ah, nice, cool grass.* He lay down, enjoying the sensation of it against his back, soothing along the wounds. Ilmar sat next to him, her legs tucked beneath her.

"Where are we?" Ilmar asked him. "Nothing looks familiar."

Danny sat, checking his surroundings. "I'm not sure." The moon had risen, but it wasn't full. A slight glowing light from the natural satellite gave off barely enough to see by in the dark. He stood. "Ugh! I'm not feeling good anymore." He reached out and held onto Ilmar for support.

"You are feverish," Ilmar remarked. "We need to get you some help."

"Yeah, right," Danny answered her sarcastically.

Reeglar joined them with Azewrath close behind. "All right, Danny, this is where my plan ends, and hopefully, yours begins."

He wasn't so sure. "Okay." He attempted to get his bearings. "Let's see... We could be anywhere. Humm... That's a radio tower... Oh... And that's a windmill. Yep, now I know where we are. Stony Brook's, Southampton College Campus." He walked away from them, slowly fading. He stopped by a small white sign and waved them over to it, checking the words to make sure. It read: Wild Meadow. "Yep, we're at the College."

"So where does that put us?" Ilmar asked again.

Danny pointed to the road ahead. "This is Montauk Highway. We're close to my place. Well, one town over."

"How far is that?" Azewrath wondered.

"Too far to walk," Danny told him. "Especially, after what we've just been through." He jumped a white privacy gate, stumbling on his way over. He hit the gravel driveway, hard. "Shit!"

Hurtling over the gate, and clearing it like a professional athlete, Azewrath helped Danny to his feet. "You are at least three hours passed your estimated time of death." He pulled Danny up before steadying him.

"Is that your way of saying, I'm living on borrowed time?" Unresponsive, they stared back at him. "Boy, it's hard to get a laugh outta this crowd."

Reeglar called to him. "So, what are we to do?"

"A short walk, that way." He pointed West. "But, I think I need you to help me, Rath."

"Ah!" Azewrath complained, holding Danny up right.

"What?" Danny worried.

"I do not think I shall ever get accustomed to you calling me by my name." They stumbled to the street, waiting for Reeglar and Ilmar to scale the gate. Both women floated and glided over it without issue.

"Show-offs." Danny laughed weakly.

XIX

To See the Stars

After just a few minutes of walking, Danny stopped them. "I have to call my friend, Aaron."

"So," Azewrath declared, "call him."

"I need a phone for that. I can't call someone the way Reeglar does. I'm sure my cell phone's dead, and I don't have it. I left in the glove compartment in my car." He noticed Azewrath wasn't paying attention. "I know, too much information."

"Will there be a phone here?" Ilmar asked.

They stopped in front of a quaint little motel; the Hampton Hamlet Inn. Plenty of motels lined the highway. All catered to the Summer tourist crowd for their enjoyment of the ocean and the ambiance.

"Yes," Danny agreed, breathing with difficulty as he limped, "but I'm sure I look like hell. I hope I don't scare anyone."

Azewrath helped Danny enter the office. When they shuffled to the front desk, the evening manager took one glance at the disheveled duo, and his eyes opened wide.

"We're all booked up," he offered quickly, hoping they didn't need a room.

"We just need to use your phone," Danny told him. "I need to call a friend." He motioned to the others behind him. "We've had a slight accident."

"Do you want me to call an ambulance?" the manager asked.

"No thanks," Danny replied. "We're okay; just a bit banged up. We just need a phone, if you don't mind."

The guy handed Danny the cordless. "Here ya go, buddy."

"Thanks again." Danny dialed Aaron's number. It rang, and the music played. "Come on, come on..." Danny whispered, impatiently. The music finally stopped, and Aaron answered.

"Hello? Who's this?" Aaron asked right away.

"Aaron," Danny said, "thank God you're still up."

"DANNY?!" Aaron yelled. "Jesus! Where've you been?"

"Dude, no time to explain. I need a huge favor."

"Shoot! What's up?"

"Is that Danny?" Sarah's voice asked from the other end. "Is he okay?"

"Sarah's asking if you're okay," Aaron relayed to him.

"No, I'm not, *dammit!*" Danny answered, frustrated. "Just take Sarah's SUV and get here ASAP! I fell into some deep shit, and I need you to bring boots, get it?!"

"Gotcha, bro," Aaron responded. "See ya in a few." He hung up.

Danny handed the phone back to the motel manager. "Thanks, we'll wait outside." Azewrath helped Danny back down the few steps. "Aaron's on his way," he told Reeglar and Ilmar.

Ilmar came over to Danny. "Can he help you?"

"I don't know, Illy, but I sure hope so. I have a nagging feeling…" Suddenly, a thought struck him. "I've got a question." Danny cleared his throat, finding it harder to breathe. "I wanna know why Rath can hold onto me and touch my skin, but you girls can't?"

Reeglar laughed. "It is all about magnetism."

"And chromosomes," Ilmar added. "Simply put, the double XX chromosome is an abstract to the male XY. Like Reeglar said. Think about your magnets. Have you ever tried to put two North attracting magnets together, or two South ones? They naturally repel each other. Think of all males as polar similarities, and then male and female as opposites. You see?"

"You're making my head spin, honey," Danny told her.

"Well, you asked," Ilmar scolded him. All at once Danny's head bobbed forward. "Azewrath!" Ilmar put her hands on her face. "I think he has passed out."

Azewrath shook Danny and slapped his face, not so gently. "Do not die, yet."

"We are losing him!" Ilmar worried.

"Aaron is coming, Ilmar," Reeglar reassured her friend.

"What will he be able to do? He is not a Healer."

"No," Reeglar explained, "yet he is a doctor."

"How do you know this?" Azewrath asked Reeglar. She didn't answer, but Ilmar did.

"Reeglar and Aaron used to –" Ilmar stopped, realizing she had said too much. "Oh, never mind."

Azewrath narrowed his gaze at Reeglar and waited for an

explanation. He got none. Reeglar turned away from him, making sure she didn't enter his mind.

It wasn't long before Sarah's Ford Escape pulled into the parking lot of the Hampton Hamlet Inn Motel. She stopped the SUV right in front of them as Aaron jumped from the passenger side, eyes wide, wondering what had happened to his friend.

Azewrath shook Danny again, trying to keep him focused. "Danny, wake up."

Danny shook his head, forcing his eyes open. "I'm up Patrick. I'm up," he said, incoherently.

"Danny, what happened?" Aaron grabbed Danny's face, hoping to get Danny to see him. "What the hell's going on... And who are you people?"

"Friends." Was all Azewrath offered.

Trying to get Aaron's attention, Sarah pointed and pantomimed through the windshield from the driver's seat. She recognized Ilmar from the picture. Aaron shook Danny's head from the grip he had on his chin.

Danny made eye contact with Aaron. "Oh, hi, Mom." Danny smiled at Aaron. "Happy Birthday!"

"Oh, shit!" Aaron cursed. "Get him in the truck." He turned around catching sight of Ilmar for the first time. Surprised, he jumped away from her. "SHIT!" Aaron tried to calm down. "Shit... All right..." Managing to get a grip, Aaron spun his finger. "Get everyone in the truck."

Reeglar slid into the back seat, with Ilmar moving in next to her. Azewrath dropped Danny in after. Practically unconscious, Danny's head fell onto Ilmar's shoulder. With the back seats full, and Sarah sitting in the driver's seat, Aaron sized up Azewrath.

"Can you fit into the back?" Aaron asked, opening the tailgate.

"Do I have a choice?"

Aaron shook his head "no," so Azewrath crawled in, making his frame as small as possible. Aaron closed the hatch and slid back into the passenger seat.

Sarah attacked him as soon as he got in. "It's her, from the picture!"

"Yeah, hon. I got that." Aaron figured that out.

Danny opened his eyes, sounding extremely weak. "Aaron?"

Aaron turned around so he could see Danny. "Hey, buddy.

What the hell happened?"

"Poison," Danny managed to get out.

"Poisoned?" Aaron worried. "Who poisoned you?" He checked to see if anyone in the truck look guilty. They all did.

"It is more like venom," Reeglar told Aaron. "He needs some antivenin. Can you get him some?" She reached for Ilmar's hand and held it tight. "We have done all we can."

"What bit him?" Aaron asked.

"Nothing with which you are familiar. Yet, I can offer the fact that it is hemotoxic," Reeglar informed him.

"Hey," Sarah interrupted. "Where the hell am I going?"

"The hospital," Aaron said. "How long ago was he bitten?"

"Not the hospital," Danny told Aaron, placing his hand on his friend's shoulder. "Atlantis…" Then he passed out.

"Danny!" Ilmar tried to revive him. She held him, but he didn't respond. "He is burning up."

"Get us to Atlantis, Sarah. Hurry!" Aaron ordered.

Sarah spun the SUV around, slapping the siren to the dashboard. "Hold on everyone!" she ordered, pulling onto Montauk Highway at full speed.

"Now, we are all going to die!" Azewrath moaned in response to Sarah's driving.

"Rath," Reeglar cautioned, shaking her head. Turning, she addressed Aaron. "Danny was stung at about 8:00 PM, your time."

"He should be dead!" Aaron yelled, incredulous.

On the other hand, Sarah wondered about something else. *Our time?*

Reeglar agreed with Aaron. "He shall be soon, but he is not yet. So – hemotoxic antivenin, you have it or not?"

"I do," Aaron added. "I just don't understand how Danny knew it."

"He is a changed man, Aaron," Reeglar stated.

Aaron took a closer look at Reeglar. "I've got the strangest feeling… Do I know you?"

"No!" Azewrath spoke before Reeglar could answer. "You do not."

"O-K," Aaron said slowly, turning around and away from them. He grabbed Sarah's hand and squeezed it, raising his eyebrows.

When they pulled into Atlantis, the building stood dark, but the lights from the parking lot blazed in the night's blackness. The moon reflected off the water from the Marina as a fish broke the surface. Aaron ran straight into the building to unlock the door and shut off the alarm.

Sarah let Azewrath out of the back of the truck, and then he opened the side door, picking up Danny's inert body. Ilmar slid out next. Reeglar followed, shutting the door. Ilmar went to the other side of Danny and helped Azewrath drag him. They draped Danny over both their shoulders, one arm over Azewrath, the other over Ilmar. As they hurried to Aaron's Lab, Sarah hit the lights and closed the door to the building behind her.

"Let's get him on the table," Aaron ordered. He and Azewrath picked Danny up and lay him gently on the exam table. Aaron put his fingers on Danny's wrist to feel for a pulse. Concerned, he brought his fingers to Danny's jugular vein in his neck. "Well, he still has a pulse, for now anyway."

Ilmar went over to Aaron. "Can you save him?"

"Yes," Aaron answered, heading into the other room. "I think so. Although, he should be dead already. I'm confounded."

"Where are you going?" Sarah asked Aaron.

"Getting what we need," Aaron told her. In the other room, two snakes moved slowly inside tanks next to a small refrigerator. Reeglar and Azewrath followed Aaron.

"What are you giving him?" Reeglar questioned.

Aaron found a large syringe, a 20 G 1 ½ needle and took two ampules out of the fridge. "Both of you take one and rub it in your palms, back and forth. This stuff needs to be warmer. Room temperature." He handed the vials to Azewrath and Reeglar, who worked the serum in their hands. Aaron continued. "These two beauties are Caucasian vipers. There from Azerbaijan, by the Caspian Sea."

Reeglar took a closer look at the tank, and one of the snakes struck the glass, its mouth wide with fangs showing. "Whaa!" She startled, jumping backward into Azewrath. He put his arms around her in a protective gesture.

Aaron motioned to them with his head to return to the exam room. "Those vipers had great success stopping the anticoagulant and the necrosis of tissue in the body. Their antivenin might counter the effect of the hemotoxic sting." He asked for the first vial. "Let me see if it's warm enough." Reeglar handed her bottle to Aaron. "We're good," Aaron said.

Aaron drew back the plunger, turning the serum bottle over. He pushed the needle in deep, expelling the air from it, so when he drew the plunger out, the light brownish liquid filled the syringe. Each ampule was a 25 mL. He withdrew the needle and squirted the remaining air out, flicking the syringe with his fingers to loosen any bubbles stuck to the sides. There could be no air inside the syringe. It could kill Danny.

Danny didn't move, but he still breathed. With Ilmar holding his left hand, Aaron maneuvered to his right arm. "Gotta do this intravenously." He made eye contact with everyone in the room. "Cross your fingers," Aaron added, as he pushed the needle in Danny's vein, injecting the antivenin. He went very slowly, making sure the liquid dispersed through Danny's bloodstream a little at a time.

Sweat beaded on Aaron's forehead, so Sarah got a cloth and mopped his brow. "Thanks, hon," Aaron praised her. "You'd make a great nurse."

"Thank you... No!" Sarah stressed. "I'm no Florence Nightingale." She tossed the rag aside, sitting on a stool.

Aaron took the second ampule of antivenin from Azewrath, injecting it into Danny. His recovery was going to take some more time. "Now, we wait."

"How long?" Azewrath asked.

"You got somewhere to be?" Sarah grilled him.

"Sarah!" Aaron reprimanded her. "There'll be time for that." He answered Azewrath. "At least an hour, give or take. I can only hope he wakes up."

Ilmar had tears in her eyes. She held onto Danny's hand like it was a lifeline to his soul. As if the warmth of her touch, even without her Healing powers, could contain him to this side of the gray line of life and death. She willed him to live with the sheer force of her love. She brought his hand to her cheek, saying a silent prayer to her Goddess.

Danny dreamed again. He stood in the middle of the street, not naked this time, but his clothes were torn and bloody. Dreaming?

Reality? The lines between the two worlds blurred for him; overlapping and seeping from one realm to the other. His mind couldn't tell the difference.

The dragottes dove at him, but Aaron and Sarah were with him. They ran and hid, trying to elude their demonic pursuers. The ground shook as they attempted to keep their balance. The dragottes circled high in the sky. As he watched them, he realized it wasn't a dragotte; it was a plane. The quaking of the ground forced him down into the dirt, only to have the earth open up underneath him, swallowing him into its depths.

And he fell.

Aaron pulled the needle out of Danny's arm and swabbed it with a cotton ball, taping it there. "Okay, gang…" He turned to the Akkadians. "I think it's time for some questions, yes?"

Reeglar approached Aaron. "This would go a lot faster if you would let me tell you things my way." She motioned him over to Sarah. "I shall need to touch her temples." Reeglar raised her hands, but Sarah slapped it away.

"I'm not going to let you touch me," Sarah warned her.

"Sarah," Aaron began, "what the hell's the problem?"

"Really? There's too much weird shit going on," Sarah answered. "My spider sense is tingling."

"O-K," Aaron spoke to Reeglar. "So, do me first."

"However you want it done," Reeglar said. She touched Aaron's temples, closed her eyes, and entered his mind.

She found his blocked memories and destroyed the wall. She touched him tenderly, giving him her memories of all that transpired in the last two days. When she removed her hand, Aaron jumped back.

"Whoa!" he expressed, scratching his scalp.

"Aaron, are you okay?" Sarah asked him.

"Yeah," Aaron managed to get out, catching his breath. "Shit! Oh, hi, Rea. Sorry for not remembering you." Aaron now recognized her.

"Rea?" Azewrath wondered.

"My name in the human world," Reeglar clarified for him.

"*Human* world? Aaron?" Sarah spoke slowly. "What the hell is going on?"

"Let Rea touch you, honey," Aaron assured her, moving to

hold her hand. "Not like I really want to go through this again, but whatever…"

"I don't trust them!" Sarah confessed.

"Yeah, well, soon… you won't trust me, either," Aaron bemoaned sadly.

"Oh, just touch her already, Reeglar!" Ilmar ordered. Reeglar extended her arm towards Sarah again.

"I don't think so, honey," Sarah repeated, jumping off the stool. She pulled out her police issue semiautomatic Glock from her waistband behind her back and pointed it right at Reeglar. "Back off!"

"JESUS, SARAH!" Aaron screamed. "Have you lost your mind?"

Azewrath laughed. Reeglar stood there, tapping her foot on the floor, and Ilmar didn't even look away from Danny. It was like they didn't care about Sarah's gun.

"Why aren't you worried that I have a gun pointed right at one of you?" Sarah asked, waving her Glock around.

Very slowly, Reeglar moved her fingers in a semi-circle, which wrenched the pistol out of Sarah's hand to land softly in Reeglar's.

"That is why," Azewrath said. "Foolish woman."

Shock took Sarah, and she stood with her jaw hanging open. Aaron approached her and helped her sit on the stool. She stared up at him, confused. "I'm missing something."

"Yeah," Aaron agreed. "Part of your memory. Would you like it back?" Sarah nodded, hesitantly. "Okay, then let Rea touch you."

"Aaron, that is not my real name," Reeglar offered. She walked over to Sarah again, tentatively raising her hand to Sarah's temples. Reeglar closed her eyes, and Sarah's eyes got wider and wider, as her memories returned. Stepping back, Reeglar released Sarah.

"Son of a bitch," Sarah whispered. Aaron wasn't sure if she was talking about him, or just venting. "So, whatta we do now?"

"We hope Danny wakes up," Aaron answered.

"Will your people come after you?" Sarah asked Reeglar.

"That is what we believe might happen," Reeglar worried. "We do not know what retaliation to expect."

"Most certainly, the Guardians shall follow," Azewrath offered. "I have at least Seen that. Pikkar shall bring the Telepath's as well." He nodded to Reeglar. "Your Father is coming."

"Of course." She sighed.

"More people like you?" Sarah referred to Reeglar's powers.

"Yes," Reeglar said.

"We're so screwed!" Sarah stated.

Ilmar listened with half an ear, looking over every now and again, but never for too long. Still holding Danny's hand in both of hers, she caught his fingers move. "Aaron!" she called. "I think he is coming around." They gathered at the exam table, as Danny took a deep breath, he moaned, turning his head a few inches. "Oh, my Goddess!" Ilmar cried, elated, squeezing his hand. "Danny!"

"Hmmm..." Danny spoke, trying to focus on everyone. He smacked his lips pantomiming a dry mouth. "Drink..." He managed.

Aaron yelled to Sarah. "Get Danny something to drink!"

Danny grabbed Aaron's arm to get his attention. "Make it a beer..." Was all Danny managed to whisper.

Aaron laughed hard. "Glad you're back among the living," he said, shaking his head.

Sarah came back with a glass in her hand, placing it up to Danny's lips. "It's just water, honey," Sarah told him. "Drink it slowly."

Danny took a few sips and then dropped his head back down on the table. "Illy?"

"I am here, my love." Ilmar kissed the hand she still held in hers, leaning closer so he could see her. "I thought I might have lost you." Ilmar motioned to Aaron. "You have a very resourceful friend." Then to Aaron, she continued. "I will be forever in your debt."

"Wow!" Aaron bragged. "I have a Princess on my side."

"I am no longer a Princess," Ilmar informed him.

"Then what are you?" Aaron asked.

"Homeless," Azewrath enlightened them.

"That's right!" Danny shouted. "We've got to get ready for the attacking Akkadian force that's coming!" He tried to sit up.

"Oh, no!" Aaron ordered, pushing Danny back down against the table. "You can't move for at least a half hour. You gotta promise me, buddy; if I let go of you, you'll lay there like a good boy."

"What am I?" Danny asked. "A child?"

"Well," Sarah interrupted. "Survey says..." She swung her arms pretending she was Richard Dawson from Family Feud.

"Ha, ha, Sarah." Danny's comeback fell short. "Trouble is coming, Aaron. I need everyone to stay at your house."

"My house?" Aaron questioned, bewildered. "Why my house?"

" 'Cuz there are three bedrooms, and it's out-of-the-way," Danny reminded him.

"Yeah, all right." Aaron gave in. "I guess I can always stay with Sarah, right?" He checked with her.

"Don't you always?" she answered him back with the question.

"All a Telepath has to do is pick up a stray thought, and they shall find us," Azewrath schooled them.

"No one knows you're here but us," Sarah retorted.

"You shall see!" Azewrath warned.

"My father is an angry man," Ilmar disclosed. "We do things his way, or else." Then she smiled. "Unless my Mother stops him."

"She shall not be able to stop him this time," Reeglar gasped. "It is the law, and we have broken it. If she did not agree with him, all the great Houses would turn against her."

"Which law was that?" Danny asked, not expecting an answer. "The law of falling in love?"

"You are a human." Azewrath sounded as if he were addressing an inferior person.

"We both have the same ancestors; I don't see the problem." Danny didn't.

"Do you not?" Azewrath asked. "We have about as much in common between us now, as you have with your chimpanzee primates."

"Hey!" Aaron interjected. "I've seen some damn smart chimps!"

"You're not helping, Aaron," Sarah offered, patting him on the arm.

"What could they actually do to us up here to get you to go back?" Aaron asked.

"The most likely scenario is they shall kill a few thousand of you humans until your people give in, find us, and turn us over to them," Azewrath informed them.

"Are you serious?!" Aaron's words weren't a question.

"We have police forces and armies!" Sarah shouted. "We won't just roll over because you're more powerful."

"No, you will not," Reeglar agreed. "It shall be ugly and bloody."

"All this, over a nasty little love triangle, or rectangle," Aaron contemplated.

"Or Pentagon!" Sarah added. "Yeah, hon, I haven't forgotten what I remembered."

"Do not blame him, Sarah," Reeglar begged. "It was not his choice, but mine."

"Whatever," Sarah defended herself. "It doesn't matter or change the facts. He did what he did."

Reeglar smiled and waved her hand. Out of nowhere, Sarah grabbed Aaron and kissed him with everything she had.

Surprised, Aaron went with it. *Kissing is better than arguing.*

When Sarah realized what she was doing, she pushed him away. "What the hell?"

"Oh?" Reeglar began coyly. "Are you saying you did not wish to kiss Aaron at this moment in time?"

"Well, it definitely wasn't my idea!" Sarah spat. "I'm still mad at him. Why would I... kiss... him...?" She spoke slowly, as the ramifications of her actions washed over her.

"Now, do you understand?" Reeglar made her point.

Sarah sighed, glancing over at Aaron. He seemed guilty, yet innocent at the same time. "I guess I owe you an apology."

Reeglar explained further. "I can make someone do anything. And then, make them forget they did it."

"Now, picture about twenty more Telepaths coming to the surface, and the mayhem they could create," Azewrath threatened.

"Well," Aaron asked, "what can we do about it?"

"I am not sure we can do anything." Ilmar worried.

"This is just speculation, right?" Sarah asked. "You don't know for sure that they're coming."

"Quite the contrary," Azewrath informed her. "They ARE coming. I have Seen it."

Reeglar explained Azewrath's Abilities. "Azewrath can See into the future. He is very rarely wrong."

"I have never been wrong," Azewrath corrected her.

"Look," Danny said trying to sit up again, "I really just want to go home. Can we do that now?"

Aaron checked his watch. "Well, yeah, but we'll move you slowly, okay?"

Azewrath helped Aaron take Danny down from the exam table. They walked from the labs through Atlantis into the parking lot until they got back into Sarah's SUV.

By the time the Ford arrived at Aaron's house, it was almost four in the morning. "You can handle this from here, right?" Aaron asked Danny. "Both Sarah and I have to be at work at 7:00, and that's only three hours away!"

"Sorry, bro," Danny apologized, as the girls helped Azewrath out of the truck's tailgate. "Thanks for not letting me die."

"You're not allowed to die," Aaron teased him. "Not on my watch!" Sarah pulled out of the driveway, leaving them at the front of the house in the dark.

Danny made it to the door. Aaron's house was a welcoming place on the water on Rampasture Road. With a meticulously manicured lawn, expensive landscaping, and more room than one man needed, it was in pristine condition. Aaron didn't spend a lot of time there in the summer. Instead, he stayed over at Sarah's. The drawback to his house was the many other houses on his block, built close together, allowing neighbors to glean too much information on each other.

The second problem it proposed was its proximity to the apartment complex next door. Some condo owners rented out their place to summer tourists, which created quite a bit of noise. As Danny approached the house, the stars were bright as the moon slipped closer to the horizon. Surprised by the quiet, Danny accepted it gladly; he could do without the drama. He unlocked the front door and reached in, turning on the lights.

"Go on in," Danny told the Akkadians. He stepped inside as

well and gave a small tour. "This is the kitchen," he said, motioning with his arm.

"What is the room's purpose? Storage?" Azewrath asked.

"We make food here and cook it on the stove," Danny explained. "Breakfast, lunch and dinner."

"You cook for yourself, in your quarters?" Azewrath turned to Reeglar. "I thought the diner was where the humans ate?"

"They eat everywhere," Reeglar corrected him.

"We're an extremely food motivated species," Danny said, adding more. "Oh, and sex motivated, too!" Without warning, Danny grew weak in the knees and braced himself on the countertop. After taking a few deep breaths, he regained his equilibrium.

Ilmar quickly went to his side. "No more exertions tonight! Let us find our bedchambers."

"Okay," Danny agreed. "I give up. We'll do the grand tour in the morning." He put his arm around Ilmar and let her support his weight. He showed Reeglar and Azewrath the first guest bedroom. "This is where you guys can sleep." He pointed across the hall. "That's where the bathroom is. See you guys in the AM. Good night."

"Danny, thank you," Azewrath called after him. "I would think we have at least 4 to 24 of your hours before we have company."

"Well, I'm hoping for the latter."

Danny shuffled away with Ilmar to their room. He turned on the lights, closed the door behind him, and pulled down the covers on the queen bed. He glanced down at his trousers. Their state was atrocious – dirty, bloody and ripped.

"These are trash."

"I agree."

He untied them and slid them off, jumping into bed, naked. "I'll shower in the morning," he explained to Ilmar. She undid what was left of her robes, dropping them to the floor as well.

She is so beautiful when she's naked. Danny thought, smiling. "We do need new clothes for tomorrow." Danny immediately reached for her when she climbed into bed next to him, but she smacked his hand away.

"No funny business, tonight," Ilmar scolded him. "But, I need you to hold me instead, all right?" She snuggled next to him and lay her head on his chest, throwing an arm over him. He sighed, pulling her close.

I'm tired, he thought. "Okay, but if I feel better in the morning, you're in big trouble." Ilmar giggled and kissed his cheek.

***

The start of the next day had all pertinent Akkadians mobilizing. Prince Pikkar's first agenda was to search his daughter's room. He stood in her quarters with the Guardians. They systematically searched all drawers. With clothes thrown everywhere, the Guardians discarded anything that was normal to their Akkadian world and attire.

Carelessly stepping on all of Ilmar's property, they rummaged through her possessions, ruining them in their wake of destruction. They found her human clothes with another pair of human pants that could only belong to a male. The Guardian held them up to show the Prince.

Pikkar snatched the pants out of the Guardian's hand and roared a growl. "Arggghhhh!"

Pikkar stormed out of the room, heading down to Azewrath's apartment. He was not pleased when he tried the door and found it locked. *Really?* He thought angrily.

Pikkar put his hand on the door, instantly commanding his Ability. His hand glowed white and faded swiftly, cutting all the electricity to the locking mechanism. The door sprang open, but he waited. When the Guardians finally caught up with him, he went inside.

"Search this place from top to bottom!" Pikkar commanded.

The Guardians tore Azewrath's place apart, enjoying the carnage they created. They set about turning the room inside out, laughing, tossing, and breaking objects that couldn't possibly be their objectives.

Finally, a Guardian called from Azewrath bedchambers. "My Prince!"

Alerted by the call, Pikkar went to investigate. A soldier came out holding a pair of footwear, most definitely human. "Conspirators!" Pikkar fumed.

Grabbing the shoes, he tucked them under his arm along with the pair of jeans he found. Angrily, he strode from Azewrath's quarters, making his way through the corridor to the Queens chambers. The Guardians knew better than to follow him inside.

Pikkar assaulted his front entryway, bursting it open as the door swung in wildly from the force of the Prince's fist. He found his wife sitting in their drawing room. Pikkar approached her, throwing the clothing on the floor at her feet. She spared him a glance but held her tongue, which fed his anger.

"Do you not see this?" Pikkar challenged.

"I see it," Alkara replied, still disinterested.

"These are the clothes that belong to our daughter's human lover!" he screamed, kicking the clothes on the floor for good measure. "Do you not see this is the proof that he was here. Right under our noses?" Pikkar paced the floor. "I do not understand how you can be so apathetic about this."

"And I do not understand why you let things eat away at you inside," Alkara retorted, rising. "Do you not remember love? How our hearts burned as the Abyss of Fire?" She took him by his hands, using her Ability to observe deep inside him. Searching.

"Yes," Pikkar answered. "I remember love. I also remember youthful exuberance and stupidity. All nonsense in the scheme of life." He pulled his hands away and continued to pace.

Distraught by her discovery, Alkara wondered at Pikkar's internal state. She had held him and regarded her husband's eyes for his Empathy, finding none. "What has happened to you, Pikkar? I just looked for the man I fell in love with and found him gone."

"The man you fell in love with was young and ambitious. All I wanted was to be your husband."

"And so you have been," Alkara added. "I could not have been so wrong about you, inside."

"No, you could not have been so fooled," he said. Pikkar scrutinized Alkara through slitted eyes. "Yet perhaps if I hid some part of myself away..." He stopped talking, letting his words sink in. "Your Mother was a resourceful woman."

He told her everything. After notifying her of an elaborate plan to wed him to the Queen to be, he pushed the knife deep into her heart. His controlled group of conspirators worked for years to get to that point; and now that he was right where he needed to be.

"I do not understand, now, Pikkar?"

"Do you not?" he said, sarcastically, laughing at her. When he turned to face her, it was if a stranger stood before her. "I am not satisfied to just rule Akkadia, my dear. I have never been. We are so much more powerful than the surface dwellers. I plan to take advantage of this fact. This present situation we have inadvertently created is the catalyst. Years of planning come to fruition."

"Do not be a fool!" Alkara warned him. "We have lived in peace with the humans for many millennia."

"We have lived in peace, only because we have lived in secret. And it has gone on for far too long, in my opinion," Pikkar boasted. "The Guardians and I shall sit idle no longer."

"And your hope is to accomplish, what? To be King of the world?" Alkara asked. The tone of her voice rose, bordering on hysteria. "Do you have any idea how *insane* that sounds?"

"To you, perhaps," he spat. "But I command many Akkadians who have backed me, and now is *our* time."

"Pikkar, please..." Alkara begged again. "How can you devalue our entire twenty-five plantings together?" She touched his arm. "Have I meant nothing to you?"

"Quite the contrary, you have meant *everything*. An end to a means," Pikkar told her. "I would not be where I am today if not for you." He walked away from her toward the front door. "But now, you are unnecessary. It is..." He hesitated. "Nothing personal."

Pikkar walked out and Drakar, the Second Seer, waited for him with some supporters.

"Have our Telepath's seal the Queen's chambers," Pikkar ordered.

"As you wish." Drakar bowed.

The Prince motioned with a wave to his Guardians, collecting them to his side as he made his way through the corridors to ready his army.

Drakar instructed the Telepaths to create a barrier around the Queen's quarters. A faint blue hue, the only indication of the force field surrounding the Royal residence. The Queen stood in her doorway and watched the twinkling of the blue energy. Alkara could no longer get out. She was a prisoner of her husband, locked in.

***

Arriving at the Healing Ward, Chancellor Torg checked on the progress of Gelfromm's mental state. He hoped to find some answers as to Reeglar's participation in her treasonous act. The Historian regained consciousness early that morning. Now, Torg stood with Mage' Rom next to the recovery bed.

The Mage' addressed Gelfromm. "We are so glad to see you have awakened from your sleep, young Historian."

"You mean a forced Telepathic coma!" Gelfromm growled harshly, glaring directly at Torg.

"I am here to try to make up for my daughter's misdeed," the Chancellor informed Gelfromm. "And help your recovery in the process."

"Thank you, no!" Gelfromm insisted. "I am sure you can understand how utterly distasteful that sounds, considering it was a Telepath who put me here in the first place."

"A most unfortunate set of circumstances," Torg agreed. "Although, I still believe I can help."

"And I disagree," Gelfromm refused again. "Mage', explain to the Chancellor that it would do more harm than good if you please."

Rom sided with the Historian. "Torg, it is my opinion that any more contact with a Telepathic inspection would be detrimental to Gelfromm's state of being."

"I need to understand what happened," Torg explained.

"I can tell you what happened," Gelfromm said. "I understand it is a strange concept for you to take someone at their word, but I did not lose my memories; they just got scrambled. A nasty side effect of your people's vile intrusions, I might add."

Rom excused himself. "I need to attend to others for just a few moments. If you both shall excuse me, I should like to leave the room with the knowledge that neither of you shall do each other harm."

"Do not leave me alone with him, Mage'," Gelfromm pleaded. "I do not trust him."

Rom glanced at Torg. "I trust him, Gelfromm." The Mage' patted the boy's shoulder. "You shall be fine, just tell the truth." The Mage' left the room.

Rom walked quickly into the next room, afraid his thoughts and knowledge would seep out and find their way into Torg's mind. *I do not wish to be under the probing mind tendrils of the Chancellor next,* Rom thought, immediately busying his mind on his task.

Torg grilled Gelfromm. "Why do you think Reeglar was with the human?"

"Reeglar was not with the human, Chancellor," Gelfromm informed him. "She was with Azewrath."

"I do not understand." Torg seemed perplexed. "Ilmartutar is betrothed to Azewrath. He and my daughter have no history."

"Yes, well, they are making some now," Gelfromm insisted. "Ilmar, it seemed, had chosen another."

"The *human?*" Torg asked incredulously.

"Yes, again." The Historian hesitated, wanting to add more. "They planned to get the Crystal Dragon, find the Stairway to Niamuck and bring the human home."

"Is there more?" Torg queried. "You appear to be contemplating something."

"I might have gleaned some other information," Gelfromm offered. "I do not know how important it might be to you." Gelfromm appeared smug.

"Gelfromm," Torg began, impatiently, his voice low and menacing, "I am only capable of so much tolerance." He leaned closer to the Historian. "It would be in your best interests to tell me everything you know!"

Gelfromm's eyes went wide, but Mage' Rom, was close enough to overhear their conversation. He came back into the room just in time. "My Lord, Chancellor," Rom interrupted. "May I have a word?"

Torg growled at the Mage'. "Not now, Rom!"

"Torg," Rom admitted," I have better, more informed information, then any Gelfromm could give you."

"And why have you not told this to me before?" Torg asked.

"I swore I would not," the Mage' answered, lowering his eyes.

Torg came around Gelfromm's bed and approached the Mage' menacingly. "I would hear this information, now Rom. Or, I shall reach in and drag it out of you."

"You may," Rom gave Torg permission. The Chancellor placed his fingers on Rom's temples.

Torg proceeded to learn the truth about his daughter and Azewrath. His face went through many changes as he accepted the information from Rom. At first, surprise, which changed to anger; and then his face softened. A smile reached his lips. Torg released Mage' Rom, nodded to the man and walked out without saying a word.

"Was that good or bad?" Gelfromm asked.

"I believe it might be a good thing," Rom inferred.

"So, does he now know?" the Historian inquired.

"Yes," Rom replied. "The Chancellor knows everything, now."

"Humm..." Gelfromm disagreed. "Even I do not know everything, and I have many more plantings of memories to choose from."

***

The morning Sun touched Danny's face, warming him. He stirred, and tried to slide out from under Ilmartutar without waking her. He stumbled his way to the bathroom to take that very demanding morning pee. He stretched as he relieved himself, much stronger than the night before.

After he had finished, Danny washed his hands and splashed water on his face. He took his finger and ran it across his teeth. With a yawn, he rubbed his hands together, thinking about Ilmar laying naked in bed. His manliness grew in the preparation of his desires.

I'm going to give her what she needs this morning. Okay, maybe I need it, Danny thought, laughing to himself, as he opened the bathroom door. He sported a hard erection when he came face-to-face with Azewrath.

"Hum... Hello." Azewrath laughed. "I am afraid I am not as excited to see you."

"Cute!" Danny responded. "I didn't plan on using this on you, either." He walked out of the bathroom as Azewrath walked in.

"Thank the Goddess..." Azewrath whispered, shutting the door.

Danny tried not to lose his happy morning rod. *Come on, buddy.* He gave himself a pep talk. *Don't fail me now.*

When he returned to his room, Ilmar's sleeping form gave him the motivation he needed, his body gladly responded. Danny crawled across the bed slowly, pulling the covers off her. He gathered the folds into his fingers as he accumulated handfuls of the blanket, exposing her creamy white flesh to his eyes.

She had rolled over after he stepped out, so her back was to him, and he marveled at the way the sensuous curve of her hips sloped downward to her waist. The dimples above her bottom and the muscles running up either side of her spine spoke volumes about her ability to make love to him. The rounded moon-shaped mound of her breast peeked out from under her arm. He moved to the nape of her neck and kissed her there.

She sighed and moaned at the same time. "Hi," she whispered as she woke, rolling over to face Danny.

Danny kissed her shoulder before moving down to her breasts. Running his fingers around one, he wrapped his lips around the other. Ilmar stretched her neck backward and let out a soft sigh. Arching her back, she grabbed his head in her hands, helping to guide his hungry mouth. He slid his tongue down further, kissing her mound and took a long taste before working his way back up to kiss her lips.

Ilmar opened to him, and he entered her smoothly, deeply, with the fervor of sexual intensity. "Oh?" Ilmar managed to get out. "Someone has gotten his strength back."

She attacked him with the same emotional lust as he thrust into her. She tightened around his shaft, holding onto him for dear life. Their bodies met and joined over and over again. The bed scraped against the floor as it moved from their extracurricular exertions.

Our love is fantastic! Danny thought as he moved inside her. *She's fantastic! We're fantastic!* He continued his lovemaking, giving Ilmar his full attention.

***

Reeglar woke after Azewrath left, assaulted by sensory overload. Naked, with her soiled robes discarded by the foot of the bed just a few hours before, excitement welled inside her.

Oh, no! She thought. *Danny and Ilmar are having sex.* She tried to block them out, but their desire for each other grew too strong.

Her body swiftly responded to their intimacy, her hands taking on an appetite of their own. She touched herself, exploring the warmth of her body. She moved her fingers over her neckline to her collarbone, sliding them down to her breasts. Cupping each full bosom in her palms, she rolled her nipples between her index fingers and thumbs. As she lowered her hands further down, she parted her thighs, and her fingers found her wet moistness. Lost to the sensation, Reeglar ran her tongue across her lips and moaned.

When Azewrath left the bathroom, Danny and Ilmar were in the throes of intense passion. *Does this man ever tire?* He thought, entering his room. Upon encountering Reeglar's odd behavior, he shook his head. She apparently enjoyed herself, by herself.

"Ah!" he said out loud, realizing what happened to her. "May I join, or are you doing all right by yourself?" he asked, getting back into bed. Azewrath soon had his answer.

"Come here!" She reached out and pulled him down on top of her. Her probing tongue found his mouth as she locked her lips on his.

He raised himself up, trying to catch his breath. "You do know your current frame of mind is artificial."

"I do not care," Reeglar breathed heavily. "Take me into your arms and finish what they started."

"So romantic!" Azewrath complained. He sighed but lowered himself to her. He entered her, pushing her up against the pillows. She reached around his back and drew him close as he proceeded to do to her what she asked of him.

***

After Danny had rolled off of Ilmar, he left for the master bedroom and rummaged through Aaron's closet. He found two pairs of old jeans; one must have been too short for Aaron. Danny put them on, pulled them up and buttoned the fly. Not that starting his day "commando" was a bad idea, he had no other choice. Next, he rifled through Aaron's drawers and found a clean white wife-beater.

Yes. Score! Danny thought, slipping into it. *Now, I need a shirt for Rath.* He found one of Aaron's preppy shirts. *This shirt will work. Humm... What to do about the girls?* He went back to the guestroom and found Ilmar sitting up in bed.

She smiled, astonished. "Oh, I see how this shall be. You have clothes, yet I lay naked."

"Hopefully, *hopefully*, I'll find something for you, too." Danny opened the closet doors. He wondered if some of Sarah's clothes were still hanging there. "BINGO!" Danny yelled.

"Bing-go?" Ilmar questioned.

"Clothes!" he explained to her.

"Ooooooooh!" She sang and jumped out of bed, running to the closet. "Let me see!" He laughed at her excitement. Ilmar grabbed a beautiful blue dress. Holding it up to herself, she spun around. "It is just wonderful!"

"Well? Put it on." Danny encouraged her.

She did. Ilmar pulled it over her head and straightened it out, holding the hemline swinging from side to side. "How do I look?"

"Like a vision," Danny complimented her. "Like a Victoria's Secret model."

"Victoria who?"

"Never mind," Danny said. "Wanna get something for Reeglar and bring these to Rath? I'll go whip up some breakfast." He passed her the clothes he held before heading to the kitchen.

"Sounds good. I am starving!" she yelled to his back. She pulled a dress off the hanger and followed him out. Ilmar knocked on the door where Reeglar and Azewrath rested. "It is Ilmar," she called through the door. "I have clothing."

Reeglar opened the door and peeked her head out, smiling. "Clothes? I need clothes."

Ilmar held the lump of linens out for Reeglar to take. "Danny

is making breakfast. Get dressed and meet us in the kitchen."
Ilmar left to join Danny.

She sat down at the table to watch his preparation. "What are
you making?"

"A real delicacy," he said. "Frozen waffles." Danny lowered
them into the toaster.

Ilmar watched as he pulled all kinds of things out of the
refrigerator. A long yellow stick on a tray, a bottle filled with a
dark brown syrupy liquid, and a package of small, round blue
things.

He placed the toasted waffles on plates, buttered them and
added blueberries. He finished by pouring on the syrup. He took
another four waffles and sent them down into the toaster.

When Reeglar and Azewrath came in, they sat at the table
with Ilmar. Danny noticed Reeglar was in a slimming coral
sundress, and Azewrath looked uncomfortable in a pair of jeans
that fit him poorly. He pulled at the crotch over and over again,
unable to find a comfortable seated position.

Danny suppressed a chuckle when they entered. "My, don't we
all look sharp!"

"I hate these clothes," Azewrath complained.

"You could always walk around naked," Danny told him. "I
won't be offended."

"Not very functional," Azewrath assured him.

"Yet, fun!" Reeglar added, giggling.

"Soup's on," Danny called, putting the food down in front of
them.

"I thought you made waffles?" Ilmar questioned him.

Danny laughed. "We are. That was just an expression. Oh,
never mind." He sat next to Ilmar and picked up his fork. They
all stared at him. "What? It's not poison. Look." He stabbed the
waffle and popped it into his mouth, chewing. "Ummm." He
swallowed it. "See? It tastes great. Try it."

They raised their utensils and tried the meal. A round of nods
sent the message the Akkadians enjoyed their food. Silver
utensils clanged against Correl plates. It was a long time since
their last meal, and everyone forgot just how hungry they were.

"I guess I better call my brother," Danny said, through
forkfuls of breakfast. "Let him know I'm okay."

"He did not know where you were?" Ilmar asked.

"How could I tell him what I was doing or where I was going?" Danny explained. "Reeglar showed up, and it was a 'now or never' sort of thing." He put his hand on top of hers, squeezing it. "I just couldn't be without you. I know… Crazy, right?"

Ilmar smiled at him. "Sweet," she cooed.

Reeglar laughed, happily. "This is really good, Danny." She held her fork up with a piece of waffle and blueberry. "What is it again?"

"Frozen waffles," Danny told her.

"Frozen waffles…" Reeglar repeated like it was a gourmet meal she needed to remember.

"So good," Ilmar agreed with her mouth full.

"Hey, this ain't nothing," Danny bragged. "Wait till you taste what I can do on a grill."

Azewrath dropped his fork, which made a loud clanking sound on the plate. As they turned toward him, they noticed he wasn't moving. He stared straight ahead, oblivious to his surroundings.

Reeglar sighed. "He is Seeing something."

"Rath!" Danny called, waving his hand in front of Azewrath face. "He really checks out, huh?"

Suddenly, life came back to Azewrath's eyes. "We have got to mobilize. NOW!"

"What? In the middle of breakfast? Why?"

"In two of your hours, perhaps… The landscape as you know it – will change."

"Two hours?" Danny checked the kitchen wall clock. It read 9:12 AM. *Oh, boy!* He thought.

"Would it be the Telepaths?" Reeglar wondered.

Azewrath nodded as he rose to his feet swiftly. "We must go somewhere safe."

"Go somewhere? Where?" Danny couldn't stop asking questions.

"Are we talking earthquakes?" Ilmar inquired.

Again, Azewrath nodded. "We – need – to – go!" He stressed every single word.

"Earthquakes?" By this time, Danny's mind soared. He brought his right hand to his temples, rubbing them; his fingers on the left temple and thumb on the right. "Okay, look. My car is still in the woods, so we've got no ride. Get it? Okay – Okay," he thought out loud. "We need a ride – and food – and supplies – I got it!"

He picked up Aaron's house phone and dialed. As he waited, he tapped his toe in agitation. "Yes, hi. I need a taxi at 48A Rampasture Road. We'll need to make a few stops. How long? Okay, thanks." Danny hung up. "I've got a plan," he told the Akkadians as he dialed another number. Danny waited impatiently for the song to end and hoped Aaron would pick up.

He did. "Hello?" Aaron asked tentatively. "It's not often my own house calls me."

"It's me, bro," Danny indicated. "This shit never ends, and we're right in the middle of it. Get Sarah from wherever she is, and both of you meet me at the hanger in less than two hours."

"What?" Aaron questioned. "Are you serious?"

"Have I lied to you about any of this so far? Do you need more proof that things are spiraling downward fast?"

"Okay, okay!" Aaron promised. "We'll be there. I don't know how the hell I'll ever be able to do this? Damn! I'm never going to get any work done..." Danny heard him complaining as he hung up the phone.

A loud beep came from outside, prompting Danny to pull back the window shade. "The taxi's here. Let's go."

"Where are we going?" Ilmar asked.

"To pick up my car, then, to the supermarket," Danny answered. Reeglar and Azewrath seemed confused.

"Supermarket," Ilmar explained to them. "It's a place to buy food and other things you might need. Like our Commonwealth shops."

"Oh." Reeglar nodded, understanding.

They left the house and piled into the taxi as Danny spoke to the driver. "We need to go to Bellows Pond Road. By the power lines?"

"You got it," the driver said. Turning the cab around, he drove off.

When they arrived at the power lines, Danny jumped out of the taxi. He asked the driver to wait while he ran off into the woods. An awkward few moments of silence passed until the excessively loud engine of Danny's Camaro warned of the car's approach. It came speeding from the parkland; the back tires spraying sand and pebbles everywhere. He waved for the taxi to follow as he raced the vintage sports car down the road.

"Oh, jeeze!" the driver said and quickly threw the cab into reverse, spinning the taxi around to catch up. "Hold on!" he yelled to his Akkadian passengers.

"Oh, no! Not again!" Azewrath moaned as the car turned sharply.

Their next destination – Stop & Shop. Again, Danny asked the driver to wait. Grabbing a shopping cart, he gave it to Azewrath, and then went back for another. They entered the supermarket hitting the water and canned food aisles. By the time they got to the checkout, they had twelve 2.5 gallon containers of water, and another full cart of quick, flip-top cans of cooked foods.

Five hundred dollars on the credit card later, with both cars loaded, they headed out to Danny's. As they pulled up the driveway toward the house, Patrick came out to meet them. Danny had the driver swipe the card again while the others unloaded the supplies.

Oh, well. It's only money, he thought. "Thanks, guy," Danny said to the taxi driver. He slammed the door and tapped the window opening. He shot the driver a goodbye with his thumb and index finger, gunslinger style.

"DANNY!" Patrick yelled. "What the *hell?!* And I don't just mean all this." He motioned with his arms. "And all these people." Patrick walked right up to his brother. "What are you thinking, leaving me and the business like that?"

"Pat, I know you're pissed," Danny began, "and you have every right to be." While he spoke, Danny carried groceries and water to the hanger.

"Hey!" Patrick called after him. "We're not done, here!" He followed Danny.

Danny put down the water and the bags. "I'm gonna tell you something, and you've got to believe me."

"Okay," Pat agreed, crossing his arms in front of his chest, waiting.

Danny sighed. "The east end of Long Island is going to get hit by a powerful earthquake, in about..." He checked his watch; it was 10:35 AM. He continued. "About twenty-five minutes, give or take. We need to be up in the air if we want to survive it."

Pat looked at him, tilting his head and gave a short disbelieving laugh. "What, Danny? Do I look *stupid* to you?"

"I give up!" Danny threw his hands up in the air and returned for more supplies. The Akkadians helped to load, so Danny met Ilmar halfway. He stopped for a brief second, kissing her cheek. "Thanks, hon!"

Patrick followed Danny back to the car. "You're not taking the planes."

"Oh, yes I *am*," Danny corrected him. "Aaron and Sarah will be here any second. We're taking both Cessnas. If you're smart, you'd call Trish right now, and get her to safety in the Dova." Danny picked up more bags and headed back to the planes.

"So," Pat turned to follow his brother again. "I should believe you, even though we have no histories of earthquakes out here?"

"If you do not believe him, then believe us," Azewrath interrupted.

"Who *are* you people?" Patrick asked.

"Reeglar!" Danny called to her. "I think my brother needs a refresher course."

Reeglar joined them and reached for Patrick's temple. Put off, Pat stepped back, away from her, but right into Azewrath's waiting hands. "Hey!" Pat struggled. "What's going on?"

"I am not going to hurt you," Reeglar told him, placing her fingers on his temple.

Reeglar gazed deeply into Patrick's ice blue eyes. "Your thoughts convert into speech, which is a two-dimensional assessment of your visual world and imagination. I can put the 'actual' occurrence directly into your cerebrum, giving you the actual memory." Within seconds, Patrick stopped fighting. She took her hand away, and Azewrath let him go.

"Oh, shit!" Pat swore, remembering everything "I've got to call Trish." Pat ran back into the house.

Danny chuckled. "I thought so…" he said out loud to Patrick's receding back. He divvied up the supplies and finished loading the planes. "Reeglar!" Danny called her to get her attention again. "You're going to have to fly the Cutlass. When Pat has a second, read his mind to find out how to fly her. He's a better pilot than I am. You and Rath can take it." She nodded to him.

"Will I be with you?" Ilmar asked him.

"Of course," Danny reassured her. "I wouldn't have it any other way. Aaron and Sarah will be with us, too."

As the words left his mouth, Aaron's truck came down the driveway. "Speaking of the devil."

"There is no devil," Ilmar told him, as a matter of fact.

"You would know! Whatever – I don't want to get into that now." He waved her off.

Aaron pulled up, and Danny ran to the driver side. "Hey, bro, just to be on the safe side, maybe we should park the cars away from the house, hangar, and the trees."

"Great idea," Aaron agreed. "I'll head to the runway, but not on the runway." Danny gave Aaron the thumbs up, as Patrick came out of the house carrying a small suitcase.

"What's in the bag?" Danny inquired.

"Toiletries! Did you load the Dova?" Pat asked.

"Yeah." Danny nodded. "No worries. Trish on her way?"

"Finally!" Patrick replied. "I had to pull the ol' 'have I lied to you yet?' card."

"As long as it works, bro." Danny patted his brother's shoulder. "Oh, to learn how to fly the Cutlass, Reeglar needs to get inside your mind again, alright?"

"Wow! She can do that?"

"Yep."

"What about your girlfriend?" Patrick elbowed Danny in the ribs, smiling. "What can she do?"

Danny smiled back. "Oh, besides her obvious charms?" Danny shot his gaze back at Ilmar. "She has an omniscient power. I hope you never need her to use it on you." Confused, Patrick shrugged, but Danny changed the subject. "Aaron moved his truck to the runway. Maybe you should park the Acura there as well."

"Do you think we're gonna lose the house?"

"Huh, I don't know what to think." Danny sighed. He brought his fingers to his forehead and rubbed it back and forth. "I've seen what these people can do. And we've pissed some of 'em off." He motioned Pat to follow him to the hanger. "Are the planes fueled up?"

"All, but the Dova," Pat answered. "Wanna help me move her

over to the pump?"

"Sure thing." Danny went to the back of the ultralight, picking up the tail section. Pat took the right wing, and they pushed together. Azewrath noticed their struggle and slid in behind the other wing, helping. They quickly moved the plane out of the hanger around the other side of the building to the fuel pump where Patrick began fueling the Skylark.

"I'll go move the cars," Danny told Pat, who threw him the Acura keys.

"Don't scratch it!" Pat warned him.

"I don't think you'll be able to tell... afterward." Danny jumped into the Acura and parked it by Aaron's Ram at the edge of the runway; then he ran back for the Camaro.

"You're moving your car?" Aaron asked, laughing. "Is it really worth it?"

"Hey! She's a classic!" Danny sulked, getting into his car.

He started the engine; its very loud roaring, screaming engine practically deafened everyone. He gunned the gas and burned rubber, driving around the hanger. He came back and joined everyone by the planes. When Trish showed up, Pat introduced her around, and Reeglar read Patrick's mind.

"Okay, what's the plan?" Aaron asked Danny.

"Do I look like I have a plan?" Danny answered him with another question.

"Well, sort of," Aaron affirmed.

Incredulous, Sarah spoke up. "You're going to listen to a plan Danny's come up with?"

"He knows what's going on," Aaron told her. "So, yeah, Sarah. Unless you got a better idea?"

"No," she added. "But I wouldn't follow Danny around the corner. No offense." She opened her hands, shrugging at Danny, who sneered.

"He's different," Aaron noticed. "Can't you tell?" No one acknowledged his statement. "I don't know if it was the dragotte's venomous poison, but he knew about the vipers I had in Atlantis. What does that mean? *Explain* it!"

"I don't know what that means, either," Danny hurried. "But if anyone cares, it's 11:00 AM."

XX

Surrender To Carnage

General Nutrion coordinated the ascent of his troops at the Reaction Lift as they readied to enter the mobile room. Guardian troops lined the corridors as far as the eye could see. A smaller group of Telepaths and Igniters were there as well, waiting for their turn to go to the surface.

Nutrion had sent the first full Lift up when Prince Pikkar arrived. He noticed the prince had donned full battle armor. Although, its makeup more for show and ceremony than defense.

"General," Pikkar addressed the soldier. "How goes the preparations for the assault?"

"The first group of Guardians has gone to the surface," the General informed him. "The rest shall join them within three more trips. There shall be a final complement of sixty Guardians, four Igniters with their air Chariots and Riders, plus twenty of our top Telepaths."

"Did Chancellor Torg pick them?" Pikkar asked.

"No, my Prince," Nutrion answered. "His Second did."

"Hum. Have you seen Torg?" Pikkar asked again. "Do you know if he shall, at least, be joining us?"

"I shall indeed." Came Torg's thought projection into both of their minds.

Pikkar jumped. "THAT is always unsettling!" The Prince stressed when Torg reached them. "I have twenty of your Telepaths who have volunteered to fight for the cause."

Torg answered unemotionally, yet serious. "And, what cause is that?"

"The safety of Akkadia," Nutrion insisted.

"I doubt that a handful of children could wreak as much havoc as you have prepared for," Torg expressed.

"Torg..."

Torg's name entered his mind from far away. Momentarily distracted, he attempted to reach out to the caller. *"Who is this? I can not feel your essence?"* Torg's thought conversation was interrupted by Pikkar.

"Watch your tongue, Chancellor!" Pikkar glared at Torg through slitted eyes. "I would hate to have you labeled a traitor to the realm, and have you confined to your quarters."

"My Prince." Torg bowed in subservience. "I did not mean to give you reason to question my loyalty."

"Torg...!"

The call came stronger this time.

"Help!"

Torg continued to ease Pikkar's bad temper. "I am behind the ruling of the Monarchy. Please accept my humblest apologies."

The pleading Torg experienced grew in intensity; more desperate. As she tried to contact his mind, he realized the thought pattern belonged to Alkara. He could never mistake her thought touch and sensed she was in trouble, but it had been a long time since she spoke to him in this fashion. By the manner in which Pikkar acted, he was up to no good.

I will deal with this, next.

"Indeed!" Pikkar granted. "Well, I accept your offer of fealty." He waved Torg off in dismissal and turned to Nutrion, stepping into the Lift. "I shall ride up now, General. You stay and organize the soldiers into groups, and then come up yourself on the last trip."

"Thank you, my Lord, Prince," Nutrion replied, watching the doors close on Pikkar. The alarm to the Lift blared.

"General?" Torg asked. "Can you send someone for me when the last Lift is ready to ascend? I have something I need to attend to, quickly." Nutrion nodded, bowing slightly. The Chancellor turned on his heels and strode away from the Guardians.

Torg took the first right turn that eventually brought him to the inner sanctum of the Queen. Stealthily he approached as he assumed she would be under guard. When he reached the Royal residence, he observed Tecma sitting guard. Tecma wasn't attending security to the Queen, but on the force field that surrounded her quarters, imprisoning her. The Chancellor could knock Tecma out with little resistance, being a Level 5 Telepath and Tecma, as a House Telepath, a Level 2.

Torg retreated down the corridor and made a left turn. He walked a little way down to the next corner, making another left turn which brought him back to the Royal courtyard. He witnessed no one else, but sensed another set of thoughts, besides Tecma's.

Hum... Torg thought. *There is another Level 2 here.*

He made his way back down the same hallway, and two lefts later, he spotted him; Torg's good friend, Rumba's child, Kumat. He needed to take both Tecma and Kumat out at once. An easy enough task for a Level 5.

The Chancellor moved out into the open. Before either Telepath could respond to his presence, Torg clapped his hands together, creating a vibrating sound wave that he pushed outward with both his arms.

One oscillating wave undulated in Tecma's direction; the other headed straight for Kumat. The force of the blast wave knocked both men to the ground, rendering them unconscious. He knelt by each man, making sure they still breathed. Torg's fingers connected to a steady pulse.

The blue force shield shimmered and fluctuated; its light fading along with the consciousness of the two men who controlled it. As the men fell, Alkara ran from her door, secure in the knowledge Torg came to her rescue.

"I knew you would be able to help me." Alkara rested her hand on his arm.

"Pikkar has gone *too far!*"

"What are we to do to defuse the situation?"

Torg considered her question. "We need to put both men in your apartments. Then I shall reignite the force shield."

Torg lifted them easily with a slight raising his hand and the power of his mind. Sending them inside, he slammed the door and created a new containment field.

"I am bringing you to Mage' Rom." Torg took Alkara's hand and led her away through the corridors. "We must be swift as I must go to the surface with the last Lift."

"I can make it to Rom by myself, Torg," Alkara assured him. "GO! Do what you can for the humans," she commanded him, pushing him in the opposite direction. He turned to leave, slowly, unwilling to leave her side. She imparted some last words to him. "And Torg, take care of both our daughters." Alkara sped away from him. Torg sighed, making his way back to the Reaction Lift as the last twenty Guardians filed inside.

General Nutrion greeted him. "Chancellor, I was just going to send someone to get you."

"As you can see, General, I am here... and, I am ready."

Torg stepped into the Lift as the door closed. Cramped and uncomfortable, the ride up took its toll on Torg. Pleased when the doors opened, he took a deep breath of fresh air. Immediately accosted by the brightness of the sun's light, he closed his eyes. Squinting, he raised his hand to shade them.

"Ah, Chancellor!" Pikkar called to Torg as he exited the Lift. The old human ball field in the parkland lay awash in Akkadians. "Search the flowing thought waves. See if you can sense anything, anything at all."

"Yes, my Prince." Torg reached out not only with his arms but with his mind to search the waves of random human thoughts. Every day, thoughts carried away from the humans and floated aimlessly on the wind. Discarded carelessly after their usefulness was over, those ideas were sent adrift into the atmosphere. Only to be caught now, by Torg.

"I am sorry, my Prince," Torg apologized. "I can find nothing of pertinence." He scanned the woods. "If they are close, then they are not close enough."

Drakar made his way through the soldiers. "I still See we shall destroy this land."

"Hum..." Torg inquired of the Seer. "Does their destruction guarantee the return of our people?"

"You mean the traitors?" Another person made their way through the crowd.

Yanni intruded on their conversation. As Torg's Council Second, she had fewer plantings than Torg, yet more than Reeglar. Tall and thin, her physique enabled her to move about with stealth. Her dark skin, hair, and eyes gave an impression of evil lurking. Yanni was the wife of Damon, Drakar's son, and held the rank of a Level 4 Telepath, the same skill level as Reeglar.

Yanni scowled. "We all know why you have joined us, Torg."

The Levels a Telepath reached in his or her life was inconsequential and of little importance down in Akkadia. On the surface world, for the purpose of interaction, it was most crucial. The complement consisted of at least five Level 4's and ten Level

3's. The last remaining five were Level 2's, and there were no Level 5's there. Except for Torg himself.

As Torg eyed Yanni, his thoughts brought him to how she became who and what she was; who all Telepaths were. A Level 1 Telepath communicated with their Abilities. Some never got further, but most children moved on to a #2 by the time they passed puberty.

A #2 could do both; communicate and move small objects. They could also control a modest force shield. A #3 could do all the things like a #1 and a #2, plus hold a substantial force shield and connect with a network of other Telepaths to become a more powerful unit.

A #4 was a mightily endowed Telepath. Possessing all the other powers of the lower levels, they achieved levitation not only for themselves but others, as well as significantly sizable objects. A Level 5 would never even bother themselves with the war.

Most #5's were so beyond the others, verging on omnipotence. With very little they could not accomplish, they were difficult to sway. Only out of sheer respect for the Monarchy, would a #5 do anything their sovereign desired.

Pikkar let Yanni know Torg did not fool him. "I have no misconception about why Torg has joined us on the surface. He is concerned about his daughter's fate, as I am about mine." Pikkar turned to the group. "Where are my Level 2's?!"

All five Telepaths came to the front, centering themselves before the Prince. Pikkar gave them their charge. "I need you to create an invisible field. You shall hold the front line for the rest of us."

The Level 2 Telepaths took up position on their way out of the parkland, their blue-hued shield blocking all who attempted to observe their passing.

Experiencing the adrenaline rush of anticipation for the upcoming attack, General Nutrion called his troops. "Guardians, fall in line behind the Telepaths!" All sixty of his ilk fell into marching step. Nutrion turned to Pikkar. "Why do we not hit the humans with a frontal assault?"

"That," Pikkar assured him, "shall be our ultimate goal, yet we must attempt all avenues first."

"I see," Yanni nodded, after scanning Pikkar's mind.

"Oh! I do *hate* that!" The Prince moaned. "It was not necessary. I would have explained all."

"Well, you may explain to me," Drakar interrupted as they marched behind the large Akkadian Army.

"If the humans do not know they are invaded, they can not defend nor retaliate against an attack. We shall go unnoticed, and they shall have assumed they have been hit by a tragic, yet *natural* disaster. That is the first part of the plan," Pikkar informed them.

"If the humans have no idea we are here, how can they point us in the direction of the traitors?" the General asked.

"Torg and his people shall find them for us," Pikkar replied with confidence. "They can not hide forever."

When the entire complement of Akkadians reached the power lines, Pikkar called a halt. He lifted his hand high for all to see, and then he climbed the tallest of the many hills and began speaking.

"Akkadians! Today is a day we shall remember in our history, forever. This day, we show the humans they are not alone, WE share this earth. In fact, we were here *first*, and we are their superiors!"

Positive hoots from the crowd of listeners carried through the air, prompting Pikkar to continue. "Be proud! For what we do today, shall change their landscape. I do not just refer to their geography, but their spirit as well. The knowledge of our existence shall shake them to their bones."

Again, cheers spread out from the soldiers. "I can think of no better way to start this process as to bring forth…" He hesitated. "An earthquake! Level 3 Telepaths!" The Prince waved his hand, singling them out and calling them forward. "Of course," Pikkar began, glaring directly at Torg from high up on the hill. "Any Level 4's or 5's may surely join in and lend their talents."

The ten Level 3 Telepaths went down on one knee, bringing their hands to the ground. Each spread them out to touch the man or woman on either side. The action connected their Abilities, making them more powerful.

Pikkar gave the order. "Open up the ground and swallow everything in our path!"

Torg shook his head. As he waited, a slight trembling under his feet marked a changed path for the human race. A distant rumble warned of the quakes arrival.

The beginning of the end, Torg thought.

***

With the planes ready and loaded all that was left to do was to wait. Patrick helped Trish into the Dova, leaving the sliding hatch open. "I'll be right back." He found Danny when he returned to the hanger. "Should we take off?"

"I'm not sure." Danny checked with Azewrath. "The planes can only keep us in the air for about 300 miles. Or, if we're not going anywhere and just circling about 2 ½ hours."

"They shall come to the surface via the Reaction Lift in your park," Azewrath figured.

"I can scan the thoughts in the area," Reeglar offered. "But chances are, they shall anticipate I might try that, and their Telepaths shall block me."

"Then, what should we do?" Aaron asked.

Sarah took the time to stare at Ilmar and Reeglar. "Hey! Are those MY dresses?" Aaron put his arm around her to keep her from attacking.

Danny gave Sarah a disgusted sigh. "They needed clothes. Stop your bitching, *if* that's possible."

At that moment something moved underneath Aaron's feet. "Uh, oh!" he shouted. "Earthquake!"

"It is happening!" Reeglar cautioned, jumping into the Cutlass with Azewrath following her. Pat ran back to the Dova, climbed onto the wing and slid into his seat. Pulling the sliding canopy closed, he fired up his baby.

"Get in the Skyhawk!" Danny ordered Aaron and Sarah. They both responded, strapping themselves into the rear. Danny helped Ilmar into the co-pilot's seat, taking her harness and fastened it for her. Closing her door, he bent over to remove the chucks from behind the wheels.

He did the same thing for the Cutlass, swinging around on his way to the pilot's side of his plane. Tossing the chucks in the corner of the hanger, they tumbled across the concrete floor and hit the wall.

When Reeglar started the Cutlass, the engine roared, and the propellers spun as she guided the Cessna out of the large building. Danny slid into the pilot's seat of the Skyhawk. It was older than the Cutlass, but as a water plane he, at least he could land it in the ocean if necessary, and all inside would be safe.

He turned back to his friends. "No time for a pre-flight checklist. We're outta here!"

He pulled out of the hangar, watching as the earthquake sent his toolkits and machines rolling away to the other side of the building. They crashed into the wall next to the discarded chucks.

"Oh, shit!" Aaron cursed, freaking out they were still on the ground.

"I can't believe I'm letting you fly me around in this old plane!" Sarah said.

"I can always leave you here on the ground, instead," Danny offered. "It's your choice."

"Thank you, no," Sarah added. "Does this heap have parachutes?" she asked Aaron, who shrugged his shoulders.

With the Dova in the lead, all three planes lined up to the entrance of the runway. Patrick made sure the wind came from the correct direction for take off. He throttled up the plane, taxied down the track, talking to himself and checking his instruments as he went along.

"You gonna be okay?" Trish asked him. He quickly shot her a glance, a stressed expression on his face.

When the Dova reached its lift speed, he and Trish were airborne. Patrick banked the plane south as she rose into the sky. He took a moment to pry his eyes away from his instrument panel to watch Reeglar in the Cutlass perform a perfect take off.

Why was I worried? He thought as he brought his attention back to his horizon line. Then, reassuringly to Trish, "we'll be safe up here."

"I would love to tell you that you're overreacting, but your place is falling apart. The ground is opening up." Trish pointed out of her window.

"WHAT?" Patrick took the plane and lowered the right wing so he could get a better look at where Trish pointed. "Oh, SHIT!!

As Pat watched a huge fissure open up at the military airport, the giant hole buckled the ground and sucked in planes and helicopters, working its way toward Pat's runway. When he followed the chasm, he observed it heading toward the last plane on the ground.

Danny's.

"He's not going to make it, Pat!" Trish screamed in panic.

"Oh, yes he will," Pat assured her.

Reeglar banked the Cutlass to the south, following Patrick, when Azewrath alerted her to the same problem. "Working the calculations with just proper math, it seems Danny shall not have enough runway to lift off."

"Hold the controls," Reeglar told him.

"I can not fly the plane," Azewrath informed her.

"So, do not fly the plane as I do not need you to FLY the plane. I just need you to hold it in place," Reeglar joked.

Azewrath took the controls into his hands. "Do not blame me if we crash."

Danny witnessed the carnage in front of him. "No, no, no!" He tried to think as the asphalt crumbled before him.

"What?" Ilmar asked. All Danny could do was point out the front window over and over again. His index finger hit the glass three or four times.

"Do we have enough runway?" Sarah asked.

"I don't think it's going to matter," Danny relayed. Buildings collapsed right in front of them, and the gaping chasm caused by the quaking of the earth ate up the concrete.

"I knew this was a bad idea," Sarah offered.

"Not helping!" Danny sang as he pulled back on the controls as far as he could. "This might not work, but I'm just gonna go for it!"

Reeglar turned around in her pilot's seat to get a better vantage point. Extending her arms, she locked her tracking Abilities onto the Skyhawk, lifting the plane before the destructive earthquake heading its way swallowed it.

The Skyhawk lifted into the air. "Woo Hoo!" Danny hollered joyfully, feeling the plane's ascent. Danny banked south, joining the other planes. "See?" he repeated to Ilmar, Aaron, and Sarah. "No problem!" He leaned over and patted Ilmar's leg. She only nodded and held onto her seat white-knuckled and eyes closed.

Reeglar turned back around, taking the piloting controls back. She turned to Azewrath, who sat still, both hands on the vertical wheel handles. "Hey!" Reeglar said to him. "Rath... I have it."

"What?" he responded, coming out of his trance.

"I have it, my love," she assured him. "You may let go."

"Oh." Azewrath sighed. "Wonderful." He let go of the handles.

When Aaron glanced out the window, he couldn't believe the destruction everywhere. Buildings collapsed and crumbled, exposing their interiors; trees toppled over, sending root bulbs toward the sky; fires and car accidents littered the changed landscape; people ran in all directions.

Aaron pulled out his cell phone, but a "no service, no signal" icon displayed on the screen. "Well, our phones are useless now."

"It's okay," Danny replied. "All our planes have Unicom. They're set to 122.95 frequency." Danny picked up the radio. "Pat, it's Danny. Everyone okay? Over." The white noise of the radio answered him.

Pat finally responded. "Danny?! Jesus! I thought you weren't gonna make it. Over."

"You and me both, bro. Over."

"You can thank me later." Reeglar picked up a handset to her radio, joining the conversation.

"Reeglar, you've got to say over when you're done speaking. Over," Danny told her.

"Acknowledged. Over." Reeglar giggled. "This is fun. Over."

"How's Rath doing? Over," Danny asked her.

"He is just fine. Over," Reeglar relayed back to him.

Azewrath leaned closer to the microphone. "We can land anytime."

"Nope, not for a while, Rath. Over." Danny addressed his brother. "Pat, I figured we should just circle for a while. What do you think? Over."

"Sounds good. Over," Pat said.

"We should stop all unnecessary communication between us. Over," Reeglar suggested.

"I agree. Over," Danny said. "Out."

"Out," Pat added.

"Out? Oh, out!" Reeglar ended with a question. She smiled at

Rath, raised her shoulders, shrugging before hanging up the radio.

Ilmar's attention drew to the window. She took the time to scrutinize the sights of the horizon. From their altitude, the world went on forever.

So much space. So much room and so much to see, Ilmar thought.

She couldn't tell where the sky ended, and the water began. Were it not for the fact the whole coastline was coming apart at the seams; she imagined people enjoying the beach.

"This is the most amazing thing I have ever seen." Ilmar smiled at them excitedly. Stoic, Aaron and Sarah didn't return her enthusiasm.

"Right... Amazing..." Sarah stated, sarcastically. "So, destruction always get you this happy?"

"Hey, Sarah!" Danny scolded. "I'm sure that's not what she means."

"It is not." Ilmar took a more subdued attitude, staring out the window again. "What is that?"

All eyes gazed out the window, witnessing the unbelievable. Flying eastward over Dune Road, or rather what Dune Road represented after the quake, they watched as large pieces of the shore slipped into the sea. As the Hampton's famous mansions lost structural integrity, giant chunks of land crumbled into the receding waves.

Broken wood, rubble, and debris scattered along the shore, exposing frames and rafters. Farther out in the ocean, a wave took shape. Rolling across the horizon, a couple of waves formed, gaining height and momentum.

"Oh, no..." Danny whispered.

"What?" Ilmar could tell the situation disturbed Danny. "What is wrong?"

"It looks like a tidal wave," Danny informed her.

"No one says that anymore," Aaron corrected him. "It's called Tsunami."

"A Tsunami?" Sarah questioned. She leaned past Aaron to get a better look out the window. "Oh – My – God!" she breathed.

They watched in horror as the first of many waves created by the landslide earthquake, slammed into the barrier road. The force destroyed restaurants, marinas, and fishing vessels along with their docks that they moored to; taken away. The waves tossed them the way children would do when playing the game of jacks. The mighty ocean breached the land and continued north.

The water slammed into the Shinnecock Bay, pulverizing the Ponquogue Bridge in its relentless forward motion. Tall streetlights that lined the bridge bent and twisted before falling into the angry sea, adding to the depredation. Danny turned away from the wreckage and concentrated on flying so his anger wouldn't get the better of him. Sympathizing, Ilmar rested her hand on his arm in a comforting gesture.

"Danny?" Pat's voice came over the Unicom. "Are you seeing this? Over."

Danny picked up the handset, clicking it. "Yeah, we see. Over." He dropped the handset in his lap, devastated.

When Patrick banked left again, heading north, the other planes followed suit. They flew directly behind the destructive wave, watching it take out the Coast Guard station.

Pat couldn't help but relay his thoughts. "I sure hope some guardsmen got out before..." He trailed off and then remembered. "Over." Danny didn't answer. He couldn't. After all, he had been through, he just couldn't believe this was happening.

"My apartment!" Sarah moaned. "All my things!" She watched the path of the waves as it headed further north. "It's trashing everything, Aaron. What about your house? It's on the water!"

"Not for much longer," Aaron bemused. "It'll be UNDER the water."

"All of this is my fault," Ilmar said with remorse.

"Kinda," Sarah agreed.

"Sarah!" Aaron backhanded her in the arm. "I don't understand," Aaron leaned toward Ilmar. "How can there still be an earthquake happening? We've been in the air for..." He looked at his watch. "About 45 minutes already."

"It is not a natural quake like you have experienced before, Aaron," Ilmar explained. "The Telepaths are moving the upper mantle, the lithosphere. They are creating the quake. It can last as long as they can."

"And how long is that?" Sarah asked.

"I am sorry," Ilmar apologized. "I do not know."

The planes circled over the Shinnecock Canal and watched the wave hit Montauk Highway. They continued to fly over the boat locks themselves as the destructive waves tossed ships and floated away cars that parked along the canal's street. The roaring water connected with the Long Island Railroad crossing overpass, decimating the steel girders.

Danny viewed the scene below, and although the wave was not high, it carried tons of debris along with it. It pushed parts of houses, businesses, and large yachts from Jackson's Marina on the east side of the canal. On the west side, the marina at Indian Cove and Spellman's Marina fared no better.

The debris became floating bulldozers that hammered the tracks that spanned the waterway, leaving a mass of hanging concrete and steel. All that was left was a gaping precipice, separating the East End of Long Island from the western land mass.

As the Skyhawk followed the other planes, they made another left toward the west, and Danny realized something. "If the waves keep coming and they take out Sunrise Highway, the entire East End will be completely cut off."

"What will those people do?" Sarah thought about their desperation. "How will they survive?"

"How will any of us survive?" Aaron asked ominously.

***

The area around Sears Bellows Park was the only land untouched by the devastating earthquake and subsequent Tsunami. The ten Level, 3 Telepaths' powers, waned, causing Pikkar to decide they needed to rest and regenerate their strength.

"Level 3's," Pikkar called from his vantage point on the hilltop, "cease-and-desist!" He motioned to the others. "Guardians, help them over to some cooler spots to rest." The Guardians took the drained Telepaths off the sandy trails and set them down under a shade of pine trees. Pikkar turned to Torg. "What are you receiving on the thought waves?"

"If you refer to the human's reaction to the destruction levels, they are horrified," Torg informed the Prince. "The death toll is high. Your satisfaction in this should reach totality."

"Good! It does." Pikkar smiled. "As planned."

"When shall my army get to face the enemy?" General Nutrion asked.

"Soon, Nutrion," Pikkar told him, placing a hand on the General's shoulder.

Without warning, Drakar stopped dead in his tracks. Yanni alerted Pikkar. "My King, Drakar is Seeing." All watched as the Seer went rigid.

"Flying..." Drakar said when he slowly emerged from his trance.

"Flying?" Yanni repeated, confused.

"They shall be in the sky... flying," Drakar stated, glancing up. "That is the word."

"Planes," Torg informed them. "They shall be in airplanes." He joined Drakar gazing upward. *I have found you, Reeglar. They shall as well.*

Reeglar's Cessna kept pace with Patrick's Dova. She witnessed the devastation all around her, but worse; she experienced the pain, the sadness, and the death. Her sensitivity made it difficult for her to continue, yet she did what she must. She had to.

She flew straight ahead, trying to distance herself from the suffering. Azewrath watched her from the co-pilot's seat, sensing her sorrow through the bond they shared.

As Reeglar flew, her father's words echoed in her head. She thought back to him. *"I am surprised to feel you so close, yet, it is not unexpected. We shall be passing over you soon. Prepare..."*

Torg entered his daughter's mind so he could get a better understanding of what she spoke. *"My advice,"* he thought to her, *"is gain more altitude, swiftly!"*

"Thank you, Father, we shall." Reeglar picked up the radio. "Patrick, I have it on good authority that we better climb higher... Quickly! Over."

"You got it! Over." Pat understood, drawing the control wheel closer to his chest, angling the Dova upward. "Get ready for some fun," he said to Trish. She gave him a look of dread.

The Dova's nose went from a 90° angle to a 55° angle in about four seconds. Patrick reached for the clouds, creating a slight G-force, but the drastic altitude change gave Trish discomfort.

"Looks like we're going up," Danny warned his passengers.

"Why?" Sarah asked. "What's going on?"

"I don't know. Whatever Reeglar just found out," Danny added. "I'm clueless."

Sarah was going to say something, but Aaron gave her a stern shake of his head, so she bit her lip. "I'm not going there, hon. I swear," she promised him. "Oh, so much material wasted…"

Ilmar made an educated guess. "We must be approaching the Akkadian army." She checked her seat belt. "Make sure you are all secured in your seat. The ride could get bumpy."

"I don't like the sound of this," Aaron worried before he checked the security locking mechanism of his seat belt.

"What are they going to do?" Sarah questioned Ilmar.

"They will more than likely try to grab the planes."

"Grab us and take us prisoner?" Aaron hoped. This time, Ilmar bit her lip, shaking her head, slightly. "Crash us?" Aaron continued to guess.

"Don't ask, Aaron," Danny warned. "Just hold on." He pushed the Skyhawk higher, following the other two planes.

Pikkar tracked Torg's gaze skyward, alerted to a faint humming. As he searched, three small specs in the sky became smaller as they climbed higher. "Yanni! Rally the # 4's. Bring those planes down!"

The Level 4 Telepaths climbed the hill. They closed their eyes, reaching out with their arms and minds. As they sent their thought tendrils upward to overtake the planes, the thought waves sailed higher. They searched upward until their ends disappeared to the naked eye. One of the aircraft flew erratically, seemingly in trouble, caught in the Telepathic field.

Yanni lowered her arms. "They are too high, my Prince. We could only shake the air around them. We almost had the last one, but…" She stopped, shrugging.

"What about the Chariots?" Pikkar's brother, Dinnac asked. "Is it too late? We could get some altitude with the Chariots."

"No," Torg said. "They have traveled out of the reach of even the Chariots."

"Hum…" Pikkar pondered. "What are our chances that they shall pass by us again, now that they know we are here?"

"Doubtful," Torg agreed. "We shall need to chase after them."

"Can you keep track of their whereabouts?" Pikkar asked Torg.

"I can," Torg stated flatly.

"Then, do so," Pikkar ordered. "We need to modify the plan. *General!*" he hollered, searching for the Guardian.

***

Trish held onto the sides of the Dova for dear life with her eyes closed and holding her breath. She seemed to be mumbling a silent prayer. Pat needed to do something. Even while he fought with the controls, he needed to make her secure.

"That's the trouble with these ultralights..." he joked, attempting to give Trish confidence in the face of danger. "Any strong wind can cause a bumpy ride."

"I appreciate the levity, dear," Trish stressed through tightly squeezed shut eyes and teeth. "But I DO know it's not the wind."

"You do? Oh, okay," he said. "SHIT! Then, I can say this out loud. We're in trouble!"

The first wave of air rushed against the Cutlass, and Reeglar immediately wrapped the Cessna in a protective bubble, creating it from her mind.

"What about the other planes?" Azewrath asked her.

"It is too late," she replied. "They shall have to fight through it. Yet it is a very feeble attempt by the Telepaths."

Danny would have disagreed with Reeglar at that moment. As the lowest of the three planes, the Skyhawk passed above the power lines and the pursuing Akkadian Army. He fought furiously with the controls while the seaplane shook itself apart.

"What the hell is happening?" Aaron asked.

"Uh, the plane is falling apart," Sarah answered, holding onto the back seat for support. "We're all going to *die!* That should just about explain it."

"The Telepaths are trying to reach out and surround the planes with their thought tendrils," Ilmar informed them. "They mean to bring us down."

"Climb higher!" Sarah screamed at Danny.

"What do ya think I'm trying to do, Sarah? You wanna fly this thing?" He turned around slightly to get a better look at her, yelling over his shoulder. "Shit!" The propeller sputtered. "Oh, no," Danny whispered. "No, no, no!" he repeated, banging on the control panel to no avail. The Skyhawk hung in the air for a second and the propeller stopped. Then the plane tilted and fell. "We're screwed!" he yelled.

"What's going on?" Aaron asked in a panic.

"Engine stall," Danny explained.

"Restart it!" Sarah ordered.

"Yeah, right!" Danny glared back at her again like she was nuts. "'Cuz I didn't try that twice already, but thanks for the flying lesson, Sarah."

The force of the fall made it more difficult to move, but Ilmar unbuckled herself. "Let me help."

"What the hell are you doing?" Danny asked her. "You need to get back to your seat. It's *too* dangerous."

Ilmar ignored him, placing her hands on the control panel. "I am restarting the plane. Unless, of course, you would like to crash?"

As Ilmar closed her eyes, her hands glowed white. The plane's controls sparked a few times, but nothing happened. That's when the plane spiraled downward. Aaron and Sarah slammed into their seats from the sudden G-force. Ilmar tried again. Going down on her knees, she braced herself between Danny's legs sparing him a glance.

"I can do this, my love." She smiled at him weakly. "Come on!" she persuaded the plane, pleading and pushing her Abilities into the controls. A small sputtering sounded entering the cockpit, as the propeller spun, and the engine engaged. "Try it now!" Ilmar yelled at him.

Danny drew the control wheel back toward him sharply, bringing the Skyhawk out of its dive. It slowly leveled, pulling away from the reach of the Akkadians.

"YAY!" He celebrated after he regained control.

"Okay, let's not come back this way," Aaron suggested.

"Ya think, hon?" Sarah added, sarcastically.

"I love you," Danny told Ilmar when she sat back in the copilot seat. He let out a big sigh. "Thank you for doing that."

"You have no need to thank me. I could not let us crash,"

Ilmar stated simply.

Pat's strained voice came over the radio. "Is everything and everyone okay? Over."

Reeglar's answer came back to him first. "We are intact. Over."

"Danny? Over," Pat questioned and got nothing but static in return. "DANNY!" His voice bordered on hysteria.

Danny finally picked up the handset. "It was rough going for a while, but we made it through. Over."

"Thank God!" Pat answered. "I saw the plane spiraling. Over."

"Did anybody get a good look at our opposition?" Danny asked. "Do we have any idea what we're up against? Over."

Reeglar took that question. "My father relayed a quick estimate to me. Twenty Telepaths, sixty Guardians, and four Igniters. Over."

"I don't know what that means. Over," Danny said.

Azewrath spoke into the handset from his seat. "It means, our troubles have just begun."

"Over," Reeglar added.

"Great!" Patrick stated. "I recommend we change our flight pattern. Over."

"I agree," Danny concurred. "Let's keep the planes by our house and the Westhampton area. Over."

"Will do! Over and out," Patrick said, closing the conversation.

"Out!" Reeglar added.

"Out." Danny hung the handset back in the radio's cradle.

***

Pikkar ordered General Nutrion to round up the troops and commanded everyone into two rows of single file. In a unanimous decision, they traveled down the power lines heading west, following the traitors. From his vantage point on the hill, Pikkar senses alerted him to something approaching from the south. Roaring and rumbling, the noise sounded like an engine.

"Torg! Nutrion!" Pikkar shouted from high on the hill. "*Something* is coming!" Torg, Nutrion, and Drakar climbed to join the Prince as he pointed in the direction of the sound. They all faced the oncoming noise. "Get ready!"

"What is it?" Drakar asked.

"You can not tell?" Pikkar wondered.

They didn't have to wait long to find out. Within seconds, a giant, rushing torrent of salt water came crashing through the woods from the south.

Torg reacted first. Reaching out; his arms wide, he threw up a force shield around everyone on the hilltop. With his arms outstretched as far apart as he could, he protected the Prince while the ocean and bay water hit the invisible field. The violent water whizzed by and over them.

"Yanni!" Torg thought to his Second. *"Erect a force field around the Army, now!"*

Yanni and the other #4's managed to whip up a shield, spreading it around the surrounding Igniters and a couple of #3's and 2's. Some Guardians managed to fall under the protection of her shield, but some were not as lucky. The flowing water took no prisoners as it smashed into the unprotected Guardians and remaining Telepaths, who were not fast enough.

Torg hoped for the best as the wave passed. Afterward, they took stock of the damage suffered by the Army. The number of visible Guardians diminished, yet most members of the other Guilds had survived. When he released his hold on the force shield, the blue hue dissipated in the breeze, slowly drifting away on the wind.

"Nutrion!" Pikkar ordered. "Go find your missing Guardians."

"Yes, my Prince." The General slid down the hill, using his hand to brace his descent as his boots kicked up the wet dirt. As he reached the bottom, the trees in the distance shook ominously. "I believe I have found them."

The large oak and pine trees swayed violently, crashing over, creating a massive opening. Many paths appeared as the trees toppled, slamming into the ground, like a child's blocks.

The things that came through the tree line would have sent the humans running. The opening revealed thirty Guardians in their metamorphosis. A stage very few ever laid eyes upon without a terminal ending. They came out of the woods and onto the sandy path.

The Guardians stood next to their fellow Akkadians, towering over them, in all of their the twelve-foot height. Giant soldiers, right down to their transformed armor, made them an invincible infantry. Lieutenant Thorium approached the hill where his General stood next to the Prince. In full "morph," he looked Nutrion in the eye, still standing at the bottom of the hill.

"All Guardians are present and accounted for, General," Thorium informed them, his voice booming loudly in his present condition, magnified by his armor.

"Good, Thorium," Nutrion praised him. "Did we lose any others?"

"We can not find a #2 and two #3's. Also, we are down an Igniter."

"Hum..." Pikkar thought out loud. "Four losses before the fight. That is not a good sign."

"The wave was a product of your own doing," Torg warned Pikkar. "Created by the earthquake. It came back and killed a few of your Army." The Chancellor slid down the hill but continued speaking. "Be satisfied if your losses remain low after all this is said and done." He made his way through the wet sand.

"You can not trust him, my Prince," Nutrion warned Pikkar. "He is only here for his daughter's sake."

"Yes, yes Nutrion," Pikkar offered, waving the General off. "We have been through this already." He started down the hill, walking westward. "Have the troops move onward."

Nutrion threw his arm out to the left. "Akkadian ranks... Fall in!" The Army moved forward, as the immense Guardians tried not to walk over the rest of the other soldiers.

NIK AUGUST

XXI

Sutters' Last Stand

The convoy of planes flew to the west. The bright summer sun took refuge behind dark clouds as if wished to escape the coming Akkadian battle. The drizzle sent droplets of water splattering against the glass, pelting the windshield. The rain ran down the window, elongated into streaks that spread to either side of the plane. Even without the storm, Danny couldn't tell where he was from the landmarks on the landscape.

"Illy," Danny began, "what have your people done to us?" He hesitated, glancing over at her. "We didn't deserve all this destruction."

"The entire town of East Quogue is now a coastline," Sarah whispered, putting her arm around Aaron. "I'm so sorry about your house, honey."

"Ah, I have flood insurance," Aaron announced. "No worries. I'll just stay with you at your house, anyway." He tried to make a joke, nudging her.

"If it's still there." Sarah hoped.

Solemn, Ilmartutar reflected. "So much loss over so little..." She trailed off.

"*Never* say that!" Danny grabbed her hand and brought it to his lips, kissing it. "This..." He squeezed the hand he held. "This is not little. I would die to protect our love."

"It might just come to that!" Sarah added, pointing to the sky. "Lightning!"

"Oh, shit!" Danny cursed. "We're gonna have to land." He picked up the radio handset and called his brother. "Pat, lightning at one o'clock. Over."

"Saw it," Pat told him. "We gotta land on solid ground. Should we go for Gabreski? Over."

"They've probably got that place locked down," Danny reminded him. "And when I took off, it looked like the ground had opened up over there too. It could be a hairy landing. Over."

"They are a search and rescue facility, Danny. I'm sure they've mobilized with the quake disaster. We're gonna have to chance it.

Over," Pat ordered. "Reeglar? Did you hear? Over."

"I heard. Landing shall be no problem for me. Over and out," she promised.

"Follow me down, Danny. Out." Pat hung up as a huge flash of lightning, and then a rumble of thunder got everyone's attention. *That was a close one,* Patrick thought. As the skies opened up, the rain came down harder.

"O-K, kiddies," Danny began. "This is gonna hurt. I can't see a thing outta the windshield."

"If I get out of this, I swear, I'll never do anything more dangerous than knitting." Sarah leaned back in the rear seat of the Skyhawk.

"Right." Aaron shook his head. "You're a cop. Every day could be your last."

"There is very little danger in Hampton Bays." Sarah glared at Ilmar. "Usually."

With the Dova in the lead, the planes made a tight circle around so they could approach against the wind. Flying south, they swung east until they traveled north. The flight plan brought them back to the borders of Hampton Bays and East Quogue.

I'm not looking down, Danny thought. He didn't want to see any more coastline he didn't recognize.

Ilmar peered down from her copilot's seat, catching the Army marching along the power lines. Ilmar had thoughts of her own. *Just out of your reach, are we, Father?* She noticed the Guardians already at full size. *I wonder what provoked the metamorphosis?*

She hoped it involved no humans, as of yet. As Danny dropped the Skyhawk's altitude, the military airbase appeared in the distance. With the lower flight pattern, Ilmar had visuals on Danny's house and the hanger for the airplanes. Everything seemed intact, except for the runway.

Thank the Goddess; the earthquake spared his house! Ilmar prayed silently.

Danny's attention was on his instruments. He had to concentrate during the inclement weather. *I've landed a million times before. Okay, maybe not a million times,* he thought, *but never in a thunderstorm.*

Refocusing, he realized he knew what he was doing and

should trust his intuition. He checked his altimeter, located over his right hand on the instrument panel, watching as the numbers fell.

Now, reduce thrust.

He pushed the controls toward the nose of the plane, slowly. As the aircraft dropped, it created pressure inside their ear canals. He poked Ilmar to get her attention away from the window.

"Illy, do a lot of yawning," he explained. "It will break the pressure inside your head." She said nothing but nodded to let him know she heard him, opening her mouth wide.

Danny lowered the wing flaps, inducing a greater amount of drag. He squinted out the windshield trying to see something, anything, that remotely resembled a runway. If the Dova or the Cutlass landed, he couldn't see them. He hoped they were in front of him, just not in his way. Visual sight was useless as the rain brutally pounded the Skyhawk.

Pushing the column forward again, Danny tried to keep the nose wheel off the ground. He waited for the jarring jolt that usually accompanied ground contact, but nothing happened. He checked the horizon line to his left and then the altimeter to his right, again. Both reported he landed, yet his eyes couldn't confirm that fact.

Am I down? He wondered, frantically. *I sure hope my instruments are still working.* With fingers crossed, he sent the wheel controls all the way forward. Slowly, the wheels touched down. *What the hell?* He thought, astonished. The plane stopped without any assistance from him. Puzzled, he checked the Skyhawks controls, but he heard laughter inside his head. It was Reeglar.

He thought back to her. *"Saving my ass, again?"*

"You are making quite a habit of this," she told him.

Danny sent gratitude over their link. *"It's like I have my own Guardian Angel."*

"Guardian?"

"No... not yours. Guardian's are a good thing here."

"Our situation is not good. My father knows where I am, and they are coming."

Danny picked up the radio. "Pat, where are we? Over."

"Looks like we're probably in the vicinity of the barracks and the air tower, near Avenue B. Over."

"Reeglar says they're coming. What are we gonna do? Over."

"We're gonna start by getting out of these planes. They stick out like a sore thumb compared to the military ones. Over and out." Pat terminated the conversation.

"Out," Danny said, hanging up. He turned around to everyone on his plane. "Well, looks like we're gonna get wet."

Groans met him in response. A flash of lightning accompanied by a quick rumble of thunder startled them. Danny sighed and jumped from the pilot's door. He traveled around the plane, his shoulders hunched against the torrent and opened Ilmar's side to help her down.

By the time the rain slowed Danny's shirt, and Ilmar's dress showed signs of a good drenching. Having Ilmar in a wet outfit was something Danny would have appreciated at any other time. Sarah and Aaron jumped down to the tarmac, and Aaron put his arm around her, shielding her from the rain.

"Let's go!" Danny grabbed Ilmar's hand and ran to meet Patrick, with Aaron and Sarah following. The storm raged on as they ran toward the Dova.

Pat yelled over the tempest. "We've got to get to cover! Come on!" He snatched Trish's arm and took off running.

"Who put him in charge?" Azewrath asked, running through the rain.

"He makes all the grown-up decisions around me," Danny answered.

The group sprinted down the runway. On their way, they jumped giant cracks in the ground, climbed over the uneven landscape before scrambling over and past toppled buildings and aircraft. Large trooper planes and smaller jets lay half buried in the deep fissures that opened up the earth, scuttled. Some untouched, standing alone like statues. Patrick waved them onward, turning right onto Rust Avenue.

"The barracks!" Patrick pointed ahead, running to the part of the building with a collapsed roof. A gaping hole in the side of the building exposed the interior, giving them access. It was wet and flooded inside, yet it provided convenient cover from the onslaught of the rain.

Reeglar put her hands out, lifting the roof so everyone could go in and get out of the weather. Once inside, they shook off as much of the rain is possible. Azewrath stood there, clothes dripping wet. His hair fell over his face as droplets of water ran into his eyes. Wiping away the wetness, he ran his hands through his dark hair, trying to wring out the excess water.

"I would have thought with all the energy from the sun, this moistness in the air would just not be," Azewrath complained. "All this hot, sticky water makes me feel unclean."

Reeglar laughed at his distress. Then out of love created a small whirlwind within the palms of her hands. Sending it around Azewrath, she dried him as best she could. The warm air wicked away the rainwater that soaked him to the skin. He checked himself over and gave Reeglar an approving nod.

"Thank you." He smiled accepting her help. "Now, at least my situation is TOLERABLE."

The others glanced at Reeglar hopefully. "Would everyone like a drying wind?" she asked.

Nods of agreements came from the group of drowned rat-looking people. Reeglar whipped up another force of air, swirled in her hands, allowing it to grow larger. She sent it out surrounding them as the airflow blasted each over and over again. Ilmar, Trish, and Sarah's hair appeared to be dancing in the strong breeze. It wasn't long before they were all dry and more comfortable.

Azewrath broke the silence again. "We do not have a lot of time before the Army finds us. They are coming here."

Reeglar agreed. "I feel my father is very close."

"I saw them," Ilmar added. "When we flew over the area. They are heading towards us through a giant path through wires."

"Power lines," Danny said. "We gotta hide."

"Hiding shall be impossible," Reeglar told him, shaking her head. "We need a plan, or we shall not succeed."

"I've got one if anyone's interested," Pat suggested. "Don't know how good it is, but –" he didn't finish, shrugging his shoulders. They waited for him to continue. "Okay, on our way to the barracks, I saw a Pave Hawk. I've been dying to get my hands on one of those, I'll tell you, but anyway… It's a combat search and rescue helicopter. Which means it's more than likely armed." He smiled, adding more information. "More importantly, it didn't look disabled by the quake."

"Can you fly it?" Danny asked.

"Pretty much…" Pat answered cryptically.

"Well, that didn't sound very reassuring." Danny worried.

"Then, I should fly it," Reeglar chimed in.

"No," Pat disagreed, shaking his head. "This is not for you to do, Reeglar. You and Rath need to stay here on the ground to protect the rest of the group. There is no reason everyone should go up. I'll be a target."

Trish didn't like that. "You can't Pat, really! It's crazy!"

"Don't worry; I'll try to stay out of reach. That Pave Hawk is definitely not the Dova."

"All right," Reeglar affirmed. "It sounds like the only plan we have."

"I'm gonna need two of you to run the guns, though." Pat glanced directly at Sarah raising an eyebrow.

"Yeah," Sarah volunteered. "Count me in. I'm so pissed at this whole goddamn thing; I could use the target practice."

Ilmar offered her assistance as well. "I should go."

"Uh, no way!" Danny told her. "I'll go instead. I can shoot a gun."

"I am confident you can, my love, but if something happens, mechanically to the craft, I will be more help than you." Ilmar put her hand on his chest. "We all need to do our part."

Patrick put his arm around Trish. "See, I'm leaving you with all this backup and muscle. You couldn't be safer."

Danny grabbed Ilmar's hand. "Hey guys," he hesitated. "Give us a second." He proceeded to pull Ilmar from the room. She turned around, threw her free hand up in the air, shrugging, as Danny tugged her along.

"What?" Ilmar's question made its way back to them, sounding surprised. As her sandals hit the concrete, he dragged her down the hallway, their footsteps echoing back to the others until they were out of earshot.

Danny drew Ilmar into the first open room. Taking her by the arm, he drove her against the wall, kissing her hard, showing his desire for her. She returned his amore in-kind and threw her arms around his neck, pulling herself closer to him. He reached under her dress, sliding his hand upward. She broke away from their kiss, confused.

"We do not have time for this!" Ilmar scolded him.

"But, what if it's our last time?" He tried to convince her, kissing her neck.

"Mmmm..." she moaned at the pleasure of his touch. "It always seems like it will be our last time."

"We don't know what's going to happen out there," Danny argued. "We could all die, or they could take you away from me again. I just want to be inside you right now. It's the only place I feel safe."

Ilmar laughed but tried to stifle a huge smile. "You are such a liar, but I can not say no to you."

Danny flashed his famous grin and unzipped his jeans, sliding them down a bit. His body responded to the sight of her. As she gathered her dress higher, he picked her up, allowing her to wrap her legs around his waist. He lowered her, and she let out a soft sigh as he parted her – her warm tightness surrounding his throbbing manhood. Danny leaned her against the wall, thrusting deeply. He hit her hard, quickly, over and over, slamming Ilmar into the hard steel wall of the building.

Ilmar worried Danny would keep going in an attempt to make their lovemaking lasts forever, but time constraints pressured them. Repositioning herself, she held onto his neck tighter with her left arm, while she slid her right hand underneath. When Ilmar found Danny's hanging tender spot, she caressed him gently. Holding his manhood in the palm of her hand, she massaged them with her fingers. That was it for Danny. Groaning, he released his seed inside her, grunting with pleasure. After, he put her down, unceremoniously.

"That wasn't fair!" Danny said, indignantly.

"What is your saying? 'All is fair in love and war'?" Ilmar retorted, straightening out her dress. "We just took care of the love part; now we must get back to deal with the war." She walked out of the room, and Danny patted her bottom when she passed. Pretending to be perturbed, she turned around and pursed her lips at him, making a face. When both Danny and Ilmar rejoined everyone, all eyes turned to their entrance and conversations ceased.

"What?" Danny asked them all. "We were quick."

"I wouldn't be bragging about that to anyone," Sarah advised him. Danny moved his head back and forth in a mocking way, using his hands like puppets, portraying Sarah.

"O-K!" Pat added slowly. "It's time to go. Are we outta here?" Pat kissed Trish, jerking his head to let Sarah and Ilmar know they needed to go. Danny released Ilmar's hand and watched her run away with Pat.

"So," Danny asked after both his brother and the girls left the building. "What's *our* plan of attack on the ground?"

Azewrath pointed from the hole in the barracks to a small building next to them. "Your brother postulated that structure over there would be an armory, of sorts." He sighed, seemingly bored. "We are going to 'blow things up,' were his exact words."

Aaron appeared sick. "I don't wanna blow things up."

"Are you sure you guys can do this?" Danny wondered. "Fight against your own people."

"We shall do what we need to do," Reeglar promised. "We have wasted enough time already." She nodded to Danny. "We need to get over to that building. I shall take the point. Rath, you take the rear. Let us keep the humans between us."

Aaron put his arm around Trish. "It's gonna be okay, Trish." They crawled out of the building, immediately assaulted by the rain once again.

"I don't know how to shoot a gun," Trish stated as they made their way to the armory.

"Don't worry; we'll teach you," Danny offered.

"And we'll all stand behind you," Aaron teased. "*WAY* behind you!"

When they crossed the hundred yards to the small building, Reeglar found the door locked, so she bent down to study it. Before she could figure out how to unlock it, Danny pulled his shirt up and tucked his elbows into it to lift it over his head. Wrapping it around his elbow, he smashed the window. Astonished, they all turned to gawk at him.

"What?!" Danny asked. "Breaking the window was quicker." He banged out the glass around the frame so it wouldn't cut anyone, and then he picked up Trish.

"OH!" She cried out, unexpectedly. "Oh, all right!" She balanced herself on his shoulders as he pushed her through the window.

"Just unlock the door for us," Danny told her. Everyone stared at him again. "What?! She's the smallest. It just made sense."

Trish went in head first, landing with a thud. She startled everyone when she popped back up in the window. "I'm all right!" She gave Danny a dirty look. "Next time, ask me first, before throwing me into a broken window, huh?!" She disappeared only to reappear at the door, opening it. "It's an armory, all right. Full of very 'big bads.'"

Danny pushed his way inside. "Wow! Jackpot!" He ran over to some rocket-propelled grenade launchers or RPG's. "This baby is mine." He picked it up lovingly before grabbing a bag and loaded it with grenades.

Aaron rummaged through the firepower until he came across a Beretta M 90 semiautomatic pistol. He decided to give it to Trish. "Found something for you, Trish. It's a little heavy, but out of all this stuff..." Aaron waved the pistol around, as he pointed to the arsenal, causing everyone to duck. He noticed everyone hiding. "What's the problem? I've got the safety on. Geeze!" He pointed the gun up in the air and squeezed the trigger. "See!" The gun fired right through the ceiling and out through the roof. "SHIT!" Aaron screamed, jumping back. He scrutinized the Beretta. "Oh," he slid the safety back on. "I thought the red dot meant it was locked."

Danny grabbed the gun away from Aaron. "O-K, Buffalo Bill Cody... Let's leave the weapons to the professionals." He handed it to Trish. "Just hold onto it. Hopefully, you won't need to use it."

"I still need a gun! I need something to protect myself from these crazies," Aaron stopped, realizing what he said in mixed company. He smiled at Azewrath. "No offense. I don't mean you guys." Azewrath just narrowed his eyes back at Aaron.

Danny searched the arsenal. He picked up two Heckler and Koch MP5 sub-machine guns. He handed one to Aaron, and the other to Azewrath. "Here!"

"This should do nicely!" Aaron went to find the ammo for his gun, stuffing his pockets with the cartridges. "Take some, Rath."

"Lovely," Azewrath replied, sarcastically, placing two cartridges in each of his pockets. "Now what?"

"I've got an answer for you," Danny continued. "We need to defend from higher ground. I think we'll be in a good position at the control tower. It'll give us the advantage of seeing them first before they see us." Everyone nodded in agreement. "Okay, let's go!" They ran from the armory and headed north on Moen Street, passing Avenue B on their way to the tower.

***

Patrick and the girls arrived at the Pave Hawk. Pat jumped into the open sliding cargo door and headed up front to the cabin. Sarah entered behind him.

"Oh, man..." Sarah whispered as she hit the cabin and ogled the side window mounted mini-guns. On the other side, a matching one waited for Ilmar.

"It's a GAU – 2B 7.62 mm machine gun," Pat yelled to Sarah from up front in the pilot's seat. "It can fire about 3,000 rounds per minute."

"How do you know all that?" Sarah asked.

"'Cuz..." Pat became giddy. "I love this baby!" he said, rubbing his hand on the instrument panel exploring the readouts. "Ho-ho!" Still excited, he continued. "She has NVG, night vision goggle capability, and FLIR, forward-looking infrared! Wow! I wonder if the base will mind if I take her home?"

"Let's just make sure we *get* home," Sarah called back to him. She turned to Ilmar, who sat with her machine gun. "You're awfully quiet."

Ilmar shrugged. "This will not be easy or fun... for me, anyway."

"Oh," Sarah voiced, and just let it go at that.

When Pat started the engine, the rotors on the top of the copter turned. Slowly at first, but soon the whir, whir, whir, from the blades buffeting the air announced take off. Pat pushed the throttle stick forward, and as the Pave Hawk left the ground, he smiled broadly.

***

As Danny got to the tower, he watched the helicopter take off.

He turned and tried to kick the door to open it, but it didn't budge. Aaron reached over, turned the handle, and pushed the door open. He smiled at Danny, raising his eyebrows.

"Yeah, yeah…" Danny moaned, running inside and up the stairs. The control tower began three flights up. A 360° perspective met them when they entered. From where they stood, they had a full view of the runway to the barracks and behind the tower toward the road as well. "I can see everywhere," Danny commented, very pleased with the decision he made.

"This was a good idea," Reeglar agreed. "We shall see the army approaching from the east."

"And, they will have to come out in the open to cross the entire airfield," Danny added. "Unprotected."

"They shall have protection," Azewrath warned. "*Trust* me." He lifted his MP5. "We might not make a difference, even with these weapons."

Aaron examined the windows on the east side of the tower. He opened them just enough to stick the barrel of his assault rifle out. "This will work, too!" He got down on one knee and demonstrated to everyone.

"I hope we brought enough ammo," Danny added. "I sure don't wanna be the one to have to go back for more."

"They are here," Reeglar informed them.

"Where?" Danny asked, running to the window.

Aaron used the sight on his gun. He squinted with one eye, as he searched. "I see 'em now. What the −?" Aaron turned to Danny. "They're coming from your house!"

"It is just a coincidence," Reeglar told them.

"Wait…" Aaron reported to them again. "Holy shit! The Guardians are HUGE!"

Danny moved over to Trish. "I want you to sit back here." He walked her to the opposite side of the tower. "And stay out of the way. Hopefully, you'll be safe."

Trish nodded, eyes wide. She slid down the wall, clutching the Beretta so hard the knuckles of both hands turned white.

"There goes Pat," Aaron warned, noticing the helicopter heading east. "Good luck, gang." He glanced away from the gun before commenting under his breath. "Stay safe, Sarah."

Reeglar rushed to the window, spreading her arms out in front of her, she sent a force shield out to surround the copter. Its blue hue sparkled around the Pave Hawk, protecting it. "That is the best I can do from here." She assured them as they all gathered around the east windows to watch.

***

Patrick took the Pave Hawk counterclockwise to the northeast. The rain hadn't stopped, but it lessened enough that his sight returned. The thunder and lightning ceased, and he hoped the storm would follow. He wasn't surprised the air around the copter glowed a pale blue.

"Thanks for the force shield, Reeglar," he thought.

"It was the least I could do." Reeglar surprised Pat by replying to him in his head.

At her mini-gun, Sarah held her eye to the sight with her finger on the trigger. She waited for the signal from Patrick. Ilmar also eyed her view-scope and spotted the Guardians leading the approaching Akkadian Army with the Telepaths just behind the massive Guild members.

More than likely #2's and #3's, Ilmar thought. She moved her sight down the line of Akkadians. There *he* was. A tall man in glowing armor. *Father! You will make us destroy you.* She blinked back a tear, wiping it off her cheek with the back of her hand and yelled a warning to Patrick.

"I don't know if these guns shall do any harm to the Guardians," Ilmar informed them. "Most certainly the Telepaths shall have a force shield around them, as we do now. Even if a small projectile might be able to penetrate this field, their armor is another story."

"Well," Sarah began, squinting through her scope and targeting, "there's only one way to find out." She squeezed the trigger and sent a quick succession of machine-gun fire straight into the center of the Guardians.

The rounds pierced right through the force shield and hit the Guardians continuously. Their armor kept them safe but showed the force of the blows, sending their giant bodies into spasms, twitching from the bullet hits.

***

General Nutrion immediately gave the orders. "Tighten the ranks!" he screamed at his troops and then warned the Telepaths. "Stop those projectiles."

"We can not!" Yanni replied. "They are too small and can penetrate easily. Our fields protect against larger attacks, like force waves."

"We are all vulnerable, my Prince," Torg informed Pikkar. "We need the Guardians to surround us."

"Give the command, General!" Pikkar instructed Nutrion.

"Guardians, surround the rest of the Army," Nutrion ordered. The giant soldiers broke ranks and spread out, creating a safe circle around the rest of the Akkadians.

***

Patrick took the Pave Hawk around for another pass. Tightening the circle, he brought the copter back in, quicker than before. Sarah yelled to the cockpit. "Shit! The bullets passed right through the force shield, but their armor is too strong."

"You're gonna have to target a weak spot," Pat yelled back to her. "Between the joining armor parts."

"Jesus Christ, Pat!" Sarah said, frustrated. "This isn't a sniper's rifle; it's a Gatling gun. How the hell am I supposed to pull off that miracle?"

"I *trust* you, Sarah," Pat encouraged. "You can do it. Just take the shot."

Sarah sighed, and then addressed Ilmar. "Illy, I'm gonna need you to spray the field with your ammo while I target a few of the Guardians. Okay?"

"Yes," Ilmar agreed. "I understand." She grabbed her mini-gun and put her finger on the trigger, resting her eye against the sight. "I can shoot at Guardians!"

Pat brought the copter in closer but stayed just out of range of the Telepath's powers. Ilmar fired and was surprised to find her bullets sent the Guardians into twitching fits.

Sarah concentrated. *Just hit a really tiny spot while traveling 40 miles an hour. No problem!* She thought to herself.

Sarah picked her mark and stared straight down the barrel through the sight, firing a round. All her bullets sprayed through the force shield. As she continued, one slipped into the seem at the Guardian's armor joints. The behemoth screamed a horrible howl and fell to the ground, de-morphing back to regular size. He did not move again.

"Gotcha!" Sarah yelled and threw her arm out, pointing at the Akkadians. "Destroy my boyfriend's house, will ya?!"

***

Everyone in the tower went wild as they watched the helicopter's successful attack. Danny and Aaron slapped each other on the back in celebration. Danny picked up his grenade launcher and loaded it, balancing it between the window and his shoulder. He turned around, yelling to Trish. "Better move, Trish. Don't wanna lose you!" Trish jumped up, ran over to Aaron and grabbed his arm, hiding behind him.

"What are you doing?" Aaron asked Danny.

"Hitting 'em while they're off-balance," Danny stated, winking.

"I thought they were too far away for our weapons to reach them," Azewrath asked.

"For your weapons, yes," Danny explained. "This baby has a 500-foot effective range for precision, but a maximum range of 1,312 feet. The runway is 9000 feet long." He smiled. "Reeglar, can you give me an extra boost? All I need to do is make a mess."

Reeglar nodded and joined him, placing her hands on his shoulder. "We are linked."

"Here goes nothing!"

Danny set up his sight and pulled the trigger. Reeglar used her Abilities to send the grenade farther than its capabilities. When it hit the ground, a huge explosive sound accompanied by a bright flash of light scattered the Army.

The grenade launcher created such a booming noise inside the tower it caused them to throw their hands over their ears. Everyone gagged on the excessive smoke from the launcher. Ducking, they tried to dodge the expelled explosion. Had anyone been looking where Danny took his shot, they would have witnessed the grenade hit its mark.

***

Guardians flew everywhere. Between the fire and smoke, Danny marveled at his handiwork. *At least the rain will put that out.* He assured himself.

"Holy shit..." Aaron whispered, getting up to see the destruction. He leaned his hands on the tower's air traffic instrument panel and brought his face inches away from the window glass. "Bonsai, bro! Nice shot!" He turned to Danny, who put down his launcher so he could look for himself.

Azewrath leaned over to the window. "Hum... Quite effective."

"Do you think I killed anyone?" Danny asked, concerned.

"Yes," Reeglar answered. "Sarah did as well."

"Wow!" Danny sat down in the chair, running his fingers through his tight, blonde spikes.

"Is that not what you wanted?" Reeglar asked him.

"Yes, but..." Danny hesitated. "I didn't know how it would feel." He focused his attention on everyone. "It doesn't feel as good as I thought it would."

"Actions and consequences," Reeglar quoted.

***

The recent attack sent the entire Akkadian Army into disarray. The remaining Guardians closed ranks around the Prince and his party. Aware they could be the next to fall; they searched the sky in trepidation of another assault from the humans. Chancellor Torg and Yanni combined their force shield and added their strength to the #3's.

"This should hold them off for a short time," Torg told Pikkar.

"What is happening here?" Pikkar asked. "We are more powerful; superior to the humans in every way. How can they do so much damage?"

"They have what they call technology on their side," Torg explained. "I must admit, I am quite impressed at their ingenuity, yet they do have Akkadian help."

Surprised at Torg's words, Pikkar attacked the Chancellor. "You are impressed by the death of our Guardians? Your fellow kinsmen?"

"No, my Prince," Torg corrected. "By the human's cunning." He glanced up at the control tower. "They have an excellent vantage point. Smart strategy. Their General is most wise."

"Enough, Torg!" Pikkar waved him off. "Yanni, get the other #4's, round up the Igniters, and mount the Chariots."

She nodded at the Prince. Turning, she ran and slapped her countrymen on their backs, letting them know it was time. Three of the Level 4 Telepaths jumped into the waiting Chariots. Three Igniters got behind the small metal carriages and touched them. A glowing white light ignited around the bottom of all Chariots. Each slowly rose into the air, carrying a Level 4 Telepath. One Chariot was left empty. It belonged to another #4, but her Igniter had died from the tidal waves.

Yanni approached her comrade. "We are down an Igniter. If I help, do you believe you can levitate the Chariot by yourself?"

"I shall do my best, Yanni."

"Excellent. Mount up." Yanni stepped back, concentrating her Ability to lift the last Chariot. Both Telepaths worked together, as the metal vehicles soared into the air. Yanni turned to Pikkar. "The Chariots are aloft, my Prince."

"Noted!" He ordered. "Commence the air assault!"

***

The helicopter circled again, heading for the advancing Akkadian Army. Ilmar sprayed the line of Guardians with the Gatling guns successive fire. "They have tightened the force shield," Ilmar yelled to Patrick. "This weapon is having almost no effect on them."

Sarah lined up her sight, searching for another vulnerable spot in the Guardian's armor where two pieces connected. She fired, and fired, and fired again until her arms hurt. The bullets just bounced off the shield, falling to the ground.

"Shit!" Sarah cursed, slapping her gun, which sent it spinning. "You're right, Illy." Sarah then yelled to Patrick. "We're done here unless you've got another idea." He didn't answer, so she called him again. "Pat? Pat?"

Pat's answer confused them. "Uh, girls… You better come up here. Now!"

After Sarah and Ilmar had exchanged glances, they jumped up and ran to the cabin as fast as they could. Objects rose from behind the Guardian's line. They appeared to be metal sleds of some sort. The four strange carriages held someone standing inside. They reminded Sarah of Roman chariots without the wheels or horses.

When she squinted, she witnessed each chariot intricately hand carved with an adorning front design. With high rounded arches at the facial facing and a sloping downward angle toward an open back, the vehicle offered maximum protection. Their glowing underside moved them at a respectable speed. They also traveled straight for the helicopter.

"Chariots!" Ilmar warned him. "Turn the helicopter around, Pat. "Quickly!"

"Why?" Patrick asked. "What are they?"

"*Dangerous!*" Ilmar stressed. "There is a Level 4 Telepath in each Chariot. We do not want to face them in the air. We will be defenseless! Hurry!"

Pat didn't need any more explanations. He hit the throttle, the cyclic, and the foot pedals, all at once, banking and reversing at the same time; creating a yaw effect. The sudden change in direction sent Ilmar and Sarah slamming into the side of the cabin. They both bounced against each other, and Ilmar rolled back into the cargo section. Falling, she slid across the floor. With the pitch of the Pave Hawk still askew, Ilmar slipped closer and closer to the open door. She tried to grab hold of anything, clawing at the floor of the copter without success.

"Illy!" Sarah screamed, trying to pull herself toward the back of the helicopter to help Ilmar.

Thinking quickly, Sarah wrapped her wrist in the cargo harness and propelled herself forward, grabbing Ilmar's hand just as the Akkadian's legs slid out of the open door. As Sarah held onto her for dear life, the rest of Ilmar dangled from the doorway. Ilmar swayed dangerously in the wind and the rain.

"I've got you," Sarah assured her.

Ilmar's panic gave way to relief as Sarah held her in place.

Taking deep breaths, Ilmar managed to regulate her heart rate back to normal. "Thank the Goddess..."

"Pat!" Sarah hollered. "Level us out now. We're losing Ilmar."

"Aw, shit! Okay, give me a sec." Patrick wrestled with the controls, leveling the copter out to a more horizontal plane.

Sarah warned Ilmar of her intentions. "I'm going to let go of one of your hands –"

"Please, no..." Begging, Ilmar cut her off.

"Yes! I must," Sarah continued. "When I let go, take your free hand and grab the side of the door opening. Then, I'll pull you up with the other one. It's our only chance. Okay?"

Ilmar swallowed, nodding. Sarah released Ilmar's right hand, allowing Ilmar to grip the door jamb. She held the steel so tightly, her knuckles whitened. Using both her hands, Sarah grabbed Ilmar's wrists and pulled her back into the cargo hold.

Once she had Ilmar back inside, both women sat against the cold steel walls. Sarah drew her knees up and wrapped her arms around them, dropping her head on her arms in spent exhaustion.

Ilmar took deep breaths until she could speak. "Thank you, Sarah." She placed her hand on Sarah's shoulder. "I will not forget this."

"Ummm..." Sarah moaned, from under her arm. "No problem..." she replied, sighing deeply.

***

"What the hell are they?" Trish asked, pointing to the objects rising into the air from behind the Guardians. Both Aaron and Danny scanned the runway through their scopes.

"They look like..." Aaron hesitated, trying to figure it out. "Chariots?"

"We are in trouble. *Doomed.* Now you may panic," Azewrath warned.

"Oh, my God!" Danny shouted, staring through his scope. Ilmar hung from the helicopter. "Illy's falling!" He turned toward Reeglar. "Do something!"

"It is all right, Danny," Reeglar stated, consoling him. "Sarah has her." She smiled. "And even if she did fall, she would not go far. The force shield would catch her so she would never reach the ground."

"Oh!" Danny sighed. His body dropped into a chair, landing with a thud.

***

The Chariots gave chase, closing the gap between themselves and the Pave Hawk. The Telepaths assaulted the copter with a barrage of blast waves, rocking the helicopter. Pikkar watched as the aircraft took a beating from the Chariot Riders. Only moments before, Ilmar had fallen from the open door, dangling precariously above the ground.

"Torg," Pikkar ordered, "relay this to the #4's. I want that flying machine shot down to the ground."

"But, my Prince," Torg reasoned, "Ilmar is still inside."

"I can see that, Torg," Pikkar assured him. "Now, have them bring it *down*. Launch the projectiles. Let us see them navigate away from the Obsidian Spears."

Torg shook his head. *This man has gone mad,* he thought to himself as he readied his mind to send out the order to the Chariot Riders. The Chancellor sent his thought waves out to the Telepaths. *"Riders, this order comes down from the Prince. Use the Spears and shoot down that helicopter."*

Torg didn't know how much longer he could continue to take orders from Pikkar. They were right in thinking he was just with the Army to help his daughter, Reeglar. He glanced back at Yanni, who stood next to him. She returned his gaze, her brows furrowed as if she picked up on one of Torg's stray thoughts. Turning his attention back to the chase, he noticed the Chariot Yanni helped to control, flying erratically.

"Yanni," Torg redirected her thoughts. "Your Chariot is falling behind. Disengage your shield and concentrate on your Level 4. She needs your full attention. I shall bear the brunt of the responsibility for our inner shield's strength." She hesitated, unsure of his true intention. "Do it! Before she dies," Torg commanded her.

"Thank you, Torg." Yanni changed her focus. She quickly used her Abilities to level out the flying Chariot, so the #4 inside could do her job.

As the Chariots closed in on the Pave Hawk, Ilmar dreaded the confrontation. Ilmar and Sarah crawled into the cabin and strapped themselves in for safety's sake, as the gap between their pursuers shortened. They watched as nearest Telepath reached down and retrieved a long, black object, shaped like a giant arrowhead. Longer than her whole arm in length, the Rider lifted the Spear, aiming.

Sarah thought about asking Ilmar what it was, but the look on the other woman's face made her stop. "What?"

Ilmar ignored her. "Patrick..." Ilmar spoke calmly. "Land! Land the helicopter, now!" Serious and insistent, Ilmar squeezed Pat's shoulder, but her warning came too late.

Once the Telepath hurled the Obsidian Spear toward the Pave Hawk, the Chariots came at the copter, one after another, streaking by at a rapid pace. They aimed straight at the helicopter. The Spears bounced off the force shield enveloping them that Reeglar controlled from the tower.

Patrick did as Ilmar ordered and brought the helicopter closer to the ground as quickly as he could, but not quick enough. A lone shard of Obsidian managed to penetrate the shield, slicing off one of the four rotor blades. The copter dove and listed, wobbling wildly.

"Aw, shit!!" Patrick cursed, struggling with the controls. "That thing sheared the rotor blade right off. We're done for!"

"No, we are not!" Ilmar corrected him, throwing herself at the instrument panel.

She went down on her knees, grabbed the control console with both her hands and the entire front end of the Pave Hawk glowed with a bright white light. Nothing changed. Ilmar could keep the engines running, but she couldn't do anything about making the rotor blades spin correctly. Thwarted, she returned Patrick's gaze.

"I can not stop the descent," she warned them.

"We're gonna crash!" Pat advised them. "Get to the back of the cargo area and hold on!" They did their best to get out of the cabin. Both women wrapped themselves up in the cargo netting, as the Pave Hawk spun and plummeted downward, falling ever closer to the pavement.

***

"You son of a bitch..." Danny cursed and loaded his grenade launcher, eying his sight. "Fire in the hole!" he yelled to clear anyone from behind him. Once Danny fired his weapon, another smoke blast discharged backward into the tower, but his speeding grenade found its target. The Chariot and its Rider Telepath went up in a fiery explosion.

Reeglar did her best to keep the Pave Hawk from crashing to the runway. She reached out with both hands, trying to hold the weight of the entire helicopter.

The heavy copter traveled rapidly, and landed hard, skidding across the runway until it finally stopped at the edge of the grass. An engine immediately caught fire, prompting Danny to throw down his weapon and run to the door on his way to the stairs.

Aaron called out after him. "Where'r you going?"

Danny turned in the doorway. "I'm going to make sure they're okay." He pointed at them. "You and Azewrath hit the Chariots, now that they're closer... And hit them hard! I'll need some cover."

"You got it!" Aaron agreed, taking up position. He pointed his MP5 out the window, weapon at the ready. Sending a barrage of successive machine gun fire into the oncoming Chariots, he laughed as he swung his barrel back and forth. "Come on, Rath. I could use your help."

Azewrath placed his Heckler and Koch on the window next to Aaron. "A short schooling session might be in order."

"Just do what I do," Aaron instructed Azewrath. "Close one eye and look through the sight, and then, when you're ready, squeeze the trigger with your finger. Like this." Aaron let his bullets fly again.

Azewrath sighed, proceeding through the motions. He pulled the trigger, but nothing happened. "My gun is broken," he told Aaron.

Aaron leaned over and checked Azewrath's machine gun. He found that the safety set to the on position. "Dude." He turned over the toggle switch from the white "S" safe mode, to the red "F" continuous fire mode. "You had the safety on."

"Are you sure?" Azewrath asked.

"Uh, yeah. I'm not gonna make that mistake again." Aaron

positioned the gun again for Azewrath. "Now try it, and hold on to the gun tightly."

Azewrath pointed his gun and fired. He wasn't really aiming at the #4's and the flying Chariots, but his gunfire sprayed the air around them, forcing them back.

"It is working!" Azewrath said, sounding surprised. He picked up the MP5 with renewed vigor, raining more bullets upon his fellow Akkadians.

***

Danny ran down the stairs of the control tower as fast as he could, skipping two or three steps at a time. Before reaching ground level, he jumped over the railing about halfway down, slamming his body into the door. He bolted out into the open at a full, flat out run.

The warm summer rain hit Danny's skin, but he hardly noticed it. He only thought of Ilmar; of her safety. The Pave Hawk went down one-hundred yards from the tower, and it went down hard.

He ran on, dodging felled buildings as he crawled over the crumbling rubble. Scrambling over upturned cars and half buried military aircraft, he spotted the helicopter laying on its side. All the rotor blades had snapped off, and a fire burned in one of the twin turbo engines.

This is bad, Danny thought. He climbed carefully to stay clear of the blaze's reach. All the while the flames licked his moist skin. "Illy! Pat!" he called, making his way to the open cargo doorway.

"We're all down here!" Pat yelled out. "A little tied up at the moment."

Danny squinted into the darkness, searching for the three of them. He found them tangled up in the cargo harness netting. "Is everyone all right?"

"Yeah. Just cuts and bruises," Sarah offered. "But not if we don't get outta here soon."

"Our injuries are nothing," Ilmar added. "I will Heal everyone as soon as I am free."

"I've gotta try ta get you guys outta there." Danny reached in, trying to unhook the harness, to no avail. "One of the engines is on fire, and it's gonna blow."

"You've got to find something to cut us free," Pat encouraged him.

Danny bit his lip, thinking hard. It was so hard to concentrate before he ran out of time. Then it hit him. "The Obsidian stones!" He realized he could use them. "HEY! I'll be right back."

"Danny, wait!" Ilmar called out to him, but he was gone. "He will never be able to hold them in his hands," she explained to Sarah and Pat.

As Danny ran, the machine guns fired from the tower. The bullets flew way over his head and scattered the Akkadian Chariots, holding them at bay. With the Army closing in on their location and across most of the airfield, the Guardians were closer to Danny then he liked.

I can't think about this now!

Instead, he scoured the landscape for any sign of a stray Obsidian Spear; challenging to spot with all the debris on the runway, but he had to try. He made his hands into fists, shaking them in desperation.

"Where are they?!" he cried out loud and squeezed his eyes tight, dropping his head. *Think, Danny. Think!* Frustrated to the point of exhaustion, it unexpectedly appeared in his mind.

He walked forward, slowly at first. As things became somehow familiar to him, he moved faster. He climbed over rubble from buildings and jumped wrecked vehicles until he found the Jeep that had appeared in his mind. A Hummer, to be exact, partially submerged in a fissure made by the earthquake. Sticking out of the hood was an Obsidian Spear. It even shined in the rain, haloed as a sign, sparkling and glistening; its edge, razor sharp.

"Yes!" Danny shook his fist again, this time in celebration. He grabbed it with both hands, trying to pull it out gently, but the sharp blade-like point cut him, as always. Blood ran everywhere. "Oh, shit! I need something strong." Searching inside the Hummer, he fumbling around the debris and found something. "Score!"

It was a Kevlar vest.

He extracted the vest, wrapping it around the spear as best he could. He put his weight into it and rocked it back and forth until the garment did its job, and the black stone pulled free of the steel. The cutting blade still managed to mangle the protective jacket, but Danny tucked the vest wrapped spear under his arm, and ran back to the Pave Hawk.

When he returned, the engine fire raged. It arched over the cargo door opening, so Danny had to climb the underside of the helicopter. When he reached the top, the heat from the flames assaulted his face, but he breached the scorching waves.

"I've got it!" Danny informed them.

"Hurry!" Pat requested, firmly.

"Okay, look out," Danny warned them. "And whatever you do, *don't* move."

He shimmied along the side of the helicopter, leaning in and carefully, but swiftly, cut the net holding Pat captive. He managed to saw one web strand at a time, releasing Patrick first. Danny reached in and helped Patrick climb out to safety.

Ilmar stared up at Danny. "You are bleeding."

"What's new?" Danny answered, chuckling nervously.

Patrick held onto the belt loops of Danny's jeans. "I've got you. You should be able to stretch further to get the girls out."

Danny nodded. Leaning in again, he attempted to cut Sarah out next. She pushed herself as far away from the netting as she could while he cut it away from her. Sarah managed to squeeze through the small opening, climbing over Danny until she was next to Patrick.

Patrick helped her down. "Run to the safety of the tower!" Sarah wasted no time getting out of danger and sprinted toward the tall building. Patrick grabbed hold of Danny one more time. "Okay, hurry up."

The flames from the engine crept ever closer, burning Danny's cheek, but he ignored the excessive heat. He leaned in for the third time to retrieve Ilmar. After a few sawing cuts, she was free.

"I've got ya!"

She grabbed Danny's hands, and he pulled her out. Immediately, her hands glowed that beautiful warm, yellow hue, which let him know she was Healing him. Pat jumped down.

"Thanks," Danny said to Ilmar, helping her down. He passed her to Patrick, first before jumping from the helicopter to the ground himself.

"Now, let's get the hell outta here!" Pat urged. "Bye, baby!" He said to the Pave Hawk. "It just wasn't meant to be."

Danny grabbed Ilmar's hand, and they ran, making it about twenty yards before the fire became too much for the fuel tanks to handle. The fuselage exploded, scattering metal shrapnel in all directions. The force of the blast sent Pat, Ilmar, and Danny sprawling to the ground.

Danny jumped to his feet first. "Get up!" he yelled, helping Ilmar to her feet.

Pat pushed himself up, following close behind him. Three Obsidian Spears hit the grass next to where they ran, missing them by inches. Cursing, they sprinted with renewed vigor.

Danny hit the door to the control room building and scaled the three flights of stairs to the tower of glass, dragging Ilmar behind. Sarah held on to Aaron as if she would never let him go, impeding his ability to fire his rifle. Danny went to the window and noticed the Akkadian Army encroached on the periphery of the control tower right outside. Pat entered the room, and Trish fell onto his chest, sobbing, her Beretta digging into his back. The experience was uncomfortable but welcoming.

"What do we do now?" Aaron asked no one, in particular, glancing from his gun sight.

Azewrath continued to fire on the approaching Army, enjoying the excitement of his new found gun user capabilities. The rain picked up in intensity, obscuring their view through the windows. Fortunate for the Army, they remained protected by their shields, keeping them safe and dry.

Reeglar moved her shield to surround the entire control tower. "I have us surrounded by my shield, but we are no longer safe here. The Army is too close."

The Obsidian Spears hit the tower, glancing off the force shield, landing in the dirt. No one knew what to do next, but the Akkadians took that decision away from them. Invading their minds, came the all too familiar warm tingling of a Telepathic intrusion. Reeglar bit her lip, and Azewrath stopped firing his MP5, unmoving, understanding the ramifications.

The invading Akkadian Army stopped its forward march about two-hundred yards from the air traffic control tower. Danny took a headcount. Thirty-five giant Guardians held the front line, with a smaller number of others behind. The Chariot Riders landed on the runway behind the Army, waiting. For what, he didn't know.

"Humans," the voice in their heads said, *"you have fought well. Now, we have come to deliver this ultimatum. Surrender the* – *the* – Torg could not adequately express the word, so he hesitated. *"The traitors, or be destroyed. The choice is yours. We shall await your answer."*

They all looked to Reeglar, sensing her affinity to the voice. In turn, she went to Ilmartutar. "It would seem we have run out of options."

"So it seems," Ilmar agreed.

"No..." Danny whispered, forcefully, shaking his head. "NO!" he repeated louder, raising his voice. "NO! We didn't do all this..." He paced back and forth, throwing his arms up in the air. "Suffer all this, to have it end this way."

Sarah let go of Aaron. "Look out there, Danny!" She grabbed him, dragging him to the window. "There are eight of us, against a whole army of..." She couldn't think of a perfect word. "... Of incredibly frightening, and dangerously powerful people." She hated what she said after it left her mouth. "Whatever! You know what I mean."

Standing, Azewrath put down his gun and locked eyes with Reeglar. "Look into Pikkar, if you need an answer. I already know what lies inside his mind, and we can not go back!"

"You want us to face them? To fight against them to the end?" Reeglar asked him.

"There is no other choice," Azewrath stated.

Reeglar finally nodded. Taking a deep breath, she contacted her father, privately. *"Father, we shall not be going back. Do as you will, for we are prepared to fight until we die."*

"Reeglar, you know I can not allow that." Torg sent his intense love for her and protectiveness across their bond. *I am aware you carry Azewrath's child, my kin. I can not lose you, nor the living male child inside you."'*

"'How?"' She searched his mind to find how he came by that information. *"Mage' Rom!"'*

"'Do not blame him, child."' Torg informed her of his plan. *"I shall come inside to you. Simultaneously, I shall drop the*

shield around the Council and the Prince. Prepare!"

Everything happened too quickly. Drakar fell into a trance, screaming out the Prince's name. *"Pikkar! Be warned!"*

Yanni jumped away from Torg, as the Chancellor wasted no time levitating himself from the Akkadian Army. He joined his daughter in the tower, floating in through the North windows.

Reeglar let both Azewrath and Aaron know where to shoot. "Pick up your guns. Now!" she commanded them.

Both men knelt at the window and aimed their MP5s at the unprotected Army. As the bullets flew, Yanni swiftly struggled to erect a shield around everyone of importance.

General Nutrion morphed into a giant, protecting the Prince. He jumped in front of Pikkar taking a barrage of fire directly into his chest plate. Lieutenant Thorium brought orders to the surviving Guardians. "Close ranks!"

Drakar addressed the Prince. "We shall not win this without the Chancellor. I have *Seen* it!"

"Nonsense!" Pikkar scoffed. "You give one man too much credit."

Inside the tower, Torg embraced his daughter. "I have missed you."

"And I have missed you as well," Reeglar answered him, surprising him with the most significant hug he received from her in weeks. He returned her embrace in kind.

Torg released his daughter, turning to Azewrath. He stopped him from his gun-play. "We shall talk later about your inappropriate behavior. If we all survive."

Azewrath nodded in reverence. "We all might not. Yet, if we do, I shall accept any and all of your wrath."

XXII

Rain of Tears

Damon came out of his trance wholly disturbed. *What to do?* He asked himself. He could turn to no one about what he had Seen. All Pikkar sympathizers were on the surface, and they were not doing well. *Unfortunate,* he thought again. He loved his father, but Damon was a pragmatist, after all. He decided to release the Queen.

He ran through the corridors to the Royal courtyard. There, he found two Telepaths unconscious and the Queen had gone. It was evident to him where she had gone. Loyalties – well known in Akkadia – gave him a location. He took off down another corridor on his way to the Healing Ward. He ran all the way until he reached the Ward entrance.

Damon stopped and placed his hand against the door jamb, resting to catch his breath. His appearance attracted Mage' Rom's attention, so he wandered over to the doorway.

"It is not every day I witness a Seer running," the Mage' addressed Damon, motioning the Seer into the room. "This must be very important, indeed."

Damon hesitated as came in and swallowed hard. "I need to see the Queen." Rom opened his mouth to protest, but Damon cut him off. "Do not even try to tell me she is not here, Mage'. She is no longer imprisoned in her quarters."

Alkara appeared from the other room and gracefully crossed the floor. "Rom," she spoke calmly, "let him speak." She approached Damon. "What is it you want of me, Seer?"

Damon noticed she didn't use his name. "Thank you, my Queen." Damon bowed low, trying to sound respectful. "The Army shall not be triumphant. I have Seen this."

Surprised, Alkara questioned him further. "Pikkar and the Guardians shall be defeated by the humans?"

"It is unclear how many Akkadians still align themselves with the Prince."

"Oh." Alkara raised an eyebrow. "I see." She gazed sidewards at Rom. "This must be uncomfortable for you to report, Damon.

As I recall, your father is up there with the Prince. I wonder what he is doing at this moment?"

"I do not know, my Queen, but I would volunteer to go to the surface and find out."

"I believe your idea has merit, Damon," Alkara agreed. "Rom, recruit as many Telepaths as you can and meet me at the Reaction Lift. We are going up." Rom nodded to her as she walked to the front door of the Healing Ward. "Oh, and Damon? Do not bother to join us. I might have had to sneak in here a prisoner, but I shall walk out a Queen." Then as an afterthought, she added more. "And a warrior."

Alkara headed to her quarters. Intending to dress for combat, she opened her wardrobe, reaching way into the back. Reverently, she pulled out a pile of thinly beaten metal. Alkara laid them on the bed and one by one strapped each piece to her body. Starting with her leg guards, fitting them tightly around her thighs, moving to her arms.

Stretching her arms, she made a fist and flexed her fingers. She needed to judge her ability for ease of mobility. Fastening her breastplate next, she was pleased it still fit her well. After, she placed her hand deep inside the shelving and pulled out a helmet, remembering the days she used to wear it. Always in training.

I never thought I would need any of this again, she thought, placing it over her head and checking her image in the mirror. Every inch a warrior Queen, Alkara turned, striding from her room to meet Rom. The twelve Level 4 Telepaths waited inside the Lift when she strode up to them.

"Alkara!" Rom exclaimed, surprised. "What –?"

"It is just for show, Rom," Alkara explained. "No one shall doubt my intent."

"Well..." Rom nodded. "Very impressive. *I* am frightened."

"Good!" Alkara stepped inside the Lift. "I would hate to have gone through all this trouble for no reason." The doors closed, and they ascended to the surface.

***

Pikkar raged in the throes of a temper tantrum. Suffering betrayal by Torg, he screamed at his subordinates.

"Incompetence!" he yelled at them from his hiding place behind Nutrion. "Drakar, my best Seer..." He pointed at the man. "And you knew nothing about Torg until *now?*" Drakar lowered his head in shame. Pikkar pointed to Yanni. "Torg was your mentor, and he gave you no indication of his intentions?" Yanni said nothing but gritted her teeth, struggling to hold and control the force shield around the Akkadian Army.

Pikkar reached the end of his patience. "All Telepaths!" he commanded. "Take down that structure!"

The Level 2's and 3's that were left knelt on the tarmac, bringing their separate Abilities together. Slowly at first, a distant rumble built in intensity until the ground visibly moved, cracking all around them. The ground tore apart, except for the area where the Akkadians stood under the dome of Yanni's shield.

"Stop!" Torg yelled to Aaron and Azewrath. Reaching out his hands he spread them outward, stopping the machine gun fire.

"Yes! Stop now!" Reeglar agreed with her father. "Quickly, everyone gather together!"

"What's going on?" Danny asked.

"They create an earthquake to take down the building," Ilmar explained. Moving closer to Reeglar and Torg, she pulled Danny along with her.

With a slight shaking under their feet, the walls swayed and buckled. The glass cracked and splintered across each window pane, creating little delicate stress veins that spread in all directions.

Torg nodded to Reeglar, sharing an inner conversation. Without warning, everyone lifted off the floor. Torg held them aloft, as Reeglar surrounded them with a force shield. As the glass windows shattered, the building fell around them. The walls disintegrated as the roof crashed down upon the force shield.

Together, Reeglar and Torg carried the group away from the collapsing tower, whisking the force sphere surrounding them away from the airfield. They sailed closer to the residential area of the base, under cover of rows and rows of buildings. The shimmering of the shield disappeared as they landed on the ground.

Danny scanned the terrain. "I think it would be smarter if we all split up." He got nodding heads in agreement. "It'll be harder for them to keep track of us."

"A wise strategy," Torg continued, turning to Reeglar. *"We might have to defend ourselves – to the ultimate outcome, my dear. Do you understand me?"*

"Yes, Father," Reeglar answered out loud. "I have already thought of that, and I am prepared."

"We gotta go!" Patrick stressed, encouraging them to make a move. "I'll take Trish with me. And – give me this gun!" He pulled it right out of Trish's hand. "Really, Danny! What are you thinking; giving my girl a gun?"

"Just in case!" Danny tried to explain.

Pat shook his head. Grabbing Trish's hand, he yelled at everyone. "Good luck! Come on, baby."

They ran off heading south, farther away from the Akkadians. Patrick didn't stop running until he and Trish got to the officer's barracks. He pulled Trish inside through a broken doorway to get them out of the rain. Once inside, Trish wrung out her hair, but Pat went to a north facing window, taking up a combat position. He watched the Akkadians from there, satisfied that they were safe for the moment.

Trish came over and knelt down beside Pat, underlining hysteria marred her face. "Is it okay for me to have a nervous breakdown, yet? I think I've held it together pretty well."

"Ummm... I'm thinking, not yet." He turned away from the window to study her closely. "Can you hold it together for me just a little while longer, Trish?" he asked her gently. She nodded, blinking back tears. He held her hand before returning his gaze out the window.

***

Aaron had both hands on his MP5 when Sarah grabbed it. "Hey!" Aaron yelled. "I was just getting used to that!"

"Well, get un-used to it!" Sarah pointed the gun upward and ran, throwing her words back at everyone. "Take care people!" She yelled out to Aaron. "Hey, lover boy, let's go!"

Aaron trotted off behind Sarah. "Well, she is better with a gun than I am." He shrugged, following her.

Danny turned to Ilmar. "Maybe you should stay with your

people. It might be safer for you."

Ilmar shook her head, wrapping her arm in the crook of his. "I am coming with you. Where ever you go, so shall I!" she stated adamantly.

"In the interest of expediency, okay!" Danny agreed.

Reeglar went to them. "Go! Both of you!" She pushed them, encouraging them to go. "We shall face them alone."

"But –" Danny started.

"No buts!" Reeglar ordered, firmly. "Get out of the rain!"

Danny rested his grenade launcher on his shoulder, taking Ilmar by the hand and headed north. They ran about 100 yards when Danny yelled for her to stop. "Illy! Look at this!" Danny grabbed her by the arm, pointing to a small motorcycle.

Ilmar checked the bike, eying Danny warily. "You are thinking something perilous, am I correct?"

"Only if it starts. You can start it, right?"

"Yes," she said, unwilling to think about the danger.

"Cool! You're going to drive it. Get on!" He helped her onto the bike.

"I knew it," Ilmar worried. "I do not know how to drive it." She threw her leg over, grabbing the handles. Her hands glowed white, and the machine roared to life.

"Just wing it. All you gotta do is steer," Danny told her, getting on behind. "And stay clear from the back of this launcher." He set the gun on his shoulder, loaded and ready for bear. Ilmar sighed, but took off, heading back toward the fighting.

**

"So, we are to hold the front line by ourselves?" Azewrath asked Torg.

"Do you have somewhere else to be?" Torg inquired back.

Azewrath bit his lip, raising an eyebrow. "Anywhere else would be preferable." He gazed at Reeglar. "Is this what you wish?"

Reeglar took Azewrath by his hand not holding the machine gun. "We do not have a choice."

"Prepare," Torg warned. "They are coming."

Azewrath raised his MP5, pointing it at the approaching Akkadians. Torg and Reeglar created a shield to separate and protect them. Six Guardians were first to come into view. Side by side, General Nutrion, and Lieutenant Thorium led the soldiers in the advanced. The sparkling of Yanni and the other Telepath's shield surrounding the Guardians blazed, informing all of their safety. From behind the Guardians came an outraged voice.

"*You dare stand and face me, Torg?*" Prince Pikkar yelled, pushing his way between Nutrion and Thorium.

The General attempted to stop Pikkar from exposing himself. "No. my Prince."

Pikkar turned to his Guardian and growled. Spinning back, he raised his hand, halting the forward motion of the rest of the Army. "Stop!"

"I do dare," Torg answered. "I wish to appeal to your common sense. I urge you to forget this campaign of destruction. Forget the human world, leave our children, and return to Akkadia, unscathed."

"Forget it?" Pikkar almost laughed. "Look around you, Torg. We caused all this." He made a sweeping motion with his arm at the destruction. "And it is just the beginning. When we are finished with the surface, it shall be unrecognizable."

"Now that is something truly to look forward to," Azewrath added, sarcastically.

"No one was talking to you, *traitor!*" Pikkar pulled back his lips in a snarl. "To think I once called you, friend." Pikkar laughed, pointing at Azewrath. "You *disgust* me."

"Yes," Azewrath added. "Well, some people grow up and move on." He had his weapon raised and pointed directly at the Prince. Sighting through the scope of the gun, he smiled. "I have never Seen you in this light before."

The Guardians made a lunging motion, but Pikkar raised his hand, halting them again. "You are going to shoot me, Azewrath? Yanni!" Pikkar yelled over his shoulder. "Bring the Level 4's." Yanni and three more Level 4's emerged from between the Guardians – their hands outstretched, creating a very impressive force shield. "You truly think your human rendered weapons can actually affect us?"

"We have done so already," Azewrath informed him. "Perhaps

you have not taken a count of your Guardian ranks."

"A mere scratch," Pikkar boasted, "you shall need to try harder!"

"By your command." Torg complied.

When Torg reached out with his arms, it seemed he gathered something from far away. He struggled with the weight of whatever he summoned. With his arms shaking, his veins stood out on his neck with the exertions.

Within seconds, Reeglar witnessed an object hover above them. It was a massive military plane, a Lockheed HC - 130 Hercules transport. Sailing overhead with its guns trained on the ground, it opened fire on the Akkadians.

Yanni and the other #4's held their shield against the barrage of projectiles trying to pierce their line. The side doors opened on the Hercules, and two 30 mm Bushmaster II cannons sent their weapons on their target. Huge explosions ripped giant holes in the runway around the shield, sending chunks of concrete into the air. Torg brought the plane around again, setting it up for another pass as the cannons attacked the Akkadian Army.

Yanni voiced her fears to her Prince. "My Prince, this weapon is strong enough to weaken the force shield!" She pleaded with him. "With our depleted numbers, I do not know if we can hold its strength for much longer."

Pikkar stormed over to her and grabbed her by the shoulders. "I do not care if you need to use every ounce of strength you have left! *Hold this barrier!* Do you hear me?" He charged the Telepaths. "This is a decree. Disobey it by threat of death!" He spun around, making sure he got his point across. His eyes burned into every one of his remaining compatriots.

Azewrath kept the MP5 trained on the opposing Army. He emptied clip after clip into the gathering troops, bringing one or two Guardians down in the process. Torg drove the giant Hercules military plane in again slowly; its large size ominous in its approach. The cannons commenced their attack, as Torg controlled the rapid firing of the weapons. Reeglar increased her shield strength, protecting them from the explosive missiles from the giant plane.

"Be careful, Father!" Reeglar warned. "The missiles get too close!"

"Indeed!" Torg smiled. "This is more difficult than it looks. Stand back. I would not want anything unfortunate to happen to Azewrath in the process." Reeglar made a face at him for that remark.

From behind the Akkadian ranks, a motorcycle sped by erratically. "Comin' in hot!" Danny yelled before launching a grenade right at the back of the shielded Army. The bike whooshed by so quickly; no one got a track on them.

"Was that Danny?" Azewrath asked.

"Woo-hoo!" Danny hollered, as he helped Ilmar steer the bike around for another pass. Once she had the bike under control, he reloaded his grenades. "Drive by as fast as you can, okay? Open the throttle all the way."

"O-K!" Full of adrenaline, Ilmar used the slang back at him. The bike took off so fast the front tire came off the road.

Pikkar had to split his attention to both sides. When Ilmartutar came toward him on the bike, he pushed his way to the rear of the Army, so that he could have a clean line of sight. The Prince laughed loudly as the cycle approached. When Danny set up for the grenade launch, Pikkar grabbed one of the Level 4's.

"Send an Obsidian Spear at that vehicle, now!" he ordered.

"My Prince, Ilmartutar rides upon it," the Level 4 stated.

"That is not your concern. Do as I ordered."

The Telepath did as her monarch bade her, and the black arrow-shaped stone flew toward the bike. Danny pulled the trigger at the same time as the spear sheered right through the rear tire.

"Oh, my Goddess!" Ilmar screamed, as the bike immediately went into a tailspin. In the pouring rain and the wet tarmac, it skidded on its side, sending both Danny and Ilmar sliding. Their bodies received a nasty case of road rash in the process.

When Ilmar stopped rolling, she sat up and placed her hands on herself. She administered her Healing Abilities to her wounds so that she could help Danny afterward. He wasn't moving. She put her hands on both sides of his face, sending the yellow light to surround him and bring him back.

"Ugh!" he groaned, once he regained consciousness. Without a moment's hesitation, Danny reached for the grenade launcher, stood, and grabbed Ilmar by the hand. They both ran to find shelter. They found it in a collapsed building, taking refuge behind it.

He got her attention. "You good?"

Breathing hard, Ilmar nodded yes as laughter took her by surprise. Danny tried to avoid eye contact. Her laughter was infectious, and he began to laugh as well. They fell into each other's arms until they caught their breath.

"THAT was stupid!" Danny stated, wiping her drenched hair from her eyes.

Ilmar nodded. "Indeed!"

***

The runway around the Akkadian Army disintegrated to the point of instability. Some of the Level 2's compensated by creating a steadying foothold. They balanced the rocking tarmac to keep the combined weight of the Akkadians centered.

"We have them in a defensive posture, Father," Reeglar thought to Torg.

Amused at his daughter's warning, Torg agreed. *"Indeed, my dear. That WAS the plan."*

Torg sent the combat plane out, circling, bringing it back in again for another attack run. It headed for the protective shield surrounding the Akkadians, guns blazing, opening holes in the ground once again. While confined to a small piece of the runway, the Army's footing wobbled.

Bringing the Hercules to a halt, Torg stopped it right over his enemies. One minute, the huge plane hovered above, the next, Torg brought it crashing down upon the Akkadians, notably, the Prince.

The plane smashed into the force shield, ripping and tearing the steel. Torg brought his hands together in a downward motion, creating enormous pressure on top of the Hercules, forcing the plane into the ground, and hopefully, crushing everyone underneath it. The momentum of the crash collapsed the field, sending the Akkadians plummeting beneath it. The wrecked hull of the Hercules covered the opening in the tarmac.

As Azewrath lowered his machine gun, Reeglar shook her head. "It is not over. Keep vigilant."

The heap of steel that was once the large plane shuddered and vibrated. Torg was not in the least surprised as the metal rose into the air, only to land on the ground with the crashing sound yards away. The Akkadian Army levitated out of the hole Torg made in the runway.

"We are too evenly matched," Torg thought to Reeglar.

"I have faith in you, Father." Reeglar smiled at Azewrath. *"And I have it on good authority that we are on the side of the righteous."*

"Indeed?" Torg was unsure whether he was slightly impressed or surprised.

Pikkar realized both sides were fighting to a stalemate, so he tried another tactic, hoping to break down their morals. "Lower us to the ground, Yanni," he ordered her, and they immediately touched down just a few feet from where they had been. Pikkar turned, taking a few steps in Reeglar's direction, but he didn't speak to her; he addressed Azewrath while training his attention on Reeglar.

"So, Azewrath, this is the paramour... Your painted woman. The one you have replaced my daughter for?"

Azewrath raised his machine gun again, pointing it right at Pikkar. "You should not go to a place you shall regret, Pikkar!" Azewrath warned him.

"You speak of my daughter, Pikkar! She is no paramour." Torg fumed. "She is a true Akkadian. At least she has not chosen a human for a mate."

"Enough!" Reeglar ordered. "All this name calling shall get us nowhere." Reeglar turned to Pikkar. "Walk away, my Prince. Return to Akkadia now, and no one else shall get hurt."

"Who do you think you are, little girl?" Pikkar asked condescendingly.

Reeglar smiled. "I am a daughter of the House of Torg. My Father is a powerful Level 5 Telepath. I am a capable Level 4. Someone to be feared."

"I do not fear you, child," Pikkar scoffed.

"Perhaps not as yet," Reeglar continued. "So, let me give you something to fear. I shall be the mother of a very powerful Seer and Telepath. One who has already shown me your end, my Prince. And your time has come."

"Now Rath!" She connected to Azewrath within their bond.

Azewrath let the continuous fire of the MP5 rip across the front line of the Army. General Nutrion and Thorium quickly jumped in front of Pikkar, taking the brunt of the bullets. Torg activated his shield and then levitated both Reeglar and Azewrath backward out of the way.

Pikkar yelled more orders. "We need a greater advantage. Chariots aloft!" The Level 4 Telepaths jumped into their flying carriages. Within seconds, the Chariots rose into the air, sending their Obsidian Spears speeding toward their enemies.

***

Danny watched the whole interaction from his vantage point behind the collapsed building, waiting for the right moment to rejoin the fray. "Stand away from me, Illy," he warned her. She did as she was asked, sliding away from him, but holding onto the bricks of the broken structure.

Danny loaded his launcher and eyed his sight. Pulling the trigger, he sent the grenade into the center of the Guardians. The explosion threw General Nutrion backward, flying into a few Igniters, his massive bulk crushing them to lifelessness. Two Chariot Riders immediately fell out of the sky, crashing into a mangled pile of metal.

Hiding behind Yanni's shield, Drakar grabbed Prince Pikkar by the arm. "This shall not end well, my Prince. I have Seen it. I implore you to give up this quest for more power. The outcome has *changed.*"

"We can gain no THING without loss, Drakar," Pikkar quoted. "The universe demands give-and-take, and I still plan on taking."

***

Sarah and Aaron ran north of the fighting, hoping to get a better position with plenty of cover. They planned to attack from the flank.

"Holy shit!" Aaron said, watching the action from under an overturned truck. "This is getting intense."

Sarah glared at him like he was crazy. "Getting?" she asked, shaking her head and rolling her eyes. The battle raged on without her, but her attention was drawn by sirens off in the distance. "Do you hear that?"

"What? All the gunplay, the explosions, and the screaming? Sure," he told her.

"No. I hear sirens."

"How the hell can you hear anything else over all that?" Aaron wondered.

"Police sirens, maybe." She listened, tilting her head. "Fire truck?" Sarah handed Aaron the machine gun. "Wait right here; I won't be long." She turned and ran off.

"Where are you going?" he asked her receding back as she jogged away in the direction of the fire. He shaded his eyes from the rain with his one free hand, trying to follow her progress.

Sarah ran from the shelter of the truck to first a building and then, to a section of small shed-like structures. She moved slowly. Leaning against the cement wall, she peered over the top.

Yep, I'm right.

From where she hid, she witnessed a patrol car and a fire truck pull up to the crashed Pave Hawk. Recognizing the vehicle from her precinct, she identified the uniformed officers that exited.

Sarah wrestled with the decision of whether to stay hidden or to procure some help for getting the hell out of the messy situation. Behind her, the battle with the Akkadians raged relentlessly.

Why can't anyone else see what's going on? She wondered, deciding to stand and hail her comrades.

"Bill! Frank!" Sarah yelled as she stepped out from behind the wall. Startled, both men turned in her direction when she called their names. It took them a few seconds to place her face. She appeared bruised, scraped, and just a general wreck.

"Sarah?" Frank asked, surprised. "What are you doing here?"

"This place has been declared a disaster zone. It's dangerous," Bill offered. "What happened to you?"

She lied. "My boyfriend and I got caught out in the earthquake. Our car got swallowed up in a fissure, so we ended up having to find someplace close to get out of his rain. I thought it'd be a safe place... Wide open spaces and all."

"Look," Frank said, "we're done here. Just had to check out the area for the firemen. They're handling that fire. We can give you and your boyfriend a ride back home if you want. Unless you need to go to the hospital."

"Yeah, thanks," Sarah agreed. "That would be great. Neither of us is seriously hurt. I'll just be a minute. I got to go get him." She jerked her thumb over her shoulder. "I'll be right back." She took off running again.

***

Aaron waited for Sarah's return, but she took longer than he expected. Becoming antsy, he decided to get closer to the action. Wanting to help instead of sneaking around corners, he got up, double handed the MP5 and then ran back the same route they had come.

Making sure to move evasively, he ran a few steps. Taking cover, he looked for an opening, then ran a few steps only to duck back under cover. He did this over and over again, all the while getting closer to the fighting.

***

As the Guardians picked up some abandoned cars from the parking lot, they threw them against the shield which held Torg, Reeglar, and Azewrath inside. Danny reloaded the grenade launcher. He stood with it in his arms.

"I'm going in closer," he told Ilmar. "They need me."

"No, Danny!" Ilmar protested, holding onto him. "They will be all right."

"Yes... " he said gently, shrugging her off. "I'm going. But please, you stay here, out of danger." She shook her head to signify no. "Promise me!" he ordered her, grabbing her with his free hand.

Ilmar sighed. "All right," she huffed, still shaking her head no as an answer.

Before leaving, he kissed her hard, parting her lips, exploring her mouth with his tongue. It was a deep kiss with meaning. After he had broken away, he put his mouth to her forehead, letting his lips linger on her wet skin. "I love you," he added, running off. His feet splashed on the muddy ground.

Danny found a suitable building, half crumbled into dust, but still offering a slight cover from the weather. Jumping inside, he set up for another grenade launch when the last remaining Chariot flew overhead and spied him. It circled, hurling its complement of Obsidian Spears at him. Danny ducked further into the destroyed building, hoping to stay out of the Chariot Riders line of fire, but the Spears sliced through the building's remains, collapsing his barrier.

Reeglar followed the Chariot's path with her eyes, witnessing the grave danger for Danny. She attempted to put out one of her arms to help him when Torg stopped her.

"He shall keep, my daughter. You must concentrate on the strength of the shield."

"I believe he needs my help."

"There are others here, who can do that for him. You must protect yourself, and the precious life you carry."

Reeglar sighed, making her force shield stronger, protecting them from the automobiles the Guardian's threw at them. The protective field sparked but held fast.

***

Alkara exited the Reaction Lift with the others into the pouring rain. "I forgot how unpredictable the weather is on the surface," she reminisced to Rom, turning to the Level 4's. "I wish to expedite this visit, so hone in on the battle, find Pikkar and levitate us there, immediately!"

The Telepaths bowed en masse, beginning their search. They reached out with their minds, their tendrils merged as one, stretching out into the air. After a few moments, they extended their arms, creating a force bubble to surround the secondary Army. The sparkling blue hue of the shield shimmered in the rain, creating a prism of colors. The Telepaths lifted the group off the ground, soaring west in the direction of their destiny.

***

As Aaron neared the fighting, he could tell Danny was in trouble. Pulling out a magazine clip, he loaded his gun, took aim and fired at the attacking Chariot, running toward Danny's location. Mud flew everywhere as he ran, and he had to use his forearm to wipe the rain from his eyes just to see.

"I'm coming, bro!" Aaron shouted as he jumped heaps of debris, sprinting at the Chariot Rider.

***

Sarah returned to where she left Aaron, perturbed he wasn't there. "Aw, shit!" she cursed, kicking the truck.

She gazed out into the rain toward the fighting, searching for him. Screams and gunfire met her ears, causing the hairs on the back of her neck to stand. Following the noise, she spotted the Chariot Rider diving toward the ground – and toward Aaron. He raised his gun and sent his bullets up, hoping to find a weak spot in the force shield. Sarah's eyes widened, and her breathing came labored as she realized what he attempted.

Oh, no! NO! She ran towards Aaron as fast as she could.

***

Danny watched as the Chariot changed direction, diving downward, swerving to face off with Aaron. A barrage of flying bullets sprayed from Aaron's MP5 and headed straight toward the Telepath in the Chariot.

Aaron screamed a loud triumphant roar, as the Chariot came within spitting distance. "Take cover, Danny!"

The flying carriage turned quicker than Aaron could compensate, spinning around. Extremely skilled at finding his target, the #4 Telepath let the Obsidian Spears soar. The Akkadian arrowhead's trajectory made a beeline straight for Aaron.

Danny sprang to his feet and sprinted from his hiding place. "Aaron!"

Propelling himself in Aaron's direction, he hoped to knock his friend out of the way. The sharp, black spear sailed through the rain straight into Aaron's chest. Sucking in a mouthful of air,

Aaron went into shock. He exhaled, as Danny caught him in his flying dive. They both landed in the mud as the spear pinned Aaron to the ground with Danny's arms still wrapped around him. A pool of blood mixed with the rain, pouring from Aaron's wounded body.

"Aaron! Aaron!" Danny shook his friend as best he could, trying not to cause any more damage. He wrenched one arm from under Aaron's body and tapped his face, attempting to stun him into consciousness. When Aaron opened his eyes, he took a deep breath, spitting up blood. "Shit!" Danny cursed. "This doesn't look good, bro."

"Doesn't feel good, either," Aaron managed, choking on more blood, drifting off again.

"No, Aaron, don't close your eyes. Stay awake! Hold on!" Danny yelled. Aaron tried to do as Danny asked, but he just couldn't.

"So tired... Let me close my eyes... just for a sec..." Aaron closed his eyes.

"AARON!" Sarah screamed, watching the whole thing as if it happened in slow motion. She almost lost her balance but adjusted by picking up the pace to get over to him.

"Aaron!" Reeglar observed what she knew to be a fatal blow and lost her concentration. Slipping through the force shield to get to Aaron, she lost her footing and landed on the ground, covering herself with mud. Regaining her equilibrium, she ran over to Danny, Aaron, and Sarah.

Pikkar smiled and then laughed at the scene taking place in front of him. "Yanni," Pikkar ordered her, "launch an Obsidian Spear, now."

Yanni picked up the black projectile with her mind and held it in place with the wave of her hand. The spear hovered as she focused on her objective. "Mark, my Prince?"

Pikkar gave another order. "Target the traitor, Reeglar!"

Yanni nodded, instantly propelling the spear in Reeglar's direction. It sped through the air about to find its mark, but Reeglar reached Aaron's side and knelt down next to him. The spear missed the kill shot, instead slicing open her shoulder. She reached up to grab the wound, but blood spilled out through her fingers onto Aaron's inert body.

"Aghhh!" Reeglar cried.

Torg watched in horror as his daughter's injury spilled her precious blood. "PIKKAR!" he hollered. *"You are a dead man!"*

Pikkar laughed at his ex-Chancellor. "I am afraid you are mistaken. I am very much alive!"

"Not for much longer!" Torg promised.

Torg barely held it together – a father enraged. Furious, he dropped his shield, bringing his arms upward toward his chest. His hands mimicked opened claws as they gathered his powers in each palm. The swirling blue air in between built to a massive energy ball. Torg focused his entire Ability into a giant shock wave made from the air surrounding him. It vibrated in his hands. Then as a man possessed, he sent the blast directly out at Yanni and Pikkar.

The weight of the pressure knocked Yanni to the ground, but her shield protected her from the worst of it. The sheer force of the blow sent three Guardians flying. Their massive weight crashed down on the few remaining Level 3's. As they fell towards Yanni, she had no time to move. All she could do was throw her arm up in a futile attempt protect herself. Lieutenant Thorium landed on her with the crunching of steel on bone.

Pikkar, on the other hand, took the full force of the blast wave. The pressure hit him from both sides, crushing his body inward, sending a mass of blood, skin, and bones in all directions. Pieces of the Prince splashed on whoever stood closest.

Torg approached the pathetic remnants of the opposing Army and stomped his way through the mud. "Anyone else feel the need to try their luck against me?"

"Oh, my God!" Sarah cried, leaning over Aaron. She glanced up at Danny, tears in her eyes. "Is he... Is he?" She couldn't bring herself to say the word.

"I don't know," Danny answered, honestly. "He can't be. I won't let that happen." Danny took his free hand and wiped the rain away from Aaron's face. He felt no resistance in Aaron's body. "Come on, bro. You wouldn't let me die."

Reeglar put her hands on Aaron's chest, sensing nothing. "I am sorry," she informed them. "He is gone."

"No!" Sarah's voice wavered as she shook her head. "No, no, no! *You're wrong!*" She grabbed Aaron's shirt with both hands and shook him. "Damn it, Aaron! *Don't do this to me!*" She held on to Aaron, trying not to cry.

Ilmartutar barely witnessed what happened from her distance, but things appeared erroneous. "Father?!" she screamed, hoping she was wrong.

Ilmar left her hiding place and sprinted toward the spot where her father once stood. Perhaps she could help. When she reached Torg, she realized she could not help at all, not any longer.

As Ilmar observed the carnage, many emotions moved across her face. She didn't know what to feel. Where her father used to be, nothing remained but indistinguishable parts. Pieces that made up her father.

He was a cruel and angry man, but I never wanted him to – to – She couldn't think the word. *Never to be able to say goodbye.* She wiped away the tears that fell past her cheeks.

Turning her attention back to her friends, Ilmar watched Azewrath scoop up Reeglar, making sure she stemmed the amount of her spilled blood. He would have no part in her bleeding to death.

"Are you alright?" Azewrath asked. "Is the –"

"Baby?" she said it for him. "Yes. We are both fine."

Ilmar ran to them, skidding in the mud. As she slid, she fell to her knees, placing her hands on Reeglar. They glowed the brightest yellow until Reeglar disappeared from the brilliance of the light. The effects of Ilmar's Healing Abilities warmed Azewrath, but he knew his love would survive. The light faded, and Reeglar smiled, still covered in blood, but alive.

"Thank you, Ilmar," Reeglar added gratefully. "But Aaron..." She trailed off.

Ilmar put her hands on Aaron, watching, waiting. Her hands didn't even glow. "There is no spark." Ilmar studied Reeglar, who lowered her eyes and shook her head ever so slightly, conveying to Ilmar the futility of the situation.

"I hear nothing inside him," Reeglar assured everyone.

Danny grabbed Ilmar by the shoulders. "You've got to be able to do something... *Heal him!*" Danny begged her. "I can't let him die."

"My love," Ilmar stated softly, "if I could do something, I would do all I could. Yet, you can not Heal death. You can Heal injury…" She stared into his eyes. Placing her finger under his chin, she lifted his head up so he could look back at her and understand. "Death is gone… Total. It is final. With death, you can only grieve and then move on. Aaron is dead, yet the memory that he loved you enough to give up his life so that you may survive will be one you shall carry with you for the rest of your life. That is what *he* gave you. That is all *I* can give you."

"It's a weight too heavy, and it'll never be enough. I didn't ask Aaron to do it…" Danny lowered his head, trying not to cry himself.

Sarah frowned at Danny and then raised her eyes to the sky. She had lost herself – her sanity gone. Staring blankly off into space, she shut out the noise of her surroundings. Her body and mind seemed to separate.

As Danny held Aaron, he noticed Sarah shook all over. He wasn't sure whether from shock or anger. He soon found out. She breathed heavily; her lips curled up and showed her teeth until she sported a full grimace. Sarah turned on Danny with a vengeance.

"YOU!" Sarah pushed him, knocking him off his knees and dislodging the arm stuck under Aaron. Danny slid across the muddy ground a few feet. "I *HATE* you! I've always hated you!" She stood, glaring down at Danny. "Aaron was all that was good, and you are all that is bad. He would do anything for you, and you were nothing but a horrible influence on him. And now he's gone. Why should you still be alive? Why didn't *you* die instead?" Sarah walked backward, giving the Akkadians a sour look as well. She still breathed deeply to the point of hyperventilating.

"Don't you think I would trade places with him if I could?" Danny tried to reason with Sarah.

"Please, Sarah," Ilmar offered. "It is not Danny's fault."

"No, you're right, it's not just his fault. It's also yours. *All of you!*" She pointed her finger at the crowd. "This has been nothing but crazy from the start. You're all murderers!" Sarah closed her eyes, trying to clear her mind, but someone yelling her name drew her. Turning, she remembered her buddies from the precinct; they called to her.

"Sarah," Frank called. "What's the holdup? Let's go! We've

got another call." He motioned for her to join them. She shot a glance at her comrades and then back to Danny, who had returned to Aaron's side. He held his lifeless body in his arms, the rain diluting the flowing blood, mixing with the mud.

Sarah shook her head, lowered her eyes and stifled a sob. Placing her fingers on her lips, she turned and ran over to the patrol car.

"Where's your boyfriend?" Bill asked.

"He won't be coming." Sarah opened the back door, gazing over at the man she loved for the last time. Sighing, she slid into the car, closing the door. Danny watched as the car drove off, taking Sarah away from Aaron forever.

***

Aaron's death and the events of the day seemed to cause the rain's end – as if the heavens spilled all its sorrow and had nothing left to give, crying its last tears. Alkara's loyal troops made their way to Pikkar's last known whereabouts. A human military base.

Fitting, she thought before addressing the Telepaths. "Bring us down, yet keep the shields up until we gage the situation." Alkara turned to the Mage'. "I hope we shall not need your services."

"I pray as well, Alkara," Rom responded as his feet touched the ground.

"My Queen," a #4 Telepath gave the Queen the information he received. "It seems there are casualties on both sides of the battle."

"An unavoidable outcome of conflict and combat," the Queen remarked, gazing around at the ultimate destruction. The terrain, marred by giant cracks in the surface, crumbled structures, and crushed transport vehicles, showed the consequences. "My husband has gone mad, just mad," she repeated to Rom. "When I get there, I shall have him suffer a memory lock, I *swear!* Even if it means he shall not be the same man."

"That might not be a bad thing," Rom agreed. "And a fitting punishment for his crime against you."

As they drew closer, Alkara focused on what remained of Pikkar's army. She caught a glimpse of Torg, her Chancellor, standing with his head hanging low, flanked by some morphed Guardians. She counted eight; all totaled, and a few low-ranking Telepaths as well.

They are no danger, she thought. She observed absolutely no Igniters left standing. *What happened here?*

Torg heard the Queen's thoughts and immediately snapped his head up to search for her. *"Alkara?"* He seemed shocked to see her. *"Your presence was not in the plan."*

"No? My mistake, then, for not telling you, but it was MY plan," Alkara informed him. *"Have you something else to relay? What is it, Torg? I can sense you're holding something back from me. Is not the fighting over?"*

"It is over... And there have been many casualties."

"So I have been told. But there is still something else..."

"Yes, my Queen."

"Oh, that did not sound encouraging."

Torg let compassion seep over the link he shared with the Queen. He didn't use words to describe what had occurred but sent images of what actually happened straight into her mind.

Alkara stopped dead in her tracks, forcing her legion to halt as well. She brought her hands to her forehead, massaging her brow and temples. Filled with conflicting emotions, she struggled to face her future.

Rom put his hand on her shoulder. "What is wrong, Alkara?"

Alkara took a deep breath; her eyes welled with unshed tears. "Pikkar is dead. So is Yanni, General Nutrion, and Dinnac, just to mention a few."

"Truly?" Rom expelled air in disbelief. "We have grossly underestimated humans."

"It was Torg who killed them all," she informed him.

"Oh!" Again, Rom showed surprise. "I do not know what to say of that."

"It does not matter." She took another deep inhale and threw back her shoulders. Lifting her chin, she honed in on Torg's location. Her armor stood out in the emerging sunshine. "Let us go collect our people."

With Patrick glued to the window, it took all his willpower not to go out and help his brother. He needed to stay and protect Trish. She wasn't doing well. She sat on the floor, her arms wrapped around her knees and her head dropped onto her arms. She rocked back and forth, making small humming sounds – vocalizing to block out the sounds of the battle.

To Patrick, things looked like they were over outside, even the rain had stopped. Standing, he tucked the Beretta behind him into the waist of his jeans and then placed his hand on the back of Trish's head.

"Hey, honey?" Pat spoke softly, and Trish became still, her rocking ended. "I think it's all over out there, plus the rain has stopped. Do you want to see if Danny's okay?"

Trish lifted her head, with her eyes still closed. She sighed. "I'm a little ashamed of my behavior," she confessed. "I'm so sorry I lost it." She opened her eyes. "Forgive me?"

Pat held out his hand. "Are you kidding? All this is like being a youngster on a bad acid trip. No apologies necessary." She grabbed his extended hand, and he pulled her up. When he wrapped his arms around her and held her tight, she buried her head in his chest. "Shhh..." Pat reassured her, breaking away from their embrace so he could see her face. "Come on; we'll go slowly." He held out his hand again, this time for her to hold. She meekly smiled back at him as they exited through the broken door back to Danny.

As Pat approached, he noticed the somber and subdued Akkadians. Their eyes drew his attention to Danny. His brother was down on his knees with his back facing Patrick, so Pat took the chance and called out his brother's name. "Danny?"

Danny turned to his name, realizing Pat and Trish stood there. He bit his lip, struggling with what to say and how to say it. "Pat..." Danny stopped. He just couldn't continue without losing it.

The pain in Danny's face warned Pat of bad news. Noticing Ilmar, Reeglar, and, Azewrath also overcome by silence, panic rose within his chest. "Is that a body on the ground?" As Patrick's adrenaline surged, he let go of Trish's hand and ran to Danny's side. That's when the body on the ground came into view.

Aaron.

Danny still held him like a child with a rag doll.

"Oh, my God..." Pat whispered. He placed his hand on Danny's shoulder for support, unsure if it was for Danny sake or his own. Overcome with dizziness; Pat squeezed Danny.

"I don't know what to do, Pat." Danny tried to hold back his tears and control his emotions, failing.

"We'll bring him home to our house," Pat promised. "We'll call the hospital or morgue from there. I'm sure the emergency services have their hands full right now, with all this other mess because of the earthquake." Danny nodded. He couldn't respond, he just didn't trust his tongue.

Reeglar offered her help. "I shall carry him there myself, Danny. I promise." As Reeglar stood, her eyes widened, 'hearing' other voices in her head. "Alkara approaches!" she stated loudly.

Panicked, Ilmar jumped from the ground, prompting the others to do so as well, all except Danny. Turning toward the second wave of the Akkadians Legion Army, the gathered waited in trepidation. Ilmar swallowed hard as the ranks marched forward, surrounding them.

Alkara pushed her way through the Guardians and Level 2 Telepaths until she faced the Chancellor, staring directly at him. Torg bowed slightly, inviting the Queen's gaze to follow down to what remained of her husband. Without speaking, Alkara closed her eyes. When she opened them again, she took a regal posture, exemplifying every inch a warrior Queen.

Torg stood from his bow. "I regret to inform you that the Prince's campaign has failed."

"A gross understatement, I dare say, and it is not a regret I share, Chancellor." Alkara understood Torg's impartiality. She glanced around, scanning the area for someone. "Where is Drakar?"

"Hum..." Torg wondered. He sent out his thoughts to search for the missing Seer, attempting to locate him. "I have not seen him in some time." Torg turned, scanning a pile of collapsed building material. Called out from his hiding spot, Drakar stood, sheepishly approaching the Queen and the Chancellor.

Alkara spoke to him as he bowed low in front of her. "It seems you and Lieutenant Thorium are the only officers left alive. How resourceful of you both," she added condescendingly. The Queen turned to Mage' Rom. "Attend to all who are injured. We shall return to Akkadia as soon as they are able to travel and use their Abilities."

All around her, her people bowed. Alkara wasn't finished giving orders, so she motioned to Torg. "I want everyone who has been to the surface to receive a memory lock. Do you understand me, Torg?"

"Yes, my Queen." He hesitated for a moment before continuing. "What about our children?"

Alkara swung her gaze over at Ilmartutar and Reeglar, for the first time, as if she had just realized they were there. She ignored Torg's question and strode over to the whole reason for this fiasco. She stood face-to-face with her daughter at last.

"Mother," Ilmar offered, bowing her head slightly. Alkara did not respond. So, Ilmar picked her head up, trying to read her mother's intentions on her face to no avail. Alkara's features seemed made of stone.

"I have a decree from the Council for the three of you," Alkara snapped without hesitation, or emotion, not an easy thing to do for an Empath. "While the remaining Council Leaders were not in favor of this conflict, they have concluded that the three of you must not be allowed to return to Akkadia. They do not condone conspiratorial actions in any way, shape, or form."

Azewrath's expression went from ashamed for being punished, to total devastation. He brought his hands to his head, sighing in frustration. Ilmar and Reeglar bowed their heads, accepting their sentence. None spoke against the decision.

Alkara continued. "There shall be a vote for new Council Leaders to replace the ones we lost. It appears there are quite a few empty seats for the next Council meeting." With the Queen's orders over, Alkara took on a softer appearance and reached out for her daughter's hand. She immediately 'felt' Ilmar's sorrow and loss. Unable to control her emotions, Ilmar hugged her mother, crying. Alkara accepted her daughters embrace and held her tightly.

"You have no idea of the consequences of your actions today," Alkara whispered to Ilmar. "With you banished, I have no heir to the Throne." Alkara pulled back from Ilmar and put her hand under Ilmar's chin, lifting it to look in her eyes. "And now, no husband to try again."

"I never meant for all this to happen," Ilmar told her mother. "I just did not want to be the Queen. I want to be with Danny."

"And so you shall be. You must accept the repercussions, and the rest of us must accept them with you," Alkara schooled her.

"Actually," Ilmar offered, "I have been thinking a lot about this." She smiled at her mother. "And I have an idea, Mother."

"Well?" the Queen asked.

"I shall discuss it with you later, privately," Ilmar told her. "Without the prying eyes and ears."

Azewrath interrupted. "So, I presume we are stuck here?"

"So it would seem," Alkara answered. "For the time being." Catching sight of Patrick, Alkara's extreme curiosity got the better of her. "Ilmar, is this your human? He seems older than I expected."

Trish held onto Pat tighter, claiming him. "No, this is his brother."

Alkara raised an eyebrow at Trish's jealous behavior. "My apologies for my mistake."

"I'm Danny," Danny said, from his position holding Aaron. The group moved aside, revealing Danny. He still knelt on the ground, muddy, bloody, with his arms wrapped around another dead human. He didn't look at Alkara but turned his attention to Reeglar.

"Reeglar, would it be too much to ask of you if you could get Aaron off the ground? I don't wanna leave him like this."

"It shall be done."

Extending her arms, Reeglar lifted Aaron's body into the air, gently. With the Obsidian Spear that pierced his chest still lodged in the ground, it was a challenging endeavor. Everyone turned their heads away as the sound of sucking and tearing made it a horrible experience to witness. Afterward, Aaron's body hovered in the air.

After Danny stood, he shook his arms, trying to get the circulation back into them. He reached out with his hand, offering it to Alkara. She took it in both of hers, even though blood covered his hands.

"So..." Alkara smirked. "You are the reason for all this havoc?"

"Yeah, I guess." Danny shrugged. "But I'd do it all again... for her." He pulled back one hand and put his arm around Ilmar.

"I see..." Alkara's voice rose as she surveyed the destruction.

"Well then, I like what you have done with the place." She turned to watch Reeglar holding the body aloft. "I am sure there are some aspects of the outcome you might be inclined to change."

Danny glanced over at the floating body of Aaron. "Yes... Well, you're right, of course. I would do anything to take that back." He put his head down again.

Mage' Rom came over and reported to the Queen. "All injuries have been Healed, and we are ready to travel at your command."

Alkara nodded. "Thank you, Rom." She turned to Torg. "Will you and the other Telepaths be strong enough to carry our fallen back home?"

"Yes, my Queen," Torg answered. "I shall personally collect all the Obsidian Spears, so none might be left behind."

"Good. Hopefully, this shall be considered just another natural disaster. Give the order to move out." The Queen told Torg. He bowed, and Alkara dismissed him, turning back to Ilmar.

"Mother, a word please before you go." Ilmar took her mother's arm, walking her away from the crowd. Hoping no one could hear, or intrude into their thoughts, they spoke quietly. Danny watched as the Queen appeared more and more surprised.

To Danny, it didn't look like Ilmar was winning her mother over. Alkara kept shaking her head as if she disagreed with whatever Ilmar suggested. The conversation heated but remained a silent interaction. Finally, the Queen glanced in the direction of Danny and Patrick, a small smile forming on her lips.

Uh, oh! Danny wondered. *I don't like the look of that! What's going on now?*

XXIII

Inception

Even though the sun shined, a heavy sadness hung in the air surrounding everyone. Before Alkara and the Akkadians returned to their city below, Torg agreed to levitate Patrick's planes back to the hangar. They hoped it was still standing, and they were pleasantly surprised when it was.

Danny accompanied Reeglar, Azewrath, and Ilmar to bring Aaron's body back to the house. They sailed him through the halls to the spare bedroom, where Reeglar lowered Aaron onto the bed.

"I do not mean to sound callous, but should you not put him in cold storage, instead?" Azewrath asked delicately.

"Rath!" Reeglar scolded.

"I was simply thinking about the sanitary conditions," Azewrath clarified. "With the smell eventually a factor."

"I'm not keeping him as a stuffed toy, Rath," Danny remarked, shaking his head. "Illy, could you take them to the cottage? They can stay there. Oh, and get some supplies from the plane to take with you."

Lifting on her toes, Ilmar rose up to kiss him gently. "All right, but then where am I saying?"

"Well, little missy," Danny joked. "You just won an all expense paid vacation to live in the Sutters' homestead." He hesitated, turning. "I'll be back in a few. I just need to make a couple of phone calls." Danny stopped and sighed. "To the coroner's office, and to Aaron's parents." He slipped out of the doorway.

Reeglar wasn't finished chastising Azewrath. "You really need to be more careful with what you say to people."

"I was careful," Azewrath assured her. "I did not say anything about how disgusting it is keeping the body here *at all*."

"All right, enough!" Ilmar interrupted them. "Follow me, and I will take you to your new home."

"I can not wait!" Azewrath sneered, sarcastically.

"We shall need supplies, remember?" Reeglar reminded Ilmar.

Ilmar nodded as they exited the house. As Reeglar brought her arms up, all the water and can goods they brought earlier rose from the Cutlass right passed Patrick and Trish. They watched it sail away behind the Akkadians on their way to the cottage.

They took the long walk to the cottage and Ilmar set a few ground rules. "I think since we have been exiled here, we should try to sound more normal, more human when we speak."

Excited, Reeglar clapped her hands. "Oh, good! I love to do this." She bounded up and down as she walked. "How shall we start?"

"Well... " Ilmar rolled her eyes. "Stop saying *shall* for one."

Reeglar giggled. "True, a dead giveaway that I do not belong here."

"We need to start using their contractions. You know?" Ilmar encouraged them.

"Oh, right!" Reeglar began. "I'm so hungry! Like that? I love the way it feels on my tongue. Try it, Rath."

"No, thank you," Azewrath refused. "I would prefer not to sound a moron."

"It's fun!" Reeglar bumped into him with her hip as they walked, startling him.

"Reeglar!" Azewrath taunted her, smiling. "You are a troublemaker!"

"One of the best," she admitted.

"Here we are," Ilmar announced, opening the door.

Azewrath stepped inside. "I can not see."

Ilmar tried the light switch, but nothing happened. "Humm... I guess the power is out. No problem." Ilmar went to the electrical box next to the door. She touched it, and white light filled the room, not from the bulbs in the fixtures but from her Igniter Abilities. Afterward, the lights came on and so did the small AC unit. "See now?"

"Oh, yes..." Azewrath agreed. "With the lights on, it is *so* much better."

"It's," Reeglar corrected. "It's much better. Try it." Azewrath glared at her, disapprovingly.

Ilmar laughed. "I will leave you two alone to figure this out. Have fun!" She stepped out of the door. "Oh, and call me through our link if you need me."

"We *will*," Reeglar told her, remembering to use the word instead of shall. She turned, raised her hands and levitated in all the supplies.

Ilmar made her way back to the house and found Patrick bringing in the last of the groceries as well. She noticed he worked alone. "Where has Trish gone?"

"She's washing up. Long hard day, you know. And she's still very freaked out," Pat explained. "I'm hoping the water will relax her."

Trish came out of the bathroom. "Hey honey, there's no electricity."

"Oh, shit. Really?" Pat cursed. He walked to the panel and checked the breaker box. "Damn. I don't know why I'm surprised. I'm sure everyone's out."

"I can help," Ilmar offered, following behind him. "Let me get in there." She snuck by Patrick and put her hands on the panel. Again, her hands glowed a bright white as the light worked its way into the grid. Within seconds, the house came alive with electricity. The appliances came back on, and things hummed. She turned, smiling broadly to Pat and Trish.

"Well, you sure are handy to have around." Pat clapped Ilmar on the back before turning back to Trish. "Go ahead and try it again."

"Thanks..." Trish kissed him but gave Ilmar a bizarre look. "Babe, I called my brother before. Let me know when he gets here if he comes before I'm done."

"You're going home?" Pat asked her.

Trish blew her bangs up. "Yep. I've got to get outta here." Again, she said that, glancing in Ilmar's direction. "I've had enough for one day... Many days actually. My brother told me Calverton wasn't hit at all. You're all welcome to come to my house and get away from all the crazy, here."

"I'm okay, honey," Pat assured her. "You go home and get some rest. I'll call you tomorrow." She nodded, heading back to the bathroom. Ilmar accompanied Patrick back to the kitchen, watching him put the canned food away in the cabinets.

"She does not like me," Ilmar stated flatly.

Patrick stopped for a second, stunned by Ilmar's remark, but continued to put his food away. "No, that's not it. I think she's just afraid. She saw a lot today."

"So have you."

"I'm different."

"Why?"

"I just haven't slowed down enough yet to freak out."

"But you will?"

Patrick laughed. "Illy, I've just spent the afternoon fighting people I never knew existed, killing them, then crashing a fifteen million dollar helicopter. Oh, and I watched flying people, and ones that 'morph' into really large giants." He looked at her. "As soon as I stop... Well, let's just say, I'm sure I'll never sleep well again."

"Oh." Ilmar worried. *This is no good. I must call out the big guns.* She called over her link with Reeglar and thought to her extremely loud. *"Reeglar!"*

There was no hesitation in Reeglar's answer. *"Yes, Ilmar? Oh, I see. We have trouble already. You are right, of course. I will be there in minutes."*

Two minutes later, Reeglar walked through the door. Patrick jumped when she came in. "Reeglar?" Pat showed surprise. "What's up?"

"You seem a bit jumpy, Patrick," Reeglar stated. "Can I help you calm down?"

"No, no. I'm good, really," Pat explained.

"All right. If not, can I ask you a question?" She came closer to him. "It is very private."

"Private?" Patrick swallowed hard as Reeglar got even closer. Placing her fingers on his temple, Pat passed out. Ilmar caught him as he fell, resting him gently on the kitchen chair.

"Work quickly," Ilmar whispered. "Trish must be next. She is unstable. Oh, and do not just erase their memories, this time make up a good reason we are here. Say we are friends or something, all right?"

"I understand, Ilmar. This is not my first mind cap." Reeglar did what Ilmar bade her. With Patrick's new memories, plus a necessary rest, he would wake refreshed and in control. When Trish came into the kitchen scrubbing her hair with the towel, she didn't see Reeglar approach her.

"Hey, Patrick. Did my brother –" Walking right into Reeglar's fingers, Trish collapsed. Ilmar sat her right next to Patrick.

"Quickly!" Ilmar whispered.

"*All right!*" Reeglar hissed. She closed her eyes, manipulating Trish's memories as well.

As Reeglar finished, a knock came at the door. Ilmar and Reeglar exchanged panicked glances, eyes wide. They shook their heads at each other, shrugging their shoulders and throwing their hands up in the air.

"Do something!" Ilmar ordered Reeglar quietly.

"Like what?"

"I do not know. Wake them up."

Reeglar brought both Patrick and Trish out of their sleep. "Well? Are you going to get it?" Reeglar said to Patrick.

"Get what?" Pat asked her, groggy and a little confused.

"Someone knocked on the door," Ilmar told him.

"Oh," Trish said. "That must be my brother." Trish stood and tossed the towel at Patrick. She bent down to kiss him. "Love you. See you later. I'm gonna spend time with the family. Make sure everyone's all right, what with the earthquake and all." Throwing her purse over her shoulder, she opened the door and walked out, blowing Patrick another kiss.

Patrick rubbed his eyes, yawning. "Where is Danny?"

As if summoned, Danny walked into the kitchen, a somber expression on his face. His eyes puffy and red told of his pain and no one wanted to ask why. He sat down at the table, placing his head in his hands.

"You okay?" Pat asked him.

"Yeah. I'm just sad. I just got off the phone with the Remingtons. They're sending a medi-transport here for Aaron's body." Ilmar put her arm around him, rubbing his back.

"I know this isn't the answer, but... Want a beer?" Pat offered, getting up. He reached into the fridge, passed one to Danny and pulled one out for himself, too. "Girls?" They both nodded, so Pat retrieved two more.

"Could I please have another one, for Rath?" Reeglar asked.

"Sure," Pat said. "It's amazing we still have electricity. I wonder who else in the neighborhood does?"

Reeglar and Ilmar shared a conspiratory look, but Danny appeared confused. "I thought you turned it on?" Danny said to

Ilmar. "What's going on here?"

Ilmar laughed, nervously. "Oh, yeah!" She spoke like a human. " 'Cuz I'm so skilled like that."

Reeglar immediately entered Danny's mind. *"We took away your brother's memories of Akkadia and the battle. Trish's as well."*

"Why?" Danny thought back to her, questioning. *"He was cool with it."*

"But, she was not." Reeglar showed him Trish's panic, letting her words play into Danny's mind. *"It was for the best, believe me."*

"Hey, bro…?" Pat worried about Danny staring off into space. "I know you've been through a lot. Maybe you should go lay down."

"I will." Danny tried to smile. "After the EMTs get here."

"Well, I better get back," Reeglar relayed. "Patrick, thank you for letting us stay in the cottage."

"No problem, Reeglar," Pat offered. "So sorry your house was destroyed in the earthquake."

When Danny heard that remark, he choked on his beer, spitting it out all over the table. Ilmar patted him on the back. "Oh, my Goddess – uh – goodness honey, be careful."

"I'm okay," Danny replied, clearing his throat. "Bye, Reeglar."

"Goodbye!" She waved and took her beer. Tucking the other one under her arm, she closed the door behind her.

Pat rose from his chair again. "I think I'll turn in early also, but I need some food first. What a day!" He went back into the refrigerator, pulling out a slice of cold pizza. As he grabbed a plate, he noticed Ilmar watched him intently. "Are you hungry?"

"Oh, yes please!"

Patrick raised an eyebrow at Danny questioningly, but he shook his head. "Not me, Pat. I can't think about food right now."

"Okay, Ilmar, do you want it cold or heated up?" Pat asked.

"I don't care," she added, using the slang contraction. She worried over how to enact her mother's plan. Paramount no one witnessed her next actions, she nibbled her bottom lip.

I've got to keep him busy, Ilmar pondered. Pat handed her a cold piece of pizza. Taking a bite, she made a face. "Could you heat it up, maybe?" She gave the plate back to Patrick.

"Sure thing." Patrick went back to the microwave and set the timer for her.

Ilmar stood and rubbed Danny's back. The grieving man still slumped over in his chair, resting his head on the table. With no one watching, she took out a small pouch, sprinkling a tiny bit of green powder into Patrick's beer bottle. Her heart beat a mile a minute, creating an adrenaline rush from her subterfuge as she put the pouch away. When the microwave beeped, she smiled at Patrick innocently as he placed the pizza in front of her again.

He sat next to her and bit his slice. "Umm..." He moaned, enjoying the oily food. "Comfort food. There is nothing like it."

Ilmar took another mouthful, chewing and smiled. She put her fingers to her lips until she swallowed, trying not to spit the food out when she spoke. "Wow, this *is* good!"

Now, to get him to drink his beer.

She picked up her beer bottle, holding it out to him. "I'd like to make a toast, to us." Pat nodded, raising his bottle as well. "Danny!" she said, nudging him with her elbow. He wasn't paying any attention, but he finally sighed and picked up his Miller Lite, like an automaton. "To good people, whether they are here, or not." She clinked her beer to Patrick's first, to get him to drink it.

"Good people!" Pat repeated, putting the bottle to his lips, drinking hard. Danny did the same, slamming the empty beer bottle on the table. Pat shook his head. "Is that where you're going tonight?"

Danny pushed himself up and got another beer from the fridge. "Yep. You got a problem with that?"

"No. Just... You have company, is all," Pat reminded him.

"She'll understand. Won't you, Illy?" His question held an edge of sarcasm.

"I'm good with it, honestly, Pat." Ilmar needed less confrontation, more merriment. She was willing to agree to anything.

From where he sat in the kitchen, Danny caught a glimpse out of the window of the medi-transport pulling down the driveway. He swigged his new beer, gulping it down. He gulped it down so quickly, the chilled liquid spilled down his chin and ran down his neck, but he didn't seem to care. Afterward, he went to the door, letting them in with the gurney.

"He's in there." Danny pointed to the spare room. The two men rolled the rack in, did their job and swiftly returned with a large black bag on top of it. Aaron's body lay inside. Patrick asked one of them about the situation.

"What's it like out there? Is it bad?"

"Yeah," the EMT stated. "Mass destruction, power lines down, gas mains exploded everywhere, and a lot of people, dead. We're swamped."

"Thanks for the update," Pat said, gratefully. "Good luck to you all."

"No problem, sir. Sorry for your loss." They lowered the gurney down the stairs, with Danny following behind.

Danny watched, as they loaded the rack into the back of the truck, shutting the doors. Both men got inside and drove away. Danny stood there, staring at the transport until it got smaller and smaller. Finally, it turned out of his driveway and was gone. Still, he didn't move.

Ilmar and Patrick walked to the back door that Danny left open. "Danny!" Pat called, but Danny's unresponsive form held its place.

Pat shook his head and went back inside. Finishing his beer, he tossed the empty in the recycle bin and went to bed.

Ilmar descended the stairs, joining Danny by his side. They watched the sunset over the military base. *Such a beautiful sight,* she thought. *No one would have known a battle had occurred there just hours before.* She entwined her fingers into his hand that hung by his thigh. Taking it, he squeezed hers back.

That's a good sign. Ilmar hoped.

Danny turned toward her, his eyes tearing up. He brought her deep into his arms and rested his head in the crook of her neck, holding her tightly. She wrapped her arms around him, surrounding him with Healing yellow light of her love.

***

Alkara approached the two Level 4 Telepaths guarding the door. They bowed, opening it up for her to pass through. Torg stood in front of someone, Drakar, she realized. The man lay unconscious, on a reclining couch.

"Is he the *last?*" Alkara asked Torg.

Torg turned away from his last memory lock, catching his first glimpse at the Queen. A raised eyebrow was the only giveaway of his surprise, having never seen the Queen dressed as such. She was not in her Royal robes but covered in a clinging, form-fitting material unfamiliar to him. It left nothing to the imagination, yet was very appealing at the same time. An overwrap rested on her shoulders which glittered like diamonds as it extended down past her rear end. To say she appeared a beautiful goddess would have been an understatement.

Her attire must be a human dress, Torg postulated. "You have plans to return to the surface?"

"You did not answer my question, Torg." She ignored his request.

"True," Torg agreed. "And you have not answered mine."

She smiled. "Only you can get away with talking to me the way you do."

"Ah," Torg replied. "That is untrue. Mage' Rom shares that honor as well."

"True indeed," Alkara repeated Torg's answer. "The Mage' is like a Father to me."

"What does that make me?" he asked, and she sensed something strange about the question. She didn't need to open old wounds.

"My best friend and most trusted counsel." Alkara defused the situation. "I need you to keep the peace while I return to Ilmartutar. The mood here is still tenuous at best."

"As you command," he responded, with a slight bow. "Shall you be leaving now?"

"I have… one more stop before I leave." The Queen answered cryptically. She asked again about his progress. "You have finished with Drakar? Then, he is the last?"

"Yes, my Queen."

"And?" Alkara prompted him.

Torg sighed. The discussion was distasteful to him. "All was as to be expected. Lieutenant Thorium was extremely compliant. It seems he was never against you, per se, just with the General and his Guild. They all have new memories. Pikkar and the others died trying to bring back our children for sentencing. No inappropriate behavior from either side – Akkadian nor human."

"That shall suffice, thank you, Chancellor," she expressed her gratitude.

"When shall you return?"

"Later," she evasively skirted his request, turning to leave, but added one last comment. "Or maybe, tomorrow." Alkara walked from the room, continuing down the corridor. She made her way to the Healing Ward, peeking inside. "Hello?"

Seeleem, Minnar, and Peony greeted her, packed up and ready to leave. "My Queen," both women said, bowing slightly.

"Oh, do not be so formal," Alkara scolded, swinging her hand in a cutting motion. "Let me see this little one." Minnar handed the baby over to the Queen, who bounced Peony up and down, cooing and rocking the child. Peony smiled up at her. "How are you feeling, Minnar?"

"I am well, my Queen. And I am heading home today," Minnar answered.

"So soon?" Alkara seemed surprised.

"Ours is a successful birth," Minnar admitted.

"Excellent!" Alkara's pleasure filled her heart. "Seeleem, please let Mage' Rom know I am here."

"Yes, my Queen." Seeleem excused herself from the room.

"I am sorry to hear about the Prince." Minnar gave the Queen her condolences.

"Thank you for your kind words." Alkara sensed the sadness in Minnar and then she felt it in herself. Uninterested in being held by her any longer, Peony squirmed. Alkara planned on handing her back to Minnar when Peony just disappeared out of her arms.

Minnar thought the shock on the Queen's face priceless, and couldn't suppress a giggle. Peony appeared in Minnar's arms one second later.

"Oh, my!" Alkara exclaimed. "You are going to have your hands full."

"Indeed, so it would seem." Minnar sighed. "But, I would not have it any other way now."

"Yes," Alkara reminisced. "Children can be our most wonderful asset and our greatest joy."

Seeleem returned from the back room. "The Mage' said to go right into his private chambers, my Queen."

"Thank you, Seeleem." Alkara turned. "Good luck with your new family," she wished to Minnar. The Queen walked through the many rooms in the Ward until she came to one lone door at the end of the corridor.

How many times have I been here as a child? Standing right at this door, waiting to be let into a world of wonder? As the memories brought a smile to Alkara's lips, she knocked on the door.

"Come," the Mage' replied from the other side of the door. Alkara pushed it open and entered. Rom waited for her – his hands on the back of his reclining chair.

"Alkara." He bowed, without need.

"Rom!" She admonished him. "That is unnecessary."

"How do you feel, child?"

"Sad, lonely, empty," Alkara answered. "Does that cover what you expected?"

"I see we are not in the mood for chitchat tonight." Rom laughed.

"I apologize, Rom." She sat in the chair. "I am trying to get myself into the proper mindset for my task."

"You just lay back and relax. I shall make sure you are very receptive in every way for tonight *task*, as you called it."

"Ugh!" Alkara sighed. "It is a chore!" Rom laughed as he placed his hands on her abdomen. "Truly!" she exclaimed.

"Think back to when you were younger, how every stolen moment brought about an adrenaline rush." Alkara did think back, blushing, but she wasn't thinking about Pikkar. Her encounter with Torg left her conflicted. "Ah, I see you do remember." Rom laughed again. "You just concentrate on having fun tonight, my child."

"Humm, fun..." Alkara repeated, closing her eyes, giving into the Mage's Healing touch. "I shall try to have fun."

***

As the sun faded, the small biting pests swarmed in force. Ilmar stood beside Danny for as long as she could without giving

403

in to their incredibly annoying bite. She itched her welts, having to let go of Danny's hand to smack them away.

"Hey!" she cried. "Something is biting me!"

Danny broke his trance long enough to see the raised bumps on Ilmar skin. "Okay, time to go inside." He led her back into the house.

"What are they?" Ilmar asked.

"Mosquitoes," Danny explained, grabbing another Miller Lite from the fridge. "They suck out your blood and use it as food."

"Gross!" She shuddered. "Where did Patrick disappear to?"

"Must've gone to bed already." Danny screwed off the top of his beer, taking a deep drink. After, he set it down on the kitchen table. "I'll be right back," he told Ilmar, heading to the bathroom. "I think I've had a few too many tonight."

Ilmar spied Danny's beer on top of the table. He hurt so badly she thought she would help. *Perhaps, if I put some of this powder that my Mother gave me in his beer...* Pulling out the folded paper, she poured the green powder into his beer and then refolded it, tucking it back in her dress. *He will sleep less fitful tonight.*

Danny returned to his chair and picked up his beer bottle. Drinking heartily, he tilted it back all the way, getting every last drop until the bottle was empty. Ilmar said nothing, biting her lips, as he tossed the empty bottle into the recycle bin, without getting up.

Danny rubbed his forehead. "I know what I'm doing tonight isn't helping anything, but I want my body to be as numb as my brain feels," he explained to her.

"It is all right, my love," Ilmar promised, putting her arm around him. "You will sleep tonight, and things will be better in the morning."

"Whadda 'bout you?" Danny asked, slurring his words. *I must be feeling the effects of the alcohol.* Or so he thought. "Never even asked 'f you'rr okay?"

"I am fine.

"Hmm..." Danny managed.

"We will discuss it in the morning if you would like."

"Maybe you'rr rright," Danny slurred. "My eyes arre gettin' heavy." He tried to get up but found his muscles unwilling.

"Whoa!"

"Come, let me put you to bed," Ilmar whispered.

"Oh, yeah!" Danny boasted as she helped him down the hallway. "I can't wait ta get ya inna bed."

"Really!" Ilmar remarked, dropping him to the mattress, to undress him. She took off his sneakers and threw them in the corner. "What will you do to me?" she asked as she unzipped his pants. As she pulled down his jeans, she realized he had no underwear on. "OH!" she gasped, startled.

"Commm 'ear!" He reached out, pulling her on top of him. She giggled as they tussled for a few seconds on the bed. Danny managed to push the straps of Ilmar's dressed down over her shoulders, exposing her soft porcelain skin, causing her breasts to spill out. She sat up, laughing, and fixed herself. He sat up as well, reaching for her again. His eyes were as wide as saucers as the smile left his lips. He passed out mid-grab, falling unconscious and face-planting into her lap.

Ilmar sighed and stroked the back of his head, running her fingers through his hair. "Sleep well, my love," she cooed, gently slipping out from under him. Laying his head on his pillow, she covered him and turned off his lights, placing the bedroom into darkness. Closing the door, Ilmar made her way back to the kitchen to await her mother's arrival.

Ilmar paced back and forth, impatiently, from the kitchen table to the back door, checking out the window glass every so often. It was incredibly bright outside, with the not quite full moon high in the night sky. She wasn't surprised her mother was visible walking down the driveway. Ilmar opened the back door and took a few steps down to greet the Queen.

"All has been prepared, Mother."

"Excellent, my daughter."

"This way." Ilmar ascended the stairs, followed by Alkara. "Will I see you before you return to Akkadia?" Ilmar asked.

"I think not," Alkara said. "I do not know how long this shall take."

"I would think not long at all." Ilmar began to smile. "You are truly a vision tonight."

"Hum... We shall see. I can only hope so." Alkara accompanied Ilmar down the hallway and right to Patrick's bedroom.

"I have given him the sleeping powder," Ilmar reported. "He is in this room alone, already under."

Alkara smiled, full of the excitement Mage' Rom placed inside her. "It was not only a sleeping powder. It was a special mixture, a Psilocybin mushroom, laced with a powerful hallucinogen, and a tiny pinch of a blood stimulant."

"Mother!" Ilmar whispered a little too loudly. "I gave some to Danny tonight to help him sleep."

"Then my little one, you shall be experiencing an interesting evening as well. I am *sure* of it." Alkara could not help but chuckle.

"Will you need to use my belly ring?" Ilmar offered. "It affords greater peace of mind."

"I shall not harm him after just one encounter. You must Heal him in the morning," Alkara promised. "I have wondered how you have managed to stave off your human's death. An ingenious apparatus."

"Thank Minnar," Ilmar suggested as she opened the door to the room. Alkara received her second view of Patrick. The bright moon sent beams of light through the window, highlighting Patrick's muscular body. "He has a good bloodline, Mother. I am sure he will be a successful donor." She added one more statement, playfully. "And he is quite *HOT!*"

"Ilmar!" Now it was Alkara's turn to scold. "This is my duty to our species. I need an heir to the Throne now that you have so forcefully refused. I shall not enjoy this!"

"No, Mother, of course, you will not. I am sorry for implying otherwise," Ilmar apologized but caught the corners of Alkara's lips turn upward into a slight smile. She glided by her daughter into Patrick's room, closing the door behind her. Ilmartutar tiptoed back to join the sleeping Danny in his bedroom.

Alkara moved into the room. She studied the light and the way it accentuated the chiseled structure of the man in front of her. Patrick turned over, rubbing his temples. Unable to fall asleep completely, he attempted to find a comfortable position.

Patrick felt strange, sluggish. He had the urge to open his eyes, and when he did, he thought something at the other end of the room moved. When he sat upright, his sheets fell into his lap, exposing his chest and abdomen.

Patrick tried to speak. " 'ello?" His head seemed full of marbles and his mouth full of cotton. "Is someone there?" His eyesight wasn't working well, either. Something, *something* stood in the darkness. White, glistening, swirling, and blowing in an utterly absent breeze. The entity approached his bed.

The moonlight struck the object, and it appeared to be human for one moment, and then it wasn't. It changed, shifting in the semi-darkness. Pat shook his head and rubbed his eyes again.

Why can't I get the stuffing out of my head? He wondered. He stared at the apparition, curious. *Yes, it is human. A vision.* Alkara's wrap flowed, twisted and turned, enveloping her in a glittering glow.

"Are you an angel?" Pat asked.

A lovely woman's voice whispered in his ear accompanied by a soft, sensual giggle. "I am whatever you wish me to be," she answered.

Pat turned, expecting to see her there, but she was nowhere near him. He was right in the middle of a complete hallucination.

The illumination from the moon bathed her in a halo as she glided closer, stopping at the foot of his bed. She seemed a moonbeam, a stream of light, sent down from the heavens to shine her soft white glow on him – just for him.

"You must be the moon, then," Patrick decided. She appeared everywhere in his room. No matter where he looked, she was in his line of sight.

"How do you feel about the moon?" She was by his side, solid, yet ephemeral. He reached out to touch her, but she disappeared only to reappear on his other.

"Ah," Patrick complained. "Stop *moving*, and I'll tell you." He tried to hold her again, surging forward. He slipped out from the covers of the sheets completely, exposing himself.

"Tell me," Alkara promised. "And perhaps I shall stop and let you put your hands on me." She took in all of him, his muscular body, and his stunning face. Alkara came closer still, moving in to gaze directly into his eyes.

Patrick sent both of his hand out, grabbing her shoulders, finally catching her. "Such elegant beauty," he mused. "I love the moon."

"Then *love* the moon, Patrick." Alkara slid into the bed next to him. She placed her lips only inches away from his ear, whispering, warming his skin. "And the moon shall love you back."

Alkara wrapped her arms around him, bringing her lips down to his. He embraced her with a desire he never thought he could possess. Pulling her down on top of him, he tried to focus on her, but his eyes betrayed him. She faded in and out. One minute there, the next not; flesh, then emptiness.Although, she seemed familiar.

"Do I *know* you?" he asked.

She laughed, a throaty, sexy laugh that made the hairs on his arms stand up, and the blood in his body fly directly to his manhood. "Can anyone really know the heavens?" she asked him back.

"Riddles and questions?" Patrick wondered.

Alkara raised herself to her knees. "No more." She slid her dress down over both shoulders, down past her waist, continuing over her hips to her thighs. Her garment fell even further until she slipped out of it entirely.

Patrick's hands followed the dress on its way down, caressing her every curve. "You're real!" he whispered, amazed.

"Real," she repeated, "available, and full of *hunger*." Alkara's craving for him took hold of her forcefully, so she reached down with both hands to take him into her grasp.

Patrick skin caught fire! He exhaled a huge sigh, responding to her touch. After his maleness became harder than any man she had ever known this way, she wasted no time. Crawling over him, she hovered for only a second, before lowering herself gently. She rubbed her warm, wet, inviting opening along his throbbing, engorged member, working him into a frenzy. Driven, he maneuvered his hips and deftly entered her, thrusting deeply into the folds of her accepting womanhood.

She moved over him, grinding, sliding back and forth. He watched her muscled legs work magic against him. *This is crazy!* He thought, needing to make sure she was still there for real.

He reached out and grabbed her hips, helping her along. Working her motion, he dragged her across his pelvis. *My hands feel like they're burning!* He spared his discomfort only a fleeting thought, and then she captured his mind by tightening her grip around his shaft.

Alkara felt his pain. She couldn't help it. *Perhaps, I should have worn Ilmar's piercing for his health. Oh, well, what is done is done.*

Patrick was so engorged and so full of excitement; he had to grit his teeth to keep from exploding. *Not yet!* He pleaded with himself. *Not yet, damn it!* He cursed his body for betraying him.

"Yes!" Alkara begged. "Now! Do it *now*, Patrick!"

"Arghhh!" he screamed, throwing his head back into his pillow. With his exertions, the veins in his neck popped out almost bursting. His body went stiff as he sent his seed deep into Alkara, and she knew right then and there, she had accomplished her goal. Smiling and satisfied, she dismounted Patrick. As she lay next to him, she attempted to catch her breath as he drifted to sleep.

***

Ilmar stood with her back to the door in Danny's room. Not that she was afraid to get close to him at the moment, but she just wasn't comfortable knowing her mother was in the next bedroom, doing Patrick.

Well, I will not think about that. Danny snored quietly, meaning he was out, genuinely passed out cold.

She smiled as she thought of him getting his much-needed rest. She tried to focus on him as best she could in the blackness of his room. This man in front of her had so changed her life and was her reason for just being. As she waited, two different doors shut, and she realized her mother had gone.

Ilmar left Danny's room and crept over to Patrick's. Turning the handle slowly, she hoped not to wake him. Stepping in, she found him unconscious hopefully for the rest of the night. When Ilmar moved to his bedside, she spotted the raised bruises that had formed on his naked body.

She bashfully looked away as she set her hands gently on him. Her Healing yellow light mixed with the waning moonlight. Satisfied he would recover, she let go, brought the sheets back up to cover his private parts, and then snuck out.

Back in Danny's room, she sighed and figured it was safe to undress and jump into bed next to him. It had been a very long and trying day, full of emotion and physical activity. Exhaustion cloaked her. Creeping in close to him, she lifted his arm and then let it fall. It dropped to the bed with a thud.

Yes, he is asleep. Convinced he wouldn't wake Ilmar gazed down and realized he did have a very "happy to see you" stiff private area, thanks to her mother's powder. *Oh, well. Such a waste.* As Ilmar snuggled up to him, draping her arm around his waist, she longed for sleep to come swiftly.

***

The next morning, Reeglar and Azewrath woke early, searching for something pleasing to eat. She finally found a box of something that seemed light and edible.

"Toaster pastries." Reeglar placed them in front of Azewrath. "Whatever they are?"

Azewrath glared up at her from his seated position at the small table. "May the Goddess help me!" He picked up the rectangular cake and took a bite, chewing carefully.

"Well?" she asked.

"It shall eventually kill me, surely," Azewrath informed her. "But it has a sweet taste."

"Hurry up," Reeglar encouraged. "I want to get over to Ilmar to see how she's doing."

"Really?" Azewrath asked inquisitively. "It would not have anything to do with the fact that the Queen was here, *again*, last night?"

"Huh!" Reeglar sighed, frustrated. "You know way too much."

"Not as much as you," he informed her. "What did you hear?"

"You do not want to know," Reeglar promised, rolling her eyes.

"I already know," he stated. "I just wanted to hear you say it."

"Beast!" She backhanded him in the shoulder. Azewrath rose from the table but left his dish. "Hey! Clean that up." Reeglar pointed to his plate. "Show some respect. This is our new home. And we have no House Telepaths here."

He picked up the plate and placed it in the sink. "Hopefully, not for long, if I have anything to say about it." They walked out the door, heading to Danny's house.

Patrick watched the news on the 21-inch flat screen TV in the kitchen, having a great morning. The kind of morning when nothing could go wrong or make him feel bad. A happy camper. He had just used the last of the milk for his coffee, confirming his good fortune, when Reeglar and Azewrath knocked on the door. He opened up the door, inviting them in.

"Morning!" Reeglar greeted him, smiling.

Patrick smiled back. "It really is, considering..." He trailed off. *It's better not to think about yesterday,* he mused.

"You are in a good mood," Azewrath wondered. Reeglar elbowed him. "OH! Ouch!" he yelled at her.

"Please come in and sit down," Pat suggested. "I'd offer you a cup of coffee, but I just used the last of the milk."

Danny rounded the corner from the hallway to the kitchen, rubbing the sleep out of his eyes. "Did I hear you say there's no milk?"

"Sorry," Pat apologized.

"Aw, man!" Danny complained. "Now I gotta go out and find some."

"Good luck with that!" Pat challenged. "I've been watching the news. The government has declared Southeastern Suffolk County a disaster zone. With the Shinnecock locks destroyed, they're letting in too much tide. The bay level is rising, flooding out the houses on the shoreline. And that's just the beginning."

"Shit!" Danny cursed. "What a mess."

"There have been many deaths, and the entire east end of the South Fork has been totally cut off. It'll be weeks before those people will get any real help. We're lucky to be able to get food and water still and have electric," Pat reminded him.

"Yeah, we're just lucky, I guess," Danny said, as Ilmar came into the kitchen. She yawned and stretched as she walked over to him, kissing him.

"Good morning, my love." Ilmar hugged him.

"Hey, babe." He reciprocated her hug, turning to Azewrath. "Wanna come for a ride with me?" Azewrath made an unpleasant face.

"Go with him, Rath," Reeglar encouraged him. "It might be nice."

"I'll bring back coffee for everyone, okay?" Danny said. They all nodded in agreement. "Cool, let's go, Rath."

As the men walked to the cars they left out on the runway, Danny was pleased to find them untouched by yesterday's destruction. He tossed the keys he was carrying up in the air and caught them again.

"We're going in the truck," Danny informed him, unlocking the passenger side door for Azewrath, who got in.

"Is this not Aaron's truck?" Azewrath asked.

"Yep," Danny confirmed, sliding into the driver's seat. Starting the engine, it roared with power. "Hemi!" Danny added proudly, realizing Azewrath didn't understand nor care. "Aaron's parents told me to keep it. They didn't want it, and couldn't be bothered selling it. Plus, I don't know how bad it is out there. The truck will be the safest mode of transportation."

Danny left the driveway and headed east to the 7-11. As they drove, they passed downed trees and power lines. Thankfully, crews were out, working diligently to get the grid back online.

Wow, this situation is bad, Danny thought, as he pulled into the parking lot.

After exiting the truck, Danny accidentally kicked a dead fish laying in the parking space with his foot. "Tsunami much?" Danny informed Azewrath while entering the store. "Their electricity is on. They must have a generator or something."

Picking up a gallon of milk, he poured out 5 cups of Sev's coffee. Handing the carryout box to Azewrath, they checked out. Danny grabbed a couple of last-minute candy bars, throwing them on the counter. He was just about to pay when Azewrath interrupted him.

"Play that. With one dollar," Azewrath requested, pointing to the lotto.

"What? Mega Millions?" Danny asked.

"Yes," Azewrath instructed. "15, 26, 45, 9, 32, 2, and 13." Danny just stared at him "Do it *now!*" Azewrath demanded.

"O-K!" Danny stressed each letter, buying the ticket. "What's Mega up to?" Danny inquired of the clerk.

"329 million," the 7-11 clerk responded.

"Hwee, hwoo." Danny whistled. "Mucho dinero! Thanks!" He put the ticket in his wallet. When they returned to the truck, Danny's sipped his coffee before heading out. "Ah! Only beer can beat the first sip of coffee for the day."

"You can thank me later for your winnings," Azewrath bragged.

"What?" Danny asked, driving back home. "Are you talking about the Mega? Yeah, right!" He laughed. "I wish!"

"You have no need to wish," Azewrath explained, calmly. "Friday night at precisely 11:00 PM, you shall win the Mega Million Lottery."

"You're not shitting me?" Danny questioned seriously.

"No. I do not think so, if I understand you correctly," Azewrath gathered.

"HOLY SHIT!" Danny screamed. With his eyes bulging out of his head, he tried not to crash the truck.

"I, however, have one condition," Azewrath demanded.

"Anything, dude! You just name it," Danny promised.

"You must buy us an exceptionally nice house. One that is befitting of my station." Azewrath continued. "Not that I dislike your little cottage," he mumbled, sarcastically.

"Yeah, yeah, whatever." Danny didn't notice the slight Azewrath meant for him. He was already living large in his head. *Boy! This is great coffee!*

XXIV

Winning

For the Akkadians, their daily routine returned to normal. With the mutinous rebellion swept from most everyone's memories, Alkara sat on the exam table in the Healing Ward, waiting for Mage' Rom to confirm what she already knew. With his hands on her abdomen, the yellow glow radiated out from him into her, covering her in its warm light.

"You are correct as usual, Alkara," Rom agreed. "You are with child. It is a female child."

"I have never doubted it," the Queen responded, smiling.

"I need to know how you feel about starting all over at your age?" Rom asked.

"Are you trying to tell me I am too old for this, Rom?" she teased.

"No, *never!*" He tried to recover from his indiscretion. "You are in the best shape I have seen for someone who has seen 450 plantings."

"That still does not sound like a compliment to me, Mage'." She sighed.

"I give up." Rom threw his hands up as Alkara slid off the table. "Torg is in the waiting room. He wishes to speak with you."

"Thank you, Rom. You are my savior, as always, my dear friend." She took his hands into hers, turning to leave.

"Remember, I want you back here every week!" Rom yelled to the back of her head as she walked out to meet Torg.

When Alkara approached Torg, he bowed in greeting. "My Queen."

"Chancellor," she replied, with a slight tilt of her head.

"I presume all is well?" he asked her.

"Indeed. I am fine, and so is the next Queen." Alkara smiled and placed her hand on her abdomen.

Torg raised one of his eyebrows, clearly uncomfortable. "I see."

"You wanted to see me for some reason?" She helped him

change the subject.

"Indeed. The new Council Leaders have been inducted." He stopped, but she knew what he would say next. She nodded only, as he continued. "They have voted and decreed to disavow all three of the outcasts, denying them any return to Akkadia."

Alkara sighed again. "I warned her about making beds..." she broke off, unable to finish her sentence as her eyes fill with tears. "I understand the Council's decision. Thank you, Torg." She made to leave but turned back toward him one last time. "Yet, they can not stop me from visiting her on the surface, often." She smiled again. Her face hurt from her experienced happiness. When she turned around, she headed down the corridor, leaving Torg standing there, staring at her, perplexed.

***

Saturday morning. Sarah stood in line in the 7-11 with a coffee in hand and her partner next to her, thinking it was way too early. She had been working hard the last few days, making sure her team found missing people, given them medical attention, and supplied them with the necessities. As the only one aware of the reason everyone suffered, she couldn't say anything to anyone. They would put her away for sure.

Who would believe me? She thought to herself. So she held her coffee cup in line, watching the TV, thankful it gave her something to do. *There is nothing but bad news all around.* She worried as she watched the story unfold on the television. Pictures of the Shinnecock Canal and the subsequent flood of tidewater rolling over houses, nightclubs, and marinas alike, flashed across the screen.

The morning anchor of News 12, Doug Geed, reported a human interest story:

"And on a happier note, a totally unexpected act of charity from two local men who won the Mega Millions last night. In a $329 million windfall, the men have decided to donate $60 million to both Hampton Bays and East Quogue, to help the towns rebuild after the devastating earthquake. Patrick and Daniel Sutters, pictured here, accepting the check from the lottery commission..."

The anchorman went on and on, but Sarah couldn't make out his voice any longer. All her mind could do was focus on the names: Patrick and Daniel Sutters.

"Hey!" Sarah's partner said. "Look at that! What humanitarians. Now, those people deserve that money."

"Oh, yeah!" Sarah scoffed sarcastically, between sips of her coffee. "They're *real* humanitarians, all right!" Sarah shook her head and threw her money on the counter. Slamming her hand into the door, she banged it open, walking out, leaving her partner behind.

***

To say the Sutters' household was a happier place now that they had won the Mega would have been an understatement. Patrick canceled the home phone service to stop it from ringing off the wall. People called at all hours, asking for money, donations, and interviews.

Promising to give 30 million to both towns to help rebuild the Hamptons, catapulted Patrick to celebrity status within the hamlets. The upper crust and the PTB (powers that be) thought of asking him to run for office. Patrick laughed at the offer.

Amid all the commotion, Danny was in his room with his suitcase on the bed, packing. As he tossed in shorts, shirts, and underwear, Ilmar unpacked, folding his things correctly before placing each item back in his suitcase.

"Are you practicing?" Danny teased her.

"I do wish I had clothing to pack as well."

Since no stores in town were open yet, she had nothing to wear. They could have driven all the way into Riverhead to buy something new, but their new-found wealth had complicated things. Ilmar had no clothing in the human world.

"But I think you look so adorable in my stuff."

He snuck up behind her and wrapped his arms around her waist. He rocked her gently, kissing her in the soft spot between her neck and shoulder.

She shrugged, giggling at the same time, trying to stop his lips from tickling her. "Oh, yes. Reeglar and I are so thankful for your workout shorts and tank tops," she moaned, irascibly.

"We'll buy you new stuff when we get to the Keys."

The Remingtons, Aaron's parents, shipped their son's body down to their home in Florida and sent an invitation for the Sutters to come to the funeral. Danny decided to attend no matter what. Pat agreed to the idea realizing they had enough money. They should get away, while the construction crew rebuilt the runway and put up a new hangar for the school. Patrick even splurged, having the house remodeled at the same time.

"The keys?" Ilmar asked, not understanding.

"Yep!" Danny smiled at her. He closed the suitcase, grabbing the handle and set it down on the floor near the door. "One whole month of fun in the sun, sand, and surf." He smacked her on her tush. "Now, go get dressed into something better. And hurry, the car will be here soon." He picked up the suitcase, closing the door behind him so she could get changed.

Danny met Patrick and Trish in the kitchen. Pat hung up his cell phone, sliding it back into his pocket. "Well, we did it!"

"What? What did we do?" Danny asked.

"We got the rental on Pecuniary Key for the whole month. And if I read the owner right, he might be willing to sell even in this down economy if we like the property."

"If? Let's hope so. Very cool, bro." They high-fived each other. Danny placed his suitcase by the door, next to Pat's. "So, I guess we're all set?"

"Yep," Pat agreed. "The crew will be here today to start the demolition and rebuild." He leaned against the kitchen sink. "I still feel like I'm dreaming, and I'll wake up totally disappointed."

"Nah," Danny said, clapping Pat on the shoulder. "This is the real deal, Pat." Danny put his sunglasses on and mimicked a Jamaican accent. "Don't worry, be happy!" He smiled his signature smile.

Coming around the corner, Ilmar joined everyone in the kitchen. She wore the only thing she owned, Sarah's blue dress from the day Aaron died. It was as clean as she could get it, and would have to do. Danny couldn't help but relive that moment in his mind. She locked his gaze and realized he thought about Aaron, and now, she did as well.

The knock on the door stopped everyone from dwelling on their sadness. Danny removed his sunglasses, opening the door to let in Reeglar and Azewrath. Danny noticed they had nothing packed either.

"No suitcases... 'cuz you don't have any clothes to pack either, huh?" He pointed his finger at everyone. "I promise, when we get to the Keys, I'll get everyone a new wardrobe."

"I do not understand," Azewrath questioned. "What are we going to do with these keys when we get them?"

"No, no!" Danny corrected him. "We're not *getting* keys; we're *going* to the Keys. The Florida Keys." They had no idea what he spoke of. "UGH!" he complained, frustrated.

Danny reached for Reeglar's hand and kept explaining with words, for Patrick and Trish's sake. He put Reeglar's fingers to his temple. "So, they're tiny islands, where the Atlantic Ocean meets the Gulf of Mexico, attached to the state of Florida." His words didn't matter; he was letting her get a picture from his mind.

"Ah," Reeglar added, inspired. She sent the picture to Azewrath and Ilmar, via their bond. Ilmar put her hands to her mouth with the vision.

"Oh, joy. More water," Azewrath stressed dryly.

Reeglar pulled away from Danny, peering out the kitchen window before turning to Ilmar. "The Qu–" She corrected herself. "Mother, your Mother is outside, Ilmar. She must be here to see you off." The expression on Reeglar's face set in grim lines and filled with concern.

"OH!" Ilmar excused herself, embarrassed. "Sorry, everyone, I'll be right back." She used the human contraction, as she went outside to confront her mother. When she closed the door behind her, she greeted her mother with exasperation in her voice. "Mother!" She pulled her aside as Reeglar and Azewrath joined them.

Alkara hugged her daughter. "I just wanted to see you. I miss you."

Ilmar sighed. "Do you think coming here is a good idea?"

"Not really, no, but you can not come visit me," Alkara reminded her. "Besides, no one knows."

"Everyone knows," Reeglar yelled over. Alkara gave her a

look, commanding her to "be silent."

"What a mess," Ilmar decided. "My would-be brother-in-law is my sister's father." She put her hand to her head. "Now, I officially qualify as a talk show freak." Alkara shook her head, not understanding her daughter's reference. "Jerry Springer? No?" Ilmar threw her hands up. "Oh, never mind, Mother. Human stuff."

Patrick and Trish came out with their suitcases in hand, followed by Danny with his. As he skipped down the steps, a long limousine pulled down their driveway; its tires sent swirls of dust into the air, creating a trail behind it.

"Where are you all going?" Alkara asked.

"Florida," Ilmar answered. "Danny's best friend, um, died in the earthquake," she explained to her mother, slowly, hoping she would follow her lead.

"I am so sorry for your loss." Alkara bowed her head to Danny.

"Thank you," Danny responded, playing along without much feeling, for Patrick's sake. "Patrick, this is Illy's mother, Alkara."

"Pleasure to meet you." Alkara offered her hand to Patrick. He took it, staring at her intently.

"Likewise," Pat said.

"Uh-hum!" Trish cleared her throat to break their eye contact.

"And this is Trish." Ilmar introduced her next. "His girlfriend."

"Nice to meet you as well," Alkara agreed. "I shall not keep you any longer."

"I'll go load the limo," Danny offered, picking up the suitcases.

Another vehicle pulled down the long driveway, followed by a truck carrying a backhoe machine. "I got this," Patrick stated, moving to greet them. "It's the demolition crew."

Alkara gazed sideways at Azewrath. "Have you done something you should not have? Change the wealth of certain people, perhaps?"

Azewrath responded to the Queen. "I no longer need to answer to you, Alkara." He hesitated. "Since I have been banished, there is a need to maintain a certain level of existence that can afford me comfort."

"We shall be more carefully restrained in the future," Reeglar promised.

"I should hope so." Alkara sighed. "You do look well."

"Thank you," Reeglar replied, smiling. "I am very happy, considering."

"Hey!" Danny called from the limo. "We gotta go!"

Patrick walked back over to Alkara. "Do you need us to drop you off anywhere?"

"How sweet, but no thank you." Alkara declined. "I have my own transportation." She kissed Ilmar. "Be safe. I hope to see you again, soon."

"Hum!" Ilmar made a semi-positive sound. "Goodbye, Mother." She slid into the limo with Reeglar and Azewrath. Alkara waved as the stretch pulled out of the driveway. Two seconds later, a Level 4 Telepath gathered Alkara up, and they sailed away together, levitating back to the park, and the Lift to Akkadia.

Patrick turned around to get another look at Alkara but couldn't find her. Perplexed, he thought about asking Ilmar, although his attention was drawn away by the demo crew. The men were unloading the big equipment.

"Take a good look, Danny," Patrick waxed nostalgic. "When we get back, all this will be changed."

Danny laughed. "You don't know the half of it, bro." Danny checked the compartments for the complimentary booze. "Okay gang, where are they hiding the beer?"

***

Sarah made the plane trip all the way to Key West International Airport in peace and quiet. Taking the early bird flight, she couldn't help but yawn as the sun came up. She exited the plane and picked up her baggage, pleased her taxi waited – a free hotel shuttle that took her directly to the Key West Marriott Beachside Hotel. Sarah was only going to be here for two days. The first day, for the funeral, and the next, to enjoy the relaxing beach. Upset from her loss and utterly spent, she needed this downtime.

When she talked to Esther and Roger Remington, she had to

watch what she said. It seemed Danny called them first with his cockamamie earthquake story.

Ha! Thinking about this still pisses me off!

Sarah dabbed a tear from the corner of her eye as she approached the front desk of the Marriott. After they had handed her a room key card, she searched for her room. Sarah booked the ground floor room directly on a private beach. As she walked to her room, she couldn't believe the view.

Yeah, she thought to herself, *I know I live on Long Island, and water surrounds me, but it's not the same. The view is breathtaking!* Sarah gazed out onto blue water as far as the eye could see. It put a smile back on her face, even though she didn't feel happy.

***

When the limousine arrived at MacArthur Airport at 7:15 AM, it took Danny and his group straight to a small jet. A giant smile spread across his face as Pat checked out the window to see if it was what he'd hoped for.

"Okay, people..." Pat announced to everyone. "Take a look at our new jet."

"What?!" Danny growled, astounded. "Get out!"

"You bought another plane?" Trish asked.

"PLANE?!" Pat pretended to be hurt. "Bite your tongue!" He pointed to the beautiful, white, streamlined aircraft outside. "A Cessna Citation X 750." Continuing to describe it Pat practically purred. "With twin Rolls-Royce engines, she can do 605 miles an hour and has a 3000+ mile range."

"You're outta control!" Danny laughed. "That's why I love ya!" Danny piled his beer on top of the other four empties. Opening the door, he got out of the limo before it was parked. "Come on, let's go."

"You can't even wait for the car to stop?" Pat sighed. "You're always in a hurry."

As they exited the car, the driver gathered their suitcases, passing them to the steward who stowed them in the Citation. After the luggage was aboard, the steward came out to greet his passengers.

"Good morning, Mr. Sutters. I'm Duncan Simms, your steward," he addressed Patrick. The steward was a young man, hardly old enough to have finished college, but he came with the plane's purchase. "The pilots are ready, and all have been prepared for you and your guests." He motioned with his arm for them to board.

They mounted the few steps and made the right turn, entering the cabin. Pat sat down in the first left-hand side chair. Trish went to sit next to him on his right-hand side, he thought about stopping her, but then changed his mind.

Danny caught the whole thing and slapped Patrick on the shoulder as he passed. "You're not the pilot, bro. Don't need to save the seat for the copilot."

Patrick leaned back and got comfortable in the incredibly plush, overstuffed beige leather seat. "Now, this is how I like to fly."

Reeglar giggled as she sat down in the third row on the right-hand side. "This is how lazy people fly." Azewrath put a finger to his lips, reminding her to keep quiet. "What?" she asked him.

Azewrath leaned closer. "You sound more and more like a human every day."

"Get used to it!" she told him, folding her arms in front of her.

Danny sat in the second row behind Trish, with Ilmar taking the seat behind Patrick. The second row faced the back of the jet, which put them face-to-face with Reeglar and Azewrath.

Danny felt the seat. "Wow! The upholstery is so soft, Pat." He had to admit it.

"How much did it cost?" Trish asked.

"Oh, honey," Pat began. "You're not going to be the type that's constantly checking on my spending, are you?"

"Well, I'm just saying, keep buying jets and you'll land us all in the poor house," she scolded him.

"What's $20 million among friends." Pat chuckled.

"That's it!" Trish warned, jokingly. "I'm taking away the checkbook."

"We're not even married, and you're already worried about what you'll get in the divorce?" Pat teased.

"Ha, ha! Very funny!" She stuck her tongue out at him.

The captain's voice interrupted their banter as it came over the intercom. "Good morning everyone. This is your Captain speaking. Our trip today down to the Florida Keys should take about two and a half hours, weather permitting. But I'm told the skies are clear, and it should be smooth flying all the way. I'd like to ask all of you to fasten your seatbelts at this time for take off. Once we're airborne, you'll be free to move about the cabin. Thank you, and have a nice flight. Captain out."

"We gotta name her, don't we?" Danny asked Patrick.

"Been thinking about it," Pat suggested. "How about Cee Cee?"

"Why? For Cessna Citation? Original, Pat. Let's go christen her."

"Not now!" Patrick remarked. "Gonna be airborne soon."

Danny yelled to the steward. "When are you serving cocktails?"

"After takeoff, sir," Duncan answered. The engines started their high-pitched whine as the jet taxied down the runway.

Ilmar warned Danny. "By the time we get to this funeral, you'll have no motor skills left."

"That's what I'm going for," Danny replied. "I want to feel no pain. I'd like to intoxicate myself into a semi-stupor. How's it going so far?"

***

The flight was quick, and the landing was as smooth as silk. Danny and company were immediately assaulted by the humidity as they disembarked the jet. Beads of sweat appeared on everyone's forehead, and their shirts stuck to their bodies, giving an overall unclean feeling.

Incredulous, Azewrath moaned. "What is it with the surface? I feel wet all the time. You people are surrounded by water with no way to dry yourselves. It is extremely uncomfortable."

"All you do is complain, Rath." Danny noticed. "Loosen up, dude. It's all good. Maybe you should have a drink."

"Later, perhaps, as I believe you drank it *all*." Azewrath appeared bored by the whole scenario.

Duncan hailed them a taxi to take them to the shops in town. They went from one store to another with the girls having fun shopping and trying on outfits. By the time they finished purchasing the vacation clothes, Danny and Patrick's credit cards were on fire from the excessive use. With still one last purchase to complete as they all needed, something black, they made their way to yet another shop. The guys were much easier to accommodate. Casual attire for all. The women, on the other hand, turned the task into a project.

Patrick put his foot down. "Oh, just pick something out, Trish!" he groaned.

"Fine!" she snapped back, grabbing a dress off the rack, sulking over to the checkout counter.

Danny stood with Ilmar and Reeglar. He handed them both a black cap with a mesh veil. "Put these on."

"Why?" Ilmar asked him.

Reeglar answered, putting hers on top of her head, adjusting it. "It is so Sarah shall not recognize us." Ilmar had to agree it was a good idea, so she nodded and did the same.

They went to the cash register to finalize the transaction and then loaded the taxi with bags and bags of wardrobe. Upon returning to the airport, Duncan waited for them in front of the helicopter.

Ilmar's eyes went wide. "Another helicopter?" She hesitated, panicked. "Truly?"

"It's the fastest way to get off, or on, Pecuniary Key Island," Duncan explained. "I spoke to the owner, and he had the whole pantry stocked with a months worth of groceries for you and your party."

"Wow!" Patrick exclaimed. "That's great!"

Duncan helped load their packages into the helicopter. After stashing the bags in the storage area, Danny, Azewrath, Ilmar, and Reeglar climbed into the four back seats. Patrick and Trish got into the two places left of the pilot.

Patrick called to the steward. "Hey, Duncan. Tell the pilots we're here for the duration. At least one month, maybe more. If they have other work, tell them it's okay for them to go. Otherwise, have a great time in the Keys. I'll call if I need the jet."

"Thank you, Mr. Sutters. I will," Duncan replied.

Pat sat back as the copter took off, bringing them to their

island paradise.

XXV

Keys to the Kingdom

After a refreshing shower, a small lunch on the island, plus a few more beers for Danny, they boarded the helicopter again, dressed for the funeral. As they strapped in, the pilot broke the silence.

"Duncan wanted me to tell you; the limo will be expecting you when we land. It will bring you directly to the cemetery."

"Thank you!" Pat yelled over the noise of the rotor blades, which made it difficult to carry on a conversation at all. The ride was a somber one, with everyone except Reeglar, stuck with their own thoughts.

Just as expected, the limo waited. Danny and company crouched low as they exited the copter, keeping away from the spinning blades. Once clear, they entered the chauffeured car and slid in.

"Good afternoon, Mr. Sutters," the driver said to Patrick in a slight southern accent, locking eyes in his rear view mirror. "The drive should be a quick couple of minutes, traffic permitting."

"Thank you," Patrick repeated. He turned to the rest of them as they settled into the car. "I don't know about anyone else but, I'm feeling pretty damn pampered today." He sat back in the seat, crossing his hands behind his head. "This is living."

"Yes, well..." Trish reminded him. "Let's not forget why we're here today." She looked around at everyone. "To lay Aaron to rest with respect."

And, to erase Sarah's memories before she does or says something stupid, Danny thought to himself.

"If you can get her alone, I shall handle the rest," Reeglar thought back to him.

"Will it work this time?" Danny asked.

"I am only capable of a memory cap, not a memory lock. If my father were here, it could be accomplished. I am not a Level 5 as of yet."

"Fingers crossed, Reeglar." Danny crossed his fingers and held them up for her to see. Pat witnessed his brother's actions also and stared at him in confusion.

"Don't just stare at me, Pat," Danny scolded him. "Pass me a beer." Patrick shook his head but did as asked.

The drive to the cemetery amazed Ilmar. The tropical feel of the Keys appeared everywhere. Busy watching the scenery, she marveled. "I've never seen so much water. It's beautiful." Ilmar enjoyed using all the human contractions.

"Yes, it is," Trish agreed. "I'm looking forward to laying on the beach."

"Did you check out the pool on the island?" Danny asked. "And the jet skis at the dock? We're livin' large." He downed another beer.

The limo pulled up to a long line of cars and parked behind them. Some people clustered in a group by an opening in the ground.

This must be the place, Danny figured.

Danny was the first out the door and none too steady on his feet. Swaying, he caught himself on the hood of the limousine. Pat got out next and grabbed Danny by the arm.

"Dammit, Danny! Straighten up!" Pat hollered. "You've managed to get yourself shit-faced drunk, just like you wanted." Pat let go of him roughly. "Now what?" He began to pace. "Don't you go over there to all those people until you are sure you can walk and stand, WITHOUT falling!"

Patrick and Trish walked off to join the funeral gathering. Danny made his way over to a palm tree, managing to lean against it. After rubbing his face with his hands, he made two fists, spinning around, and punched the tree trunk. Ilmar confronted him, leaving Azewrath and Reeglar by the limo.

"You were hoping for another outcome?" she asked him.

All the sadness returned to Danny's eyes. "I don't know what I was thinking. Maybe I wasn't… Thinking, I mean."

"You do not look well," Ilmar informed him.

"Ha!" Danny laughed. "Ya think? I feel like I'm gonna to throw up."

Ilmar ran her hands up his very muscled arms. "It shall pass," she assured him, sending a small amount of her Healing Ability into him. Ilmar moved closer to him to hide the yellow glow from prying eyes. She placed her hands on his chest, and let the light fade. He smiled. "Feel better?" Ilmar asked him.

Danny took both her hands in his. "How did I ever get by without you? I don't deserve you."

"That is *exactly* what I have wondered many times." Ilmar waved Reeglar and Azewrath over to them. "And sometimes you do not."

Danny caught a glimpse of Patrick and Trish standing next to the coffin. Watching, the Remingtons placed a rose on top of the wooden casket. Then, so did Sarah. They all retreated as the chest lowered into the ground.

"We missed the service?" Danny asked out loud, to no one in particular.

Patrick gave his condolences and shook Roger Remington's hand. Danny observed Ryan, Aaron's older brother, there as well. *Oh, no,* Danny thought. *That means she'll be here, too. Why didn't I think about that before?*

"Illy!" Danny called to her absentmindedly, even though she was standing right next to him. "Take Reeglar and Azewrath, and go stand behind all the guests. Please. We don't want Sarah to see you all, yet."

"All right," Ilmar agreed. "Be careful."

Sarah took one glance at Patrick, and her head snapped around to search for Danny. She spotted him immediately and stormed over to him, every inch of her, screaming an agenda with a vendetta. And it wasn't good for him.

Sarah poked him in the chest. "How *dare* you come here?" She whispered forcefully, not wanting to draw too much attention to the confrontational argument with which she prepared.

"What?" Danny went on the defensive. "I don't have a right to pay my respects?"

"*Pay your respects?*" Sarah's voice rose higher in a hiss. "That's a good one. You caused this! You're the reason he's dead! Are those *freaks* here with you?" She checked the area when a young woman's voice called Danny's name from behind Sarah. She turned to see who it was.

"Danny!" Megan screamed, breaking into a sprint even though she was in a dress and high heels. When she reached him, she pushed Sarah out of the way and jumped into his arms.

Megan was Aaron's little sister. She held a huge crush on her big brother's best friend growing up. Danny could never get away from her. Obviously, she still suffered that crush.

Danny thought she sobbed a little, into his chest. "Hey!" he cooed, trying to soothe her. "It'll be okay, Megs." That's what he always called her.

"Nothing will ever be okay, again," Megan sniffled, melodramatically, gazing up at him. "But I feel better... Now that *you're* here."

Danny gently released himself from her grasp and really studied her for the first time. *Wow!* He thought, wishing someone would smack him for thinking the thoughts he had. Megan had changed. She had grown into a woman, and it made him very uncomfortable. *Or, maybe too comfortable?* He smiled.

"I haven't seen you since you were in high school," Danny reminded himself. "How old are you now, Megs?"

"Twenty-three," Megan answered. "I just graduated college."

"Twenty-three, huh!" Danny repeated. *Same age as Ilmar,* he thought again, trying to keep his mind out of the gutter. "My, have you grown up!"

Sarah seethed inside. "Enough with happy family reunions," she spat, biting her tongue for Megan's sake. "Megan, go back to your mother and father. Danny and I need to talk."

"Okay, Sarah," Megan replied, happily. "I'll see you later, Danny. Don't leave without seeing me, okay?" She grabbed his hand when it seemed like he was going to protest. "Promise!" she urged him.

"Okay, Megs, I promise... Now get!" Danny smacked her on the bottom, hoping Ilmar didn't see that. *Oh well, I've got bigger problems right now.* "Sarah, let's go somewhere less crowded. Especially, if you're going to yell."

"I wish, just for once, you could feel what I'm feeling." Sarah started. "And telling the Remingtons their son died in the earthquake... Really!" She walked next to him, going on and on. "I've lost the only man I've ever loved. What am I supposed to do now?"

Danny wasn't listening anymore; he was going deep inside his mind to get word to Reeglar about where he was. *"Reeglar, we're walking toward the water's edge. Meet us there."*

"We are coming, but you shall not see us."

When Danny came back to his reality, he realized Sarah had

stopped walking and so had he. In fact, she was right in his face, standing in front of him with her hands on her hips.

"Danny? Did you *hear* me? Are you even *listening?*"

Danny moved closer to her. "Oh, I'm *tired* of listening to you, Sarah," Danny began. "I've been listening to you for *years*." He hesitated. "Listening to you, and letting you treat me like crap for Aaron's sake. Well, honey, this ends now!"

Something grabbed Sarah by her arms and held her in place. She struggled fiercely against it. "What the hell?!" she demanded.

"Where are you trying to go?" Danny smiled at her. "I thought you wanted to talk?"

"It's them!" Sarah screeched, searching for the Akkadians. "They're with you, aren't they?"

"Yes, they are," Danny assured her. "I didn't want to do this, but you forced my hand."

"What are you going to do? Take away my memories AGAIN?" She struggled harder, and this time the Akkadians became visible to Sarah.

Danny let her know what he planned on doing. "By the time we're finished with you, I'm going to be your new best friend."

"You wouldn't *dare!*" Sarah breathed.

"It's the only choice I have, Sarah," Danny said sadly. "You've brought this on yourself." He nodded to Reeglar. "Don't worry. I promise not to take away your memories of Aaron."

"*You bastard!*" Sarah screamed.

Reeglar entered Sarah's mind, an unfriendly place, at that moment. Sarah's memories assaulted Reeglar as she tried to collect any trace of the Akkadians. Bright red in color, filled with electricity, and moving very quickly, Sarah's memories shocked Reeglar every time she grabbed one.

"*Oh, no! You can not escape me!*" Reeglar warned the memories.

She gathered them one by one, locking them behind a wall. This time, she made sure the barriers she erected were doubly secured. No spaces, nor tiny cracks that could leak any errant thoughts or memories. She would not make the same mistake twice. Whether or not it would hold was another story, but at least this time, it would not be her fault. When Reeglar was satisfied, she left Sarah's mind. Azewrath let go of Sarah when Reeglar nodded to him.

Danny was the first person Sarah laid eyes on when she came out of her trance. "Danny?" It took her a moment to realize it was him. "Danny!" She threw her arms around him. "I'm so glad you could make it."

"We would never miss this. Aaron was too important to me and so are you," Danny lied to her. "We all wanted to be here to support you."

Sarah gazed at the Akkadians and smiled. "Thank you all; you'll never know how much this means to the Remingtons and me." She let go of Danny's hand and began to walk back toward the cemetery. "Come on. Let's get back to the family. You're all coming back to the Remington's house afterward, right?"

"Of course," Danny agreed. They mingled with the rest of the people gathered at the funeral before making the trip to Aaron's parent's house. As the night wore on, Ilmar had her hands full trying to keep Megan away from Danny. They stayed well into the evening, spending their first night in the Keys in the company of friends and family, remembering Aaron.

***

Six weeks passed since they arrived at Pecuniary Key. In that time, Pat kept in touch with construction company rebuilding his house and the flight school. The foreman informed them they had completed all the work was and ready for them to return home. So, he and Trish decided that morning was going to be their last day on the island. It was time to take the Citation back to Long Island and return to their lives.

Danny, on the other hand, fell in love with Pecuniary Key and convinced the owner to sell the island to him. Patrick couldn't argue. He realized Danny had to follow his own heart and if it wasn't working for the aviation school any longer, so be it.

On a beautiful South Florida morning, from the vantage point in his bed, Danny was able to watch both the sunrise and the sunset, fifteen hours apart.

It doesn't get any better than this, he thought blissfully.

Ilmar still slept by his side, peaceful and glowing from her new suntan. Startled by all the noise coming from the kitchen, Danny realized what the banging must be.

Patrick and Trish, trying to get as much in as they can on their last day here. In my home! The thought of his own place sounded wonderful in his head.

Danny jumped out of bed and threw on a pair of swim trunks – his new daily attire in the south. Ilmar rolled over, causing the sheet covering her to slip down, revealing the sensual curve of her back, hips, and rear end. He couldn't resist, so he crept over, brought his lips to the sweet spot on her lower back, right next to her dimple. He ran his hand across the upswing of her hips.

"Mmm..." Ilmar moaned, rolling to face him, reaching out to embrace the man she loved. "Good morning, my love."

He kissed her belly, grabbing the ring in his teeth. She mouthed the word "ouch," silently as he moved up her body – his hair tickling the bottoms of her breasts. She laughed. His arousal grew as his body responded to hers, but his brother broke the mood by calling his name from outside the door.

"Danny!" Pat yelled from the other room. Ilmar and Danny stopped moving. "Danny?" Pat knocked on the door. "You guys up yet?" He leaned his head against the door.

"If we don't answer, maybe he'll go away," Danny told her.

Ilmar giggled. "No," she scolded him. "Do not be so selfish. Today is his last day on your island paradise. He wants to spend it with you." Ilmar called out to Patrick. "We will be right out, Pat!" Danny playfully smacked her on the arm, so she laughed and smacked him back. "Danny's excited to spend the day with you!" She yelled again.

"Oh, yes..." Danny yelled through the door "See ya soon, bro!"

"Okay," Patrick answered proceeding to walk down the stairs and back into the kitchen.

"You know," Danny remarked, moving back on top of Ilmar. "We could still take a few minutes to ourselves."

Ilmar smacked him again. "I am afraid the moment has passed." She frowned.

"Aw, man!" Danny stood, adjusting his shorts. "Can I pencil myself in for later?"

"Ass!" She laughed, got out of bed and jumped on him.

"Look out, little lady," he warned her as she moved to the dresser. "You're gonna start something you can't finish."

"Oh, I can finish it!" she teased him, putting her suit on and her skirt wrap. "And I *will*... Later." She opened the door. "You will be begging for mercy!"

"Oh, have mercy!" Danny overreacted in a southern accent, walking from his room to join his brother for breakfast.

When Danny and Ilmar made it downstairs, Patrick greeted them. "Good morning. Trish made bacon and eggs!"

"I thought I smelled something delicious!" Danny complimented Trish. He pulled up a stool for Ilmar and then one for himself, sitting next to her at the central island in the middle of the kitchen. Immediately attacking the bacon, Trish slapped Danny's hand away.

"Wait for everyone else to get here." As if on cue, Reeglar and a none too awake Azewrath, strolled in and took a seat next to Danny and Ilmar.

"Something smells good," Azewrath managed, examining the food.

"Good morning to you, too," Danny added, sarcastically.

"Hum," Azewrath moaned. "I have nowhere to be, so why am I awake at this hour?"

"To share in the joy of being alive." Trish smiled at him.

Reeglar kissed him on his lips before he could say anything else.

"What was all that about?" Danny asked, wondering about Trish's comments.

"I just got a call from our broker," Pat informed Danny. "He said the stocks you told me to invest the rest of our money in, has soared."

"And?" Danny coaxed. "Don't leave me hanging."

"And, in the last six weeks, we've made another $150 million."

"What? *Dude!*" Danny stood up so quickly; he knocked the stool to the floor.

"Who would have thought you'd be such a great investment strategist?" Pat offered. "I'm proud of you. Keep it up. We're rolling in the dough."

"He'll have to, the way you both have been spending," Trish

teased.

"We are rich?" Ilmar asked Danny, who bent over to pick up the stool.

"Yep, honey. We are." Danny laughed.

"It is a good thing." Ilmar wasn't asking.

Azewrath leaned closer to Danny. "You can thank me again, later."

"For what?" Danny asked, whispering back.

"For giving you this lifestyle," Azewrath explained.

"A completely selfless act, on your part," Reeglar joked.

"I am used to a certain level and standard of living," Azewrath added. "And in my eyes, the ends justify the means."

"How's the breakfast?" Trish asked.

"The best!" Pat kissed her.

"We will clean up, Trish," Ilmar offered. "It's the least we can do since you've cooked. You and Patrick go to the beach, and we will be out to join you soon."

Trish smiled at Patrick, picked up her sun hat and placed it on top of her head. "Oh, let's beat it before they change their minds!" She grabbed Pat's hand and their towels before running out the back door as Ilmar cleaned up.

***

Later in the day, Trish and Patrick lay in the lounge chairs, soaking up the sun, relaxing. Danny and Ilmar sped around the perimeter of the island on the jet skis. As they zipped by, Danny hollered. "Woo-hoo!" He sent a massive wake rolling toward the shore.

Pat shook his head at Danny's behavior as he reached for Trish's hand and held it. "Have I made you happy?"

Trish eyed him lovingly, yet puzzled. "Of course!" she insisted. "You don't think I'm here only because of the money, do you?"

"No, not really." Pat shrugged. "Well, at least I hope not!"

"Oh, you!" she scolded him. "Haven't we been through enough together?"

"Yes, yes," Pat admitted. "Just making sure you're not a Gold-digger." He smiled at her.

"Really?" she asked. "A Gold-digger, huh!" She smiled back, but her expression held mischief. Jumping up, she pushed him out of his chair, and he fell to the sand. "I'll give you Gold-digger!"

"Oh, yeah?" Pat yelled. "You just wait till I get up!"

He struggled to get to his feet, and Trish ran away from him, holding onto her hat for dear life. Unfortunately for her, Pat was faster and caught her. They both laughed as he picked her up and spun her around. The warm breeze blew her large sun hat off her head. Placing her down, they both gave chase after the headpiece as it rolled along the shore just out of their reach.

Danny and Ilmar watched the whole thing, and they laughed, circling the jet skis around and heading back to the dock. They blew by Azewrath and Reeglar, who enjoyed themselves paddle boarding. The wake the jet skis created sent both Akkadians plunging into the warm Gulf waters.

As Danny and Ilmar walked down the jet ski dock, they met Azewrath and Reeglar coming up the beach. They dragged their paddle board equipment from the water, dropping it to the sand. Danny couldn't believe how much the Akkadians had changed in the last few weeks. They all appeared tan and healthy.

"*That* was uncalled for," Azewrath stated, dripping wet.

Ilmar giggled. "We are sorry."

"No, you are not!" Reeglar teased, also dripping from her dunking. "It is never a good idea to mess with a Telepath." Reeglar raised her hands.

"No! Wait, wait!" Danny pleaded.

"No, Reeglar, truly!" Ilmar also begged.

The Telepath shook her head, lifting both Danny and Ilmar off the ground. Slowly, she sent them over the water. "What do you think, Rath?" Azewrath stuck out his arm and made a thumbs-up sign, but spun his hand around, pointing his thumb downward. He smiled wickedly. "All right." Reeglar let them fall, and they landed with a giant splash.

Danny and Ilmar broke the water's surface, gulping for air. They wiped their eyes as they walked back up to the beach, laughing. All four of them sat down in the waiting lounge chairs. It had been a day full of happiness, and much needed relaxation.

Azewrath hit the chair, staring out at the endless ocean,

unmoving. Reeglar noticed he remained unresponsive to the environment around him.

Uh, oh! She thought to herself.

Danny reached for a beer in the cooler next to his chair, handing one to Ilmar and then offered one to Reeglar. "Reeglar?" He held up the beer when she finally reacted.

"Oh, um, sure," she said, absentmindedly, taking the bottle from Danny.

"Hey, Rath! Rath!" Danny called.

Azewrath came out of his trance. "Yes?" he answered.

"Wanna beer?" Danny passed another bottle to Reeglar. "I don't know about anyone else, but I think it's a great idea to sit here for the rest the afternoon and drink beers." he declared, leaning back in his lounge chair. "Who's with me?"

Azewrath took this opportunity to agree. "Yes! Wonderful idea!" Reeglar shared a conspiratorial glance in his direction, nodding. She read his mind aware of what he had Seen. Azewrath repeated the idea. "We should sit here and enjoy the sun for the rest of the day."

Reeglar agreed. "Yes, I agree. I do like this new skin tone and nice bronze color."

"Now you're getting it, Rath!" Danny encouraged, happily.

So they sat and drank. Pat and Trish finally joined them, enjoying a few more beers, but by late afternoon, Pat got hungry.

"I think I'm gonna start the grill, and get dinner barbecuing." Pat glanced around, counting heads. "Anyone else hungry?" It seemed everyone was.

"I'll come with you," Trish offered.

"We'll be up soon," Danny added, finishing another beer.

Ilmar remarked to Danny about Patrick. "He truly is a wonderful brother to you."

"Hey," Danny admitted, "it's not a one-way street, you know!"

"True," she agreed. "But you have *definitely* caused Patrick more trouble than he has caused you."

"Uh, that's not ALL my fault." He specifically gave the Akkadians the eyeball. "I've had a little help, present company included. What about what you and your mother did to him?"

Reeglar giggled, and Ilmar shot her an angry glance. "That was necessary!" she assured him. "Unless you wanted me to return to Akkadia and leave you, never to see you again? Is that not how this all began?"

Danny had to admit he didn't want that. "No, I'm glad you're here... with me."

Ilmar pressed him. "Will you tell him?"

"WHAT?!" Danny replied. "Tell Pat that you and your mother, whom he slept with while drugged, by the way, are actually not human, but are from an underworld kingdom?" His voice raised an octave at a time. "And, are going to raise his love child, schooling her to become the next Queen of Akkadia? You mean, tell him that, ever?" Ilmar nodded. Danny smiled that famous smile of his. "Nope! No way in hell! I think I'll just keep that tidbit of information to myself, thank you."

"Well, when you say it that way, it does come across a bit unsettling." Ilmar smiled back, coyly.

Danny gazed out into the endless water. "A perfect end to a wonderful day."

As the tide moved in, their lounge chairs appeared right at the edge of the water line. Danny splashed his toes in the surf, sending droplets of water everywhere, getting everyone wet.

Azewrath leaned forward. "I have had enough water for one day, thank you."

"What's with you and water?" Danny asked. "Why don't you like it?"

"I like it enough," Azewrath explained. "It is just not dry here like it is in Akkadia. Even the air here holds moisture."

"It's called humidity. You'll get used to it," Danny assured him.

"Oh, joy," Azewrath replied, without joy. "Wonderful."

"I am getting hungry," Ilmar said. "Should we check on dinner?"

"No," Azewrath ordered quickly. "No one is getting up now. We are just going to sit here."

"Why?" Ilmar asked. "What's wrong? Reeglar you have to be hungry."

Reeglar answered Ilmar through their bond. *"Yes, but Rath has had a vision. We should keep Danny here as long as possible."*

"Is it bad?"

"No, just complicated."

"Oh." Ilmar understood. *"What should we do?"*

"I am finally comfortable here," Azewrath said out loud.

Danny pondered Azewrath's decision but got up from his lounge. "Uh, okay, but I gotta go."

Azewrath stood confronting Danny. "It was your idea to sit and relax, so, let us enjoy the afternoon!"

"I feel like I have to *go*." Danny turned, gazing at the house, distracted.

"What if I asked you not to go?" Azewrath asked him.

"Okay, what's going on?" Danny inquired cautiously. "Why do you care about my travelin' feet?"

"Ask yourself... Why must you go?"

"How the hell should I know?" Danny shrugged.

Reeglar cleared her throat. "It is the venom of the dragotte. Your mind's eye controls you."

"So... Now what are you saying?" Danny asked. "I'm a divining rod for the weird?"

"Never mind." Azewrath gave in. "I tried, just remember that. Reeglar, bring the oar. We are going to need it."

Danny had given him another quizzical look before he turned, walking toward the house. They followed behind; parading past a beautiful rock waterfall, obviously man-made. Danny trekked past, but something made him stop. The falling water rushed down the face of the rocks, emptying into a deep, oval well. Danny reached into the pool of water, tasting it.

"It's a saltwater well?" Danny stated, confused. Azewrath took the paddle from Reeglar and held it out to Danny. "How did you know I was going to ask –?" He stopped and thought for a moment. The expression on Azewrath's face told him. "You've Seen something."

"Nothing gets by you," Azewrath told him, sarcastically. "Just take the paddle."

Danny snatched it from Azewrath's hand and explored the back of the well's rock wall. Fighting his way through the palm fronds, he came face to face with white coral. The coral created the Florida Key islands, and someone had built the well over it.

Taking the butt end of the paddle and using it as a battering ram, Danny hit the soft coral over and over again. It crumbled away from the force of his blows, slowly revealing a hole. Underneath the well, a hollow area appeared. A cave. He hammered at the coral until the opening was large enough for him to get through.

"I'm going in," Danny informed them.

"We are *all* going in," Azewrath corrected him.

"Oh, okay," Danny responded. He dropped to the ground, and slid down into the dark hole, not knowing what to expect. He stopped, checking with Azewrath first. "Am I going to be all right?"

Azewrath couldn't resist the comment. "Have you ever been all right?"

Annoyed, Danny yelled impatiently. "Hello? Hanging here! Get serious."

"Sorry," Azewrath asked for forgiveness. "There is a solid bottom. You shall be safe."

"Thanks." Danny dropped down into the darkness. He hit the floor, unable to see a thing but was ankle-deep in standing water. "I can't see down here," Danny yelled up to them. "Send Ilmar down, first."

Ilmar sat on the grass and Azewrath passed her into Danny's waiting arms. "Do you have a good grip on me?" she asked Danny.

"Yep, I got ya," Danny answered, pulling her down into the blackness. "Turn off your piercing, and hold on to me. We need some light." She wrapped her fingers around his upper arm, and he immediately broke out in blisters. "Ow, ouch!" he complained.

"Sorry, my love," Ilmar apologized.

Azewrath came down next, and even though he knew what he would find in the cave, he still lamented about getting wet. "Will this torture never end?"

Ilmar's Healing light brightened the cave and made it easy to see Reeglar float down gently. She hovered, so as not to have her feet slosh around in the water.

"Come over here, Illy." Danny stared at something on the other side of the cave wall. She moved closer to the wall, studying it carefully. "Damn..." Danny whispered.

Azewrath sighed. "It can not be."

"It is..." Ilmar assured him. "It is a dragotte."

Reeglar disagreed. "No, not quite."

Danny had to agree with Reeglar. "You're right; it's not a dragotte." He ran his fingers across the fossil on the wall. "The dragotte is a flying creature, like a bat, or dragon. Here, this animal isn't all bone. There are areas where the organic material could have been cartilage. And look here, no real limbs." He turned back to them. "See the outline, here?" He traced a large diamond shape. "It does have a long tail, like the dragottes, but don't you see it? It's a sea creature of some sort. An offshoot of a dragotte that has evolved into something else. I don't know, like a stingray, maybe?"

"What does this mean?" Ilmar asked.

"I think it means; there might be another way down to your subterranean kingdom of Akkadia."

"Are you sure?" Reeglar asked.

"No." Danny shook his head, growing weak, suffering from the blisters on his skin. "I need to check this out." He rubbed his hand on the fossil again. "I've got to go down... Into the well."

"Your brother is still here," Reeglar reminded him. "Yet, he leaves tomorrow. Can this not wait?"

"Wait until tomorrow?" Danny complained.

"Tomorrow," Azewrath repeated.

"Damn," Danny cursed. "Okay, but I am going down. Tomorrow I'm getting diving gear, and anything else I need." Wondering, he asked them all question. "I don't suppose any of you know how to dive, right?" Azewrath and Ilmar shook their heads. "Of course not."

Reeglar nodded. "I can come with you. And I shall not need diving equipment."

"Okay, so, diving gear for one, then," Danny decided.

Reeglar gazed up at the hole as if she read someone's thoughts, so she warned them. "Pat is looking for us. We need to get out of this cave."

"Ah, we better go," Danny agreed. "But we're coming back here tomorrow, right?"

"Yes, tomorrow," Azewrath repeated. "Have you forgotten the meaning of the word?"

"Geeze, Rath..." Danny moaned, as he reached for the cave opening.

They climbed out of the cave and brushed themselves off. Ilmar quickly Healed Danny, making him well and full of renewed energy as Patrick called Danny's name.

"We're coming, Pat!" he yelled back. "I'm starving!"

"Me too!" Reeglar admitted. "I could even eat some animal meat at this point."

"Truly?" Azewrath asked.

"Do not worry," Reeglar assured him. "I shall not turn into a barbarian."

"Ya think?" Danny said. "I'll turn you all into barbarian meat eaters!" He put his arm around Ilmar as they walked up to the barbecue pit. "And, I could sure use another beer." He slapped Azewrath on the back. "How about you?"

As they reached Patrick and Trish, Danny stopped one last time. He spun – his eyes focused on the water in the well. Sighing, Danny wondered what mysteries lie below the island. He shrugged, and turned back toward the house, continuing up the path on his way to dinner.

If he stayed a little longer, he would have seen bubbles breaking the surface of the well. They expanded and popped, disappearing into the depths.

THE END?

About the Author

The first child of two very talented parents, Nik spent the formative years at an advertising agency alongside a father who allowed and encouraged creative expression. With an affinity for illustration, Nik immersed in any form of artistic conduct. Whether it be writing and performing short plays for the family, or memorizing movie dialog and old radio shows, Nik also found imagination enhanced within the pages of books.

Science Fiction held much mystery and possibilities. Nik read and read until the desire to make the fantasy come to life grew too strong. Nik created over 40 comic book characters and then wrote and illustrated four original comic books. A local magazine published some of Nik's comic book characters. Nik also helped write a Star Wars film spoof, that won a contest.

Nik's recent novel writing is not a passion, but an obsession. The words never stop. All in hopes of creating a spectacular world of science fiction/fantasy, enjoyed by many.